Land Of My Sojourn
A Trent Carter Novel

RICHARD TRICE

DEDICATION

For my family, who gave me my own history and continue to honor me with theirs: My father Calvin, my sister Cheryl, my brother Jeffrey – already in their Heavenly sojourns; my mother Betty;my wife Linda; my children Nathan, Lauren, and Jillian and their spouses; my amazing grandchildren;

And last but not least, for all the readers who enjoyed the first book of this series, ACT OF CONTRITION.

CONTENTS

ACKNOWLEDGMENTS

When I sat down to write the first novel of what is now a planned trilogy, *Act of Contrition,* it was a process I can only imagine as being akin to giving birth. Once I got it out of my system, I predicted that it would be the last book I would ever try to write. Little did I know that the ideas for a sequel would begin to germinate in my mind almost immediately, culminating a year later in the volume that you now hold in your hands.

No project of this scope would be possible without the help of several people, who I would like to hereby acknowledge:

 Deep and profound thanks go to my wife Linda, who gets the dubious honor of reading the very first draft of each and every chapter as it leaves my printer, warts and all. She reads "like a reader," and therefore is able to clue me in to her invaluable wisdom of where the story is not flowing correctly, or worse, isn't working at all.

To Phillip A. Scott, grammarian and story doctor extraordinaire, one of my long-time best friends, partners in many crimes, etc. (oh . . . and also happens to be my brother-in-law), goes my deepest gratitude for an editing job well done. I cringed with delight each time I opened up and read his voluminous red-noted corrections/suggestions; it was most humbling, as if I were taking a graduate level writing class.

To all the faithful "beta readers" and supporters of my *Land Of My Sojourn* page on Facebook, a forum through which I experimentally shared rough first drafts of much of the book as it was written, thanks bunches for your ongoing interest and encouragement. Your feedback has also improved the final version of this book tremendously.

Richard C. Trice
Raton, New Mexico
December 2019

PROLOGUE
Field Of Holes

(Present Day – three miles south of Raton, New Mexico)

His breath came in ragged gasps. Sweat poured into his eyes, almost blinding him. He paused to swipe the back of one grimy hand across his face. As he did so, he rested from his work and leaned shakily on the handle of the pickaxe he had been wielding. He winced as he rubbed the bloody, broken blisters of his hands, wondering for the hundredth time that night why he hadn't brought a pair of work gloves.

"That, and another bottle of water," he muttered to himself.

He was not completely unaccustomed to hard work, but perspiration seemed to pour from every part of his body. Even though the late autumn night air was chilly, he had shed coat, scarf, and pullover sweater and had tossed them aside somewhere in the dark behind him. The brilliant stars in the pollution-free sky and the dim light of a waning half-moon working its way inexorably toward the western foothills shed scant illumination on his feverish work.

He froze, sucked in his breath, held it, and listened into the darkness. *Had that been a foot kicking up a distant loose rock?* He strained to listen intently for almost a full minute, squinting up the hillside ahead as a dim figure moved slowly along the ridge above him, silhouetted against the star-strewn New Mexican sky. The nondescript figure plodded purposefully, dislodging a few more stones and sending them clattering down the slope toward him, followed by a faint lowing that drifted down to reach his ears.

He let his head drop thankfully and slowly blew his breath painfully out of his lungs.

"Damn cows! Almost gave me a heart attack!"

He rubbed the raw palms of his hands painfully onto his jeans and looked around him, barely making out the nearest of half a dozen holes he had hammered out of the hard clay earth tonight, the meager results of his feverish labors. From here he could also just make out the ruined remains of a nearby adobe chimney, all that was left of the 150-year-old stagecoach station on the Santa Fe Trail known as the Clifton House. He knew that what he was looking for had to be within just yards of the famous old ruins. All the old stories had pretty much said so.

He grasped the pick as firmly as he could and hoisted it up and over his head before resuming his work. He slung the bit heavily into the hard soil below, then again, and again, trying to pace himself. He was approaching the point of

1

exhaustion, bone-tired from his endeavors, willing himself beyond all reason to continue. He really didn't know how much longer he could continue digging, but knew that he just couldn't give up the search.

Not now.

Not after so much had happened, and not without really knowing who else might also come looking.

It just had to be here, somewhere. He paused, bent over, and tried to gauge the depth of this current hole. It had to be three, maybe four feet deep now. He was about spent and couldn't go on much longer. He stood up, took another deep, pounding breath and swung again with what little strength remained.

The metal blade thudded into something less solid.

He paused, his heart quickening even faster than his exertions had caused, and then swung again, a little less forcefully.

Another solid thud as the pick punched into what felt like rotten, spongy wood—exactly what he was looking for.

He tossed the axe aside and excitedly lay down on his stomach, leaning as far as he could into the hole until his hands touched the bottom, then scrabbled like claws into the loosened earth. He then reached into his shirt pocket and produced his mobile phone, switching on the flashlight feature, and trained it eagerly back into the hole. The light played over the rough ground for a moment before clearly illuminating what he had hoped to see--splinters of old wood protruding through the disturbed earth.

Could it be? He stood up again slowly, wiping sweat from his eyes as he kept the light trained on the hole. His breathing gradually returned to normal, but his heart continued to pound with excitement. He instinctively rubbed his left wrist, glanced down, and in the soft reflection of the flashlight glimpsed the faded tattoo there. From here it appeared to be a mere smudge, but he knew it was the figure of a fossilized shell, once an important symbol to him, but now only a dreaded reminder of the past several weeks and months that had drawn him like a magnet across continents and oceans to this abandoned location on a high desert cattle ranch in Northeastern New Mexico—an historic place long forgotten by all but a select few. And now, had he really been the lucky one to finally locate it? Had he finally found the long-lost grave of the old gunfighter? And did it hold the secrets that he suspected it did?

He blew out his breath once more. *Only one way to find out for sure.*

He stooped back down to confirm what he had found, then stopped as he heard the sound of yet another dislodged rock, this one quite nearby, and behind him. He slowly turned to follow the arc of his light as it traversed the ground before him, and then froze as it suddenly illuminated, just a few feet away, a pair of expensive-looking cowboy boots and the cuffs of dark pants. He squinted, curiously aware that the shadowy figure balanced something familiar in its hands. He raised the light slowly upward, and his eyes widened as he recognized the person who was now holding the pickaxe he had tossed aside.

"You!" he blurted out with a shocked gasp.

The other person only smiled.

He stood paralyzed in place as he watched the pick slowly rise, as if of its own volition, then blur as it flew forward. His breath burst from his lungs for a final time as something massive hit him in the middle of his chest.

He dropped his cell phone, its light skittering away to finally stop nearby and shine straight into his eyes, momentarily blinding him. He gasped in vain to catch his breath, shuddered, and began losing his balance as his legs turned to rubber. He looked down incredulously at his trembling hands closing around the blood slick head of the pickaxe now imbedded in his sternum. His feet began to lose traction and he stumbled backwards, then fell straight back into the old grave, slamming unceremoniously onto his back.

His eyes went in and out of focus, his sight fading as he thought he saw the silhouette of his murderer loom over the edge of hole, blotting out the beautiful stars.

"I thought it was only the cows," was his last thought, and he felt a rush of relief that his laborious digging was finally at an end.

CHAPTER 1
This Promised Land

(Letter from María Consuelo Delgado to her brother, Manuel Delgado)

April 19, 1868
Sr. Manuel Diego Delgado
El Rancho de las Golondrinas
Santa Fe,
Territorio de Nuevo México

Dearest Mannie,

I do so hope this letter finds you soon and finds you very well and happy. Even though it has been only a few months, it seems like years now since we have laid eyes on one another. Our situation here continues to improve and prosper. The land that Papa obtained from Sr. Maxwell is quite beautiful and sits in such a beautiful valley located north of Cimarrón, here in the Sangre de Cristo Mountains. Oh, if you could only come see it, Mannie! You would never want to ever leave the endless grasslands, almost 1200 acres—well, almost endless to me—that flow gently up hill to disappear into fir trees on the hillsides, and lush ancient cottonwoods that line a clear mountain stream that runs just south of where the house is going up. Papa says it runs from the river that flows from the mountains in the west and joins an even mightier river that runs east of here—I believe it is named the Canadian River—and so, therefore, our little stream will never run dry! Our cattle are going to feel that they are in paradise, as indeed I am beginning to believe.

Papa and the boys are almost finished with the stonework chimney and fireplace and started last week to lay the logs for the walls. Oh, I wish you could see it, Mannie! It is going to be such a beautiful house! I am so tired of living in this tent, although I must remain thankful for whatever shelter we have. God has, indeed, provided so well for all our needs. Mr. Maxwell even brought out a team of horses to help drag the timber, and some experienced Indian loggers—Utes, I believe—to help properly notch and fit the logs.

They are very hard workers, these Indians, and not quite so fearsome as the Comanche and Apache that roam south of Santa Fe. Papa says to be watchful of them, however; that they will steal anything we leave lying around.

Oh! And some other excitement the other day, Mannie: some vaqueros rode through, headed west to hunt for gold at a place called Elizabethtown, and stopped to ask for water from our stream. They shared the news that more cattle are moving through from Texas, following what they are calling the Goodnight-Loving cattle trail, just a few miles to the east of us, and named after the two Tejano gentlemen who blazed the path a year or two ago. They say that it runs all the way from the Llano Estacado along the Pecos River, all the way up through Colorado Territory! What a busy place this Norte Nuevo México has become! When we answered Lucien Maxwell's advertisement just a couple of years ago to come homestead this land, it was considered so wild and untamed!

Papa is so excited and is making plans to ride over toward the Canadian River, a few miles to the east of us, the next time we hear of these cattlemen coming through. He hopes to buy another bull and a few more heifers—although our money is getting very tight. I cannot disagree that it would be a good investment, although we already owe so much to Mr. Maxwell on the land lease, as well as others in town, for goods and supplies. Most are very agreeable, and Mr. Maxwell has told us time and again not to worry and that we may begin to pay as we get income from our calves and crops next year. So, I suppose growing our own holding of cattle is the only way we will survive.

Oh, dear brother, how I do miss you! Please write back and tell me you are well and prosperous there at the rancho. It was so hard leaving you, but I know you have your obligations there already as foreman, and to your precious family. Please pass along my warm love to dear Ana and little Patricio. I am sure he has grown much by now, and probably does not remember me at all! I have had to pause to wipe away the tears before they spill onto the page.

I pray daily to the Blessed Virgin and Our Savior for all of your safety and well-being—and that someday, one day, we may be reunited.

Papa, Antonio, and young Pepé—who has been hanging over my shoulder as I write and forcing me to read everything to him—all send their love. Please write back to me soon.

In the meantime, I remain
Your most sincere and loving sister,
María

(June 23, 1865 – Doaksville, Indian Territory)

Captain Jonathon S. Carter, CSA, stood his horse just inside the tree line of silver maples, peering down the slope of knee-high grama grass that rippled in the early morning breeze. He couldn't see the river from here, but he could hear the rush of water rising and falling in harmony with the breeze in the leaves around him. He caught an occasional whiff of wood smoke, and once or twice he thought he heard the distant murmuring of voices.

He stiffened, one hand on the butt of the pistol shoved in his belt, as the soft steps of another horse moved behind him. He twisted in the saddle, then relaxed.

"Anything, Salal?" came a familiar voice, using the name his friends and family called him.

"Nothing in particular yet, General." Jonathon paused, sat up straighter, saluted his general, and then nodded downhill. "But they're down there, I'll wager."

Cherokee General Isaac "Stand" Watie had been awarded the rank of brigadier the year before, the only American Indian in the Army of the Confederate States of America to be so promoted. This followed, among his many other accomplishments, his successful raids on a large Union supply train at the Battle of Cabin Creek, and the capture of a Union Army steamboat making its way up the

Red River to Fort Towson. Four years ago, upon the commencement of hostilities, Watie, having himself owned Negro slaves and a plantation in northeastern Oklahoma, had immediately declared his allegiance to the Confederacy and formed the Cherokee Mounted Rifles. He had led his troops of combined Cherokee, Choctaw, Chickasaw, and Osage tribal members—some of the so-called "Civilized Tribes"—through many successful military operations and was highly regarded. Now, at 59 years of age and after many years at war, he felt worn-out—old and tired.

General Watie painfully dismounted with a slow groan. He tied his horse's reins to a low branch as Jonathon handed down a pair of binoculars, and the general squinted through them. He had indeed aged greatly, in Jonathon's opinion, seemingly all in just the past few months.

Jonathon Carter had been born near a small place called Honey Creek, Oklahoma, and orphaned after his Cherokee mother died giving birth to him and his English fur trapper father was stabbed to death in a saloon brawl three years later. The boy had been informally adopted by Watie and given the Cherokee name "Salal," which meant *squirrel*, and at the age of 14, with no objection by his adopted father, he had been one of the first to answer the call to arms. Though now only 18, Jonathon had advanced through the war to his current rank as captain and had earned a good reputation of leadership in the opinion of his general, and more importantly, among the men. Only his cool demeanor under fire outweighed his strategic and tactical abilities. Like his Cherokee namesake, he seemed to be everywhere on the battlefield at once, darting first here, then appearing somewhere else entirely, encouraging and leading his men into the fray by calm example. Bullets seemed to avoid him entirely, and his men, convinced he was invulnerable in battle, were more than willing to follow wherever he led.

General Watie lowered the field glasses and sighed. "I cannot do this any longer, Salal." He looked down at his feet, then back over his shoulder through the thick grove of trees where he knew the remains of his battalion sat hidden and waiting, and nodded. "I cannot ask them to do any more."

Jonathon took back the binoculars, and then, without being asked, handed down a canteen. Watie took the water without looking up and drank gratefully.

"General, the men will always follow you," Jonathon said, admiration filling his chest as he watched his old chief, friend, and mentor carefully, "anywhere." He then added, almost sadly, "Even to death."

Watie plugged the canteen and handed it back up, but then held it and caught his son's eyes intensely.

"Yes, I know. And that's the real tragedy of all this." He then looked away, almost embarrassed. "You know, don't you, Captain, that Lee has already surrendered? Someplace in Virginia called Appomattox Courthouse—months ago, they say."

Jonathon met the general's misty gaze. "Yes sir, General. I have heard that."

Watie shook his head slightly, let go of the canteen, then stared back down the grassy slope.

"Then why in God's holy name are we still here," he muttered under his breath, "fighting for this—this, no man's land?

"Excuse me, General?"

Watie motioned with his hand and spoke up. "A killing field. How in the name of all that's decent can I ask men to go down that slope and cross that river—straight into those Yankee guns again? For no good reason!"

Jonathon Carter followed his general's gaze, out across the grass, then squeezed his eyes shut, listening to the leaves rustling. He sat thinking for several long moments before opening his eyes again and looking around wearily. Like his general, Captain Jonathon Salal Carter felt old beyond his years, and so very tired of this war.

"General, I await your orders, Sir."

#

(April, 1868 – Fort Worth, Texas)

The bright yellow stalks of grass dripped in blood, and his ears filled with the screams of wounded and dying men as the guns of the enemy filled the air with the acrid stench of gunpowder and death. He saw himself leaning forward in the saddle, digging his boot heels into the flanks of his warhorse—and screaming a deafening war cry. His saber pointed straight out over the head of his horse, whose hooves pounded through the long, sloping plain of bloodied grass and then splashed into the river beyond. His horse was now screaming and thrusting forward powerfully through the surging current—straight into the rifles of blue-clad soldiers lining the far bank, the muzzles exploding into his face with fire, smoke, and lead.

Then deafening silence and complete darkness.

Almost three years after Robert E. Lee's surrender, Jonathon Salal Carter, captain and warrior, late of the Cherokee Mounted Rifles, lay squirming and tossing through yet another nightmare. It always ended the same way and Jonathon would jerk wide awake, covered with sweat, eyes wide, and lungs heaving for breath. The roar of guns and screams of men would gradually fall away and merge into the raucous laughter and distant music emanating from the saloon across the street, and he would finally awaken to his current life now—that of a drifter and seeker of his fortune, stranded and living hand to mouth in the bustling cow town of Fort Worth.

And in that reality, General Stand Watie's Cherokee Battalion did not fight that day, nor ever again. Instead, under a flag of truce they had marched out onto the open field of grass and laid down their arms in final surrender. General Watie held the dubious distinction of being the last Confederate general to do so, and seven years later the old chieftain would be dead, a broken and ruined man.

The small room that Jonathon lived in at the livery stable wasn't much bigger than a broom closet and was even less soundproof. He lived here rent-free as part of his wages for cleaning the stalls, hauling fresh hay and feed, and currying the dozens of animals that passed through the busy stable weekly. The few additional coins he earned were scarcely enough to buy one good meal a day, a weekly bath in the back of the emporium up the street, and perhaps a drink or two at the nearby Cattlemen's Saloon. It seemed that a half-breed Cherokee could find no better work around here, even as busy a town as this was.

As he raised himself up and kicked his damp bedclothes off, he had no idea what time it was and didn't need to know, for the noise from the bar across the street told him it wasn't late at all. He rolled back over with a pillow over his head and tried to go back to sleep. It was no use, and he finally sat up on the edge of his bed, which was barely big enough for a large child, and rubbed his face. He ignored the sound of a rat scampering across the floor, sighed, found the chamber pot underneath the bed, and relieved himself into it. He stood up, stretched, and stumbled over to the washbasin to dunk his face into the tepid water there. He dried his face on a worn towel while pulling the dirty excuse for a window curtain back and peered outside. The half-moon cast a pale wash of light over the silent streets and buildings behind the stables.

He slowly pulled on his clothes, buttoning his shirt and neatly tucking it into his dungarees. The clothes were worn, but he prided himself on keeping them clean and as presentable as he could. He reached over to the wall for his gun belt hanging on a bent nail, and buckled it on. The heavy Army Colt .45 revolver hung reassuringly down his right hip.

He now felt fully dressed.

The door to his room was tight in the frame and protested loudly as he wrenched it open and stepped out into the sawdust alley that ran between the horse stalls, which were dimly lit by one gas lamp on a nearby post. He ran his hands through his thick black hair and tucked his head into a worn, gray campaign slouch hat—which besides his pistol was his only memento from the war—and stepped out of the livery stable into the cool night air. A stray dog yapped at him as he crossed the dry, dusty street and stepped onto the board sidewalk where he stopped for a moment.

The mingled sounds of tinkling glassware, piano music, and boisterous laughter greeted him, mocking him like the outsider he was. The odor of liquor, sweat, cigar smoke, and cheap perfume drifted like ghosts around him. He pulled some coins out of his pocket and examined them in his open hand. Enough for one drink, maybe two; but that meant no good eats tomorrow. *Payday on Friday, though.* He sighed, hitched his pants up, and pushed through the swinging doors of the saloon, into yet another type of isolation.

Almost immediately a drunk fell into him and Jonathon caught the man by the front of his suspenders to keep him from falling over. The man's face was pressed against Jonathon's chest, drooling. "'Scuse me," the drunk belched, and then roughly pushed himself off of Jonathon and staggered on. Jonathon grimaced, took a folded handkerchief from his vest pocket, and dabbed away the spittle on his collar. He did not consider himself to be overly fastidious, but he had just soaped his clothes off during his bath a few days ago, an added luxury.

He picked his way through the loud tables filled with conversation and laughter and caught the occasional eyes of saloon girls who appraised him up and down and just as quickly dismissed him. Some of them probably recognized him and knew he was not easily drawn to the well-worn charms of their pleasure trade; others probably wanted nothing to do with a half-breed. He eased up to one end of the bar on the other side of the room, leaned on his elbows, and surveyed the scene. He preferred the corners of crowded rooms, where he was able to take in almost everything and everyone at a glance; the large mirror behind the bar served to double the effects of his vantage point.

"The usual, Jonathon? Kentucky bourbon, right?" The bartender had appeared and began pouring the drink before Jonathon even answered.

"Yes. Thank you, Pete. That will be fine." He slid a twenty-five cent piece across the bar. The bartender took it and just as quickly disappeared, giving Jonathon his privacy. Pete was the only person Jonathon knew in the room, at least by name, and he was always impressed that Pete the bartender remembered his drink of choice. He took a slow, appreciative sip of the whiskey, then set the glass down as he allowed his eyes to wander. The noise and terror of the recurring nightmare had finally faded to the back of his mind and some other part of his brain kicked in—the cold and assessing part. As had often occurred during the war, he seemed to have an innate ability to recognize dangerous situations long before they became obvious. He had always assumed that this was his Indian nature, but he had soon discovered that most of the other native soldiers in his battalion had not been so endowed. Whatever this skill—this gift—and wherever it came from, Carter no longer questioned it. It had saved his life on more than one occasion.

A small movement further down the bar caught his eye, and he straightened up. The movement seemed out of place, and it soon evolved into a commotion that began to broil among a group of men gathered there. Jonathon felt himself tense up, then a strange calm descended upon him—a calm before the storm. The level of voices steadily rose to a crescendo of shouting, arms began to flail, and the knot of men began to shove and pulse as if it were one thrashing beast. It noisily lurched away from the bar and just as suddenly disentangled itself as a lone figure was pushed to the floor, falling face first. Curses as well as boots began to fly, kicking the defenseless form as his arms covered the back of his head and he began to curl up into a ball.

"Get him outa here!" came a yell, and arms roughly raised the man off the floor and half walked, half dragged him across the room, knocking into tables and chairs, which elicited more angry shouts of displeasure. As the man was jerked to a standing position, Jonathon finally saw that he was an Indian wearing ragged, dirty skins of some sort and sporting long, greasy black hair that was pulled back and tied by a leather thong. The man winced from pain. There were cuts on his face, and blood reddened his puffed and swollen lip.

As the native was thrown through the swinging doors, Jonathon clenched his teeth and turned back to his drink. He slowly rubbed his jaw, then had another sip, which burned pleasantly in his throat but did nothing to dissipate his feeling of imminent danger. No sooner had he set the tumbler back down than the door flew open and the bloodied Indian sauntered back in, the back of one hand wiping his lip. The noise of the room dropped to low murmurings as he defiantly walked back up to the bar, motioned to the bartender, and quietly ordered a beer. Pete frowned at him, continued wiping out a mug he had been working on, and shook his head slowly.

"Now Chief, you know I can't serve you anything. You best get on out before it gets worse for you. I really don't want to see you hurt any more than you have been already."

"But I have money," the Indian said softly, holding out a dollar coin. "I work hard and mind my business, and I would like a beer, please."

A few more muttered curses floated around the room, and a chuckle or two rose as the men who had previously manhandled the Indian sidled up to him once again. "Friend," one of the larger men said evenly as he put a meaty hand on the Indian's shoulder, "I do believe you are either lacking in wisdom, or else hard of hearing." He reached across, knocked the coin out of the outreached hand, then squeezed the Indian's cheeks hard as he brought his face around to him and continued, enunciating each word. "The man told you to get yourself out of here!"

On this last word, he backhanded the Indian hard across the cheek, the sound mixing now with the uttered *Oh!s* that rose from the room. The Indian said nothing but slowly turned back around and glared at his tormentor. The man raised his hand to deliver another slap, but this time the Indian whipped his own hand up and took hold of the man's fingers, squeezing them tightly in his fist before shoving them away from him.

The bully backed up a couple of steps, shocked and holding his painful hand. He then swore and jerked his good hand down to grab the butt of a pistol that was shoved into the front of his pants. He had it drawn halfway when another strong hand suddenly gripped his elbow hard and a low voice came from somewhere right behind his ear.

"Mister," the voice purred. "You don't really want to be pulling that iron, do you?" It was more of a statement than a question. The man whipped around, the surprise on his face turning to anger as he thought he recognized the speaker, who had appeared out of nowhere. His hand paused uncertainly, fingers loosening a bit on the butt of his gun.

"I know you," the bully said. "You're that damned half-breed rebel that sweeps up all the horseshit, ain't ya?" The frown on his face began to split into a grin, which he turned and shared with his pals.

Jonathon rested his thumbs on the edge of his belt. He glanced at the Indian, whose face betrayed no emotion, but whose dark eyes twinkled at him. "Yes," Jonathon answered quietly, and looked the bully up and down.

"I am that half-breed—who shovels the shit."

His adversary straightened suddenly, uncertain of his next move. He glanced warily down at Jonathon's Colt, still holstered but dangerously near Jonathon's right hand. "Well, I would think you would, yourself, be a little more cautious— half-breed." He stuck his chin out a bit with the insult. Then, keeping his eyes on Jonathon, he addressed the bar. "Pete, I would think you wouldn't be serving half-breeds in here, neither."

Pete kept his eyes locked on Jonathon's. "This one here's earned his right to be here, Jasper, much as you have, I reckon," he replied, giving the bully a name at last.

"How you figure?" Jasper snarled. "He's got Injun blood in him, don't he?" He kept his eyes locked on Jonathon's and his forefinger twitched, as if hankering to stroke his gun handle.

Pete nodded toward Jonathon, then answered. "You see that gray officer's hat he's wearing?" He pointed down at Jonathon's hip. "And that big Army .45 tucked into that well-oiled holster?" Jasper's eyes darted down, then back up, but he said nothing. "Well, I'd say that there half-breed, Bob, probably wore those accoutrements proudly for the past four or five years, in service to a grateful Confederacy, and he probably knows how to use them, too. And Jasper," he paused to spit into the mug he was cleaning, then wiped it again before continuing, "that there half-breed has got a name, and you ought to use it, instead."

"Oh yeah?" smirked Jasper. "What name would that be, do you think?"

There was a pause and the room seemed to shift a few inches and collectively draw closer. A quiet voice spoke from Jonathon's right. It was the Indian he had stepped in to protect.

"His name is Captain Jonathon Salal Carter, of the Cherokee Mounted Rifles, Oklahoma Territory." The crowd in the saloon held its collective breath as the shabby Indian drew himself up tall and straight and pulled his right arm up into a smart salute. "It is very good to see you again, Captain," he said, a smile playing at the corner of his lips.

Jonathon squinted, then smiled back. "Your name is Mangus, isn't it?" he replied. The Indian nodded, but kept the salute in place. Remembering his etiquette, Jonathon returned the salute and then stepped up to shake the ex-soldier's hand. "I am very glad to see you again too, Mangus."

Jasper the bully stared first at one and then the other.

"Screw this shit!" he muttered, then suddenly drew his pistol; but Jonathon was quicker. He drew and whacked the barrel of his heavy Colt loudly across the top of Jasper's hat, then stepped back as the man collapsed with a loud sigh into a pile at his feet.

Chairs scraped as a few men jumped angrily to their feet, and the murmurings and exclamations grew louder. Some shook their fists toward the two Indians while Jonathon, pistol still drawn, touched Mangus's arm, ready to make a hasty retreat for them both toward the back door.

"Salal, huh?" a voice called out from somewhere in the middle of the room, stopping them in their tracks. The room grew quiet again as all other heads swiveled toward a tall man dressed in a sharp, dark gray suit and a black hat slowly stood up and sauntered forth. He sported a well-trimmed goatee with mustaches to match that he now stroked thoughtfully as he seemed to size Jonathon up.

"Why, if I am not mistaken," the man said with a thick, unmistakable Southern drawl, "back where I grew up in Tennessee, the name Salal was Cherokee for *squirrel.*" The Southerner stopped halfway across the floor, which was now clearing between him and Jonathon, and pulled his long coat back to reveal twin pearl handled revolvers strapped to his sides.

"So, is that what you are, Captain?" he continued. "A squirrel?"

Jonathon turned and faced this new possible threat.

"It is indeed my name," he answered quietly, but proudly, "and one, I might add, given to me by my father."

"Your father?" smirked the gunman.

"Perhaps you have heard of his father, Mr. Allison," Mangus interjected into the conversation. "General Isaac Stand Watie?"

The man's face grew motionless, and he cleared his throat. "You are General Stand Watie's son?" he stammered, a degree of respect entering his voice. He removed his hat, let his coat close over his guns, and took a non-threatening step forward. "I am well aware of the accomplishments of the great General Watie during the late War of Northern Aggression!" He took another couple of steps, extending his right hand. "I apologize for any rudeness; and may I be so bold as to introduce myself, Captain? I am Robert Clay Allison, late of General Bedford Forrest's cavalry. But you may call me Clay; all my friends do."

Jonathon slowly holstered his pistol, then tentatively took the Tennessean's hand and shook it. "Mr. Allison," he replied evenly.

Clay Allison quickly turned and gestured toward his table, where another man was seated and calmly watching the exchange with great interest. "Won't you allow me to buy you a drink, Captain Carter? And please, come join my friend and me here at our table." He moved toward the table, then stopped when he noticed Jonathon had not moved.

"I would be pleased to, Mr. Allison," he replied, and then nodded to Mangus, "if my friend here is welcome to join you, also." A tide of fresh murmurings rolled across the room, but this time they were unaccompanied by any fist shaking and died away just as quickly when Allison scanned the faces with a sudden frown.

"Why, of course, your comrade-in-arms may join us," he gestured grandly toward two additional seats. "How do they say it? *Any friend of yours,* et cetera?'" He then motioned to the bartender for more drinks.

Jonathon and Mangus approached the table. Jonathon could now see Allison's companion, a swarthy giant of a man with a dark beard that matched his dark, short-cropped hair, who was already standing up and extending a hand.

"Charles Goodnight is my name, fellows," he offered, a huge grin splitting his face as he shook each of their hands briskly in turn. "And may I say I am proud to meet two more veterans of the noble cause, which I also served."

Pete interrupted them all by quickly setting brimming shots of whisky in front of them as they took their seats. Jonathon and Mangus exchanged bemused glances at this odd and quick turn of events.

"Mr. Goodnight here is a cattleman," Allison said, moving the conversation along. "Er—you have, no doubt, heard of the Goodnight-Loving Trail that runs from here through western Texas and straight up along the river into the New

Mexico and Colorado Territories?"

Jonathon shook his head. "No, I have not." Allison started to say something else but was stopped by Goodnight placing a hand on his arm.

"Let me cut to the chase here, Clay." He turned back to Jonathon. "Captain Carter—Jonathon, if I may—I appreciate that you don't know me from Adam, but suffice it to say I fancy myself a good judge of men and of character." Here he nodded at each of the three of them. "And I reckon that the three of you are solid. Now, my partner Oliver Loving and I are about to make our third run, trailing three to four thousand head of prime beef to the military and settlers in the territories. It's a hard trail to ride, I won't lie. There's drought, and dust, and desert, and long days, short nights, and sometimes bandits and Indians—oh pardon me, I meant nothing by that." Jonathon and Mangus said nothing. Goodnight coughed, embarrassed, then continued. "But what I meant was wild Apaches and Comanches, not you civilized ones." He waved his discomfort away. "What I mean to say to you is, I need solid men of integrity for this drive. Now, for some reason, I am finding the pickings a little slim around here." He cast a disparaging look around the saloon. "And I have already spoken to Mr. Allison here, so what I am offering you two are good jobs to come along and help get my cattle to market, if you'll have any of it." He paused, looking again from one to another. Allison leaned back in his chair and stroked his goatee thoughtfully, while Jonathon and Mangus exchanged another glance. "Like I said, it will take a few months, and I will expect a long day's work, each and every day—sometimes sixteen hours in the saddle—and I will tolerate no arguments, fist fights, nor gunplay. First sign of it, and you will be gone!" He punctuated his words with a stiff forefinger on the table.

"But in exchange for all that, I will provide you a fresh rig—saddle and tack, if you ain't got one, and ammo for your guns—fresh mounts every day, the best grub you can fill your stomach with, and fifteen dollars up front so's you can get your affairs straightened up before we leave," and here Goodnight paused and sniffed. "And to get yourselves some decent clothes; a dollar a day after that, and another twenty-five dollars bonus when we successfully deliver the cattle—plus you get to keep a horse of your choice from my remuda when you're done."

The three former Confederate soldiers stared blankly back at Charles Goodnight, who finally slapped the table.

"Now, there's no one else around gonna pay you those sorta wages, and—well dammit to hell—are you boys going on this cattle drive with me or ain't ya?

CHAPTER 2
A Peaceable Kingdom

(Present Day – Montaño del Sol Ranch)

Trent Carter took a long, grateful gulp of the amber liquid that had filled his tumbler to the brim and sighed deeply. He rubbed the cold glass against his warm forehead, allowing the condensation to mix with the perspiration that lingered there after the warm afternoon. He exhaled, propped his boots up on the heavy split railing that surrounded the veranda, and examined the glass's contents.

Trent only occasionally missed the bourbon now; and besides, Maggie's special sun tea always hit the spot on these warm Indian summer days. The fresh sprig of crushed mint from her garden gave the refreshment just the right little kick as it played on his tongue; at least, that's what he told himself.

He allowed his gaze to wander across the manicured yard, across the large drive and plaza, to the outbuildings and barns, and finally to the corrals beyond where Maggie was working with a young gelding she had been training. From here Trent could just barely hear her calling out firm but smooth commands as she led the animal through its paces around the arena, motioning occasionally with her free hand while her other firmly grasped the long lead line fastened to the horse's bridle. Maggie wore men's ranch clothes as usual—jeans, old work boots, and a red flannel shirt. Normally, she would be wearing the old jean jacket that now hung on the corral fence along with an old slouch hat. She had pulled her long, dark hair back into a ponytail that played enticingly down the back of her neck and shoulders as she moved. She cooed to the winded animal and slowed him to a halt before easing up on the rein. She moved toward the horse, removed a leather glove, and reached up to stroke the animal's soft nose and face. The gelding bowed his head in submission to Maggie's gentle and assuring touch. She reached into her pocket and rewarded him with a raw carrot.

Trent never tired of watching his wife work, especially with her horses. Maggie was the consummate horsewoman, and he took pride in her abilities to confidently and soothingly build the necessary trust of the animal to bend it to her will.

"Much as she tamed me," he mumbled and then took another long sip of iced tea.

"What was that?" Walter Carter looked up from the chessboard that sat on a small table between he and his son.

"Nothing, Walter. Just recalling an impossible situation," Trent answered. Walter grunted and returned his attention to the board, pondering his next move.

Mostly at Maggie's insistence, she and Trent had moved his aging, often cranky father to live with them at her family ranch at Montaña del Sol shortly after they were married. Before that time, Walter had been living in a rehabilitation center after a work-related accident in the Raton train yards had forced him into early medical retirement. Trent even now felt a twinge of shame at having left his father in the retirement home for so long after the rehab was complete—or as complete as it was going to be. He and his father had become estranged after the death of Trent's mother from cancer, followed shortly by the murder of Trent's first wife, Victoria. Trent and his father had each blamed the other for the deaths of these strong women who had anchored their lives. Trent's excuse for maintaining the estrangement had been his own disabilities of body and spirit from injuries sustained in the same horrific attack that had taken Vicky away from them all.

As Trent had continued to heal, his feelings toward his father had gradually softened, to a certain extent, although he still found it difficult to call him *Dad*.

The fall color was still in full glory on the cottonwoods, elms, and oak that surrounded the ranch headquarters compound; but further up the hills behind the corrals, Trent could see that the aspens scattered among the tree line of pines were beginning to lose some of their gold. The afternoons had grown shorter, and he shivered a bit now as the temperature noticeably dropped and the sun disappeared into a glitter of light playing through the trees to the west. His joints and old injuries ached fiercely.

Winter would be here sooner than later.

He glanced back over to the corrals, now empty. Maggie must have led the gelding into the barn; he could picture her giving the animal a welcome rubdown and a can full of oats. He smiled to himself, envying the horse, and looked forward to his wife finishing her work, coming back to the house, and calling it a day. He pulled his boots back off the railing and swung back around to the game.

"Give up yet, Walter?"

Walter twitched his lip and glanced up. "Give me a minute, will ya?" he growled.

"Well, you have had several," Trent answered, then shrugged, "but what's a few more?" He grimaced as he got up stiffly from his chair, stretched his back, and proceeded to stroll along to the other side of the veranda, where a fat, orange-dappled old tomcat lay napping in the last patch of sunlight that he could find on the porch. As Trent neared, the cat twitched, lazily opened one eye questioningly, and then rolled over onto its back and purred, lifting three legs accommodatingly in the air. A forepaw was missing, owing to a bad experience involving an animal trap.

Trent bent down and scratched the cat's exposed belly for all of three seconds before it decided to attack him with its remaining good paws and a mouth full of sharp fangs. It was a game they often played with each other and one that Trent frequently lost.

"Dammit, Jarhead!" he exclaimed, thrusting a bleeding knuckle into his mouth.

"What'd you expect?" muttered Walter from across the way, still absorbed in the chess game. "It's just a stupid, damn cat."

Jarhead leapt off the veranda and scampered across the yard. Trent noted that the cat made pretty good progress on just three legs now, only a year or so since the incident with the trap. He sipped his tea again before rolling the cold glass against the side of his forehead. The cold felt good against the burning scar that disappeared into his hairline there, a souvenir from the bullet that had grazed him when Vicky had been killed. It had left him with an occasional lapse—a glitch—in his cognitive skills. At other odd and inexplicable times, the wound seemed to give him an extra bit of deductive reasoning abilities, bursts of odd clairvoyance, and unexplained visions. But this combined curse and blessing remained something mostly out of his control, something that his doctor had told him he would probably never fully recover from, and something extremely frustrating to Trent, as the visions sometimes involved dead people.

These uncontrollable events were the main reason he had finally resigned from the Colfax County Sheriff's Department—that, and Maggie's urging.

Consequently, he had retired to live the life of a gentleman rancher in the pristine and quiet canyon lands of northeastern New Mexico. Montaña del Sol had been in Maggie's family for decades and lay nestled among the verdant valleys lying between Raton Mesa and Johnson Mesa, several miles due east of the old railroad town of Raton, where Trent had been raised and where he had returned after retirement from the New Mexico State Police. After marrying Maggie, he had deeded the old family home in town to his only daughter, Sophie, a newspaperwoman who could've had a brilliant career in big city journalism somewhere had she not come home to care for Trent following the horrific events that had taken the life of her mother.

Without the two strong women now in his life—his daughter and his new wife—Trent knew that he would have permanently disappeared into the bottom of a whiskey bottle —or worse. They and a newfound faith in God had led him through the horrendous minefields of physical and spiritual recovery.

"Check!" Walter hollered, slapping his knees and grinning ferociously at his son. Trent looked at his father, shook his head, and sauntered back to stand over the chessboard. Chess was a game that Walter had become obsessed with in the retirement home, playing often against a kindly old priest he had befriended there. Trent had learned to play only within the last couple of years, mainly to give Walter and himself something constructive to do with one other—something besides arguing—to help them bond. Trent rubbed his chin thoughtfully for a moment, studying Walter's move of a white bishop upon his black king, leaned over, and moved his own queen to take the bishop, while simultaneously putting Walter's king in undeniable jeopardy.

"Check and mate," said Trent, tipping Walter's king over. Walter's obsession did not necessarily make the game his strong suit.

"Dammit!" Walter exclaimed. "Dammit all to hell—piece of shit game!" He jumped up and allowed his hand to tip the board and let the pieces fly across the porch. He stomped off into the house, slamming the screen door behind him, muttering all the way.

"Language, Walter, language!" scolded Maggie's voice as she made her way up the rough-hewn flagstone walkway that meandered through the lawn up to the steps of the veranda. Trent turned around and walked over to the edge of the top step and waited for her there. She had donned her jacket and the old slouch hat was pulled down to her eyebrows so that as she stopped at the bottom of the steps, she had to tilt her head back to gaze up at her husband. He hooked his thumbs in his jeans pockets and smiled down at her. Even dressed in her ranch work clothes, she always took Trent's breath away. Margaret Van Ryan had long ago mastered the delicate balancing act of single-handedly running a working cattle ranch while at the same time wielding the charm, mystique, and coquettishness of a beautiful woman—almost like a weapon.

"Hello there, Mr. Carter," she said, her slightly husky voice like honey being spread on toast. A strand of dark brown hair flecked with wisps of grey strayed from under her hat and down her cheek to flirt with him.

"Hello back, Mrs. Carter," Trent murmured. "Hard day at the office?"

"Nah," she answered, now making her way slowly but methodically up the steps. "Just the usual pointless meetings and phone calls," she joked back.

She stopped at the top of the steps and, having no other place to go, slipped her hands under his arms and gripped his lower back. He winced slightly, and then stopped as she tiptoed up until her lips just met his with a soft kiss.

"What's for supper, Cowboy?"

"Well," he answered, "we can go with whatever Walter might be in there rustling up—except that he's just a little perturbed right now."

Maggie pouted for a moment.

Trent scratched the back of his neck for a second. "Or, we can go in to the Supper Club Steakhouse in town. I'm buying," he continued, and her pout turned to a sweet smile. She stepped back and slid around him.

"Well, you'll have to give a girl some time to get dolled up, then," she called back at him as she headed for the door, but not before whipping her hat off and slapping him possessively on the butt. "Some of us have been working for a living today, you know, and could use a good wash." Her voice drifted sweetly away as she disappeared into the house.

As she did, Trent's pocket buzzed. He retrieved his old-school cell phone, flipped it open, and frowned at an all too familiar number.

"Carter," he answered, annoyed.

"Why, as I live and breathe, you actually answered this time."

It was his old boss Ben Ferguson, the county sheriff.

"What brings you into my ear this time of day?"

"Oh, nothing much. Just out here wandering around the boonies south of town, scratching what little hair I have left on the top of my head, and wondering whether I should even bother a burnt out old retired cop or not."

"Aw, gee, Ben, and here I thought you just missed my charming wit and pleasing personality."

"More like your sharp tongue and uncanny bullshit filter." Ben paused, then continued. "And I'm thinking I just may need some of that uncanniness of yours right now, Trent."

"What's up Ben?" Trent sighed. He could hear noises in the background of Ben's call—sirens, other voices. "Where are you?"

"Stockton place. Couple of bodies, out here at the old Clifton House ruins. You know the place?"

"Yeah, I know it. What do you mean 'couple of bodies?' Who are they?"

"No idea. Pretty bizarre, actually. But *bizarre* always seemed to be right down your alley."

"Murders?" Trent pressed. He was becoming curious—and for some reason a little guilty about it.

"Well, you might say that. At least one of them definitely is. Has a pickaxe sticking out of his chest." Ben hesitated once more. Trent waited for a second or two.

"And the other one?" he finally asked.

"That's the bizarre part. The other one is, well, let's just say he's a bit seasoned. You'd have to see it to understand, exactly."

There was a silence from both of them for a while.

"Trent, you there?"

"Yeah, I'm here."

"Think you can come on out for a little bit? This new medical examiner from Santa Fe is driving me bat-shit crazy. I need someone here that speaks my language."

"What happened to Bill Emerson?" Trent asked, referring to the old M.E. who had helped him on several previous cases.

"He retired and bought a bungalow on the beach in Mexico or some gosh-awful place, where his wife could work on her suntan while he ogles the bikinis without getting into too much trouble."

"What about Hector? Isn't he your star deputy now? Isn't he available?"

"Yeah, Hector's here. But he's . . . well, hell, Trent. He's your son-in-law. You know, Hector is . . . *Hector.*"

Trent chewed his lower lip, touched the scar on his forehead, and glanced back at the house. He was more than a little intrigued. His days, recently, had not been that much of a challenge. He sighed and put the phone back up to his ear.

"Come on, Trent—you act like you're not interested."

"Okay, I'll give you thirty minutes. Be there shortly." He almost hung up, and then thought of something else. "And Ben, if Maggie finds out, you know that you're the one who's going to pay hell for it. I *will* throw you under her bus. I hope you realize that."

There was a significant pause on the other end before Ben spoke again. "So, what are you going to tell her?"

"I don't know. I'll think of something." He snapped the phone shut just as Ben started to say something else, and went into the house.

Yep, he thought. Sometimes he really missed the bourbon.

CHAPTER 3
Desierto de los Muertos

(A letter from Maria Consuelo Delgado)

July 12, 1868

Sr. Manuel Diego Delgado
El Rancho de las Golondrinas
Santa Fe,
Territorio de Nuevo Mexico

Dearest Mannie:

I was thrilled to receive your letter last week! I have read it over and over so many times, I think the ink must be wearing off the paper. Papa and the boys have also had me re-read it to them several times. Thank you so much for all the news, my precious brother.

I am still laughing over your description of little Patricio trying to catch the rooster, only to be chased himself. I can just picture it. I shall have to give him a new nickname: Gallo!

And how exciting to hear the news that my dear sister-in-law is going to have another baby! How I am tempted to jump onto the next train of wagons that heads down the Santa Fe Trail and surprise you all with a long visit! I would time it, of course, with the arrival of the new little one. I feel certain that Ana is wanting a little girl now, to even things out. Ana and I being the only women right now, I would love to have a beautiful little niece. But no, having said that, I quickly add a prayer that God may have His way and give us a sweet girl or a precious boy, as He chooses. Either one shall be welcomed into the bosom of our family.

Oh, I so wish Mama was still alive to see her preciosos nietos!

Some more wondrous news: I must tell you that Papa has said I may accompany him to Willow Springs when he goes to buy more livestock, the next time one of the big herds come through from Texas! I am so thrilled, not only because I have been no farther from our new home than the small town of Cimarrón but also because it will be such an adventure!

In the meantime, write to me soon, dearest one. I miss you all so terribly, but I especially miss our talks, as only brothers and sisters have.

I remain,
Your loving sister,
María

(June 1868 – West Texas)

"Hey, Squirrel! Wake up! You have a couple of stragglers over there!"

Jonathon jerked awake. He had been daydreaming and had dozed off on the back of his gently swaying gelding. It was a skill he had learned long ago in the cavalry, where they often had to catch their sleep wherever, and whenever they could. But it was not a skill that was too well thought of when one was herding cattle.

He turned and looked behind him where Clay Allison was trotting up to him, a big grin on his face. Jonathon rubbed the back of his neck and adjusted the brim of his hat. He clucked at the gelding and directed it with his feet as it trotted away to intercept the errant steers. He didn't press the strays too hard, as he had learned from the more seasoned hands that so long as the cattle—even the strays—kept moving generally forward, such hard pushing would actually stress them and accomplish little. Instead, he allowed the steers to wander a little further while he made his way steadily below them and away from them.

"It is the odd psychology of the herd animal," Oliver Loving had lectured more than once, "to actually want to go in the opposite direction you and your horse are headed." He would then aim and spit tobacco juice on some bug ambling across the ground beside his horse. "Damndest thing to try and understand," he would continue, knowing the young cowhands were hanging on his every word, "so don't even try to. Just believe it."

Jonathon continued to give ground as he was taught, and thereby coaxed the animals back into the *invisible box* that made up the boundaries of the herd. He stood his horse still for a while, letting the cows plod methodically past him. They seemed content to know that he and his horse were just there and part of their perceived safety zone. A cloud of dry desert dust boiled up from their hooves and hung no higher than the animals' knees, so long as they moved slowly and steadily; but dust was still dust, especially on a hot, dry day. Jonathon had his red bandanna pulled up over his mouth and nose as he worked the cattle.

After a few more minutes, he pulled his gelding back and slowly made his way over to Allison, who had also stood his mount several yards back from the herd.

"Don't call me *Squirrel*," said Jonathon evenly as he pulled up next to Allison.

"Why, Jonathon—I thought you said you were proud of that particular sobriquet."

"Not the way you say it. And the correct Cherokee pronunciation is Sa*lal*, even if I don't understand that other word you said."

Clay Allison chuckled. "You mean *sobriquet*? Why, let's just say it means *funny-as-hell-name*."

"How should we know, Clay?" called out Mangus, who had just ridden up, trailing yet another stray from a nearby arroyo. "You could be saying anything, fancy whorehouse words like that." Mangus skillfully stopped his horse, allowing the steer to find its own way back into place. "Mr. Loving says we will hit Horsehead Crossing soon. Maybe this evening, things keep moving."

Jonathon squinted to the south, where a dark band of dirty clouds was gathering. He nodded in that direction.

"Better be sooner than later. That squall there's moving faster than I'd like." He frowned as a distant white tongue flicked underneath the cloud line. "That lightning moves in on us, you and I will not be spending any bedroll time tonight."

Jonathon, Mangus, and the Allison brothers, Clay and John, had all left Fort Worth together at the beginning of May with fresh duds, new mounts, and even a few dollars left in their pockets, with instructions from Mr. Goodnight to meet him and the herd on the Brazos River, south of Fort Belknap, in four days. There they had met up with Goodnight, 3,800 head of nervous cows, several other cowhands, and Oliver Loving—a feisty, wiry old cowboy with a quick wit, a quick smile, and a quick laugh at his own terrible jokes. Well into his fifties, Loving was as seasoned a cattleman as they came and a die-hard Texican, even if he had been born in Tennessee; and even though he and Goodnight were co-owners of the entire herd, Loving liked to hang out in the bunkhouse with the cowboys, sharing his good whiskey, tall tales, and talk of bawdy women. Jonathon had observed that the old gent could pull a cork with the best of them—but once the real work began the whiskey had better be well hidden away or Loving would be the first to make sure that there was hell to pay for it. He held his own liquor well but did not personally know anyone else who could, and he did not tolerate anyone shirking hard work at 4:30 a.m. because of anything so ridiculous as a hangover.

Loving had put the herd together over the previous few months, wheeling and dealing, cajoling and even stretching the truth, plying sellers from Kansas City to Fort Worth with a mouth full of smooth talk and a saddlebag full of gold and silver coins. Having worked closely with his friend and colleague Charlie Goodnight for a few years now, he knew exactly what sort of trail-hardy animals they both needed for this important drive, he knew the eager markets that lay ahead of them, and he knew how to get the beef to those markets.

Goodnight had put the talent together, gathering seasoned and non-seasoned trail hands alike with as practiced an eye as Loving had for the animals. They had all come together as one unit a hundred miles west of Fort Worth on the Brazos River. Here, not only were the cattle sorted out, but this new and often rowdy bunch of saddle tramps were also quickly weeded through and molded by the skillful hands of Goodnight and Loving into a well disciplined, skilled team of trail hands.

Now, six weeks later and 300 miles further southwest of their starting point, they had hit the edge of what the old Spanish explorers had named the *Desierto de los Muertos—Desert of the Dead*. The vast Chihuahuan Desert, which stretched from El Paso to the border of Norte México, was magnificent in its stark, rugged beauty but could be sudden death to those who neither understood nor respected it.

Just up ahead, they had been told, was the landmark ford over the *Rio Pecos* called Horsehead Crossing, supposedly named by ancient plains Indians—probably ancestors of the Comanches—who had marked the river passage with the skulls of dead horses.

Such was the tale. All Jonathon knew was that the crossing offered welcome relief with much needed water for men and animals and marked the point where they finally turned northward and followed the river into New Mexico Territory and onward to Fort Sumner. There they would find their first major market, where they would sell hundreds if not thousands of beeves to the U.S. Army.

"Well, storm or no," Mangus replied, "I will be happy just to fill up my canteens again. Fort Sumner is over 200 miles away yet. Many a dry desert to cross and many a savage's arrows to avoid before then."

"Oh hell, Mangus," smirked Clay. "You have nothing to fear from a savage's arrow. Why, they'll take one look at you and give you the road out of professional courtesy—young Squirrel here too, I expect." Allison turned his horse and moved away toward the rear of the herd, calling out over his shoulder. "Why do you suppose I hang around both you Injuns? For good luck!"

About 4:00 that afternoon their luck finally ran out.

The squall they had been nervously eyeing finally boiled up and over them, just as the outriders had come through a gap and sighted Horsehead Crossing a mile or so ahead. Some arroyos were already trickling streams of water, which grew faster and deeper by the minute. The cattle had begun to bawl and had gotten skittish, jumping with each distant flash of lightning, eyes rolling white with the cracks of thunder that followed. Voices up ahead began to shout back to the flank riders. Jonathon and Mangus strained to hear the shouted instructions.

"What's that they say?" Mangus called over.

Jonathon strained again, finally making something out.

"I think they're trying to circle the herd—get it milling about." He realized if that were the case, the trail bosses were going to try and bed them down right here, but he knew that was going to be difficult. The cattle had already caught a whiff of water ahead and caught the fear of lightning behind.

Suddenly, Jonathon pulled up short, his sixth sense tingling madly. Something was amiss and a wave of danger, like nausea, rose within him. He twisted in the saddle, this way and that, scanning the scene wildly. He had not experienced a feeling like this since going into battle in the face of Yankee guns during the war. If he had learned one thing, it was that he should trust his feelings, as illogical as they might seem. All he knew for the moment was that this was no mere lightning storm he was dreading—this was a portent of war.

Up ahead, he could see that half the herd had already pulled tightly into the sloping walls of a draw, a ravine-like passage that sent shards of alarm stabbing through Jonathon. If the cattle got themselves bottle-necked here, particularly in this storm—or worse—the entire herd would be in danger of disintegrating. They would be all night gathering it back together.

"Mangus!" he finally called out, his eyes wide and his free hand gesturing wildly toward the draw. "Stop them from going on. Something's not right!" Jonathon dug his heels sharply into his horse's sides. The experienced beast jumped forward, sensing as well as responding to the urgency in its rider's body language.

Mangus turned at the sound of Jonathon's voice and immediately recognized his former captain's movements in the saddle, whipping his mount back and forth in a zigzag motion, manuevering away from some danger yet unseen but as real as anything the eyes could see; and Mangus knew it was to his best advantage to respond immediately and unhesitatingly.

A brief feeling of satisfaction welled up in Jonathon's chest as he watched Mangus move into action, just as he had seen him do countless times during battle in the hills of Oklahoma. There was at least one cowhand he didn't have to worry about right now. The gelding was puffing with exertion, and Jonathon skillfully turned it in a long arc around the western slope of the draw. If he could outflank the geographic feature and come back out upon the head of the herd, he might just also catch the attention of the trail bosses and alert them to the impending crisis— *whatever it was,* he thought frantically to himself.

And it was then that he saw exactly what *it* was.

As heavy raindrops began to pelt his back, a streak of lighning crashed not a mile away, lighting up the darkened horizon of a small, flat mesa nearby and revealing the unmistakeable silhouettes of several riders against dark clouds. At this distance, it was at first hard to identify them, but Jonathon knew by the way they sat their mounts they were not cowboys—certainly not military—and then he caught the flashes of light from sharpened lance points and saw fluttering, decorative feathers. He watched in grudging admiration as these lords of the plains loped casually along an intercept line, straight toward the herd—a Comanche war party, whose riders knew exactly what they were doing. They melded so easily with their ponies that each had become one beast, and all together they had become one experienced, well-seasoned, self-assured troop of cavalry like few others in the world.

And he could sense at first glance the verification and culmination of all the rising tension in his heart and throat.

The loping, lance-brandishing war unit picked up speed now, seemingly carried along on the wind itself. Jonathon was sure he heard their war cries, ululating across the earth, vying with the clapping thunder for attention—and getting it. Up ahead, Jonathon could see that the other outriders had finally seen the imminent danger and were turning to face it as the warriors barreled toward them from out of the belly of the stormcloud. The cowhands darted this way, then that, most of them unsure and inexperienced in the battlefield tactics they needed to confront this threat.

But Jonathon knew what was needed. He whipped his horse into a frenzied gallop, bisecting the line of approach of the enemy war party while screaming out at the cowboys.

"Get to the high ground!" he shouted, but felt that his words were whipped away on the rain. He fumbled now behind him, searching with his free hand for the scabbarded Winchester rifle he knew was there and finding it right away. He swung it around and cocked it hard in one movement, then brandished it over his head, back and forth like a battle flag, shouting once again as a few of the cowboys finally noticed him and pointed his way.

"The high ground!" he repeated at the top of his lungs. By now the cattle were panicking, no longer plodding or trotting, but working themselves up into a full-blown stampede, the cowhands helpless to stop them. "Get out of their way—let them run for it!" Jonathon yelled, whipping his rifle to the left, motioning them away from the dangerously running herd. The more experienced of them recognized the danger and whipped their mounts away from the roiling, slashing hooves of their charges, now a dangerous, single-minded machine that would mow down anything alive in its path.

Out of the corner of his eye, Jonathon saw Mangus paralleling his own run on a line that would intersect with him and the other cowhands shortly. They had both swung their horses up the gentle slope, darting past mesquite bushes, jumping over small ravines. At a point where they were just yards apart now, Jonathon pulled up hard on the reins, then swung off his horse, still at a full lope, planted both heels and slid through the sandy soil, pulling his horse's screaming head almost 180 degrees around with one hand and firmly gripping the rifle in the other. The horse bounced to a stop and dropped over onto its side, almost in one fluid motion, as Jonathon fell over the neck and face of the frightened animal, cooing repeatedly and stroking its neck. The horse quieted down, soothed by the weight of its rider splayed across him. Jonathon slowly slid off the animal, still stroking and comforting it, his eyes glued to the horizon and the blunt force trauma of the approaching Comanche war party. He risked the luxury of quickly glancing around to take stock of his people, and his heart sank as he counted only Mangus, himself, Allison, and one other outrider who had had the wisdom to copy his movements and now lay behind their own prone horses, rifles cocked and aimed over their mounts' necks. They caught Jonathon's glance and he nodded briskly at them. It wasn't until this moment that he noticed the ground shuddering and thundering beneath them; at first he surmised it was from the thunder and lightning crashing around them, but soon he realized it was from the pounding hooves of the stampeding herd, just out of sight behind them and below the escarpment of the draw.

The war party had all but disappeared in the clouds of boiling dust and deepening shadows of the storm, which had already moved in and was pelting them steadily with wild sheets of rain. The visibility was terrible, but the ominous sound of war cries grew steadily nearer. Suddenly, distant gunshots could be heard repeating faster and faster, the sounds mixing with the overall cacophoany swirling around them. For a moment Jonathon was transported back to his recurring nightmare of the final charge of his vaunted Confederate Cherokee Mounted Rifles: pounding hooves, swirling waters, screams, the explosions of gunfire in his face, and finally the welcome peace of silence—and death.

"Captain!"

The voice shook Jonathon back to this dreaded reality, and he turned to see Mangus rising on his knees behind his horse and motioning frantically ahead. Jonathon looked to see the shadows of strange shapes moving in a surreal dance within the swirling dust just ahead, in the direction where all the gunshots had come from—gunshots that had now grown eerily quiet.

"Get down, Mangus!"

Suddenly war-painted men and beasts burst as one through the outer veil of the dirty cloud, their arrows and spears arcing gracefully upward and then falling inevitably in slow motion toward the cowhands along with the heavy sheets of rain.

"Capta . . . !" Mangus's shout suddenly cut out with a gurgling noise and Jonathon twisted his head again in time to see his old comrade-in-arms, a startled look on his face, an arrow straight through his neck and blood spurting from around the shaft, slump and collapse across his horse. Jonathon sucked his breath in hard, his eyes wide, and turned back to await for himself the imminent, deadly impact of these archaic but effective weapons. He pulled on the trigger of his Winchester over and over, a warrior's scream rising and then bursting from deep in his throat.

The Comanches were upon them.

CHAPTER 4
Sheol

(Present Day – Colfax County, New Mexico)

Three miles south of town, Trent took the first exit from I-25, then immediately swung back north onto the frontage road that paralleled it. Half a mile farther, a ranch gate lay open in the barbed wire fence that bordered the road on the left. Trent slowed his old pickup, turned into the gate, and stopped. He was vaguely familiar with this property. From here, a poor excuse for a ranch road trailed away to the west across a wide open pasture and disappeared down the hill into a grove of ancient cottonwood trees about a hundred yards away. A few hundred yards beyond that arose the foothills of what was known as the Raton Range. He knew that between the trees and those hills, just out of sight, ran the Canadian River, and that on the opposite bank the land slanted uphill again for several yards until it flattened out. He couldn't see it from here, but somewhere on those flats sat the ruins of the old Clifton House hotel and stage stop, a once thriving frontier destination that had mysteriously burned to the ground at the turn of the previous century. The only thing he could see from here was the distant flashing of emergency vehicles reflecting through the trees.

He sat for a moment, pinching his eyes. How did he get himself talked into this mess?

Maggie had not been at all pleased when he told her where he was going, even after he assured her that he would finish up quickly with Sheriff Ferguson and afterward meet her and Walter back in town for dinner.

"Just wait until I get my hands on that Ben Ferguson!" she had breathed heatedly, her neck turning a pretty shade of pink. "He knows just what buttons to push with you, doesn't he, Trent Robert Carter?"

This reaction was just what Trent had expected, especially her use of his middle name. Since he had retired, he knew that the one fear an otherwise fearless Maggie had was that he would start to miss the challenge of detective work and be enticed to go back to it someday.

He had started to answer her, but she held up one hand to stave off any attempt at excuses. Instead, he had stood looking at the floor between them, stammering in the back of his throat, and shifting his feet like a teenage boy caught sneaking out the window at night.

"Well, go on then!" Maggie had finally conceded. "Go get yourself all worked up, sniffing around yet another dead body."

"Oh. Okay then," he had blurted out, wondering whether he had heard her correctly and whether or not she had just granted him leave. "I'll see you for dinner in about an hour, then?"

"Oh sure," she had responded, her voice dripping with sarcasm. "Like that's really going to happen!"

He had beat a hasty retreat while the getting was good.

Now he let out his breath slowly, along with the clutch, and steered his truck through the gate and on down the path toward the cottonwood grove. Here, he meandered around the massive tree trunks, careful not to run over any of the large branches that lay about. As the afternoon sun dipped further on its journey to the horizon, the shadows cast by the trees created a spooky atmosphere. It crossed his mind that this was, indeed, a prime area for a murder to have taken place.

He continued a couple hundred yards before he left the trees behind. The road dipped suddenly down an embankment before it veered abruptly to the right. He slammed on the brakes and slid to a stop right at the river's edge. Here the river was somewhat narrow, only about ten or fifteen yards across, but the water ran fast and was deep enough to give a person pause. Trent opened the door and stepped halfway out to assess the situation. He was just about to get out completely when he heard a shrill whistle and spied a figure in uniform on the opposite rise, waving a flashlight at him.

"Hey!" came a shout, almost drowned out by the sound of running water. The person was shouting something else but Trent couldn't make out the words just yet. As the figure got nearer, he recognized him. It was Hector Armijo, a deputy with the Sheriff's Department—and also the man who happened to be married to Trent's daughter Sophie.

"Hector?" Trent answered, cupping one ear and shaking his head.

"The ford's right straight across," Hector shouted, when he got close enough to be heard. "The bottom's kind of dropped out of it, though, and it's awful muddy. But just throw it into four-wheel drive and gun it on across. You'll be fine."

"You're sure?" Trent asked cautiously.

"Yeah, well. I mean, *I* made it." By now, Hector was standing on the far bank of the river, just where the road came out of the ford, and was waving him across.

"*Yeah, well,*" Trent answered, mockingly. "You'll drive anywhere, Hector."

Trent got back in, looked upriver, then back downriver, and cursed under his breath. *Doesn't mean a sane person would do it,* he muttered to himself, then shifted into four-wheel drive and gave it the gas. The truck wheels spun as they plowed into the swirling water; the tires slipped and slid on the muddy bottom. At its deepest, the water came halfway up the door. The truck fishtailed back and forth a time or two before Trent gunned it one last time and it finally lurched up on the other bank and came to a halt on dry ground—but not before dowsing his son-in-law's trousers up to the knees as he remembered too late to jump out of the way. At that, Trent allowed a smile to play across his mouth.

"Jump in, Hector," he offered affably.

As they topped the rise a minute later, a familiar scene greeted them. Trent slowed down. They were now bathed in alternate red and blue flashes from the police units parked at various intervals around the ruins.

"Watch out for the holes," Hector cautioned.

"The holes?"

"Yeah, somebody was up here digging around. Wouldn't want you to run off into one of them. Figure he was looking for something. "

"You mean the vic?"

"The what? The vic?" Hector looked confused.

Trent sighed and rubbed his forehead. "I forget you haven't been on the job too long. 'Vic' is just police slang. 'Vic.' You know, as in 'victim?'"

"Oh, yeah. Okay." Hector said, peering ahead, still worriedly watching for holes.

Trent glanced at him for a second. Hector was a sweet kid, if a little impulsive at times, but Trent still often wondered what Sophie saw in him. He supposed he was a good husband to her although the jury was still out on whether he would ever make a good detective someday.

"Stop!" Hector shouted, bracing himself on the dashboard.

Trent slammed on the brakes hard. The truck slid to a stop. *Just as he had thought—impulsive.*

"Dammit, Hector!" he exclaimed. "You could give me a little warning!"

"I did! I said to watch out for the holes, didn't I?"

Hector looked at him, made a clucking sound with his tongue in exasperation, and quickly got out of the vehicle. Trent followed suit. He glanced up at the setting sun and leaned back through the window to grab his flashlight.

As he did so, he spied Sheriff Ferguson moving toward him, illuminated eerily by the bright red and blue flashes. He had his head down as he threaded around large holes there.

"Ben," Trent greeted as the sheriff drew near.

"Just like old times, Trent."

"Why so hangdog?

"Looking out for the damn holes," Ben muttered.

"So I've heard. Where did they come from?"

Ben jerked his thumb over his shoulder. "Well, that's just one of the questions I thought I'd save for *you* to figure out—among other things." He shook hands quickly with Trent, then took him by the elbow and led him back along the meandering path from which he had come. "Watch your step."

Trent stopped suddenly as he accidently stepped into fairly fresh cow manure. "For the holes or the cow patties?" he grimaced.

"Both," Ben answered. As they walked, Trent thought he saw a frown cross his friend's face. "How'd Maggie take it?" Ben finally continued in a worried tone.

Trent didn't skip a beat. "Well, Ben, she said to tell you next time she lays eyes on you, she's going to put her boot so far up your ass that you'll always have a spare."

Ben nodded but didn't break his stride. "Yep. That's just about what she would do, too." He paused now to lift up a long strand of yellow police barrier tape so they could step under it. "Of course, you did take up for me, didn't you?"

"Valiantly, Ben. Valiantly, but completely in vain."

They were coming up onto a group of uniformed officers from several branches of law enforcement—New Mexico State Police, Colfax County Sheriff's Department, Raton City Police. They were all quietly watching as someone squatted and worked at something in front of them. The person was clad neck to feet in a light blue protective jumpsuit with the word *"Forensics"* spread across the back in big yellow letters. Portable lights, powered by a small, quietly humming of a small generator nearby, lit the bizarre scene.

"Dr. Fortner," Ben spoke quietly to the jump-suited person. "I'd like you to meet someone." As the doctor stood up and turned around, Trent saw that she was a young woman, about his daughter's age, maybe a little younger. She appeared to be more than a little irritated at the interruption.

"Trent Carter, this is Dr. Nancy Fortner, forensics. Nancy, this is . . ."

"Yes," she interjected abruptly. "I recognize you." She peeled a latex glove from her right hand and tentatively shook Trent's, continuing to frown. "Your reputation precedes you, Deputy Carter."

Nancy Fortner was attractive, probably in her early thirties, of slight build, maybe all of 99 pounds, about five feet two inches tall; but she had a firm, professional grip to her handshake. Her blonde hair was pulled back into a ponytail, more to keep it from interfering with her work, Trent guessed, than for any sort of preferred hairstyle.

"Well," Trent smiled, going for a bit of levity, "I hope you haven't believed everything you've heard, Ms. Fortner. And it's simply *Mr.* Carter. I am recently retired."

The levity failed and Trent thought he saw Ben roll his eyes.

"Then it's Dr. Fortner, to you," she corrected him, with no change of expression on her face, "and I'd like to know what this civilian is doing here, mucking up my crime scene?" This last question was addressed to Ben.

If Trent was at all insulted, he was even more surprised to see Ben take a half-step back, his hands coming up in a defensive posture as if Fortner were about to punch him. It was only the second time, and both in the same day, that Trent had seen Ben intimidated by a strong woman.

"Dr. Fortner here has come in from Santa Fe to process the site," he finally stammered, giving Trent a look that said *I told you so,* "particularly with such an interesting case as we seem to have stumbled upon here."

"From Santa Fe?" Trent asked. "That's a bit odd, isn't it, Dr. Fortner? I mean, in my day, getting anyone from Santa Fe to respond in less than a week would be highly unusual."

Fortner folded her arms and continued to stare at Trent defiantly. At this close range, she had to tilt her head back to look up at him, and it reminded him briefly of Maggie. Trent had decided to stand his ground and stared right back at her blankly.

Dr. Fortner blinked first.

"Well, if you must know," she finally said, turning back toward her work and gesturing, "this is a highly unusual crime scene, and unlike my predecessor, *my* department tends to respond much more quickly to important cases." She interrupted herself and turned back to Ben. "You didn't answer my question, Sheriff. Why is he here, again?"

Trent, now also getting perturbed, turned and stared at the sheriff as well. "Yeah, Sheriff. Just why *am* I here, since you already have such heavy hitters to aid you?"

"So now I suppose you're both going to be difficult?" Ben shoved his hands in his jacket pockets and frowned. "Dr. Fortner, I do appreciate that you responded so quickly. Couldn't do it without you. But as talented as you are, in this case I felt that we needed another set of skills on hand." Dr. Fortner rolled her eyes. "So, yes. I have personally taken it upon myself to ask *former Deputy* Carter here to come join our little team and provide some, uh . . ." He paused here, searching for the right words.

"Special insight?" offered Trent, helpfully.

"Clairvoyance?" interspersed Dr. Fortner, sarcastically.

"*Clairvoyance?*" Trent blurted, clearly perturbed. Fortner turned to him.

"Well, what else would you call it? I mean, as I said, your reputation precedes you—*former* Deputy Carter. I've actually read your case files," she scoffed. "I mean, it *is* you, isn't it, who not only seem to get innocent people killed by your actions, but who also evidently has the ability to talk to dead people?" She shook her head scornfully and turned back to her work. "Those right there are some stellar skills, if you ask me. Can't imagine why you retired."

Trent couldn't believe what he was hearing. He turned, a little embarrassed now, and glanced at the other police officers, who had grown quiet and were intently watching the exchange. He suddenly grew angry.

"Don't you people have anything important to do?" he barked. "Some clues to look for; some more holes to go look at, or something?"

The group of uniforms suddenly moved around, almost bumping into one another like pinballs, acting busy and murmuring to one another. Trent turned back, looked from the sheriff to the good doctor, shook his head, and quietly chuckled.

"What's so funny?" demanded Fortner.

"Ferguson and Fortner," he laughed. "That would make a great name for a law firm, don't you think?" Trent stopped laughing abruptly and looked back at Dr. Fortner. "You were absolutely correct, Ben. This one *is* a real piece of work."

Ben started to say something, but Trent cut him off and continued.

"Dr. Fortner," he began, placing undue emphasis on the *doctor*, "you may be a crackerjack at what you do, and I am sure you are paid very well to do it and have received many accolades in your *brief* career to have earned you complete and total carte blanche in most situations."

"*Most* situations?" she blurted.

Trent suddenly leaned in close to her, so that only she could hear him, and lowered his voice somewhat menacingly. "Dr. Fortner, you happen to be about the age of my own daughter, so don't make me speak to you as I would to a child. You don't know half as much as you think you do. Those incidents you are referring to were in the past. I couldn't explain them then, and I sure can't now, but they happened to involve my dead wife. And Nancy, . . ." he paused here and raised a pointed finger for emphasis, "don't you ever bring those things up in my presence again or make light of them, or I might have to put you over my knee. We clear on that?"

Dr. Fortner's eyes grew wide; her fists clenched at her side. Her mouth opened and closed a couple of times in shock, but no words were forthcoming.

"Good!" He smiled, straightening up again. "I'll take that as a *yes*." He sidestepped around her and approached the hole in front of them.

"So, Dr. Fortner. What you *can* tell me right now—since I have no immediate 'clairvoyance' to apply here, yet—is what you make of *your* crime scene so far."

Trent had squatted on his heels and let out his breath slowly. Before him, lying outside the rim of a large hole, was the bloating body of a man. It was hard to tell his age with half his face missing from the buzzards and ants having feasted on it. The victim's lips were pulled back and grinned at him with a well-cared-for set of teeth; his hair was close-cropped and sandy blonde; he was wearing fairly new jeans, new Nike running shoes, and a dirty blue denim shirt—dirty primarily because a pickaxe was firmly imbedded in the center of his chest and a lot of dried blood had caked on his clothes.

"How long's he been here?" Trent asked, continuing to stare down at the body.

No one answered. Trent turned his head to look at the doctor who was still fuming. He raised his eyebrows questioningly. "Well?" he added. "We on speaking terms yet or not?"

Dr. Fortner, her arms still folded, shifted her weight to the other leg and cleared her throat. "I put the time of death as two days ago," she answered quietly, "given the amount of rigor mortis and the general decomposition due to the wildlife."

"The rancher saw buzzards circling this morning," offered Ben, leaning over Trent's shoulder. "He found the body; figured it must've been one of his cows at first."

"Who is he?"

"No idea," Ben answered. "Searched his pockets, but nothing. No wallet, no ID. Nothing. Hoping his prints will turn something up."

Trent didn't answer. He was now shining his flashlight into the hole itself and squinting.

"This is no ordinary hole," he muttered.

"Yes, we know," said Fortner smugly. She had moved over next to Trent and was bending over his other shoulder. Trent turned and looked at Ben.

"This that *other thing* you were referring to then?"

Ben nodded and rubbed his chin.

"Who moved the body?" Trent asked.

"What?"

"The guy there wearing the garden tool in his chest—he was originally lying down here, in the hole, wasn't he? On top?" He pointed to the victim. "Who moved him out of it?"

"I had him moved," answered Ben. "Just before Dr. Fortner arrived. I mean, we had no idea that— "

"That there was another body buried here underneath?" Trent finished for him.

He let his light play back down into the hole to reveal what it really was—a grave. Fragments of rotten boards had been picked away and moved aside. A partial skeleton lay in the bottom, bony hands folded at the chest and the face of the skull turned away as if in shame at being exposed. Patches of dark hair were still visible in places. From here a large hole was visible at the back of the skull. Trent peered more closely at the jagged edges of bone protruding from the hole. *An exit wound, perhaps?*

"Well, at least now we know what your vic was looking for out here." Trent looked around again at some of the other nearby holes and scratched his forehead. He scanned the grave again. The bottom half of the skeleton had not yet been fully exposed, but the corpse still wore remnants of clothing: an old vest of some type, just visible underneath a worn canvas overcoat; a partially decayed leather belt with a tarnished buckle; a torn and crumpled hat tossed to one side; and, wedged underneath one of the hands, a rusted pistol.

"Something's not right," he muttered.

"What's that?" asked Dr. Fortner.

Trent stood up, sighed deeply, and continued to peer into the grave.

"Something's not right, here. Something's wrong. Can't put my finger on it."

He squatted back down and stared into the grave for a long while.

"Either of you disturb the clothing?"

"No," they both answered at once.

"Well, somebody sure did. This grave has been carefully searched." He looked back over at the murder victim. "And you say you have nothing on this guy?"

Ben shook his head again.

"Well, Doctor Fortner, you're right about one thing," Trent said without looking at her. "Here are definitely a couple of dead men that really need to start speaking to me." He then slowly turned, smiled at her, and tapped the side of his head. "But so far, neither of them have said a word."

Dr. Fortner opened her mouth to say something but then closed it and frowned at him.

Trent stood up, wiped his hands on his jeans, and looked at his watch.

"Damn," he muttered, then turned to walk quickly back to his truck. Ben followed him.

"So just what did you say to her?" he asked, catching up with Trent.

"Who? Maggie?"

"Well, I was referring to Dr. Fortner," he answered, glancing back at her. "I don't know what you said, exactly, but if looks could kill. . . ."

Trent chuckled, then glanced at his watch again and grimaced.

"Well, speaking of dead men, now Maggie is definitely gonna kill us both."

#

The tall, almost middle-aged stranger at the bar was dressed in black jeans, black button-down shirt, gray sports coat, and flashy cowboy boots. Longish blonde hair was well groomed, had been brushed back from the face, and fell back over the ears. A small gold cross on a delicate gold chain was just visible beneath the open collar of the shirt.

The stranger sat quietly nursing a beer, the third of the evening.

A woman, perhaps in her late thirties and somewhat a little worse for wear, but still attractive, materialized on the next barstool. She quietly ordered a drink, glanced at the stranger, and then softly cleared her throat.

"Whew, long night!" she murmured softly.

"Excuse me?" the figure responded. "You talking to me?"

"I said it's been a long night," the woman repeated, self-consciously touching her hair, and then looked away.

"You don't say," the other muttered and sipped at the beer.

The woman fumbled in her purse and produced a cigarette, which she held motionless between two fingers.

"Got a light?"

"I don't smoke," came the terse response, which betrayed a slight foreign accent.

The woman pouted for a moment, then produced a lighter of her own and lit up, blowing the smoke in front of her. "Say, I like your voice," she said. "Where you from, anyway?"

"Not from here."

"Wish I had a sweet accent like that. Might help business a little." When there was no further response, she kept quiet for a while.

Presently, the stranger pulled back a sleeve of the jacket to look at a watch. The woman reached over tentatively and touched the stranger's wrist.

"Ooh, what's that?" she asked. "Tattoo? I love tattoos. Let me see."

The sleeve was jerked back down and the arm pulled away.

"Oh, come on. No need to be rude. What was that, anyway? Looked like some sort of seashell, maybe?"

"Yes," came a gruff reply. "Seashell."

"What's it mean?"

"Nothing."

"You just liked the way it looks, then?"

"Yes, I like the way it looks."

The stranger drained the rest of the beer and caught the eye of the bartender who uncapped another bottle and slipped it across.

The woman also picked up her now-empty glass and shook it at the bartender so that the ice rattled. "Don't be stingy, Ray." The bartender came over to refill her drink. "Say," the woman asked after another long minute, "you waiting for someone?"

The dark-suited stranger guzzled beer, continued to ignore the woman, and glanced at the time again.

"I said, are you waiting for . . ."

At that moment, a cell phone rang loudly. The blonde, middle-aged stranger gratefully reached into a pocket, stood up, moved away from the bar, and answered the phone.

"Is it done, then?" came a voice on the other end.

"Yes, it is done. Last night."

"Can the authorities identify him?"

"No," the stranger answered coldly, rebuffing an apparent challenge to professionalism. "I cleaned out his pockets and disposed of his car. Besides, his real identity is impossible to trace."

There was a brief pause.

"Do you think he found what we're looking for?"

"No. He tried, but I don't think he found anything."

"You don't think? You mean you're not sure?"

"Yes, I am sure," came the slightly exasperated reply. "He found nothing. Only a lot of empty holes. I am sure of it."

There was silence on the other end for a long while.

"What do you think he was looking for, precisely?"

The stranger thought carefully for a moment—perhaps for just a moment too long.

"I am sure that is not for me to know." Another pause. "That is not what you pay me for."

"No. No, it is not what I pay you for, is it?" There was another long silence.

"So, what shall I do now? Do you want me in Santa Fe? Or back in Amsterdam?"

"No. I have other work for you there. You must prepare for Mr. Bouwmeester's upcoming visit."

"But I thought that was not until next spring?"

"He has moved his timetable up. I am afraid he will be there by the end of the month." The voice paused again, then went on. *"Something has happened. I am not sure yet exactly what, but Mr. Bouwmeester is now, for some reason, more anxious than ever to make the trip. He is, in fact, most adamant. He wants to inspect the entire area for himself—up close. For what reason, I am not yet sure. But I will find out. And when I do. . . . Well, I'll be in touch again— soon. In the meantime, you must prepare for his arrival. I will wire some funds for your additional expenses, and I will handpick more men myself. I will send them to you soon, and the others will accompany Mr. Bouwmeester. Am I clear?"*

"Quite clear. I will take care of all the arrangements."

"I know I can trust you. You know exactly what has to happen, after he gets there. With your help, we will get all this behind us, yes?"

"The sooner the better. This is turning into very bad business."

There was a moment of silence on the phone, and then, *"It will be very bad business—for you, my friend, if this doesn't get handled. And quickly!"*

The phone went dead; the stranger looked at it vacantly for a second, and then placed it back in a pocket. Fingers touched something else there, pulled out a small sealed plastic bag, and held it up to the neon lights above the bar.

The stranger gazed at the contents, turned the bag over, and smiled slowly.

Perhaps this was what everyone was looking for.

CHAPTER 5
Valley Of The Shadow

(A letter from María Consuelo Delgado)
July 28, 1868

Sr. Manuel Diego Delgado
El Rancho de las Golondrinas
Santa Fe,
Territorio de Nuevo México

Dearest Brother:

Thank you for your beautiful letter! I just received it yesterday. I read it over quickly, then again to Papa and the boys. I must read it over again more carefully.

But I must tell you, Mannie, Papa is a little disturbed over your talk of maybe coming north to hunt for gold. I am sorry if I somehow flamed your imagination with my previous letter. As much as I would love to have you closer, I can tell you that the gold camps—Elizabethtown in particular—are no place for a wife and small children; and I cannot imagine you leaving dear Ana, in her condition, and little Patricio. Don't be angry with me, Mannie, but I am afraid I have to agree with Papa on this. Your first duty is to your precious family.

I can tell you that the gold rush has brought such a low element to our beautiful territory. There is news of terrible depredations daily, and of cold-blooded murders almost on a weekly basis! Even on our occasional trips to Cimarron for supplies, the number of drunkards and ruffians I see on the streets has more than doubled. I refuse to go anywhere to shop by myself, for fear of being accosted.

Mr. Maxwell's beautiful wife, Luz Beaubien Maxwell, accompanied him one day and brought a wonderful meat pie she had baked herself. Don't you know that we ate it most gratefully! I know your little brothers are growing weary of my poor cooking!

Señora Maxwell saw the Ute Indians Papa has working on our place, and she took me aside and warned me about them. She says they are thieves, and worse yet, she even heard that they occasionally steal children and women! I was alarmed at first, but later, after she had gone, I sat and watched them. They are such hard workers and seem so eager to please that I can hardly think they would do us harm. Papa treats them well and pays them in food and other supplies. But they also look like such a pitiful lot—their clothes are often threadbare and they always seem so hungry. When we finished our lunch, I gave one of them the remainder of Mrs. Maxwell's meat pie, which he immediately wolfed down gratefully.

From the other women in town I hear such disturbing stories of how the Indians elsewhere in

Nuevo México have been so woefully treated! There was even an article in the local newspaper, detailing the horrific conditions in some sort of prison camp located at Fort Sumner, in the southern region of the territory, where the Navajo Indians have been placed. Have you heard of this, Mannie? I pray that it is not true.

Write to me soon, mi querido hermano. I miss you all so terribly.

I remain,
Your loving sister,
María

#

(July 1868 – Fort Sumner, New Mexico)

"Get the hell on out of here, then! You are both about as verbose and tiresome as that useless sawbones." Oliver Loving glared up from his bed at the two cowhands, the fever bright in eyes as his outburst quickly turned into a wracking cough. He turned to gaze out the window. A faint afternoon breeze had finally moved the curtains, but the air in the small room was close and thick with the odor of sickness, or worse.

Jonathon Carter and Clay Allison exchanged quick looks, then waited at the foot of the bed until Loving's hacking subsided.

"Well," said Allison finally, slipping his black hat onto his head and stepping to the door. "That sounds plain enough for me, Squirrel." He paused when he noticed that Jonathon had not moved. "You coming?"

"Doc says your leg has got to come off, Mr. Loving," Jonathon said evenly, ignoring Allison.

His afflicted boss did not respond and continued staring out the window, his breathing a ragged wheeze. Jonathon looked down at his hat in front of him as he twisted it in his hands. It was evident that Loving was finished with this conversation, but Jonathon was concerned that his boss was not thinking clearly. He breathed through his mouth to try and avoid the putrid stench of gangrene that seeped from the swollen and bandaged leg lying exposed on top of the blanket. Jonathon had seen many such terrible wounds during the war and, what's more, he knew first-hand what happened when a soldier refused the standard treatment, amputation.

"Mr. Loving," he insisted, "if you don't let Doc take that leg, you will surely die, and sooner than you think. Is that what you want, Sir?"

Loving continued to ignore him, but now raised his arm and fluttered the back of his hand at him in tired dismissal. Jonathon turned to follow Allison out the door, but stopped when he heard Loving stir.

"Charlie here yet?"

"Haven't seen him yet, Mr. Loving."

Loving coughed into the bed sheets again, then quieted for a moment. "That sombitch said he'd be here," he growled, squeezing his eyes shut. "Better get here soon, is all I got to say."

Jonathon shut the door softly and followed Allison through the small, cluttered office of the army physician and on through the outer door to the wooden porch, where they found the doctor leaned back in a chair on its hind legs and smoking a pipe.

"Well?" the doctor quizzed them. "You get through to him at all?"

Jonathon shook his head and pulled his hat on while Allison rolled his eyes, took a fresh cigar out of his coat pocket, and bit the end off of it.

"Nah, not that old buzzard," he muttered, spitting out the tobacco nub before lighting the cigar. He leaned casually against one of the wooden columns holding up the veranda roof.

Jonathon sat down on the edge of the plank porch and drew lines in the dirt with the toe of a boot.

"I thought as much," mumbled the doctor, sucking on his pipe. "Hard-headed cuss ain't gonna listen to anyone other than Mr. Goodnight, I reckon." He stopped and looked at the other two. "When'd you say you saw him last?"

"A week—ten days ago," answered Jonathon softly, gazing now across the square as a group of sadly dressed Navajos shuffled around the corner of the large adobe commissary building and joined a growing crowd there. "He should be here just about any day now," he assured himself absently, watching the Indians stirring up the dust of the dry street with the soles of their worn moccasins as they walked. Some of the more pitiful natives were barefoot and ragged as they slowed and lined up at the doorway where they waited patiently for the evening rations to be doled out. It was a daily routine that they knew well.

The dust reminded Jonathon how dry his throat was and he fished into his shirt pocket for the remains of a peppermint stick he remembered was there. He stuck it into his mouth and continued to watch the sad spectacle across the street. Beside him, Allison puffed his cigar and wiped the sweat from his eyes with his bandanna before tying it neatly around his neck.

The horizon to the north had filled with large clouds to tease them with a promise of rain, just as it had every afternoon at this time but had not produced a single rainstorm since the two had arrived at Fort Sumner three days ago with their wounded cattle boss. They had hauled him here in a wagon from Horsehead Crossing, where an arrow had imbedded itself deep into his femur, just above the knee, after a Comanche war party had attacked them as they tried to drive 3,000 head of cattle across *Río Pecos* in a thunderstorm. Thanks to the defensive tactics that Jonathon had put into play during the battle to save the herd, the cowboys had managed to fend off the attack, shooting down several of the marauders before forcing the remainder to turn tail and run. But not before the herd had been woefully scattered in the waning thunderstorm, and not before Oliver Loving had been gravely wounded.

And not before Jonathon's old friend Mangus had died in his arms with his chest and neck full of arrows.

Although the herd was badly scattered, Charles Goodnight had quickly assessed the damages and decided that he and most of the hands would spend whatever time it took to gather the animals back together, but that Jonathon and Clay should get Loving to Fort Sumner for medical help as soon as possible. He then planned to join them in just a few days.

The military facility was no longer as busy as it had been in recent years. Across the *Río Pecos* lay the squalid Navajo Indian settlement at what was called *Bosque Redondo*. In retaliation for alleged atrocities against the American and Mexican settlers of New Mexico and Arizona, the army had established a prison camp there five years earlier, in the middle of the Civil War, in a misguided attempt to punish and relocate the *Diné*—the name the Navajo tribe had given itself—from their ancestral homelands roughly 400 miles northwest of Fort Sumner. Subsequently, on what became known as the "Long Walk," the tribe was promised that it would be humanely cared for, with plenty of food, water, shelter, and medicine. But the tragic truth was that more than 2,000 *Diné* men, women, and children had died on the brutal forced march, freezing to death in the savage northern New Mexican winters or starving when inadequate rations became the reality. The number of survivors who finally stumbled into the *Bosque Redondo* concentration camp eventually swelled to over 12,000 souls, and the U.S. Army continued to find it next to impossible to properly feed, clothe, and shelter its prisoners. Forced to try to grow their own food crops in the inhospitable soil, the natives dug miles of irrigation ditches only to see them washed out by the frequent floodwaters of the *Río Pecos* or to watch as their meager crops were consumed by plagues of insects. Often, whatever rations the military was finally able to provide came in the form of rancid meat and insect-infested grain, and whoever survived the various illnesses and hunger found themselves victims of attacks from the neighboring enemy tribes of Mescalero and Comanche, who would mount raids into the fringes of the compound, stealing children, women, and livestock and murdering the men.

"They'll be leaving soon," remarked the doctor, absently staring at the hundreds of Indians now patiently massing across the way. "Army's given up on them. Can't keep them fed nor healthy." He paused to strike another match on the heel of a boot and relit his pipe.

"I'd heard such," answered Allison.

"About damn time," muttered Jonathon. He felt the gall rising up from his belly again. Each day he had spent here, he sat and watched the pitiful exercise of the Army doling out inadequate foodstuffs to these scarecrows. In the presence of the *Diné,* the native half of him felt a deep kindred connection, and shame from being as well-fed and moderately successful in life as he was, while his white half felt as inadequate and helpless as his Army hosts to do anything about it.

"Doesn't help none that you boys don't have those beeves delivered yet," the doctor scolded. "The Army sure does depend upon you cattlemen to get some fresh meat onto the supper tables. And all you two showed up with is that dying, crotchety old Texan."

Jonathon knew what the doctor was referring to: in recent months, the beaten and downtrodden *Diné* had begun pleading with the American government to release them to return to their homelands in the fertile high canyons of northwest New Mexico, where they could start their lives over or at least die in peace and dignity. In response, just a few weeks ago in the spring, General William T. Sherman himself had come to Fort Sumner to investigate. To his credit, he was immediately appalled at the conditions of the natives and quickly agreed to open negotiations with the tribal leaders. His resulting decision was to put an end to the incarceration of the Navajo people, give them a military escort back to their ancestral lands, and send with them enough tools and seed stock to begin life afresh. Indeed, the military post with its adjacent prison camp was even now showing signs of increased activity as preparations were being made to accomplish the supposed repatriation.

Suddenly Jonathon became acutely aware of someone staring at him. He focused his eyes to the middle of the line, where a small *Diné* boy, not much older than five or six, gazed across the street at him. The boy licked his lips, then stuck a finger in his mouth, sucking on it. Jonathon became self-conscious of the peppermint stick in his own mouth. He slowly pulled it out, keeping eye contact with the boy. He held the candy out in front of him, smiled, and nodded to the boy, who took a couple of timid steps before his mother stopped him, glaring in Jonathon's direction. Jonathon paused for a moment, then stood up and walked across the street to the boy. He tipped his hat at the woman and said something to her in Cherokee, not certain at all that she would understand. She didn't.

"A gift for the boy," Jonathon repeated in English, but the woman knitted her eyebrows and kept a protective hand on her son's shoulder.

Jonathon squatted down to the boy's eye level and again handed the peppermint stick out to him, glancing back up at the suspicious woman. *"Un regalo para el niño,"* he repeated in Spanish, and this time the boy's mother smiled and nodded. The boy grabbed the candy and immediately began slurping on it. Jonathon stood and tousled the happy child's filthy head of hair.

"Maybe, just maybe," he thought to himself, *"the United States of America might finally keep one of its promises to these people."* But he seriously doubted it.

"Hey, Squirrel."

A voice called from behind him and broke his train of thought. He turned to see Allison stepping off the porch and peering up the street into the distance. Jonathon followed his partner's gaze and squinted until he spied a long cloud of gray-white dust billowing from the rim of high ground on the horizon, about a mile or so to the east. At first, dark specks moved into view like a line of ants. Then he smiled as a two or three of the dots disengaged themselves and materialized into silhouettes of cowboys on horseback, waving their arms and coaxing lines of cattle that soon spilled down the slopes into the river valley. Shortly afterward, he could also hear the distant murmur of bawling animals as they caught the scent of the nearby river.

Indians began to break away from the orderly crowd at the commissary and were soon joined by soldiers and merchants, all of whom began to meander down the street, pointing, grinning, and cajoling one another as they went.

Charles Goodnight and his long-awaited cattle had finally arrived in Fort Sumner.

Oliver Loving died the next morning.

#

"Charlie, don't you dare let them bury me in this gawd-awful desert!"

Charles Goodnight stood staring out the window with his arms folded, his back turned to his dying friend, and watched the sun claw its way over the same eastern bluffs he had just pushed their remaining 2,763 head of cattle over the previous evening. He had then made a beeline to Loving's sickbed, only to discover that it was now a deathbed. Goodnight had spent the whole night keeping vigil with his best friend. He had also nearly worn out his voice in arguing with him over the pros and cons of amputation, but they both knew the gangrene was too far spread by now. The argument had gradually turned to funeral arrangements.

"By gawd, Charlie, I swan I will just stay alive and lie here in my own stench until you promise me!" Goodnight continued to stare out the window and mumbled something in reply. "What's that you say?" demanded Loving, weakly. "Turn around here so's a fellow can make out what you're saying!"

Goodnight turned around, his arms still folded defiantly, and frowned down at his friend.

"You want me to wrap up your dead, stinking carcass, drag it on up to Colorado with me while I finish this trail drive, then haul you all the way back down to Fort Worth to bury you? I mean, dammit all to hell, Oliver—where is the logic in that?"

Loving looked away, coughed weakly, then turned his face back to Goodnight.

"Charlie, you are the best friend a man could wish for. I know I am asking an awful lot of you, but at this point I am way beyond caring. My final wish is to be buried at home in Texas, where my family and friends can come sit and visit and have a drink or two with me—or hell, even piddle on my grave if they want. And last time I looked around here, you are the only one I know stubborn enough to make that all happen."

"Stubborn enough—or fool enough?"

"Both. But just you promise me, . . ." Loving tried to continue but was stopped by another bout of deep coughing. Goodnight sat down in a nearby chair, wet a cloth in the washbasin next to the bed, and leaned over to wipe his friend's sweat-drenched forehead and face. The smell in the room was unbearable, but he had long since managed to ignore it. He comforted his friend, who grew gradually still, his breathing ragged and shallow.

"Oliver," he murmured finally, his voice barely above a whisper as he leaned nearer. Loving's eyelids fluttered and his feverish eyes held Goodnight's for a moment longer. "Oliver. . . I promise."

#

Jonathon Carter and Clay Allison exited the saloon, where they had just finished what passed for breakfast. They had spent the night keeping the army doctor company as he drank himself into a stupor. They had all been well aware that Charles Goodnight was going to do his damnedest to talk his mortally wounded friend into letting the doctor amputate his leg, and Doc had decided that whichever way that argument went, he needed to be good and drunk at the time.

Jonathon stretched, yawned, and breathed in the cool early morning air that he knew would disappear into a blazing July heat later in the day. He heard a door slam across the way and caught sight of Charles Goodnight as he left the doctor's office. Jonathon motioned to Allison and they crossed the road.

"Doctor's sleeping it off," Jonathon said as they approached their trail boss, who just stood there staring at them blankly. "Want me to go get him?" Jonathon asked uncertainly.

Goodnight rubbed his eyes hard, took a deep breath, and cleared his throat of a lingering emotion they were both suddenly reluctant to identify.

"Nope," he finally replied, blowing out his breath, then squinting and looking toward the sun, now several degrees above the horizon. "Oliver's dead. Doesn't need no doctor anymore." He swiped his nose, took another deep breath, stepped off the porch, and walked away from them, continuing to talk as he went. "And I am going to bed, and you boys best get some rest, also. Because tomorrow morning, we are cutting out a few hundred head to sell to the Army, then right after that we are leaving to take the rest to Colorado as planned. We have lost enough damned time on this drive."

Goodnight suddenly turned back at them. "Oh—and ya'll best go find an undertaker, if there is one around here. In most towns, you will find the local barber does the job. Or maybe the Army has one. Whoever it is, send him on over to Doc's pronto and get him to embalm Mr. Loving there right away—and have him wrap him up tight in some canvas, tight as a tick. Seems we are taking him with us." He turned, all business again, and marched briskly up the street. Carter and Allison looked after him in shock.

Goodnight continued loudly as he walked away. "And make sure he drenches him real good in some strong foo-foo water, or whatever the hell he has that will cover up the stench. I *do not* want to be smelling him for the next couple o' months."

CHAPTER 6
Buffalo Hunters

(Present Day – Vermejo Park Ranch)

There was a definite crispness in the afternoon air as Trent rolled the window down and leaned out to press the button on the intercom at the security gate. The Indian summer they had been enjoying was quickly coming to an end and fall was descending upon them.

"May I help you?" came the smooth, professional female voice from somewhere at the other end of the electronic device.

"Yes. We're here for the Governor's Reception," Trent answered.

"Names, please?"

"Mr. and Mrs. Trent Carter."

There was a long pause as he pictured the gatekeeper's forefinger sliding down a long list of invited names. Trent tapped his own fingers absently on the steering wheel of the large cream-colored Cadillac Escalade, an overly resplendent vehicle that he would have never purchased for himself, but which had belonged to Maggie since before they were married. He would have been just fine with driving his twenty-year old pickup, but he knew better than to assume that Maggie would agree to arrive at a fancy party chauffeured in such a conveyance. Trent glanced around in the late afternoon silence surrounding them out here, forty-five miles up the rugged forested mountains west of Raton. Parked in front of the massive iron gates of the Vermejo Park Ranch at the end of a dirt county road, it was easy to feel that they were isolated in the middle of nowhere, save for this black metal squawk box on the top of a metal post linking them to civilization.

"I am sorry, Sir," came the metallic female voice again, dripping with unction. "I'm afraid I don't have you on tonight's guest list. Might there be a mistake?"

"Try under *Margot Van Ryan.*" Maggie had leaned over and aimed her voice loudly across Trent, making him flinch.

There was another, briefer pause, before the voice returned, this time oozing conciliation. "Ah, yes. Here we are. *Margot Van Ryan and guest.* Come right in."

There was a sudden loud buzz, followed by a metallic clank as the massive gate unlatched itself and began to roll back noisily on its track. During the few seconds it took, the electronic woman returned with another question: "Do you know how to get to *Casa Grande?*"

"No." "Yes," answered Trent and Maggie almost simultaneously.

"Follow the road around. You will go five miles along the side of the river until you—,"

"Yes, I think we'll manage fine, dear. Thank you," Maggie cut her off, her voice asserting itself with more than a bit of authority. Trent glanced at her with a smirk as he moved the large SUV through the yawning gates.

"What?" Maggie responded to his raised eyebrows. "I can summon up condescension too, you know, when it's called for. Comes in handy at times."

"Don't I well know it," he chuckled, before his smile turned back into a slight frown. "But why *Margot Van Ryan?*" he asked. "You couldn't be bothered to reserve under both our names?"

"Oh, stop your pouting, Cowboy. I didn't make the reservation—just RSVPed to the governor's invitation, that's all. And it's obvious she doesn't even know that I'm now married. She only remembers me from college, from our sorority. And I'm probably one of the few Democrats she knows by name around here."

"Oh, well, that explains it then, since I voted Republican. Doubt I will even get past the parking lot tonight. You can just sneak me out a sandwich later, one of those little tasteless cucumber thingies with the crust cut off—you know—Democrat food."

Maggie backhanded his upper arm, not entirely playfully. "Hush up and drive. Do you even know where you're going?"

"No, Ma'am. I am just playing chauffeur and enjoying the scenery. And besides, I was just told to hush up and drive."

"Keep going another four or five miles," she continued, ignoring his quips. "I'll let you know when we get there, though I doubt you'll miss it."

Maggie took a deep breath and blew it out slowly. "And don't mind me," she said finally. "I'm just a little nervous, is all. I haven't seen the Governor in over fifteen years, not since I helped her campaign for Secretary of State—Watch out!" This last exclamation came just as Trent slammed on the brakes and slid to a stop to allow four large elk to continue across the road, just feet in front of them now. The big one, a bull, turned and stared at them, his huge antlered head as high as the roof of their vehicle.

"Go on ahead there, big boy," Trent breathed, his voice betraying a thrill of admiration. "After all, you do own this particular road."

They watched with awe as the small family sauntered dramatically down the other side of the road and splashed into the middle of the shallow river crossing, stopping for a while to slurp at the clear, cool mountain water. Trent eased the gas pedal down and let the vehicle move away slowly. As it picked up speed around the next bend, they ran over a hidden pothole.

"You'd think they could afford to at least pave the road," he winced.

A mile or so later, they rounded a bend and spied a group of well-built, modern bungalows nestled along the edge of the valley underneath the shade of large fir trees and fronted by nicely landscaped lawns. A variety of company 4-x-4 pickups and other outdoor utility vehicles were neatly parked in the driveways. The windows of the houses were already ablaze with light, and could've been located on any suburban estate instead of incongruously spread out on this massive compound in the rugged wilderness of northern New Mexico. Trent slowed down.

"Keep driving. That's not it," Maggie announced. "Employee housing."

"Yes, Ma'am."

Farther down the valley, spreading out ahead of them now, appeared a large, dark mass of slowly moving animals. At first Trent thought that they were more elk, but as they neared, he saw that they were part of the ranch's famous buffalo herd. He slowed the SUV once again and almost held his breath. A multi-millionaire communication mogul and his family owned Vermejo Park Ranch. Trent had read somewhere that this was just one of a few ranches that the family had set aside as a preserve for the majestic animals. They roamed and grazed freely across the thousands of open range acreage, much as they had more than a hundred and fifty years ago. To see them in such huge numbers struck a chord deep inside Trent.

Suddenly, off to the left, just inside the tree line of blue spruce and oak, he noticed other movement. He squinted for a moment, not sure of his own sanity. Two tall, elegant men dressed in beautiful buckskins, their dark hair long and tied behind their necks, stepped out from behind the trees where they had evidently been lying in wait. The waning afternoon sunlight infused their bronze faces with an almost ghostly glow. They carried strung longbows, and were raising them as they slowly knelt and aimed, arrows ready to loose upon their approaching unsuspecting woolly prey. Trent took his foot off the gas and started braking again, his attention rapt upon the hunters.

"You seeing this?" he breathed quietly, not trusting his own eyes.

"Seeing what?" Maggie asked impatiently. "Why are we slowing down? You haven't seen buffalo before?"

"No, I just. . . ." Trent stopped himself, turning back to the strange scene that had been before him. Trent absently touched the scar at his hairline, closed his eyes, and shook himself back to reality. The ghostly Indian hunters had now vanished, leaving the unmolested buffalo calmly grazing below the evergreens.

They drove on as the waning light of the day began to draw long shadows into the valley around them. A mile or so farther their car topped a ridge and a cluster of massive stone and glass edifices hove into view to their right.

"Here we are." Maggie nodded toward one of the two mansions that loomed just ahead. The smaller employees' bungalows they had passed a mile or so back didn't hold a candle to this breathtaking estate. Trees of every genus that could be supported at this altitude decorated the expansive landscaping, and festive lights spilled through the floor-to-ceiling veranda windows and on out across the football filed sized manicured lawn to compete with the fading sunset.

"That first one there is where the family stays—the owners—whenever they're here, which I think is seldom anymore," Maggie offered.

"I would sure hate to pay their electric bill," Trent mumbled.

"What was that? Stop muttering."

"I just said that judging by all the lights on, I imagine your friend the governor is taking up residence there tonight," Trent replied. "You reckon she's got a spare bedroom for us?"

Maggie shot him another sharp look.

"Sorry," he said, sheepishly. "No more jokes. I promise."

He drove slowly past the second huge building—the main guest lodge—the one with the large stone-covered veranda that extended the two-hundred-foot breadth of the front and hung out over the lawn. A crowd was already milling on the veranda, drinks in hand and grins on faces, celebrating what already appeared to be a very enjoyable occasion. At the end of the yard, the road split, the main branch continuing up the valley until it ran out of sight beyond the buffalo herd meandering there, and the other turning and passing immediately under a huge stone gateway that led to a tree-shaded double-lane drive. Trent noted with relief that at least the driveway was paved.

He shook his head incredulously. The majesty of the huge herd of buffalo—and his vision of the ghost hunters—in juxtaposition with such examples of modern wealth boggled his mind. He followed the drive another hundred yards uphill until it curved around the side of the building and spilled them into a large parking area. A young man wearing a company baseball cap and a reflective vest motioned efficiently to him with a flashlight, directing him where to park. There were probably sixty or seventy vehicles already in place, leaving room for maybe forty or fifty more. Other late arrivals were disembarking and threading their way chattily on foot toward the big lodge, most of them trendily dressed and expensively jeweled in what he would call Santa Fe chic. Trent slid the Cadillac into an empty space, turned off the engine, and sat quietly for a few moments, trying to convince himself that he didn't really hate crowds of people—especially crowds of snobbish, condescending, well-to-do people. Maggie opened her door to get out, then turned to him.

"Well? You coming?"

"This is really penance for me sneaking away to help out Ben the other night, isn't it?"

"Yes. It is," Maggie answered, matter-of-factly, then slammed her door.

"Maybe I really should just let you bring me a sandwich," he muttered, although she could no longer hear him.

\#

Governor Cha'risa Thompson had not only been one of Maggie's best friends from college, but was also the state's first Native American female governor. Among the inner circles of her party, on the national level, her name was already being whispered as a strong possibility for the second position on the next presidential ticket.

But Trent had learned that the real reason for tonight's shindig was to welcome and honor a visiting minor dignitary from the Netherlands. As they made their way through the throng of people crowding the veranda, Trent dutifully followed a half step behind his wife, the palm of his hand dutifully touching the small of her back, and a smile pasted dutifully on his face. He dutifully nodded as they met up with one familiar face after another, and at one point Maggie stopped to whisper up at him.

"Will you wipe that chimpanzee grin off your face, for gosh sakes?"

"That what it looks like?" he muttered back at her. "Guess that works just as well as any other animal. I mean after all, it is a jungle in here. Oh, hi, Ben!" he called out thankfully, as Sheriff Ferguson suddenly extricated himself from a nearby group of people who seemed deep in self-absorbed conversation.

"At last," Ben said, as he stepped quickly over to Trent and Maggie. "Someone here with the same lack of importance as me."

"Ben," Maggie said, her voice abrupt and cool as she flashed her eyes once at the Sheriff.

"Uh . . . Hi, Maggie! Of course, I was referring to your husband." Ben blinked in Maggie Carter's icy glare. He gratefully gestured to the pretty young woman walking up beside him, dressed smartly in a dark blue pantsuit.

"Trent, Maggie, I'd like to introduce you to my daughter, Jennifer. Jenn's down here for a short break from college, from Denver—studying political science and business." The pride that beamed from Ben's face was unmistakable. Jennifer pulled her shoulder-length blonde hair behind one ear, smiled at them warmly, and shook each of their hands firmly. "Pleased to meet you," she said pleasantly. "Dad's told me a lot about you both."

"Oh my," Trent responded slowly, raising his eyebrows in mock concern. "Well, we shall certainly have to correct your thinking then, Ms. Ferguson, on a few of those critical facts."

"Oh, never mind these two clowns, Jennifer," Maggie interrupted, taking her by the shoulder and steering her away. "Let's go get you properly introduced to a few really important folks around here, shall we? It could help your poli-sci career." Maggie turned and made a slight face at her husband, which he knew was code for *behave yourself.*

They watched the ladies move away. Trent admired his wife as she gracefully and artfully worked the room, interspersing herself into conversations and making introductions. He also noted that Jennifer looked completely at home in the rarified atmosphere. A waiter passed by with a tray of drinks. Ben deftly took a fresh one while depositing his empty on the tray. Trent shook his head when the waiter turned to him.

"May I get you something lighter, Sir? Club soda? A nice sparkling water, perhaps?

Trent furrowed his eyebrows at the waiter.

"Well, what the hell would be so nice about that?" he blurted. The waiter beat a hasty retreat.

"Not drinking tonight?" Ben asked. Trent waited a beat, thrust his hands in his pockets, and cleared his throat.

"Not tonight," he finally answered. Giving up alcohol was still a daily, almost hourly decision for him. He nodded back toward Maggie and Jennifer, as much to change the subject as anything.

"She sure seems quite at home," he said.

"Jennifer? Yeah, she takes after her mother," Ben replied.

"I was already thinking that very thing; especially in the looks department—thankfully."

"Amen to that."

Trent was about to say something else when he noticed Maggie motioning to them.

"Um—I believe we are being summoned."

"We?" asked Ben, uncertainly. "I thought I was still on your wife's shit list."

"We both are—I think rather permanently," Trent muttered. Maggie gestured again, this time insistently, pointing toward a double doorway where a knot of important looking people had just entered. "And I think this is all part of our ongoing purgatory."

As they re-joined Maggie and Jennifer, it immediately became evident that Maggie was navigating them all strategically through the crowd toward a receiving line that included the governor, a tall and rather distinguished-looking middle aged gentleman in a conservative business suit, and a younger woman next to him, all smiling and shaking hands sincerely. The small group was anchored at both ends by athletic-looking types in dark suits who continuously scanned the crowds with squinty eyes, occasionally touched their ears, and talked mysteriously into the cuffs of their jackets. Trent found himself taking more of an interest in this security detail than in the dignitaries they were protecting.

"Wonder how you get a gig like that?" he said quietly to Ben as they made their way methodically through the queue and nodding toward one of the security detail. This particular guard was a woman with short blonde hair, perhaps in her late thirties, about five feet eight, maybe a hundred twenty pounds, and who carried herself quite professionally. The tailored cut of her buttoned suit coat effectively hid the heavy-caliber semi-automatic handgun that Trent knew was there, just under her armpit. He watched admiringly as her cool, practiced eye appraised each person approaching the group. He knew that she was not so much seeing people as she was seeing potential threats—even targets, if necessary; that she was, in turn, checking out the position of each person's hands, quickly scanning their clothing for any signs of bulkiness that would indicate hidden weapons, and finally peering intently into the subject's eyes for just the few moments it takes a skilled professional to see into the soul of a potential attacker. He smiled slightly, knowing that it was exactly what he would do.

"That one right there sure knows what she's doing," he continued before Maggie jabbed him once in the ribs.

"A little chunky, if you ask me," Ben said.

"What do you want to bet there's not an ounce of fat on that frame, though."

Maggie gave Trent *the look* again, which dissolved into a magical smile as she turned and stepped up to the governor.

"Margot, how in the world are you?" Governor Thompson took Maggie's hand, grasped her forearm familiarly, and pulled her close to kiss her cheek lightly. "I am so glad you could make it; it's been much too long!"

"Madam Governor," Maggie said.

"Oh, *Cha'risa*. Please."

"Cha'risa," Maggie repeated. "It is very good to see you, too."

"Margot, allow me to introduce you to our real guest of honor tonight: the Minister of Education and Science of the Netherlands, Laird Bouwmeester." The tall, middle-aged man next to the governor turned, beamed warmly at Maggie as he took her hand, and gave her an abbreviated bow of the head.

"Minister Bouwmeester, I am honored."

"Oh, I am only the Second Minister," Bouwmeester chuckled. "Not so much a dignitary; merely a functionary."

Trent had pasted the dutiful smile back on his face as Maggie discretely pulled him forward by his arm.

"Governor, Minister—may I introduce you to my husband, Trent Carter."

"Ma'am, Sir; my pleasure."

Maggie went on with the introductions of Sheriff Ferguson and his daughter, Jennifer, after which Minister Bouwmeester turned to the attractive young woman beside him. "And this is my own daughter, Ilsa. She is taking a brief holiday from her university studies to accompany me on my trip here to the American West."

"Business, or vacation, Sir?" asked Trent. Maggie gave him a quick, sharp look of warning. He twitched his eyebrows as if to ask, *"What?"*

"A little of both," answered Bouwmeester. "Ilsa is studying paleontology, and I am somewhat of a history buff, especially of the American West. Ilsa is eager to search for fossils in the area, and I—well, neither of us has ever visited this part of the United States before, so it is a marvelous opportunity for us both. You are, of course, familiar with a company that had some importance here for a while—the Maxwell Land Grant Company?"

He paused as fewer nods than shaking heads responded.

"Vaguely know of it." Trent answered. "It owned a lot of country around here at one time, didn't it?"

"It certainly did! The largest of the old Spanish land grants, dating back to when this area was still a colony of Mexico. The company owned a huge amount of land right around us here, and it was purchased in the last part of the nineteenth century by a group of Dutch investors. As it so happens, my grandfather himself was the president and CEO of the Maxwell Land Grant at one time. I have heard his stories all of my life: of the company, the wild shootouts in this area, the eventual battle in the United States Supreme Court, all beginning in this very county. Very exciting." Bouwmeester paused again in amazement at a few of the blank faces around him.

"*The Colfax County War?*" he continued, incredulous. "I am amazed some of you have not heard of it. This was the longest and bloodiest land dispute in the history of your entire country! And you are privileged to live right here where it all took place!" He looked out beyond the veranda and waved a hand toward the darkening expanse in front of them. "Why, even this very valley we are standing in right now was the heart of the homeland of the Ute Indian tribe."

Trent took a deep breath, suddenly remembering the two ghostly buffalo hunters he thought he had seen earlier.

"Yes, I've heard of the history," he said. "Even think I might've had an ancestor or two of my own involved back then."

Minister Bouwmeester glanced to his right at the growing line of people waiting impatiently to greet him. He turned back to Trent.

"I am afraid I must return to my official duties. The Governor and I have some rather pressing business we need to meet over yet tonight. But I would be very interested in continuing our discussion, Mr. . . . um. . . ."

"Carter," Trent finished for him. "Trent Carter."

"Mr. Carter. Thank you. I will look forward to visiting further, and maybe picking your brain, yes?"

Doubt there's much there to pick through, Trent wanted to say, but instead said, "I look forward to it, too, Sir," although he didn't really mean it. Right now, he only wanted to find a quiet corner for the remainder of this already too long evening.

His head throbbed once and he was suddenly keenly aware that amongst the many impatient people in the reception line glaring in his direction was a particular set of eyes scrutinizing him. He knew even before he glanced around that those eyes belonged to the tall blond-haired security agent, who seemed to have taken a sudden interest in him. She quickly looked away when he turned in her direction. Was it only his imagination, or had he done something to raise her suspicion? Maybe she was simply paying more attention to him because of his close proximity to the minister.

Yes, that had to be it, he realized, shaking it off as he moved away to find Maggie.

#

Later, Trent had found his quiet corner table where he now sat with Ben. He was sipping on some bottled water he had found in a tub of ice and counting the number of gin and tonics his friend had consumed. Trent was ready to call it an evening, but as he watched Maggie continue to skillfully navigate the crowd, doling out smiles, handshakes, and hugs, he knew that his exit wasn't happening anytime soon. Ben followed his gaze.

"Quite a gal you got there, that Maggie," Ben said, only slightly slurring his words.

"You can say that again," Trent nodded, continuing to watch his wife with admiration.

"I mean, look at her go," Ben continued. "If I didn't know any better, I'd say *she'll* be running for governor soon."

Trent frowned as his friend flagged down a server for yet another drink.

"Or sheriff, if you don't slow down there."

Ben took a large swig, set his tumbler down, and squinted at Trent. "You know what your problem is, Carter?" he asked, pointing his finger. "You are turning into one of those tiresome and prudish reformers, now that you found Jesus, got remarried, and stopped drinking."

"I only found what I needed to find, for me. What I profess or do—or do not do—does not require anybody else to do the same."

"Then why are you being so damned judgmental tonight?"

"Well, I'll answer that by asking why are you drinking so damned much tonight? And I am not being judgmental; drink yourself into a well, for all I care. I'm just concerned that you still have to drive forty-five miles back to town tonight down a mountainous highway, with your precious daughter in the car with you."

Ben grew quiet and studied the ice in his glass for a long moment.

"You ever wonder if you were really a good father, Trent? I mean when Sophie was Jennifer's age."

"I think that's in the job description, isn't it? To wonder how badly you're screwing up as a father? Goes with the nameplate."

"Yeah, but my situation is a little different; you guys were together, as a family. I haven't been around Jenn much for the last few years, since her mom divorced me. And now I find I have all of this pent-up advice to give her, but I don't feel I have the right anymore to give it to her. I mean, who the hell am I to her anymore, other than the biological part of being a dad?"

Trent looked at his friend with compassion. "Well hell, Ben. Do you love her?"

Ben took another drink and scoffed. "What the hell kind of question is that? 'Course I love her."

"Then stop trying so hard. I mean, she's almost grown; she sees that you care. But don't push things at her. Nothing you can say will matter anyway, until she's ready for it. If she needs your advice, she'll come to you. In the meantime, just be there for her, and listen. That's the sort of father she really needs at this stage in her life."

"So, did that work for you? With Sophie?"

"Oh, hell no. Not at first, because I didn't know better. And a lot of it didn't take place until much later, after her mother, um . . . passed away, when Sophie was already on her own." He paused for a moment, reflecting, and then looked back up at Ben. "But, you know, I do wish I had had someone like me around to tell me all that, while she was younger."

Trent heard a small commotion behind him and turned to see heavy double doors open and the Dutch Minister of Whatever-It-Was, Governor Thompson, and another man with Native American features and dressed in a western cut jacket, turquoise bolo tie, and expensive snake-skin cowboy boots come out of another room where they had obviously been holding some sort of private meeting. They shook one others' hands warmly, smiled, then parted company. Trent noticed curiously that the smiles disappeared, almost immediately. Beowmeester looked around, and then, to Trent's immediate regret, caught Trent's eye and began making his way toward their table, smiling once again, and shaking a finger at him. A couple of bodyguards were in tow closely behind him, including the tall blonde bodyguard. Her head swiveled imperceptibly as she scanned the crowd around them. Trent and Ben stood up.

"Don't look now," Ben leaned over and said quietly, "but I think you're about to get your brain picked."

"Carter . . . Carter," Bouwmeester repeated as he approached, still wagging his finger. "*Jonathan Carter*, the famous Sheriff of Colfax County?" he asked, pulling out a chair between Trent and Ben. "Please, gentlemen, be seated." He sat down and slapped the table with his hand. "Why, of course. I should have gathered it before! Your great-grandfather, I suppose?"

"Yeah, I suppose. Come to think of it," Trent paused, mentally counting his fingers. "Maybe my great-great. Don't know much more about him beyond that. At least, nothing I can recall that anyone else ever said about him." He paused as he looked at the agents. "Um—would your, uh, bodyguards also like a seat?"

"That won't be necessary, Sir," answered the agent, seemingly the one in charge, and with only a hint of an accent. Trent assumed she was Dutch and continued to look at her thoughtfully. She intrigued him for some reason.

"Suit yourself," he finally said, raising his water bottle in salute. The agent cocked her head and furrowed her eyebrows above steely blue eyes that stared into his evenly. He had the distinct feeling she was scanning his soul, and his sixth sense tingled again.

But beneath her hard professionalism he also detected the softness of her femininity: a glowing, clear complexion; full mouth with only a hint of lipstick; only a trace of eye makeup; and short, full-bodied collar-length blond hair combed back behind the ears. She exuded confidence and an overall attitude of no nonsense. Her hands were clasped easily in front of her black suit jacket and she appeared completely relaxed. But Trent knew she was poised to jump into any action that might suddenly be required. He himself had often found himself in the same position of coiled readiness in his former military and law enforcement careers.

"Ah, allow me to introduce to you Ms. de Jaager, my head of security. She is like you, Mr. Carter, a former marine—in the Dutch military, of course. Britt, this is Trent Carter, also like you, a retired law enforcement officer."

Trent extended his hand to her. "Ms. de Jaager," he said. "Welcome to New Mexico."

"Mr. Carter," she replied, shaking his hand briefly, her voice low and even. She returned to her former stance, her hands clasped easily in front of her. Bouwmeester chuckled.

"I am afraid Agent de Jaager here is all business and can appear quite formidable at times. But then, that's what makes her so good at her job, yes? From one professional to another, Mr. Carter, I am sure you'll agree that's an invaluable quality to have in someone whose job it is to protect your life."

"Impressive," Trent responded.

"Now, back to the subject at hand: your great-grandfather Jonathon."

"Great-*great*-grandfather," Trent corrected him. "And I'm afraid I don't know much else about him."

"Oh, he was a key figure in the Land Grant conflict, Mr. Carter, I assure you." Bouwmeester then almost scolded him, as if he were a child. "And speaking of which, I am shocked that you do not seem to know more of your own family history."

Trent started to make some excuse about part of his memories being lost forever in the scar tissue left behind by a would-be assassin's bullet years ago, but he thought better of it.

"Well, guess I had better study up on my family history, then," he said instead. He looked over their heads, searching impatiently—and unsuccessfully—for his wife to come rescue him.

"Yes, Jonathon Carter had much influence throughout the entire affair. Why, I have even read that he was close friends with many of the other key individuals of that so-called war: Frank Springer, Thomas Stockton, the cattleman Charles Goodnight, the gunfighter Clay Allison—you do know the famous quotation attributed to him, don't you? *I have never killed a man who didn't have it coming!*" Bouwmeester clapped his hands excitedly and chuckled. "Oh, it is a marvelous history! Why, a person could not make these stories up if he tried."

He must have noticed Trent's raised eyebrows, and then with a brief chuckle, regained some composure. "You must excuse my exuberance, Mr. Carter. I am just a bit overwhelmed to be walking the same ground that up until now I have only been able to read about or heard about in my grandfather's stories."

"No apologies necessary, Sir."

"Ah, what have we here?" Bouwmeester beamed as his daughter Ilsa appeared at his elbow, along with Ben's daughter Jennifer.

"Papa, you remember Jennifer."

"Oh yes, your daughter, I believe, Sheriff Ferguson." He shook hands again with Jennifer. "It appears that you two have gotten to know each other a little. I am so pleased." Bouwmeester turned to Ben. "These receptions can become quite stifling for a young lady, you know. Nice to find someone her age." Ilsa smiled and blushed, then pulled Jennifer next to her.

"Papa, I was telling Jennifer about our planned trip this week—the helicopter ride over the mountains, to see some of the old Land Grant property?"

"Yes?"

"Well, I was hoping that—you see, I was telling Jennifer, and she seems very interested in the history, and—well, I was hoping. . . ."

"You were hoping that Ms. Ferguson could go along with us on the tour, yes?"

"Yes, Papa, if that would be fine with you."

"Hmm, I am not entirely sure," Bouwmeester replied, rubbing his chin thoughtfully, teasing his daughter. "What are your thoughts, Sheriff Ferguson?"

Ben put his glass down, having a little trouble focusing on the conversation. Trent rolled his eyes.

"About what, Sir?"

"About your daughter accompanying Ilsa and me on a helicopter tour of Colfax

County; specifically, the old Maxwell Land Grant lands—I was just discussing some issues of mutual interests with your governor. . . ." Beowmeester stopped himself suddenly, and Trent was sure he caught a quick exchange of looks between the minister and his blonde head of security. "Well, that is neither here nor there," he quickly continued. "I'm sure it will be most enlightening for her, and Ilsa would love the company."

Ben looked at his daughter. Jennifer glanced quickly at the number of empty glasses on the table and back at him. Ben turned red and rubbed his face.

"Yeah, Dad? What do you think?" Jennifer folded her arms and waited.

"I'm really not too sure, Jenn. I should probably give your mom a quick call . . . ."

He stopped himself as he caught Trent glaring at him.

"Yes," he continued, making a decision. "I think that would be great. Good chance for you to see something different."

"Wonderful!" exclaimed Minister Bouwmeester.

#

"I hope you are calling to tell me you have taken care of things."

"We may have an unexpected opportunity—a better opportunity, that is," said one of the dark-suited security agents, who had managed to slip away from the veranda, back into the main room of the lodge, and was speaking quietly into a mobile phone.

"Yes?" came the voice on the other end, after a pause.

"It seems our target is planning a little air tour soon."

Another pause.

"Continue."

The agent stopped and waited as a couple walked in from the veranda, their heads close together and giggling. They soon disappeared up the stairs.

"I think it would be much cleaner to have something else happen—something just as final, but less apparent."

Another pause.

"You mean a well-timed accident, rather than a well-timed bullet?"

"Yes. Exactly." The agent waited. "Are you still there?"

"Yes. I am here. And I like the way you think. Better than trying to manage the authorities, and the press—although the press occasionally has its uses. Nothing like a good, old-fashioned assassination to stir things up. Still, a nice conspiracy theory can work the same magic."

"Shall I proceed, then?"

"When is this tour scheduled?"

"In a few days. Plenty of time to make things happen."

"Well then, go and make things happen."

CHAPTER 7
Land Of My Sojourn

(A letter from María Consuelo Delgado)
September 12, 1868

Sr. Manuel Diego Delgado
El Rancho de las Golondrinas
Santa Fe,
Territorio de Nuevo México

Dearest Mannie:
    I was thrilled to receive your letter last week! I have read it over and over so many times that the ink must be wearing off of the paper. Papa and the boys have also had me re-read it to them several times. Thank you so much for all the news, my precious brother!
    Oh, Mannie! As I shared with you previously, I must tell you I was thrilled to accompany Papa on his cattle buying expedition. We had learned that a large herd was coming north and were also told that such herds often rest at the water holes at Willow Springs for a few days before making the demanding trek over Ratón Pass into Colorado. We certainly timed it well! We were able to meet a Señor Charles Goodnight from Téjas and talk to him about purchasing some of his cattle. We met him at the new hotel on the Canadian River called The Clifton House. Oh, it is such a wonderful place, Mannie! It is as if a genie magically picked up one of the magnificent hotels from El Paso, or even Santa Fe, and deposited it out here on the prairie! Señor Tom Stockton, another Tejano cattleman, had the place built on his rancho just a few miles to the east of us, right on the Santa Fe Trail, as a stagecoach stop to take care of the wagon trains and the stagecoaches coming through.
    He held a great feast and a wonderful party in celebration of his grand opening, and since Papa and I just happened to be there at the opportune time, he invited us to stay for the festivities! He said he still has much work to do, but such a wonderful meal we enjoyed, and there were even musicians and much dancing, although you can be sure that Papa kept me close to his side. It seemed that every young man there was eyeing me. It made me blush! But Papa was giving out such stern looks that no one dared come close—except for one young vaquero, a handsome young man who had accompanied Señor Goodnight, and who was there when we discussed the cattle business. He introduced himself to Papa, very politely, and asked his permission to speak to me. Papa was, of course, flustered at first; but then he relented, I think only because the vaquero was an associate of Señor Goodnight.

And he was so well mannered! He actually did not want to dance but just to talk to me, so he sat down at our table and we talked through the evening. His tales of the war and of the cattle drive enraptured me. Why, he told me they had even fought with Comanche Indians, and that some of his people had been killed!

That night, of course, it was too late for us to make the journey home, so Señor Stockton allowed those of us still there to spend the night in his new hotel! The men, of course, all slept in one room and the women in another. Papa, I think, did not sleep a wink but sat in a chair in the hallway, guarding my door. I was so embarrassed! But then, I could not stop thinking of this handsome young vaquero. Alas, when I awoke the next morning and quickly dressed and went out on the great balcony along the front of the hotel, there was no sight of the cattlemen. We were told they had arisen hours earlier, while it was still dark, because they had to get their herd over Ratón Pass that day. Other vaqueros brought over the cattle we purchased—one hundred head of fine, young heifers to breed to Papa's bulls!

But alas, my handsome young vaquero was not with them.

I can still see his beautiful bright eyes and his chiseled chin . . . and his quick smile. I wonder if I will ever see him again.

Oh how awful of me, to mention such things to my own brother! But who else am I to talk to about it? I am giggling to myself. Mannie, I know you will share my letter with Ana, but please do not say anything to Papa or the boys. I will never hear the end of it.

Write to me soon, dearest one. I miss you all so terribly. And give my sweet little "Gallo" a hug from his Tia!

I remain
Your loving sister,
María

#

(September 2, 1868 – Colfax County, New Mexico)

Jonathon Carter and the Allison brothers had been riding drag and now unsaddled their tired horses and hobbled them in with the rest of the *remuda* grazing on the slope of Capulin Mountain, an extinct cinder cone volcano situated just a few miles south of Colorado. Jonathon tossed his saddle on the ground, slapped the dust off his clothes with his hat, then plopped down and leaned back against his rig with a long sigh. He chewed on a long stem of grass as he gazed back down the slope to the west, where the sun was beginning its final dip toward the distant snow-capped peaks of the Sangre de Cristo Mountains. He knew that the nearest town, *Cimarrón,* lay sixty or seventy miles in that direction, in the foothills. He tipped his hat way back on his head as an easterly breeze from those same mountains wafted up and over him, quickly cooling the perspiration from his face and hair. He allowed his gaze to wander to the northwest, toward where Ratón Pass topped out at over 6,500 feet, and where he knew that they would soon be driving the herd, finally, into Colorado.

But here where he sat, the volcanic flows had created lush grasslands; the grass grew waist high in some places, a welcome change from the rugged and sometimes barren path the Goodnight-Loving Trail had taken from Southwest Texas. Through rocky canyon lands the last couple of weeks they had pushed the remaining 2,300 head of ornery cattle ever northward from Fort Sumner, skirting the desolate escarpment to their east called *Llano Estacado,* or Staked Plains, leaving the Pecos River at the old Spanish town of *Las Vegas,* merging there with the Santa Fe Trail for last hundred miles into *Norte Nuevo México,* and finally arriving in this peaceful and beautiful place.

Jonathon Carter breathed deeply again, thinking that this was a land he could quickly grow fond of.

"Damn . . . I can smell that fatback and beans cooking from here." Clay Allison had scooped up his saddle rig, shuffled past Jonathon, and followed his brother downhill through the high grama grass without a single look back. "You're not hungry, Squirrel?"

"Think I'll just sit and enjoy the view for a minute. You boys go on."

"Suit yourself. But you had best not fall asleep there. Best get your ass down to the chuck soon, for I am not going to protect your portion from young mister John Allison here and his voracious appetite." Clay reached over and good-naturedly cuffed his brother on the back of his neck, causing his hat to flip off his head.

Jonathon ignored them.

What an absolutely beautiful country this is! He was eager to get the cattle up into the foothills of those mountains in the next few days—eager to compare those hills to the rolling woodlands of his home in eastern Oklahoma. He wondered, not for the first time today, whether a man like him could find opportunities and make a good life out here in this relatively untamed land.

And he also wondered vaguely what his adoptive father was doing this evening, hundreds of miles away. Was the old general sitting on his porch, back on the reservation at Honey Creek, smoking his pipe and watching this same sun traverse across the afternoon sky? Jonathon felt a pang of remorse that he had not written to him in months. He made himself a promise to do so once they got near another settlement.

He felt his mind drifting and had begun to nod off when he heard a shrill whistle and jerked his head up to see figures down at the chuck wagon waving their hats in his direction, gesturing to him to come on in. He sighed, hefted himself up, and groaned as stiff muscles tightened. He grabbed his saddle, and made his way downhill to supper in the fading evening light.

#

"We got ourselves another three days to get these 2,317 head of prime Texas beef up and over Ratón Pass, right over there about twenty-five miles or so, as the crow flies."

Charles Goodnight was standing near the small cook-fire beside the chuck wagon as he pointed and then shoved the tips of his fingers back into vest pockets, pontificating like a schoolmaster. Several cowboys sat or lay in various positions, some still sopping up the savory juices of their supper with warm biscuits and honey, but all of them listening intently to their trail boss. Most had learned the hard way that *not* to pay attention to Charles Goodnight when he was holding forth would bring an immediate and embarrassing chastisement in front of everyone else, or worse, a dock in pay for the day. It depended on his overall mood. Jonathon sat cross-legged, a full plate of meat and beans on his lap, chewing thoughtfully and trying to absorb what his boss was really saying. Sometimes you had to read hard between the many lines of verbiage Mr. Goodnight loved to hear himself utter before you could get to any real nuggets of useful information.

"Now the bad news is, gentlemen, if you think you have worked hard up to now, and for those of you youngsters who have never had the pleasure of punching a mean cow up and back down a 6,000-foot mountain pass, you are all in for the ride of your life. And I pity the idiots amongst you who will most certainly lose one or two or several of my cows off the side of that gall-darned mountainside yonder because you weren't paying attention! On top of that, there is a land pirate goes by the name of 'Uncle Dick' who lives on top of that damned pass, and who is going to try his damndest to rob me blind with his ridiculous tolls against my herd."

Goodnight continued with his curse-laden diatribe against the owner of a twenty-seven mile toll road he had built over Ratón Pass and who made a pretty good living off each and every soul—two- or four-legged—who needed to continue travel east or west on the Santa Fe Trail. Some of the cowhands began to chuckle as Goodnight rambled on, until suddenly they all straightened up as they heard the sound of approaching hoof beats. Some scrambled to grab weapons.

"Hello the camp!"

The approaching horseman was a well-dressed middle aged man in dark leather boots over gray trousers and a matching vest over a ruffled shirt collar with a red kerchief around his neck, topped off by a long brown overcoat of expensive cut and a flat-brimmed black hat. The man had well-groomed mustaches and long sideburns and carried himself well in the saddle as he pulled up to a stop just outside the ring of cowhands. Goodnight broke into a broad smile.

"I thought that had to be you, Stockton!" he chortled, stepping between two of his cowboys to reach a meaty hand up to shake the visitor's hand in welcome.

Thomas Stockton was yet another *Tejano* who right after the war had come out of East Texas with a herd of prime cattle headed for the Colorado markets but had instead stopped right here in the high plains of New Mexico, where he had built himself a ranch and stocked it with his own herd.

"Charlie, you old cattle thief. How in the hell are you?" Stockton got off his horse and tied the reins to the branches of a short scrub oak near at hand. "Got anything resembling a good cup of coffee there?"

Goodnight gestured to the cook, who quickly wiped out a mug with the dishtowel tucked in his belt, filled it with the remainder of whatever was in the blue enameled pot that sat on the cook fire, and handed it over to Stockton.

The two *Tejano* cattlemen stood off to one side, sipping their scalded coffee, grimaced, and made small talk for a few minutes.

"Where's Oliver?" Stockton eventually asked, looking around the camp.

Goodnight hesitated, turned and spat out some loose coffee grounds, and frowned back at Stockton. "He's gone and got himself shot up and killed— Comanche—down at Horsehead Crossing."

"Well I'll be danged!" Stockton took another long sip of coffee as he stared down into the embers of the fire. "Sumbitch owed me some money, I do believe," he muttered absently. He came out of his reverie long enough to realize that he had just been insensitive and stared at Goodnight, who held his gaze for a long moment.

"Yeah, well he got me better than that," Goodnight said, breaking the silence. "Would you believe he made me promise him I'd haul his decaying carcass back to Texas?" He gestured toward a nearby supply wagon sitting at the edge of the camp. "Got him embalmed and wrapped up tight as a drum in that wagon there. Want to see him?"

"Nah, I believe that I will pass on that experience."

They continued to stare at one another. Then Goodnight snorted and they both burst into laughter.

"Well, damn!" exclaimed Stockton. "Sounds like that old bird got to both of us real good!"

The discomfort passed, and they continued to visit in low tones for a while before Goodnight looked up and called out.

"Carter, Allison—no, not you John but your brother. You two come here for a minute."

Jonathon and Clay glanced at one another from across the campfire, set their supper plates aside, and stood up.

Goodnight introduced them to Stockton. "Tom, these are probably my two top hands—but don't get in the habit of telling them that or it goes to their heads." Stockton shook hands with Jonathon, then turned slowly to Allison. Both faces were expressionless.

"Small world, Clay."

Allison stepped up and extended his hand. "Lieutenant. Very good to see you again, too." The shook hands slowly, then smiled.

"Last I heard you was wanted for murder of some Yankee soldier boy, back home in Tennessee.

Son of a bitch busted up my Ma's place. I merely sought to teach him a few manners, was all." Clay stroked his chin in thought, then shrugged, and grinned sheepishly. "Those Yankee fellers got softer heads than most the boys I grew up with."

"Clay here fought by my side at Chattanooga and Chickamauga. Pulled each other out of many a scrape." Stockton clapped Allison on the shoulder and smiled again. "Good to know you're still upright and functioning, Clay."

Goodnight spoke up again. "Boys, the reason I called you over is that Tom here has gone and built himself some sort of fancy digs just over here to the west of us twenty or so miles—some sort of stagecoach station or some foolishness—what is it you called it, Tom?"

"Clifton House."

"Yeah, that's it. Anyway, he has just finished it up over there—stables, hotel, restaurant, bar, the works—and he's having a big old soiree over there this week, with food and partying."

Jonathon and Clay exchanged looks as their eyes lit up and smiles spread their faces. Goodnight frowned at them and continued in hushed tones. "Wipe that smile off your faces! And if it were just a shindig, I wouldn't be talking to you numbskulls right now and nobody would go. Can't leave the herd untended just so's everybody can go to some big old bar-b-q. But what I do have here is an opportunity to sell a few head of cattle to some of Tom's friends and neighbors who will be there kicking up their heels. I am sure you can see the significance and advantage of my doing so."

Jonathon was the first to speak. "I would assume that would be fewer head you have to wrangle over that mountain?"

"Exactly," Goodnight answered, slapping his knee. "Tom, you see why this half-breed is my top hand? He's got a brain, too."

"Half-breed?" Stockton asked, his eyebrows raised. "What tribe, son?"

"Cherokee—Oklahoma," Jonathon answered warily. The question usually led nowhere good.

"Huh. Good tribe," Stockton grunted, and that was the end of it.

Goodnight went on to tell the two that he needed them to accompany him to the Clifton House, where they would be useful in negotiating with prospective buyers, and to make arrangements for the delivery of any purchased livestock.

"When do we leave?" Jonathon asked.

"Well, guests have already begun arriving today," Stockton answered, taking another sip of his coffee before grimacing again and tossing the remains on the ground. "Dinner and dancing will take place the next couple days. Figured if I was going to throw this wingding, better drag it out for more than a day—get more folks involved that way."

"Which is also the best time to get us a good price from these yahoos," Goodnight added, "after they're all good and liquored up!"

"So, Mr. Goodnight—this here dinner and, um, refreshments. . . ." Allison paused as Goodnight interrupted him.

"Clay Allison, you are like an open book. I can read you clearly, and *yes,* you can expect to be amply rewarded with food and drink—but *only* if you two manage to get me a good price on my beeves! Now go lay out your bedrolls—get a good night's sleep. We're leaving early in the morning for the Stockton Ranch."

#

"Gentlemen, if you would please hold still for a few seconds—deep breaths, please—and now…*hold!*"

Jonathon had tried to do as instructed, but he felt himself jerk as a brilliant flash of light and smoke filled the room and blinded him for several seconds. The acrid odor of the white smoke billowing up from the flash pan in the photographer's hand smelled like rotten eggs. The man's other hand held a black metal cap of some sort that he had quickly removed from the front of a large wooden box on legs—something he had called a *camera*.

"Hold . . . hold still . . . steady now." The cameraman quickly snapped the black cap back in place. "Good! You are now free to move. Thank you, gentlemen."

Jonathon blew out his breath, waved away some of the smoke floating around him, and turned back to the bar for his beer, which he slurped gladly. He glanced down the bar at his companions. Three of the four other men drinking beside him were Goodnight, Allison, and Stockton; but the man on the end he didn't recognize. He was a well-dressed, tall, and barrel-chested man with a finely combed walrus mustache whom everyone in the room except Jonathon seemed to know. *Some local official of some importance*, he surmised.

"Ever had your photograph made, Captain Carter?" Goodnight asked.

"No, Sir, I have not." He thought for a second. "And I'm not too sure why I have just done so." He had heard of the newfangled art form of photographs, but had seen only a few, in Fort Worth, when some man named Matthew Brady had displayed some very realistic—and disturbing—photographs, supposedly taken on various battlefields of the war.

"First time for everything, son. Might as well catch a little glory when you can."

Jonathon took another sip of beer, then nodded to their right. "Who's that fellow down there on that other end, had his picture taken with us—the governor, I presume?"

"No, but I heard the governor and he do move in some of the same circles." Goodnight set his glass down and called out. "Frank, you got a minute? Come on down here."

The tall stranger disengaged himself from a conversation he evidently was just as happy to be disengaged from and stepped toward them, a friendly smile on his face.

"Jonathon Carter, meet Frank Springer."

Springer put his hand out and Jonathon shook it. He had the distinct impression that Springer had already sized him up, and he wondered idly if the man approved of what he saw.

"Carter," Springer greeted.

"That's *Captain* Carter to common people like you and me, Frank," Goodnight chuckled, poking an elbow into Springer's upper arm. "Frank here is visiting with a view of relocating out here. From Iowa, I believe you said?"

"Yes, that's correct." Springer turned back to Jonathon. "Captain? A war veteran, then?" Springer asked, narrowing his eyes as if to study Jonathon more closely. "Let me guess: no remarkable accent, measured tone, good vocabulary—

yes, I confess to eavesdropping on some of your earlier conversations; my stock in trade as an attorney, I'm afraid. Let's see, my first guess would be that you fought for the Union."

Jonathon knitted his eyebrows and visibly bridled. Springer quickly noted his error. "Oh, my. I see that I misjudged. Please don't get me wrong, Captain; I'm not being judgmental here. I am a scientist as well as a lawyer. Detecting a person's background from their obvious characteristics is just a little hobby of mine. Bear with me a moment longer."

Springer cocked his head, too a step back, and peered at Jonathon once more.

"Your manner of speaking would suggest Northerner, but I would have to revise my assessment to say that your ruddy complexion, dark eyes, and good posture—yet at the same time your lightness of foot—would all indicate at least a partial indigenous blood-line. I know of only one regiment of soldiers in the late war that was made up of tribal warriors, and that would be from the Five Civilized Tribes, mostly out of Oklahoma." Springer spread out his hands in conclusion. "You fought for the Cherokee Mounted, am I correct? Obviously a staunch Southerner. General Watie, I believe. A fine legacy, Sir, if I might add."

"Stand Watie is Jonathon's father, Mr. Springer." Clay Allison had stepped over and joined the conversation, evidently proud to have shared something that few here knew. "Why, I myself served with General Bedford Forrest." He hoisted his glass of bourbon and started to toast, but then paused, cautiously. "For whom did you serve, Mr. Springer?"

"I, regrettably, did not serve on either side, Mr. Allison, but spent the war engaged in my university studies, in Iowa."

Allison looked at Springer evenly for a second, and raised his glass again. "A toast, then, gentlemen, to the glorious Confederacy." He allowed his glass to pause at his lips long enough to confirm that Springer had indeed raised his own glass, then drained the tumbler of whiskey. Allison turned to Jonathon and lowered his voice.

"I was just chatting with some of these fine gentlemen over there, Captain Squirrel. Why, did you know that there is actually a gold strike going on in these parts, as we speak?"

"No, I was not aware of it."

"Well, I have certainly made you aware of it now," Allison slurred, setting his empty glass down on the bar with a loud thud and tapping it with his forefinger to get the barman's attention, "and I think it bears further conversation on our part."

Goodnight smiled thinly, excused himself to Springer, and then took Jonathon aside by the arm.

"Our friend Clay, here, is clearly enjoying his refreshments this evening, wouldn't you say?" Jonathon started to speak, but Goodnight continued. "Jonathon, we have yet to get our livestock contracted this evening. I have no time for further distractions. I fear Mr. Allison is not going to be of much help, so it falls now to you and me to push forward."

Goodnight turned Jonathon with a nudge so that they both had their backs to the bar and could survey the tables in the large, festive room. They were filled with laughing men and women eating—and drinking—and a few of them were dancing to the marvelous four-member string band that Tom Stockton had spared no expense in hiring from *Las Vegas*.

"Now then: Mr. Springer over there certainly has amazing intuitive skills, wouldn't you say? Something I believe him to have in common with you, my friend. So, what do *your* amazing skills tell you tonight?"

Jonathon shook his head at his boss's cavalier approach. If he had any abilities at all, they usually came to the fore only under stressful situations, such as in the heat of battle. He dutifully scanned the room, taking in and analyzing the guests' various movements, attitudes, and demeanors.

His attention was suddenly drawn to a table near the corner, where a distinguished Spanish-looking couple sat, an older man and a much younger woman—possibly a daughter. Jonathon felt an odd twinge go through him when he looked at the girl more closely: hair black as coal and pulled back attractively with a blue ribbon that matched her simple, high-collared dress; smoldering wide, almost liquid dark eyes; the olive skin of her face smooth and free of blemish; full, almost maroon lips. The fingers of her hand tapped out the rhythm of the music, and he spied a toe of her shoe tapping as it peeked out from under the hem of her skirts.

"There," he breathed, and nodded once across the room.

"What's that?" Goodnight asked.

"Right over there, Mr. Goodnight, is a gentleman who is ready to buy some of your cattle, I do believe." Jonathon removed his hat, smoothed his hair, and moved off to thread his way among the tables of partiers, his employer in his wake.

#

Her name was María Consuelo Delgado, the only daughter of Señor José Delgado, late of Santa Fe but now homesteading a small ranch on the Maxwell Land Grant north of Cimarrón, New México; and she was the most beautiful woman Jonathon had ever laid eyes on. Indeed, as Señor Delgado and Charles Goodnight bargained over livestock, Jonathon barely comprehended a word they said, enraptured as he was over his proximity to the girl. He had frequently regarded a pretty lady here or there and had agreed with his fellow cowboys whenever they pointed out an attractive woman. But until this moment, Jonathon had not felt anything like what he was feeling now: a deep, distinct thrill that thudded in his chest and swelled up into his throat so that he could hardly breathe; and a thrill that simultaneously filled him with joy, fear, and pain, His mind swirled right now and contained only four thoughts:

He knew what it must feel like to have been hit by lightning.

He had never felt this way before.

He never wanted to let this girl out of his sight.

He was sure that he was about to pass out.

"Carter!"

Jonathon came to his senses and looked up. Goodnight was standing next to him, his hand squeezing Jonathon's shoulder.

"We're finished here. Let's go." Goodnight turned back, bowed slightly, and shook Delgado's hand firmly. "*Señor* Delgado, it's a pleasure doing business with you. We'll cut out a hundred head tomorrow and deliver them here to you, as agreed. And I'm certain you can hire a couple of Mr. Stockton's hands to drive them back to your place."

María Delgado was looking at Jonathon with those dark eyes, which she now lowered briefly. He felt his heart sink until she raised them back up and smiled at him.

"Thank you," he stammered, unsure of his feet as he stood up. "I mean, it was sure nice, um, that is, a pleasure to meet you." He was staring at María's dazzling face as he spoke, then quickly addressed her father. "And you, of course, Sir— *Señor*, also."

He felt ridiculous. Something inside his head told him to shut his mouth, *now*, and leave, which he did, following Goodnight back to the bar.

"Fine bit of good you did for me back there," Goodnight growled at him, ordering another drink from the bartender. "Sitting there making puppy-dog eyes at Delgado's daughter all night. I would've done better with Allison, even as in-his-cups as he was."

Jonathon ignored his rambling boss, choosing instead to lean back against the bar and attempt to catch the beautiful eyes of *Señorita* María Consuelo Delgado from across the room at least one more time.

#

"Ten cents a head?" exclaimed Charles Goodnight, glaring down from his saddle at Richens Lacy "Uncle Dick" Wootton, whose smug smile was beginning to irritate Goodnight as much as what he had just heard. "Last herd I brought through, you only charged me seven cents, you damned highwayman!" Goodnight fumed some more, then continued. "Why, I have half a mind to turn them around and go back to Fort Union and sell them all there."

"Go on ahead," Uncle Dick answered. "That's your right, for sure. Only owe me half as much then."

"Half as much! How do you figure that?"

Wootton gestured back north of the tollgate.

"Because half of your cattle is already through my gate into Colorado. You owe me ten cents for them ones already."

"Dammit all to hell!" exclaimed Goodnight, spluttering and turning red in the face. "You are worse than a horse thief. Wouldn't be surprised to find you strung up by your own purse strings one day!"

Wootton scratched his ear, and looked up at the apoplectic Goodnight. "Of course, if you do insist on taking that attitude with me, Charlie, you can pay me for the cows that already went through, and then pay me again when you turn them back around to the south. That would only be fair."

Goodnight's mouth hung open, wordlessly, as his face turned a deeper shade of crimson.

"But, being as I am a man of my word," Wootton continued, "and seeing as my dear wife and children are watching . . ." He pointed at the doorway of his adobe ranch house across the way, where his family stood, being entertained by the spectacle of the cattle herd passing by. "I will only charge you the half—this time."

"Fine then!" Goodnight roared, jerked on the reins, and turned his horse as it reared up slightly on two back legs. "Fine, fine, fine! Just piss-on-my-back-and-say-it's-rain. *Fine!*" He spun his horse away in a fast trot, splattering Wootton's legs with dirt and small stones as he went. "Jonathon!" he shouted.

"Yes, Mr. Goodnight?" Jonathon trotted up to meet his boss. Goodnight tossed him a small leather pouch, none too gently.

"Pay the man! Ten god-forsaken cents per head. Worst money I will ever spend in my entire life. That's ten times 1,093 head, mind you, after those piddly few we sold at the Clifton House the other day. *You watch him count, then you do the math!*"

Jonathon sat his horse for a moment as Goodnight galloped past him, crossed through the tollgate, and disappeared around a bend in the trail. He turned in his saddle as Clay Allison rode up next to him. Clay crooked one leg over his saddle horn, pulled a cigar out of his vest, and lit it. He looked over at Wootton.

"Say, why does everyone call you 'Uncle Dick?'"

Wootton shrugged, and continued counting noses. It was clear he was not to be deterred from his accurate counting.

His obviously pregnant young wife had stepped out of the doorway and moved up beside her husband, her hand caressing her bulging belly. "It's on account of he almost got hisself lynched up in Pueblo couple years back, by a bunch of hard cases," she paused and spat tobacco juice on the ground, "much like you boys, I reckon."

"I don't rightly follow, Ma'am," said Clay.

"Well, he had a couple of good kegs of Taos Lightnin' in the wagon, so he broke them open and give them boys all they wanted." She spat again, this time almost hitting a hoof of Clay's horse. "By the end of the evenin', they was all laughin' and happy, like family. Henceforth, he became 'Uncle Dick.'"

"Seems an appropriate name for him."

"You mean 'Uncle?'"

"No. I mean the other one."

Jonathon shook his head and chuckled, loosed the reins, and allowed his horse to wander and graze on some nearby grass. Clay clucked at his horse and followed him.

"You tell Goodnight?" Clay asked when they were out of earshot.

"Yes. I told him."

"That why he's so pissed off?"

"Partly, I reckon."

"How'd you put it to him, then?"

"I told him that a few of us had decided to go back to Colfax County and hunt for gold. I told him it was too good an opportunity to pass up." Jonathon paused and took a deep breath. "I also told him," he continued, looking Clay right in the eye, "that we would stay with the herd until we got it safely to his sorting station at Apishapa Canyon, at Spanish Peaks there." Jonathon nodded to the north, where two perfectly formed twin mountains sat on the Colorado plains, forty-five miles away.

Allison met his gaze coldly. "I never agreed to such a damn thing. Why, that means a couple more days, at the very least."

"More than that—there and back, not counting the time it will take sorting the herd once we get there."

Clay snorted, and threw the stub of his cigar away. "Sorting the herd?" he blurted.

"It's the right thing to do, Clay. Can't leave the man in the lurch like that, after all he has done for us."

"We're talking eight, ten days then."

"Easily that," answered Jonathon. "That gold will wait a few more days," he added, noting his friend's sour countenance.

He looked back toward the Spanish Peaks. From this altitude he could easily see the two perfectly formed mounds rising seductively on the southern horizon, above the Sangre de Cristo range. In fact, the collective proper name had been given them ages ago by the Ute Indians: *Huajatolla,* meaning "two breasts," or more specifically, "breasts of the earth."

And they reminded Jonathon right now of the real reason he had decided to return to *Nuevo México.*

CHAPTER 8
Icarus Rising

(Present Day)

*T*he *boy finds himself lying painfully on sharp rocks. Darkness envelops him, but lights flash sporadically, revealing that he is in a close, damp space, hemmed in on all sides by hard immovable objects. Smoke clings to his nostrils and with each sobbing breath he feels a raw wetness slither down his throat like a snake. His eyes sting; he finds that wiping them only makes it worse.*

He tries to pull himself upright, but his foot is jammed underneath something heavy. He pushes on this weight with his other foot, harder and harder, until he finally wrests his leg free. He squints as another light illuminates whatever it was that had trapped him; he gasps when he sees that it was the body of a man wearing a white jacket that is now torn and dirty, with blood smeared down its side. The man stares back at him with lifeless eyes. His breath catches as he thinks he recognizes the face of this man—someone he has seen just recently.

Various sounds suddenly echo in the distance: footfalls of people running, unmistakable weeping, a shout, and a sudden shrill scream nearby. He gasps and his heart races, fear grabbing his throat, the walls of the already tight space closing in on him. He has to get out of here, wherever "here" is.

He cries out, but strangely, no sound comes from his mouth.

He screams. Nothing.

Now in full panic, he scrabbles like a crab on all fours, climbing across the hard stones until he bangs his head hard. His hands shakily feel their way up the side of a solid stonewall that he has run into. He twists around and crawls the other way, coughing now as the acrid smoke fills his throat once more. His outstretched arms and hands grasp ahead of him to protect himself from banging into anything else. He feels the coldness of metal now, a frame of some sort, and runs his fingers across it before jerking back his hand. Something jagged, broken glass perhaps, has ripped across his fingers. He puts them in his mouth and immediately tastes his own blood.

Panicking now, he tries calling out again, but his voice comes out as only a hoarse whisper. "Help me," he wheezes. "Somebody."

He suddenly remembers that he had not been alone; others had been with him, but who? And where had they been? Then he remembers. "Timmy? Where are you, Tim?" He looks around again in the dimness, and in another flash of light he sees it: a possible path of escape, a narrow space just ahead, about his size—if he squeezes himself small enough. Maybe his brother Timmy went that way, too. His mother is going to be furious if he can't locate him. He stretches himself out on the rough gravel floor and inches his way forward like a worm, bare knees scraping now, and flesh tearing on the stones. Then he feels another cold smoothness of metal, like a long rail.

"Rail?" he thinks suddenly, and stops, sliding his hands gingerly back and forth along the metal. "Rail? Train?" he whispers excitedly now, remembering more. "That's it! We were on a train! Mom and me—and Timmy!" But something had gone wrong—something bad, something terrible. What was it?

He commences his escape again, crawling underneath what must have been a railroad car, hoses hissing nearby, spitting hot steam his way, electrical wires snapping and popping somewhere, and always the rocks underneath his body, which is almost pinned between the car and the rail bed. He slides over another rail and then takes an involuntary ragged breath as cool air whips past his face and hair.

He has made it! His fingers touch the opposite concrete wall now. "Tunnel?" he thought to himself. "Yes, we were in a tunnel." But something happened—something terrible. He still can't think straight.

Mom. He has to find his mom.

He blinks, trying to make out objects through the prism of tears welling in his eyes. Something—or someone—is moving down the way there, through a dim light of some kind. Daylight?

He pulls himself shakily to his feet. He looks down and discovers that he has only one shoe. His head throbs, and his hand and knees sting where he has cut and scraped himself. He shuffles forward, seeking the light, stumbling toward the fresh air that flows wonderfully across his face. He has one goal now: Get out. Find help.

Find Mom.

And Timmy.

He follows the voices, the cries; the movements he can just make out against the brilliant light ahead that is growing steadily larger. The hissing of steam grows louder until he finds himself opposite a hulking black locomotive. He is now almost out of the darkness. He rubs his eyes with his knuckles, and this time his vision clears noticeably; but he wishes it hadn't. A nightmare scene unfolds in front of him as he finally stumbles out of the wrecked tunnel into the daylight: men and women and screaming children are stumbling about in a daze of confusion, just as he is. And like him, they have torn and bloodied clothes. Some are sitting on the ground, rocking themselves or each other, as if they want to go to sleep. He recognizes no one.

Suddenly he remembers the man in the tunnel with the white coat. He was the waiter in the dining car. The man had been a bit rude to his mother, but he had also given Timmy and him ice cream.

But then, he remembers that his mother left them there, to go back and get something.

And then Timmy ran away, to go find their mother.

And then he went to find Timmy.

And then. . . .

He can't remember what came next. Only that it was terrible, otherworldly. And then all of this came next.

And he doesn't like what he is seeing. He begins to sob, upset. He feels completely lost, alone, isolated. He needs to find someone he knows. The screams and odor of smoke begins to fade as the sweet fresh air bathes over him. He turns away and stumbles across a field of grass, toward some trees. They look peaceful, safe, inviting. He continues toward them.

But again, something is terribly wrong. The feeling of peace eludes him, and in its place he feels dread—fear.

He stops just yards from the nearest tree and looks slowly up into its branches.

Something is there.

Something is wrong.

Something is terrible.

A dark shape, barely distinguishable from the shadows behind the trees, is moving there, very slowly—a hulking presence of some kind, swinging in the cool breeze.

He takes another faltering step and then falls suddenly to his knees, both hands covering his mouth to stifle a scream. A dead man is hanging from a rope tied to a lower branch of the tree, swinging gently back and forth.

The body swings slowly around until it faces the boy, whose eyes grow wide with recognition.

He screams, again and again, and this time his screams fill the evening air.

The dead man is his father.

#

"Walter!"

Walter woke up, crying out. He felt a deep, implacable sadness in his chest; tears crept out of the corners of his eyes and down the side of his face. His hard breathing and his racing heart gradually slowed down.

He flipped the sheet and blankets off angrily and sat up on the edge of the bed, rubbing his eyes. It was the same damn dream he always had, the same feeling of tremendous loss that seemed ever-present.

Such loss. I am so weary of it. Why, after all these years, couldn't he get over it?

And why do they always occur within the same dream?

Both his little brother Tim and his mother had perished in the explosion of the train tunnel under Raton Pass at the end of the war in 1945. Walter himself had barely survived.

And his father had also barely survived after being wounded in the South Pacific. That's why they had been on the train journey to begin with, to finally pick him up from the Naval Hospital in San Diego. Walter had been only twelve at the time and had hardly remembered his father before he had left to fight. *But later, after he had returned. . . .*

A light tapping sound on the door interrupted Walter's memories. The door squeaked open a few inches.

"Walter? You okay in here?"

Trent stepped into the room and turned on a small bedside lamp. Walter sat with his back to him. He wiped his nose roughly between his thumb and forefinger.

"I'm all right," he answered brusquely. "Sorry to disturb you—bad dream is all."

Trent stood looking at his father's back.

"Want some coffee?" he asked. Walter was silent for a moment.

"You having some?" he finally asked.

"Thought I might. I mean, it's already 4:00 a.m. Might as well get my busy day started."

"No need to be a smartass," Walter muttered, his back still to his son.

Trent sighed and left the room to go make coffee. Walter listened as the sound of footsteps receded down the stairs, and then faded as they moved into the kitchen before disappearing altogether.

Someone was always disappearing.

#

Trent gingerly pushed the door open with his toe, two steaming mugs of coffee in his hand. He moved around the bed and carefully set one on the bedside table by Walter, next to a packet of old letters that lay there.

Walter had turned on his bedside lamp and was stretched out on the bed, his head propped up against two pillows. He had reading glasses perched on the end of his nose and he was peering closely at something in his hand.

"What's all that?" Trent asked, nodding to the table where an old wooden box sat with its lid open, revealing what seemed to be old letters, photos, and newspaper clippings.

"Never you mind." Walter grabbed the box, slammed it shut, and moved it onto his lap protectively. He glared at his son for a second before returning to scrutinize what Trent could now see was an old photograph, nicely framed, that Trent recognized as one of his father's oldest possessions. For as long as he could remember, it had hung on the wall in the hallway of their old home in Raton along with a few other family photos. But unlike those other photos, Trent had never had any idea who the five strange men were in this one, which looked as if it were taken from the footage of some old black and white, silent western movie. All he knew was, it was never far from Walter and these days normally hung just above the bedside table, except for when Walter often had it off the wall and was studying it closely.

Like right now.

Trent stood there for a few seconds before sighing and putting his hands in the pockets of his robe. He had often, since he was a little boy, asked his father about the photo but always got the same answer.

"Don't suppose you want to finally tell me about that old photo."

"Nope."

"Then I don't suppose you would be interested in any of these, either?" He pulled a hand out of his pocket. It held a napkin wrapped around several Vienna Fingers sandwich cookies, Walter's favorite.

Walter's eyes flickered for an instant as he saw the cookies. He glanced up at Trent.

"This some sort of bribe?"

"Nope. No bribe—no tricks." Trent held them out to him. A smile creased the corner of Walter's mouth as he grabbed the cookies and set them next to his coffee. Then meticulously, like a child, he twisted one of them apart, licked the icing off one side, dunked both halves into his coffee, and gobbled them up. Walter suddenly looked up with concern.

"You're not going to tell Maggie, are you?"

"About what? The cookies, or the bad dream?"

"Either one—but I guess the cookies, mainly."

"Nope. Our little secret." Trent sighed again and pointed to the photo in his father's lap. "But, come on, Walter. Don't you think it's high time you let me know about that old photo? I do know it's very important to you."

"So?"

"So, that makes it very important to me, too, don't you think?"

"Why should it?"

"Well, because maybe those people there are important. Anyone in it I might be interested in?"

Walter narrowed his eyes and reached to protect his cookies.

"So, it's blackmail then, is it?"

Trent chuckled, scooted his father's legs over a bit, and sat down on the bed.

"No, Walter. I promised—no tricks." He looked away for a second, then back. "But I do see you with that picture a lot, and that box of old letters there." He scratched thoughtfully at the stubble on his chin, thinking about what Bouwmeester had chastised him for at the reception the previous night. "I haven't bothered you lately about them, you know. But I have to wonder if they have anything to do with your history—*our* family history."

Trent let his voice trail off and touched the scar on his forehead, out of habit. Walter watched his son quietly.

"You seeing ghosts again, are you?"

"No, not for a while now. Not since. . . ." He didn't finish the sentence.

"Not since Victoria?"

Trent looked up at his father. There was sadness in his eyes that he usually kept well hidden; a sadness that was one of the few priceless treasures they had shared, each in his own way. Trent knew how close his late wife had been to her father-in-law, how she had been there for him during difficult times.

Trent started to say something about the two ghostly Ute Indians he had seen a couple of days ago, mysteriously stalking the buffalo at Vermejo Park Ranch, but then he thought better of it.

"No, not since Victoria," Trent echoed softly. "But I do still have trouble filling in the gaps sometimes, the memories. Some are just . . . gone, I guess. But others come back, usually without warning. Anyway, my doctor says anything can trigger a lost memory: a word, a smell." He nodded again to Walter's lap. "A photograph."

Walter glanced down at the old framed photo. He then slowly handed it to Trent, who took it very carefully. Trent had, of course, studied the faded photograph many times, since he was a boy, and had always been curious about the sullen men staring back at him.

It appeared to have been taken at some sort of saloon, maybe over a hundred years ago, judging by the age of it and the attire of the subjects in it. Five men—six, if you counted the ghostly image of a bartender moving in the background—were posed in front of a bar, eyes wide, and faces frozen in various states of seriousness. Most of them were cowboys; real ones, not the dime store versions that roamed the West today. Their faces were ruddy from weather, their clothes and hats flamboyant but very practical. The one on the far left looked barely out of his teens, but his eyes held the camera with seriousness beyond his years. The next fellow was heavyset and appeared quite successful. The fingers of one hand were held stiffly inside a vest pocket. A shiny watch chain looped out of the other pocket, a sign of success. The third man was dark, not only from weather, but from his soul. His dark eyes stared back at Trent with a hint of malevolence—maybe even a touch of insanity.

Trent suppressed a shudder.

The fourth man held himself smartly, his chin up and his trimmed mustache stylish for the times. He wore an expensive-looking overcoat and a black flat-brimmed fedora. His eyes sparkled with pride and achievement. The fifth man was a departure from the other four: he looked like a young businessman, his suit simple and worn, but clean. His hair was neatly combed; his lip sported a large walrus mustache, also neatly groomed. His eyes looked intelligent, again beyond his years. In short, he looked ready to take on the world.

Trent flipped the photo over. The back of the frame, like most professionally framed works, was sealed with brown paper which was still tightly attached to the weathered wooden frame, except for a missing corner about an inch square through which you could just see another piece of backing paper of some sort underneath. "Pretty decent shape, for an old one," he noted.

Some smudged writing appeared in a couple of places on the back and was somewhat decipherable. At the bottom edge was printed in archaic, fancy calligraphy the name of the photography studio—Timothy H. O'Sullivan, Washington, D.C. Centered at the top were simply the words *Clifton House, 1868,* that someone had penned in ink with an elegant handwriting style. Below that were listed five names, evenly spaced out; obviously the names of the men in the photograph. Some of the names were more legible than others. Trent started to read what he could.

"Springer . . . Goodnight. . . ." He looked up at Walter, whose eyes were shining at him. "Goodnight? Like the famous cattle drive trail?"

"One and the same," Walter answered. "Goodnight-Loving trail. That other one next to him there is Frank Springer."

"Like the town of Springer?"

"I suppose so." Walter reached a finger over and pointed at one of the others— the one with the evil eyes. "That one there is Clay Allison. You remember hearing about him, don't you?"

Trent studied the dark man—the one who had made him shudder. He could see the man's hand fingering the butt of a Colt .45 stuck in his belt. He seemed to recall something and looked up at Walter. "Gunfighter, wasn't he? Killed a bunch of folks over at Cimarron? Bullet holes all up in the ceiling of the old bar at the St. James Hotel, as I recall."

"Yep, that's him, all right." Trent glanced at his father and shook his head slightly. Walter was having a good time at his expense. It occurred to Trent that this was probably the most meaningful thing they had talked about in years, besides coffee and cookies.

He turned the photo back over and tried to read more names.

"Tom something or other—too faded. Starts with an S. *Stanton? Stilton?* I can't read it." He showed it to Walter, who adjusted his glasses and held it close.

"Stockton," he said. "Never heard of him."

"Well I have," remarked Trent. "He's the one who built that Clifton House— I'm guessing it's where this photo was taken, and where that murder took place a few days ago."

"You mean that guy I saw in the papers? Digging holes?"

"Yep. That one."

Trent leaned forward to point to the young cowboy at the end. *Something in those eyes.* They peered straight back at Trent, looking into his soul, almost familiarly.

"What about this young guy? Can't make out his name there."

Walter just smiled and watched him. "Keep looking. He's the real interesting one here."

Trent glanced on the back, reading silently with his lips moving, trying to make out the smudged name.

"Jona—something, something, then O-N." He shrugged and looked up to see Walter watching him closely. "*Jonathon?*"

"What about the last name?" Walter urged. "Can you make it out?"

Trent squinted again at the faint letters, sounding them out.

"Come on," Walter chuckled, obviously toying with him. "I thought you were a trained detective!"

"S, no—a C. O—wait. That's an A. Small one." He struggled to make out the rest. "A small R, then…"

Trent's eyes went wider. He couldn't make out the other letters, but then he suddenly knew.

"It's *Carter,* isn't it?" He looked at his father who was beaming at him with pride.

Walter tapped his finger at the photo. "That is none other than your great-great grandfather, Jonathon Salal Carter!"

#

Trent and Walter continued to talk for almost an hour, with Walter filling in more of the story of what had happened following the explosion at Raton Pass in 1945—how he had been found wandering the tracks by a truck driver by the name of Jim Peters, who saw that his injuries were tended to, and then later took him in for several weeks, until Walter's father finally made it back home and they were reunited. Walter grew quiet at this point.

"I remember Jim Peters," Trent said, with a hint of surprise in his voice. "You mean *Uncle Jim?*" Walter nodded. "I guess I always thought he was really my uncle. Never thought about it. But he was always coming around, I recall, when I was a kid. Always had some kind of little present, or piece of gum, or something on him." Trent looked off in the distance. "What ever happened to him, anyway?"

Walter sighed and said nothing for a moment. "Died. Truck accident. He was hauling cut stone off of Johnson Mesa. Brakes went out, truck left the road and went straight into an arroyo embankment at sixty miles an hour. Might've survived it, too, if the stone he was hauling hadn't also slid in on him." Walter now grew very quiet, his eyes misty.

Trent stood up and went over to hang the old photograph back on the wall. He turned and studied his father for a few moments.

"He was a lot like a father to you, wasn't he, for awhile?"

Walter nodded, unable to speak.

Trent took a long gulp of his coffee and watched him; he decided to go ahead and ask the question he had always wanted to ask.

"Uh, Walter, you're a junior, aren't you? Tell me about Walter Senior, your dad—my grandfather. What exactly happened to him? You never talk about him."

Walter looked up and stared at Trent for the longest time, a cloud like a veil dropping over his face. He then shook his head slowly and squeezed his eyes shut, unable—or unwilling—to speak. Trent immediately regretted asking.

"It's all right, Walter," he sighed. He turned to leave. "It's not that important, I guess."

"You guess?" Walter exclaimed. "*You guess?* What the hell would you know about it, anyway?" He sat bolt upright on the bed, grabbing the old photograph back and pulling the box further away.

Trent sighed and stood up. *Another mystery; perhaps for another conversation—another time.*

"My father was a war hero! He loved us! He would've done anything for us, except that he. . . ." Walter stopped suddenly, unable to say anything else. Instead, he reached over, opened the drawer of his bedside table, shoved the box of documents inside, and slammed it angrily.

"Go on. Just get out," he growled, folding his arms defiantly, refusing to look at his son.

Trent walked to the door and stopped, studying his father. Something was terribly amiss in their family story, a subject that Trent had been reluctant to broach for all these years, and evidently for good reason.

But just when would be the right time?

#

(Colfax County Sheriff's Department — Raton, New Mexico)

Ben Ferguson sat staring at the folder on his desk. It was early afternoon and he was doing some investigative work on the bodies found at the old Clifton House ruins. He was having trouble keeping his mind focused on the project at hand.

At 8:00 that morning he had driven Jennifer to the Colfax County Airport to meet up with Minister Bouwmeester and his daughter. They pulled up on the tarmac of the small airfield where they were directed over to a large helicopter parked near the terminal, and where he immediately began having second thoughts. The chopper was a vintage Bell HU-1, nicknamed "Huey," famous for its exploits during the Vietnam War.

"Oh, wow, Dad! I've always wanted to see one of these up close!" Jennifer gushed over the antique. Ben, on the other hand, felt sick to his stomach.

"You know what this is?" he asked, surprised she would recognize vintage aircraft from fifty years ago.

"Of course! I just studied a segment at school on the American involvement in Southeast Asia.

American involvement. Is that what they were calling the Vietnam War these days? He shook his head. It seemed a poor attempt to sanitize—rationalize—all the madness of that era in one politically correct phrase. He placed the palm of his hand on the side of the iconic war machine.

"Well, this can't be at all good. It's a wonder it still flies," he muttered. At that moment, Bouwmeester came up beside him, obviously having overheard.

"Oh, the owner assures me this aircraft has been completely rebuilt and has passed all of its current inspections with flying colors—no pun intended," Bouwmeester smiled.

"Yeah, but it's just that it looks so . . . old," Ben complained. "Who's flying this thing?"

"I am, Sheriff. How ya doin'?" the pilot said as he walked past them both and opened the doors of the Huey. Ben vaguely recognized him. He was a wealthy landowner from neighboring Union County and originally from Texas who had made all his money in oil and now didn't know what to do with it all, except maybe buy a ranch he didn't really work and stock it with vintage aircraft and other toys he didn't really need. He did have a reputation as a good pilot, though, which really did nothing to soothe Ben's churning stomach.

"You see, Daddy? It's going to be just fine." Jennifer stood on tiptoe and kissed his cheek, grabbed her knapsack, and climbed aboard with Ilsa and the Minister of Whatever from the Netherlands. Ben stood by his car, watching his daughter laugh with her new friend as they buckled in, and reflected on how time sure speeds up when people are separated from one another, even for just a few months. Jennifer was no longer his little girl, and the lost time with her dragged on his spirit like a lead weight hung around his heart.

He continued to stand there for several minutes after the Huey had taken off, its powerful twin-blade rotor churning the air with an iconic sound that shook him to the soles of his feet and to the depths of his soul. It gradually shrunk to a flyspeck in the sky and finally disappeared into the foothills nearby.

At his desk now, he sat perplexed and tried to concentrate on his work. The forensics had come back inconclusive on fingerprints or other DNA on the murder weapon, the pickaxe imbedded in the victim's chest. However, the fingerprints of the victim himself were what intrigued and puzzled him. They came back from an Interpol database as belonging to one Cobus de Groot, a citizen of the Netherlands, which was another coincidental fact, given the nationality of the currently visiting dignitaries. But the most disturbing fact was that the late Cobus de Groot had also been a lieutenant in the UN Peacekeeping Force, stationed most recently in Kosovo, and had been reported as dead once before—killed in a skirmish in Kosovo during the unrest there in 2004.

But according to the facts of the case, Lt. Cobus de Groot had just died a few nights ago, in Colfax County, New Mexico, USA.

So just who had died in Kosovo in 2004? And who had died in Colfax County, New Mexico, with a pickaxe through the chest?

Ben scratched his head and stared at the copy of the soldier's official military photo and ID in the file in front of him, willing the man looking back at him to say something—anything.

He was still peering at the photo when the phone on his desk rang.

"Yeah, Molly."

Molly Swindoll, the department dispatcher, paused. Ben heard her take a deep breath.

"Ben, Line 2 is for you. You need to take it right away."

Ben didn't care for the serious tone in Molly's voice. She was usually sharp, sarcastic, and sweet, all at the same time. But never this serious. He pushed the button for Line 2.

"Ferguson," he said.

"Sheriff Ferguson, this is control at Colfax County airfield."

"Yes?"

There was a pause on the line. Ben glanced at his watch. It was a quarter to noon. He wasn't supposed to pick Jennifer up until 1:00. "There a problem?" he asked slowly.

"Sheriff, I really hate to disturb you, but yes, there has been an issue."

"An issue? What the hell is an issue?"

"Sir, I'm afraid we have a situation that involves an HU-1 helicopter that departed from here this morning at 08:16, and proceed on a northwesterly route—"

"Son, how about removing the official lingo from out of your mouth?"

"Uh—excuse me?"

"I mean, what the hell exactly is the *problem?* Just spit it out, please."

"Sir—we received an S.O.S. from the HU-1 helicopter twenty minutes ago."

Ben stared off into space as parts of his mind felt like they were shutting down.

"Sheriff Ferguson, we are no longer in radio communication with the chopper. We believe it has gone down northwest of here, somewhere in the Sangre de Cristo

Mountains."

#

(Montaño del Sol Ranch)

Trent stepped out onto the veranda and blew into his hands. The late September air continued to grow cooler almost daily, and even now at noon he had donned his wool-lined denim jacket against the cold. He held a small brown bag full of warm egg, bacon, and cheese sandwiches and a thermos of hot coffee and stood for a moment looking over at the corrals where Maggie was working the bay gelding again. He went down the steps and across the large plaza that separated the house from the barns and other outbuildings of their working ranch. He walked through the alley of the horse stables, clucking softly to the few horses that greeted him from their stalls with soft nickering, and stopped at the open half-door at the other end that opened directly into the corral.

"Lunch time, Cowgirl," he called softly, not wanting to spook Maggie or the gelding.

"Hey there, handsome," she cooed back at him, holding the halter line firm in her gloved hands.

"How's he coming?" he asked, nodding at the horse. "He about ready for my soft butt?"

The gelding had been the one attacked by a cougar last year, and Trent had always had a soft spot for him. He hoped he would actually be able to ride him one day.

"He's coming along. Almost there, in fact." The gelding blew his breath out and nickered, rolling an eye in Trent's direction in recognition, almost as if he knew they were talking about him. Maggie pulled gently and walked the horse over to the door where she handed the line to Trent while she removed her gloves and examined the contents of the brown bag.

"What do we have here, Chief?"

"Simple bacon and eggs, ma'am. All I really know how to cook, you know." The gelding moved up close and nuzzled Trent's shirt with his soft nose, blowing its warm breath on his sleeve. Trent patted the animal's neck.

Maggie leaned back against the door and took a bite of her sandwich. She nodded at the animal. "I do think he's in love with you—and I do believe I am jealous."

Trent smiled, looked away, studying the horse's face, scratching his ears, and looking distracted. Maggie watched him for a moment, and then laid her hand on his arm. "How's Walter?"

"Oh, he's okay. He actually opened up a little this morning, more than usual."

He proceeded to tell her about his conversation with his father, concerning their family history. Trent smiled, and then grew reflective again.

"Walter still won't talk about his own father, though—my grandfather."

"Walter Senior?"

"Yeah. All I really know is from Walter, that he was a marine who fought in the Pacific, was seriously wounded, came back home, and died shortly thereafter. He got very emotional about him for a second—defensive even, and then clammed up. Something happened that he refuses to talk about. Whoever my grandfather was, he's still a big, blank page to me."

"Sounds familiar, doesn't it?"

Trent frowned at her. "What does?"

"Walter and his dad—you and Walter. Seems like a generational thing, this disconnect between fathers and sons?" She squeezed his arm affectionately. "I mean, you still insist on calling him *Walter*, not *Dad*."

Trent looked down at his feet, nodding slowly, but not answering. He knew she was right, but there were some things that he was not ready to concede or change—yet.

Instead, he changed the subject.

"Maggie, about the other night, I really do apologize for taking off like that."

She took another bite of her sandwich and chewed thoughtfully. "I know it's just your nature. You and Ben are sort of like a messed-up Sherlock Holmes story—*The game's afoot, Watson!*—and all that stuff. And I know I can't change that."

Trent stroked the gelding's face gently.

"I just don't want you upset with me. I really am trying to settle in here and leave all that police stuff behind."

Maggie turned around and leaned on the lower door, facing him now. She peered intently at him with those gorgeous hazel eyes.

"You know what upsets me, don't you, Mr. Carter?"

"No idea—really," he replied.

"What upsets me is," she paused and blew her breath out slowly, then started over. "What really upsets me isn't that I know solving crimes is in your DNA; not that I know you won't ever change and turn magically into a happy little rancher. No, what really upsets me is that I know you are going to continue to run off at every whim and opportunity to be this big, rugged crime fighter, and that one day—" She choked on her words, squeezed his forearm sharply with her fingers, and went on. "One day, my phone is going to ring, and some stranger on the other end is going to tell me that you are not coming back that day . . . or ever."

She turned away, and swiped the back of her sleeve against her nose.

"And *that's* what upscts me, Mr. Carter."

Trent reached over and wrapped his arms around his wife as she leaned back against the door. When he opened his mouth to try to say something profound, his cell phone rang. Maggie sighed deeply and stepped away as he looked at the caller ID.

"It's Ben," he said softly. "Could be something."

"Well, you'd better answer it then . . . *Dr. Watson*."

But before he could answer it, she turned around and abruptly and marched back to him, grabbed him by the lapels of his jacket, and pulled herself up as far as her face could reach. She kissed him hard and fast on the lips, and then pulled back to search his eyes deeply.

"*Whatever* the hell it is that Ben wants, you had better come back to me in one piece, Mister!

CHAPTER 9
Valley Of The Ancients

Letter from María Consuelo Delgado
April 22, 1872

The Honorable Marsh Giddings
Governor
Santa Fe,
Territory of New Mexico

Dear Governor Giddings:

I shall begin by apologizing for being most presumptuous in writing to you, and I will come directly to the point of my concerns.

No doubt you are aware of the deteriorating situation here in Colfax County regarding land rights. Law--abiding settlers, like my family and me, who have homesteaded the land for years now under a long-time arrangement with the previous owners, Mr. and Mrs. Lucien B. Maxwell, now find ourselves under unreasonable efforts of the new landowner, The Maxwell Land Grant and Railway Co., to evict the leaseholders for non-payment if we are not able to complete the cash purchase of our land in short order.

Your Honor, my family, as well as many others, are certainly unable to raise the amount of cash moneys required for such a purchase. The prior arrangement was, indeed, a godsend; and over the years we have gradually prospered in cattle and crops, a generous share of which is paid annually to the current landowners as part of the original contract. Unfortunately, this contract was totally verbal and is being completely denied by the company, whose enforcers have already visited our ranch twice now, demanding full payment, or threatening eviction!

The violence elsewhere in the county is escalating, with several shootings and lynchings. I cannot believe it is your wish, Governor, to see such lawlessness continue. As a lawful citizen of this territory, I implore you to intervene on behalf of all the lawful settlers and enforce our prior contract, allowing us to continue to honor our previous agreement to pay a share of our crops and livestock to the Maxwell Land Grant and Railway Company for the continued privilege of homesteading.

I await your favorable response.

Most humbly,

María Consuelo Delgado
Cimarrón, Colfax County
Territorio de Nuevo México

#

(April 1872 – Elizabethtown, New Mexico Territory)

Jonathon Carter, the Allison brothers, and their new friend Henri Lambert had all arrived about the same time in Elizabethtown, New Mexico, a bustling mining boomtown built near the western slopes of Mount Baldy and the Cimarron Range goldfields, to try their hands at prospecting for gold. Now, scarcely three years later, Jonathon was tired of having little or no luck at all. Over drinks one night at Lambert's saloon and hotel in "E-Town," as the local citizens had nicknamed it, he announced to his friends that he was throwing in the towel and going back to Texas to return to a more successful life as a cowhand.

He was broke, dejected, and perhaps worst of all, broken-hearted.

María Consuelo Delgado had been on Jonathon Carter's mind ever since that morning long ago when he had ridden away from the Clifton House with Charlie Goodnight. Her dark eyes and full smile tormented his heart during the day, and unconsummated dreams of her warm closeness tormented his nights. Once he had finished his contracted work with Mr. Goodnight in Colorado, he had ridden back over Raton Pass, paying Mr. Wootton his required toll on the way, and made his way hell-bent for leather to the Cimarrón country. Here, it hadn't taken long to find out where the Delgado ranch lay, and bolstering up his nerve, he had cleaned himself up, ridden over one afternoon, and knocked on her door.

Jonathon had been wise enough in the ways of fathers of daughters that he knew to ask formally to speak to Señor Delgado right away. He had brought as gifts a box of expensive cigars, shipped all the way from Cuba, and a bottle of good tequila, both of which had seemed to smooth the frown from the man's face somewhat, and Señor Delgado had reluctantly given permission for Jonathon to begin to talk to María. Since then Jonathon had called on her several times, riding almost weekly the thirty miles or so from E-Town to visit her.

The problems arose when he eventually spent most of his savings from the wages he had earned from trailing cattle. With only the meager remaining earnings from barely scratching enough color from his gold claim, he could hardly afford to continue courting María, especially in the style that he knew she deserved and that her stern father expected.

So it was without any real surprise, but to Jonathon's ultimate shame and dishonor, that Señor Delgado was waiting for him and sitting on his porch one afternoon as he came calling.

"María is not available today, Señor Carter," he told him brusquely, puffing on one of Jonathon's expensive cigars.

"Oh, is she away in town?" Jonathon twisted in his saddle and squinted back up the road. "Odd that I didn't spy her when I rode through Cimarrón."

"No, she is here—and again I tell you, she is not available."

"Oh. I see," said Jonathon, but he didn't really see. "She is not ill, is she?"

"No, she is quite well, I assure you."

"Then, what seems to be the problem, Señor Delgado?" He was now suspicious.

Delgado had shifted on his wooden bench a bit uncomfortably. "You don't, by chance, have any more of these marvelous *cubanos,* do you, Jonathon? It seems I am nearing the end of the first box."

It was Jonathon's turn to shift uncomfortably, now beginning to understand.

"No, Sir, I do not. I would not be able to, um, afford them. At least for the moment." He had cleared his throat, embarrassed. "But I am sure that I will soon be able to save some more money, and I would be more than happy at that time to order you some more."

Delgado tapped the ash from his cigar and squinted up at Jonathon.

"And I am just as sure that you will *not* be able to do so, Señor." He had finally uncrossed his legs, stood up, and straightened his jacket. "Perhaps I am being rude to you, Señor Carter. After all, you have been nothing but polite to me and honorable to María. So I shall not play games with you, either. María needs a husband who can care for her every need, give her a good roof over her head, and reliably provide good food on her table as well as a good name. These things cost money, and let us face the cold truth: you have no more money, Señor." Delgado had pointed with his cigar to the northwest, to where Mount Baldy lay. "And pretending that you will be anything more than another desperate miner scrabbling for a hard living in the dirt up in those mountains does not assure me of a future for either María or for yourself."

Jonathon suddenly saw movement at a window, a white curtain being closed quickly. His heart melted in his chest.

"Señor Delgado, I don't know what to say . . . I love your daughter, more than anyone else could. I will quit the mining—I will come to town and get a good job, make enough money eventually. You will see—"

"No, I will not see, Señor Carter," Delgado debated. "The time is past. The opportunity for you is gone, I am afraid . . . And my daughter is not getting younger."

Jonathon couldn't believe what he was hearing.

Delgado cleared his throat. "I have given permission to another young man, a settler from the borderlands with *México,* who has his own farm and many good prospects. He will begin courting María, in view of becoming her husband." Delgado turned to enter his house but then looked back. "You will please honor my wishes and not attempt to see María again, Señor."

As Delgado shut the door behind him, Jonathon was sure he heard weeping from within.

Now, months later, Jonathon sat nursing his beer and his shattered heart.

"You are nothing short of crazy, Squirrel," pronounced John Allison, Clay's younger and less industrious brother, who had followed them out from Fort

Worth, Texas, herding cattle up the Goodnight-Loving Trail in 1868. "Have you forgotten what it's like to choke on the dust of three thousand stubborn-as-mules cows, or sit a saddle for eighteen hours a day until your ass is one big blister, or waiting to get your hair lifted by the Comanch or Mesc'leros?"

"Well, I wouldn't know about that last part, Johnny, because I still have my full head of hair. Secondly, no matter how ornery they get, I always tended to get paid real regular when I was trailing those cows. And thirdly, . . ." Jonathon took a long slurp of his room-temperature beer and set it down slowly, " . . . don't call me *Squirrel*, Johnny."

Clay Allison, his feet propped on the table, chuckled and took a sip of his whiskey John Allison glared at them both.

"Well, how come Clay calls you that? You don't chastise him for it!"

"That's because I gave up chastising Clay a long time ago. It does not do a bit of good. Besides, he has a certain appreciation for what the name means. But I'll be damned if I am going let his kid brother get away with it."

"Well, what's it mean, then?"

"You don't ever want to find out, John," Clay chimed in.

"Why not?"

"Because that would mean the bullets are flying and Death is knocking."

"Oh, well, all right then," John muttered, chagrined.

Henri Lambert had come over with a pitcher of fresh beer. "You seem particularly irritated this evening, Jonathon."

"No more than usual, these days, Henri," he replied, using the French pronunciation of his friend's name.

"That's Henry," Lambert corrected.

"*Henry*? Why Henry all of a sudden?"

"Because I have decided to Americanize my name, in honor of the country where I have made my fortune, that's why." Everyone around the table knew that Henri had been the most successful of them all. Henri Lambert had once been the personal chef to Abraham Lincoln in the White House, having left Washington, D. C. following the great man's assassination, and ending up in the Colfax County goldfields. But Henri had soon, and sensibly, given up gold prospecting to open up a saloon and restaurant, to do what he knew best, and to take what little money the other prospectors had left.

"Hmph," snorted John. "I like *Henri* better."

"Give up, Johnny," advised his brother. "You clearly have no idea what you are talking about when it comes to proper names."

Lambert changed the subject, which, in the long run, also changed Jonathon's life.

"Jonathon, why don't you come to Cimarron with me?"

They all stopped drinking and looked at Lambert.

"You mean for a couple of days?" asked Jonathon.

"No. I mean for a couple of years, at least. I am going to build a hotel there—the biggest around—and you can help me." He looked around the room and then lowered his voice. "Elizabethtown is dwindling."

"Dwindling?" rebutted Clay. "Last count, there's 7,000 people lives here. One of the largest towns in the territory."

"For now. But if you go out into that street right now you'll see 70 of them leaving by the wagonful, and 70 more yesterday, and tomorrow, and the days after that. It's adding up." He cleared the remainder of empty glasses and walked away. "You mark my words: in a year or two, there won't be 700 left."

#

(1872 – Cimarrón, New Mexico Territory)

Jonathon soon took Lambert up on his offer and came to Cimarron to help him build his hotel palace. The gold was, indeed, playing out and Elizabethtown had dwindled to fewer than 2,000 souls and was still shrinking, while Cimarron was growing. The Allison brothers had stayed on, occasionally scraping up enough ounces of gold or silver to get by. But Clay Allison had also begun to make another reputation for himself, and not necessarily a good one. His skill with a pistol had already cut short the lives of a few young cardsharps who had made the mistake of trying to cheat him—or other perceived offenses. The explosive outcome of his strict, if unique, Southerner's moral code of honor, coupled with his mercurial temper, usually spelled doom for any who crossed Clay Allison.

Jonathon Carter wiped the sweat from his forehead, stepped back, and surveyed his work. He had just put the finishing touches on painting the trim on the first floor windows of the newest hotel in New Mexico. His friend Henry Lambert had planned at first to call his new Cimarrón establishment The Lambert Inn, but recently had hit upon the name *St. James Hotel*. As a former chef to an American president, Henry felt the name evoked the amount of class befitting his reputation, and the right appeal he hoped to market far and wide. Indeed, the new two-story Spanish Colonial-style hotel was like nothing ever seen in the region, eclipsing even Tom Stockton's popular Clifton House near Willow Springs, thirty-five miles to the east.

"I could never have done this without you, Jonathon."

Henry Lambert had walked up from town and was admiring Jonathon's handiwork. Jonathon was squatted on his haunches, sucking on a piece of peppermint.

"Oh, anyone can sling paint around."

"Paint, carpentry, hauling supplies from as far as Pueblo. I would say you have more than earned your keep, my friend. Why don't you call it a day and take the rest of the week off? Hell, we're all but finished. The remainder of the new furnishings should be arriving from Denver next week."

"Well, then, don't mind if I do," said Jonathon. He cleaned his tools and brushes and then went inside, where he took a good long hot bath in the indoor bathroom, the only one of its kind for miles around. Lambert had given him a room in exchange for his labor and had indicated that it was still his to use, rent-free, for as long as he wanted, in exchange for providing a little security work around the place.

After cleaning up and dressing in fresh clothes, and still having the better part of the afternoon, Jonathon walked the few blocks of residential streets to the main street of town. He stopped in the mercantile to look at a rack of new shirts that had just arrived from New York. As he held one up to size it to himself, he heard shouting from the street outside. He put the shirt back and wandered out to the plank sidewalk, where he saw some sort of altercation taking place next door at the grocer's market. Two women shoppers were backing out of the doorway, their bags held in front of them protectively, and their hands up to their open mouths in apparent shock.

Jonathon sauntered over to see what the ruckus was, excusing himself to get through the doorway. Inside, the shouting was much louder, most of it coming from the proprietor, who was yelling and shoving an elderly Indian, a Ute by his appearance.

"I'm not telling you another time! Get your ass out of here—and now!" He shoved the old Indian again, forcing him to lurch backward into the corner and almost fall over a mangy dog that was wolfing down meat scraps thrown there by the grocer.

"What's the problem here, Matthias?" Jonathon had hooked his thumbs in his belt. He had chosen to leave his gun belt back in the room, because he had seen no need to wear it this evening. The old Ute's clothes were threadbare and hung on a very skinny frame. He turned a pair of rheumy, sad eyes up at Jonathon, lifted his hands imploringly, and then holding them up to his drawn face to mimic eating.

"Damned Indian knows they ain't allowed in my place, Jonathon. I've had to chase him out before, but he keeps coming back in time and again."

"Looks to me like he's starving, Matthias." He nodded at the dog. "Your worthless mutt eats better than he does. You can't give him some scraps too?"

"He'd just be back next week, and you know it. I ain't gonna have no filthy Indian scaring off my customers."

Jonathon stared at Matthias, then at the Indian, and then started looking at the shelves filled with tins of food, crackers, and dried fruits and vegetables. He turned back to the door, smiled, and tipped his hat to the ladies still standing there gawking.

"Ma'am, if you don't mind." He took an empty shopping bag from one of them. "Only because you don't seem to be in need of it right away, ma'am," he continued, tipping his hat and giving her another big smile. He started filling the bag with various canned goods, vegetables, and bread before stepping behind Matthias's meat counter, where he added a side of bacon and some goat's cheese for good measure.

"Now, see here, Jonathon," protested Matthias, rushing over behind the counter. "You can't just give that old deadbeat those good foodstuffs. I paid good money for those . . ."

"And you'll get your money back, you skinflint. Put this all on my bill."

"But you ain't got a bill here."

"I guess I do now," said Jonathon, moving his face within inches of the grocer's. "Unless you want me to ride out to Ute Valley and bring the rest of his family shopping in here."

Matthias was breathing hard and his face had turned red. He stared back for a few moments, and then pulled a pad of paper and a stub of pencil out of his pocket and peered into Jonathon's bag. "Well, let me see what all you took, so's I can make account of it!" he blurted. He looked up at the crowd pushing in through the door on top of each other, clearly entertained by the proceedings. He waved his pad at them angrily. "You all can just go on about your business! There ain't nothing concerns anybody else here!"

A few minutes later, Jonathon escorted the old man out of the store, one hand steadying him under his elbow, the other holding the full bag of groceries for him. The poor soul had already torn off a chunk of bread and was chewing it slowly with the few teeth he had left in his head. They stopped on the sidewalk and Jonathon looked down the street to where a tired pony that seemed to be about the same age as the old man was tethered to a hitching post. A couple of young boys were tormenting the old animal with sticks and laughing.

"That your horse?" he asked the old man, nodding that way. The Indian didn't comprehend at first, so Jonathon made sign language. The old man nodded and pointed, then said something in Ute.

"You boys knock it off," Jonathon called out. "Before I take one of those sticks to you."

The boys looked at Jonathon with worried eyes that indicated they knew he was quite capable of following through with his threat. They dropped the sticks and ran. Jonathon started to help the Indian onto his horse, but was surprised as the spry old fellow sprang right up on its back with no aid.

Jonathon handed the bag of food up, took the rope bridle, and led the horse and rider down the street to the stables to fetch his own horse.

#

(Ute Encampment, Cimarrón Canyon)

Having been told by Henry Lambert to take some time off, Jonathon spent the next three days at the old Indian's camp as his honored guest in the Valley of the Utes, under the shadow of Mount Baldy. The old man, whose Ute name was roughly translated Walking Elk, had once been a proud chieftain of his tribe, but younger bloods had long since taken his place and his ragged lodge had been relegated to the extreme outskirts of the village. Here he vied with the dogs and other old people for whatever scraps of food and game the tribe felt like throwing their way, whenever they remembered. Some of the old ones still had family who would bring them food and blankets, but Jonathon soon learned that all of Walking Elk's sons had died in battle and his daughters had died either in childbirth or of white men's diseases. Having no one left whom he could call family, he was on his own, which was why he risked his life going into town to beg for food.

They conversed in sign language, although a few of Walking Elk's words were similar to Jonathon's Cherokee tongue, and Jonathon began to make note of the simpler words he could commit to memory.

The old man had many stories to tell of his life, of his childhood relatively free of conflict with the Whites and the Mexicans, and of the many years when he was free to range far and wide, hunting his elk namesake and the buffalo. That was before the big trail came through from the white men's world far to the east, bringing hundreds of the big wagons filled with their worldly goods, their women, and their children. The white men stole the land and built their ugly towns, and, finally, they attacked the Utes' villages, raping the women and bashing in the heads of the children.

The Utes had, of course, fought back; taking what they felt was their rightful revenge upon the isolated farms and ranches, and occasionally raiding small towns. And then the miners had moved in, uninvited, cutting away the trees or burning them, scraping their ugly swaths through the land and carving out the mountains, searching desperately for the shining yellow stones. At first, the Utes had tried to steer clear of the filthy interlopers, but it was of no use. The miners were worse than the white settlers, in their own way: they didn't raid, but they would come and barter with the Utes, trading whiskey and guns for their women, whom they would then take away to cook for them and to sleep with them and to become their wives, to further pollute their bloodlines and culture.

And it didn't help that the young braves would be jealous, raid the miners' camps, and scalp and kill the hapless miners when they caught them alone upstream panning for the yellow rocks.

And now the men in black coats and long guns had started coming, demanding that Utes leave their ancient homelands and move to one of the white man's reservation camps, somewhere to the north, in Colorado. The tribal elders had tried to reason with these men, who said that they represented the real owners now, and that the Ute People must leave as they were told or else they would send the feared Buffalo Soldiers from the blue army camp to the south to force the Ute People to leave.

"How long do you have before you all are to leave?" Jonathon had signed.

"I do not know, because we will not leave, of course."

"Then you will surely die, for they will surely kill you."

"Then yes, we will surely die."

#

(Cimarrón, New Mexico Territory)

"How'd you like to be my deputy?"

Jonathon was at the bar of the St. James Hotel, idly sipping a beer when Sheriff Rinehart stepped up beside him.

"Excuse me?" Jonathon looked around him. "I could have sworn you just asked someone to be your deputy. You certainly couldn't have been talking to me."

"Why not you? I mean, I have seen how you handle a gun. I have seen your diligence in helping Henry build this fine place, I have heard of your reputation during the long unpleasantness with the Union, and I witnessed first hand—from my chair on the porch of the jail office—how you effectively calmed everyone down and handled that old Indian the other day.

Jonathon looked at the Sheriff over the rim of his mug and took another slurp.

"I happen to be part Cherokee Indian myself, Sheriff. Let's see . . . what do you white's like to call it . . . 'half-breed?'"

Rinehart choked on his beer, turned red, wiped his mouth, and stared back at Jonathon for several seconds.

"Well, I'm not, uh—I mean . . . " he stuttered, trying to compose himself. He suddenly slapped the bar. "Oh, the hell with it. I don't care about that, Carter. And I believe that, in your case, your qualifications all outweigh that . . . particular issue."

Jonathon shrugged. "Never been a *particular issue* with me," he said.

Rinehart turned to face Jonathon fully now. "Listen, Jonathon. I really need some help around here, and good help doesn't often come into this town. What with all this trouble brewing with the Land Grant Company starting to evict folks from their homesteads, and with the Utes about to go on the warpath again, I need you bad. So what do you say? Give it a try, will you? I know you were born to be a lawman!"

Jonathon finished his beer, set the empty mug on the bar, and hitched up his belt. "Well Sheriff, you know what you just said? About 'good help doesn't come easy?'"

"Yeah?"

"Well, it doesn't come cheap either."

#

Two months later, Deputy Sheriff Jonathon Carter was put to the test twice in the same week and apparently passed with flying colors. He was still alive.

The first case was when he came to within a hair's breadth of either arresting his old friend Clay Allison or having a shootout with him in the street.

Two days earlier, the good citizens of Elizabethtown had broken into the jail there and sprung an innkeeper and serial killer named Charles Kennedy, who had been accused of murdering some of his guests, as well as his entire family, and hiding their bodies in his cellar. It wasn't until the newer guests had complained of the smell that his crimes were discovered. But the mob wasn't satisfied to await a trial and had hauled him out in the street and lynched the poor bastard.

Not happy with just a lynching, a drunk Clay Allison had stripped off his own shirt and pants (so as not to get them dirty), cut down the hanged Mr. Kennedy, and proceeded to saw off the corpse's head, which he then tied up in a burlap sack that he slung on his horse. That night, still naked, he rode the 27 miles to

Cimarrón, whooping and hollering the whole way. He pulled his exhausted horse in front of the St. James Hotel, where he jumped off, opened his grisly bag, and mounted Kennedy's head on a post outside the door, possibly as a warning to other innkeepers.

Jonathon met his old friend downstairs in the closed saloon, having been awakened by all the cacophony and having examined the monstrosity out front.

"What the hell, Clay?" he said, coming back inside.

"Come on in, Squirrel! Drinks on me!" Clay reached over the bar and helped himself to glasses and a bottle.

"It's 5:30 in the morning, Clay. Too early for drinking. Besides, you have a real mess to clean up. Seems like you left your 'friend' out there a little worse for wear."

"He was a murderer, Squirrel. A real doozy. Left his family butchered in the basement. For all I know, he was tenderizing them for a barbeque later on. Hell, I used to eat dinner in his place there in E-Town. Who knows what ended up on my plate!"

"Well, you can't leave him there, whatever it is he did."

Clay Allison drained his glass and stared back at Jonathon, his jaw suddenly dropping. "What the hell is that on your shirt? Is that a badge? Oh, for the love of gawd!"

Clay Allison scoffed, poured another drink, sipped it, and shook his head. "Never thought I'd live to see the like of it—young Captain Squirrel is now young Deputy Squirrel."

"Clay, I'm telling you, you need go take care of that head out there, then you need to come with me."

"*Come with you?*" Clay Allison's demeanor changed, subtly, in a dangerous way that Jonathon immediately recognized. Allison slowly set his drink down and straightened up from the bar. He gently touched the butt of his pistol with one finger and turned toward Jonathon. "I think that's a request you are going to want to rephrase—Deputy Carter, *Sir.*"

As usually happened for him in a stressful situation, Jonathon's head began to swim with visions of several options and outcomes. Whatever happened in the next few seconds could change both of their lives, perhaps forever and fatally. While Clay Allison continued to lightly finger his pistol butt, Jonathon mentally surveyed and quickly dismissed each possible course of action, all of them clearly acted out in his head like a play, within the space of only a few moments. The possibilities all left his head, except for one, and that was what Jonathon acted on now.

He slowly and meticulously reached his non-shooting hand to his gun belt, unfastened it, and let it drop to the floor. He then held his hands out away from his body.

"Kennedy was a cold-blooded murderer for sure, Clay," he murmured, taking one step back out of Allison's personal space. "But you sure aren't."

Jonathon slowly reached down, scooped up his gun belt, slung it over his shoulder, and started back upstairs. "And for mercy's sake, Clay," he called out over his shoulder. "Put some damned pants on. Parading around town stark naked like that could be considered an assault on the good senses of some of the better-classed folks in this town."

When Jonathon came back down an hour later, the head had been removed, and Clay had left town, presumably headed back to E-Town.

The second testing of Deputy Carter's new law enforcement skills came a week later as he sat in the Sheriff's office, going through dispatches and newspaper articles. The sounds of raucous laughter from somewhere outside, followed quickly by shouting and cursing, brought him to his feet and out the door. Here he found something not too disruptive but at the same time very disconcerting to him personally: across the street, three ruffians—out-of-work miners, by the look of them—had accosted a Mexican family as they walked down the boardwalk, blocking their path, shoving, and grabbing shopping bags from them. Not a huge problem to resolve, and Jonathon knew he was up for it.

Except for the disconcerting part.

The family was the Delgados—the father, his two younger sons, and María on the arm of a young man Jonathon could only assume was her new fiancé. He had not seen María for over a year now, and his breath caught short in his throat. He had forgotten just how beautiful she really was. He stood stock-still for a moment, completely enraptured and surprised at the depth of the feelings he still had for her.

"You damned greasers need to pack up and get on back south!" snarled one of the men, pulling an apple out of one of the bags, biting into it, and spitting it back out at one of the Delgado boys. María's escort, who had kept his temper up until now, bridled and drew himself up into the ruffian's face, his fists clenched. Jonathon glanced at the escort's waist; he was unarmed. His tormentor, though, did not suffer from that lack. He whipped his hand down to his sidearm, drew it out, and began to level it off, when María and the gunman screamed simultaneously—María, because her young man was about to be shot, and the gunman because Jonathon had appeared out of nowhere and slammed the barrel of his own pistol hard against the man's forearm. The attacker's pistol clattered to the walkway as he bent over to moan and mewl like a cat, holding his shattered hand to his chest and backing away.

"You busted my hand, you piece of half-breed shit!"

"Not the first time I've been called that," Jonathon replied calmly, and then leveled off against the other two miners whose hands lingered dangerously close to their own holsters. "And not the first time I've found more than one use for this." He knew from their suddenly widened eyes that his Army Colt .45 must look like a cannon to them as it steadied itself twelve inches from their heads, and the three men finally turned tail. He calmly holstered it as they disappeared around the corner, even though his heart was anything but calm.

He picked up a few scattered grocery items and put them back in their bags, then turned.

"Señor Delgado, I am sorry for your trouble here today. Hopefully those particular three won't bother you again."

"At least today. I cannot be sure about tomorrow!" Delgado caught himself and held his hand out. "Please forgive my manners. Thank you, Jonathon. I don't know what . . ." He paused, looking at Jonathon's badge. "So, you are a lawman now? I didn't know." He tilted his head as they continued to shake hands, a look of suspicion crossing his face. "This means you will be aiding the eviction processes of the land grant people, will you not?"

Jonathon looked at his feet and answered. "Sir, I will do what I need to uphold the law. It's why I took the job. But rest assured that in the performance of those duties, I will see to it that no harm comes to anyone who is cooperative, and I will see that everyone is afforded the full protection of the law." Jonathon looked straight into Delgado's eyes. "Sir, there are legal remedies to your land situation. Are you aware of them all?"

"Yes. I am aware. Most of them are, in my case, impossible. But thank you again, Jonathon. Thank you." He turned to gather his family. "Come. We must be going."

"Goodbye, Jonathon," María called out, her voice as soft and musical as ever.

He didn't answer but tipped his hat as he turned to leave. He had yet to meet her eyes, and he dared not do so now, but he had made note of the sharp glare he had just received from María's new fiancé.

#

Later, back in his office, Jonathon sat down at his desk and let his breath out slowly. He picked up the small photograph he kept there in a cheap cardboard frame and studied the smoky image of five men, including a slightly younger version of himself leaning against a fancy bar and peering quite seriously into the camera. Like the old stories Walking Elk had shared with him, the photo now seemed a lifetime ago.

As he placed the photo back, his hand brushed a telegram lying on the desk, his name scrawled hastily across the envelope that he had not noticed until now. *Who would send me a telegram?* He tore it open carefully, and spread it out on the desk.

The telegram had originated from Oklahoma. It had been signed by one of his Cherokee stepsisters and the message was brief.

General Stand Watie, his beloved stepfather, was dead.

CHAPTER 10
Brother of the Moon

(Present Day – Somewhere in the Sangre de Cristo Mountains)

H er tore at him.

A vicious fight over a dead elk earlier in the summer had left him badly injured, had slowed him down in his subsequent hunting endeavors, and had made him half-crazed and ravenous. Although he had managed to get away with a large piece of his prey, the duel with the Mexican gray wolf pack had come with a price: he had lost one eye and had come away with a badly mangled forepaw that had never healed completely. Now, the constant pain and hunger made him vicious, and every minute of every day kept him occupied in finding food.

On this brisk autumn morning, at a height of seven feet and weighing six hundred pounds, the twelve-year-old cinnamon-colored male American black bear had no trouble standing on his hind legs, stretching his massive frame full length, and pushing over the remains of a lightning-charred trunk of a pine tree with his good foreleg. His nose had detected the promise of a nest of grub worms buried in the upturned root system of the tree trunk. He thrust his snout hungrily into the moist, musky earth and lapped up the worms, but his grumbling stomach already told him they were nothing more than an appetizer.

Soon, he would seek a den in which to hibernate, and he instinctively knew that the frozen sky would soon fall; at this point in the late season he needed to gorge, and would resort to any sort of easy prey.

Anything.

A distant and growing rumble caught his attention. The bear pulled his huge head up from his meal and looked angrily with his one good eye into the sky at this intrusion as the noise popped and spluttered and turned into a fast-approaching growl. At first he thought it was the rumbling of the sky that often preceded the falling of water and the brilliant flashing of lights in the clouds. But this intruder was something entirely different. A growl formed deep in his chest and roared out its challenge into the sky, where it mimicked the answering roar of a huge dark, bird-like creature that now suddenly appeared overhead, with hard-looking smooth sides, belching smoke and fire like a dragon. Its thudding, dragonfly-like wings beat the air with a frenzy that hurt the bear's ears and caused him to snarl and bat angrily at the strange bird with his one good paw, although it was out of his reach. The strange creature flapped away and soon sailed across the valley, growing smaller but continuing to breathe smoke until it disappeared completely over the next ridge.

The bear snorted as the acrid lingering smoke wafted down to him. He then sneezed, licked his jowls, shook the fur around his massive neck, and plowed his face back into his meal. He lifted his eyes only once more when a distant wrenching sound reached his ears, like the crashing noise the tree had made when he had shoved it over earlier—only much louder.

He chewed and squinted his good eye nearsightedly toward the ridge where the beast had flown, thinking idly that he would seek it out later; it had been an awfully large and noisy bird, but it had looked tired as it had flown past him. And if it was tired, it was weak, no matter its size.

Perhaps he would go find it, kill it, and eat it.

#

At an elevation of just under 12,500 feet, Baldy Mountain—or Old Baldy, as the 19th Century gold and copper miners had called it—is the highest point in the Cimarron Range of the Sangre de Cristo Mountains. Sitting atop rugged slopes about six miles northeast of the town of Eagle Nest, New Mexico, Baldy drops abruptly into the Moreno Valley to the west; spills dramatically down its east side into a series of ridges, ravines, canyons, and rugged forested lands for miles; and lords over 70 square miles of abandoned gold, copper, and silver mining camps spread around its skirts. To the south spread even more sparsely populated mountains, ridges, and canyons for miles; and to the north lie the ponderosa and spruce woods of the Carson National Forest, which eventually spills across the Colorado state line.

The summers can be balmy and pleasant, the winter storms short and brutal, the habitat perfect for a variety of hardy flora and fauna, and the area a paradise for outdoorsmen, hunters, hikers, skiers, and other adventurers who know and respect this wild, breathtaking landscape. It spells disaster for those who don't.

It was mid-afternoon and low, scudding clouds were already gathering in the west as Trent pushed the half-ton, four-wheel-drive club cab pickup through the sleepy town of Cimarron, speeding up as Ben and he barreled out of the town limits and continued west on U.S. Highway 64, headed for Cimarron Canyon just ahead. Behind the pickup he pulled one of Maggie's horse trailers carrying two horses and their gear. He had no idea what sort of terrain they were going to find ahead, so horses were the best fallback resource.

Because of the added burden of the trailer, Trent cautiously tapped the brakes as the truck entered the first of many curves and switchbacks. Beside him, Ben Ferguson let out a sigh of exasperation.

"Can't push it any faster, Ben," Trent answered his friend's unspoken impatience. "Isn't going to help anyone at all if we roll this rig.

He glanced over at Ben, who alternately squeezed his knees and rubbed the bottom of his face with his open palm. Ben's face was drawn tight, and the usual smile had abandoned his face.

"Why the hell did I let her go?" he muttered for the tenth or twelfth time since they had left Raton.

And for the tenth or twelfth time, Trent didn't bother to answer, or try to rationalize things with him. Instead he glanced at the mileage marker they had just passed.

"Twelve miles to Ute Park," he commented, changing the subject. "Then we head north on County B-13, and then as far as we can drive up Ute Creek. I figure somewhere there is where we have to continue on horseback." He glanced up at the sun. "Either way, we're camping out tonight, for darn sure."

He glanced over at Ben once more, trying to get his friend's mind engaged on details and freed from his emotion. "Tell me again about the last known position of the chopper."

Ben chewed a knuckle nervously. "Airfield control had them just north of Baldy at their last good contact point. After that, he got a garbled signal that could've been a Mayday, but it cut out almost immediately."

"And tell me again where they last pinpointed that signal."

Ben sighed, starting to lose concentration again.

"Damn it to hell!" he said, rubbing his eyes.

"Ben, just focus. Right now we have to look at the facts at hand and use them—make a plan. Nothing else helps right now, okay?"

"Yeah, I know, I know." Ben worked to regain composure. "Um . . . controller said he triangulated the Mayday signal with Angel Fire airport, and it appeared at that point that the helicopter had circled around to the east of Baldy before dropping out of range."

"Which would make sense if he was losing some altitude."

"Shit," muttered Ben.

"Which," Trent hurriedly continued, "could mean the pilot was simply dropping down to conserve fuel, or looking for a clearing or ranch headquarters to set it down on."

"Sure, any of that sounds possible right now," said Ben. "But not highly likely, is it?"

Trent geared down and slowed through another steep curve, feeling the climb drag them back as they gained elevation. The twisting two-lane highway was well maintained, mainly for the summer tourists, who had grown scarcer now by the late fall—a temporary lull until ski season would bring the Texans west once again. It crisscrossed the Cimarron River, which ran invitingly clear and full. At any other time on a quiet afternoon like this, Trent would have been tempted to pull into a turnout, grab his fly rod out of the back, and lose himself for a couple of hours along the gurgling, crisp waters.

But not today.

"We're going to find them, Ben. I promise you."

He squinted behind his sunglasses as the truck gently swerved through curves, causing the sun to swim back and forth through pine trees that shot thickly skyward on either side of the road. He felt a familiar twitch in the front of his head and held his breath softly. The feeling was often a portent of something, a vague hint, which gave Trent a clue of things to come. He felt something like cool fingers slide softly through his hair, brushing his scalp, comforting and quieting his mind. He wished he could somehow pass this feeling physically on to Ben. "I promise you," he repeated. "I know it's going to be okay."

Ben turned and studied his former deputy. "You saying you can feel it? They're alive?"

Trent bit his bottom lip, regretting that he had said anything. But too late now.

"I'm just saying that . . . I don't feel anything in particular to the contrary." He looked at Ben. "You know? I mean, that's usually what I feel, right? When it's bad news, I can usually tell right away." He turned his attention back to the road just as they passed a small family of deer grazing on the grassy shoulder. He slowed accordingly. "I'm not feeling any of that right now." Trent's odd ability—his infamous sixth sense—was at times both a blessing and a curse.

Ben squeezed his eyes between his fingers.

"And that, I suppose, is all we have to go on, then, isn't it—until we get there."

He paused and looked at his friend again. "I'm sorry for being such an ass. Thank you, Trent. However this turns out—before I forget to say it—thanks. I mean it."

#

When Ben had called Trent earlier, informing him that the helicopter carrying Bouwmeester and the girls had disappeared somewhere northwest of Cimarron, he was already barreling through the gates of the ranch at Montaño del Sol. By the time the department cruiser slid to a stop near the house, Trent had already relayed the news to Maggie and all three jumped into action—Trent backing the pickup to tie onto the horse trailer, Maggie loading two of her best mounts into the trailer, and Ben pulling ammo, guns, and other gear from his vehicle.

Trent hopped out of the truck and slowed down as he eyed the gelding Maggie led up the ramp.

"You sure he's ready?" he asked uncertainly. After all, this was the animal that had been previously attacked by a cougar and Trent had yet to try him out.

"Freshest mount we have," reasoned Maggie. "Besides, I've ridden him several times now. Mild as a kitten!" She smiled a little mischievously.

"For you, maybe."

Maggie grew serious again, gently stroking the animal's neck. "Sweetie, you don't know what to expect up there. But I do know this little guy is about the best I've got right now," she reached over and squeezed Trent's forearm, "and I want you on the best, especially if it gets rugged. Besides—can't you see he loves you?"

"Yeah, we're a real match made in heaven," he said as he patted the horse's soft nose as it nuzzled him back.

"How did you guess his name?"

"What name?"

"*Angel.*"

"Hmph. Not much of a name for a guy."

"Well, he's not really a guy—he's a gelding," she smirked. "Besides, you're the one who mentioned heaven."

"Where do you want all this?" Ben asked as he strode up with an armful of weapons and gear.

"You really think we'll need all the heavy artillery?" Trent asked as Ben walked up.

Ben didn't say a word but went ahead and threw the guns in the back seat of the club cab then jumped in on the passenger side, ready to go.

"Let's go, Trent."

As Trent started the truck, Maggie leaned into the window, grabbed her husband's hand, and kissed the back of it.

"Remember what I told you earlier."

"What was that, again?"

She gently squeezed his arm, stepped up on the running board, and planted a soft kiss on his lips.

"You come back to me in one piece, Trent Carter." She gave his forearm a sharp pinch. "Or I will hurt you!"

#

"Did you happen to call Search and Rescue?" Trent asked.

"Yes," Ben answered in a monotone, staring out the window as the highway finally spilled out of the lower Cimarron Canyon into Ute Valley.

"And?"

"And what?

"Are they meeting us up here somewhere, or what, Ben?"

"They were going to take a while to organize, and frankly, I didn't have time to answer all the guy's questions."

"So, you're saying we're totally on our own."

"Yes . . . for now, anyway. Figured we'd make better time, just the two of us. I mean, you do know this country around here, right? You were raised here."

It was Trent's turn to get aggravated. He was beginning to get exasperated with the sheriff's ill mood.

"Ben, I might've been raised here, and yes, I have camped and hiked these mountains since I was a kid. But there are hundreds of ravines and canyons an aircraft can lose itself in, never to be found. Even a city boy like you should appreciate that. We need to be prepared for anything up there."

Ben turned a distressed face to him, and Trent immediately regretted the tone he had taken.

"Look, Ben, all I am saying is there's a big mess of mountains up here. Parts have been settled, from way back in the old mining days. But much of it has remained terribly remote, or abandoned. We're liable to not run into anybody up there, at least anyone who can help us if we get in a jam." He jerked his thumb over his shoulder. "That's why we've got the horses."

He looked at Ben and squinted his eyes. "When's the last time you rode, anyway?"

"Me? Oh I guess a few years ago, on vacation. Jennifer was probably nine or ten . . . ." Ben's voice trailed off and he chewed on a knuckle again.

"That's okay. I'm sure it's like riding a bicycle. You know—once you fall off and get back on, it's a lot easier the next time."

"Don't you worry about me. I can ride." Ben gazed out the side window again.

The miles drifted by along with the majestic scenery around them. Finally, Trent could wait no longer to ask the question that he had to ask.

"Did you drink today?"

Ben continued to look away and idly scratched the lobe of his ear.

"You know I've got to ask, Ben. And you know how I went down that rabbit hole myself for so long. Sometimes you just need someone to throw you a line and pull you out."

"Go to hell, Trent," Ben muttered, and continued to stare out the window.

Trent started to respond, then thought better of it. He left Ben alone with his own thoughts and demons for now.

The county road he was looking for loomed ahead, and he slowed down to turn off the pavement. The graveled road looked fairly well maintained, and he was able to pick up a little speed again as they now headed north up the old Valley of the Utes, named for the tribe that had once called these mountains and hills home. As Trent remembered his history, they probably would still live here, had they not become yet one more group of Indigenous Americans displaced by a group of land-grabbing gold miners and settlers backed by a corrupt state governor and his cronies more than a hundred and thirty years ago.

At least that's what he thought he had read somewhere. Or maybe it was just his smattering of Cherokee blood expressing indignation.

The county road dipped and curved with the rolling hills and meadows as they passed by summer tourist cabins and second homes tucked into the ponderosa forest. Many were already boarded up against the looming winter months. Occasionally, the truck topped a rise to reveal cattle dotting the grasslands on either side of the road as they passed through a small ranch. Trent knew the animals would soon be shipped to the lower plains, if not directly to nearby markets to be auctioned and eventually slaughtered for hamburger and steaks to feed the nation's insatiable appetite for beef. Whenever he caught sight of cattle grazing, he still marveled at how they continued to be such an important cog in the economic wheel in this part of the country, even more so now than a hundred years ago.

By degrees, the road became rougher, the ruts deeper, and their advance slower. At times it turned them sharply to cross the narrow banks of Ute Creek, which flowed steadily from somewhere higher up on its journey to spill into the Cimarron River where they had left it far below, near the highway. Their ascent had been gradual but steady, and Trent could feel the truck wheels slipping and dislodging larger stones as they searched for traction. Ben braced himself against the dashboard and peered down at the creek rushing just beneath his doorway. Trent put the transmission into four-wheel-drive and felt the front tires bite sharply and the truck lunge forward, sure-footed once again—for now.

"We stopping soon?" Ben asked.

"Not quite yet," Trent said quietly. "We can get a little further up, I think."

He studied the diminishing road ahead, not caring for how it increasingly disappeared around a sharp corner or faded down another drop to the creek bed. But so long as the four wheels kept traction, he would push a little farther. It would save time, and that was the priority right now.

They had left behind any signs of civilization a few miles back, their isolation broken only occasionally by a herd of deer or a flock of wild turkeys that would stop their nibbling of roadside grasses to warily watch the strange vehicle pass by. Trent glanced back at the sun, trying to gauge their direction and determine how much daylight they would actually have to begin their search. He did not like what the sun told him and certainly didn't like the fact that they had no real idea of where to begin.

The truck suddenly lurched when he wasn't paying attention. He had misjudged a sharp turn in the road, slammed on the brakes, and slid to a jarring stop with the front left wheel off the ground and spinning in space over the edge of the precipice. Their position wasn't life threatening, but if the truck had gone on over and jackknifed the trailer, it could have spelled a quick end to their mission. Trent closed his eyes and blew his breath out as he gripped the wheel, the engine idling. He began shaking his head in slow frustration.

"We still okay?" Ben asked sarcastically, his voice pinched and impatient.

Trent slowly opened his eyes and looked at his friend for a long moment before finally losing his own patience and answering.

"No—no, Ben, I don't think we are." He nodded and gestured out the windshield. "I mean, just look at us: sliding around precariously out here on this blown-out road; no idea, really, where we're supposed to go; no one else around. And it'll be getting dark in three or four hours. So, no, Ben—I think we're getting pretty far away from *okay,* don't you?"

Ben frowned back at Trent, nodding slightly. "So, just who do you suppose needs to focus now? I mean, we've come this far—and you're the one's been repeating over and over how *it's going to be okay.*"

"We don't have time for this, Ben."

Ben suddenly opened the door, got out, slammed it, and moved to the front of the truck. "Well, then, don't you think it's time to get on with it—and *find my daughter?*"

Trent shook his head again before getting out to join his friend. Ben was right: this was as good a place as any to saddle up their horses, load their gear, and get going further up into the high country before they lost any more daylight.

And both his and Ben's crappy attitude was not helping the problem.

#

Trent let Angel, his sure-footed gelding, have his head and pick his way up the ravine ahead. Maggie had been right, and he had had no trouble whatsoever getting comfortable in the saddle on this animal right away. He had Ben following a few paces behind on the gentler bay mare, far enough back in case the gelding lost footing and slid backward. No need to wind up with both of them injured in a pile up of horses, men, and equipment in some rugged draw with no help nearby.

Getting out in to the crisp afternoon air seemed to clear Trent's head and calm is earlier irritations. One of the first things he had done after they had stopped was to try and get a cell signal, but to no avail. Whatever cell towers might be in the area was either too far away on a remote peak or else hidden behind tree lines and ridges. Hand-held police band radios might have fared better, had either of them thought to bring them along. Trent's next hope was to try and gain some elevation on a nearby ridge to possibly find a signal there. Then, he might be able to get someone at State Police dispatch in Raton to ping the tower and maybe triangulate his phone with another one nearby—hopefully, one of the passengers' phones in the downed chopper, if one had its location software turned on. He knew it was a shot in the dark, but it was one he needed to try. The sun was now only two or three hours from dipping below Touch-Me-Not Mountain just south of Old Baldy as Angel scrambled up the last few feet and over the lip of the ravine to a level spot. But again, no success: Trent's phone showed no cell service at all. He grimaced, switched it off to conserve power, and pocketed it.

He waited patiently while Ben's horse finally crawled and lurched out of the ravine and came alongside. From here they had a clear view of rolling hills and sharp ridges to the northeast, separated by countless canyons and ravines. Twisting to look behind and up, Trent could see the same scenario rolling away to the west, only this time straight uphill for several miles until the trees thinned out toward the upper reaches of Baldy Mountain. At any other time, he would have been struck with the timeless beauty of the wild land enveloping them and been thrilled thinking of all the amazing history that had occurred around them—from wild Indians, lost mines, and probably outlaws who had roamed these same hills and forests, all searching for whatever their passions drove them toward: livelihood, riches, or just a good, remote hideout.

But none of this interested Trent at all right now. At this moment, he felt like the smallest, most insignificant creature on God's earth, about to be crushed into oblivion by the sheer dangerous magnitude of the unknown that pressed in all around them. It didn't help that the temperature was dropping by the minute and the chill already was finding its way through the heavy, down-filled parkas that Maggie had made sure to throw in for them both, through his other layers of shirts, and finally on into his very bones.

Trent had never felt so useless or without a clue, but he knew that Ben—and anyone possibly still alive on that helicopter—was counting on him alone. It was time for them to get moving— somewhere—anywhere, but where?

And suddenly, he saw him.

Seeming to materialize out of nowhere was the shadow of a tall figure, dressed from neck to knees in what appeared to be an elegant, if old fashioned, deer skin overcoat, with a fur-lined collar. The figure was on foot and wearing ornately decorated, booted moccasins that covered his calves. He was carrying something in his hand and as he moved closer, out of the shadows of the scrub oak bushes that dotted the ridge, the light began to touch his features. Trent warily touched the pistol he had shoved into the pocket of his parka, not sure what the silent man wanted and more than a little spooked that his dark eyes burned with some intense internal light that held Trent's steadily. Trent sucked his breath in softly and held it, mesmerized. "Can I help you, Sir?" he asked, his voice barely audible. His heart began to thump in his throat and he became increasingly uneasy.

"What did you say?" Ben asked, just behind his shoulder.

"I was asking this gentleman down here a question."

"Gentleman? What gentleman?"

It was now obvious that Ben had not seen the man, and Trent began to suspect why. *Here we go again,* he muttered to himself.

The tall man had stopped suddenly when Trent spoke, clearly in response to him, although at thirty yards away he couldn't possibly have heard. Trent could now see the man clearly, with long dark hair braided down his shoulders and handsome bronze, aquiline facial features—and he caught his breath again, his eyes suddenly wide in recognition.

This elegant apparition was one of the Ute Indians he had seen hunting buffalo in Vermejo Park a few evenings earlier.

What the hell is happening?

For a second, Trent was transported back to a time when ghosts and visitations ruled his days and nights until he thought he would go mad. And even though he now often joked to others about being *the man who talked to dead people*, he had never again experienced anything like the ghostly visitations of Victoria, his deceased first wife—until now.

"What do you want with me?" Trent asked in a low monotone, not daring to raise his voice and awaken himself from this obvious trance, if that's what it was—or scare away this shade of another time.

Ben said something else behind him, but Trent no longer understood him. It was almost as if he could no longer decipher spoken language.

The silent Ute warrior knelt now on one knee and seemed to study the dirt. The item he carried was now recognizable as a strung longbow, an arrow notched on the rawhide string, and he now gestured with the slender weapon off to the east. The man's lips moved, clearly saying something to Trent, but no audible sound came forth. Instead, Trent felt the communication somewhere in his spirit.

It is there.

"What is there? What are you telling me?"

The huge beast—the one with the body of a large locust and the faces of men in its eyes—the one that flies low and breathes smoke and fire. It is just down there.

"The beast?" Trent's breath became shallow and he experienced tunnel vision. The mountains, trees, sun, and all else had faded to an iridescent, shimmering wall, and nothing else seemed real except for the Indian, whose lips now moved again.

Yes. The one you seek; the one that vomited out the sky-riders. Most are dead. Some of them yet live. The warrior stood slowly, turned his face to the north and south, as if smelling the air. Then he looked upward and closed his eyes, took a deep breath, and peered intently at Trent again. *But you must hurry, before Brother of the Moon gets there . . . and the others.*

Trent frowned, and shrugged his hands in a sign of confusion.

"But I don't understand what it is you're saying to me—the others? What *others*? And who is *Brother of the Moon?*"

"What? Who are you talking to, Carter?" Ben had leaned over and was shaking Trent's shoulder. "Now who's been drinking?

The Ute warrior turned away, stepped off the ridge, and slowly walked back into the shadow of the ravine he had come from; but Trent could still sense the ghost warrior's thoughts.

You must hurry now. Hurry, Squirrel!

CHAPTER 11
Fire And Brimstone

(Letter from María Consuelo Delgado)

February 15, 1873
Jonathon S. Carter
Deputy Sheriff
Colfax County
Territory of New Mexico

Dear Deputy Carter:

I am writing to you to express my sincere thanks for your intervention in the troubles that have recently plagued my family. Given my recent experience—that law enforcement has not always come down on the side of the local colonos, that is, us land grant settlers—imagine my relief when you came to our defense in Cimarrón the other day. To have you stand up to such a group of unruly thugs was both surprising and welcome.

I understand your reluctance to engage me in conversation, given the estrangement my father has forced between us, and I am not a little saddened by it. I do so wish that things were different! Please know that I think about you often and pray for you always.

Most sincerely and humbly yours,
María

#

(February, 1872 – Cimarrón, New Mexico)

In the nightmare he sat on his tall warhorse as it stamped its hooves, impatiently awaiting the touch of the master's spurs signaling the imminent thrill of battle. Jonathon stared through the lightly waving grass toward the creek not a half-mile downhill, beyond which lay the Yankee encampment—and his fate.

He was momentarily all alone, but when he motioned with a small wave of his gloved hand, a line of his Cherokee Cavalry emerged miraculously like silent spirits on ghost horses from the silver maples at his back. Not a sound was made: no jangle of spurs, no voices, no creaking of leather—nothing but the muted scraping sound of Jonathon's own saber as he gently drew it from its scabbard.

All eyes along the line glanced as the sun glinted off his blade, held first at port arms at his shoulder and now slowly extended straight out at arm's length just over his mount's right ear. A whisper of metal against leather trembled up and down the line as his Indian troopers pulled carbines from saddles, cocked them, and tensed for his signal to advance into the line of battle.

Then it came. A dip of his sword, accompanied by a quick tap of his boot heels against the stallion's flank, and the horse jumped forward at a quick trot, excitedly tossing its head and snorting, ready to be cut loose into the full charge it knew was coming.

Jonathon sensed rather than saw his soldiers on horseback following him at a slow trot with military precision and dressed ranks. There were three files of riders and horses with fifty to seventy-five men in each file, no more than a horse's width and length separating them side-to-side, front to back.

His heart swelled into his throat, not from fear but from a combination of pride, confidence, and, yes, dread: pride and confidence in his warriors' experience and ability in battle, and dread over the premonitions that flooded his soul—premonitions of defeat and of senseless death. Confederate General Isaac Stand Watie, Jonathon's adoptive father and commander of the Cherokee Mounted Rifles, had so far refused to surrender, even though Lee had already done so.

Death over dishonor—Jonathon could not really find fault with the idea. And so, as always in this recurring night terror, they had charged the Yankee guns.

But this time, for the first time, the outcome of the dream was different.

This time, for the first time, the guns did not explode in his face to awaken him.

For this time, for the first time, a tall, elegant young warrior of about Jonathon's age stepped out of the reeds that grew along the stream bank. The warrior was dressed in a beautifully beaded deerskin shirt and leggings, his long black hair braided and hanging down his shoulders. There was something disturbingly familiar about the man, but the custom and style of his dress did not belong to any of the Five Civilized Tribes that made up Jonathon's troop of cavalry. The man carried a long-bow, advanced erect and completely unconcerned for the enemy's guns that had to be just yards behind him, and walked straight toward the center of Jonathon's advancing lines—straight toward Jonathon, his dark gaze unwavering.

Halfway between the line of cavalry and the river, the warrior stopped, held up his bow with both hands high above his head in a universal sign of peace, and spoke Jonathon's Cherokee name.

Salali—

With a mind of its own, Jonathon's horse planted its rear hooves and skidded to a stop, just feet away from the strange warrior. Simultaneously, the other two hundred horses behind him also stopped as one. Mangus, Jonathon's first lieutenant, rode up next to him.

"Cap'n Carter? Is there a problem, Sir?"

Jonathon's mind swam with nausea and confusion. He glanced at Mangus and silently pointed at the warrior who blocked his path. Mangus looked to where his captain pointed but he registered nothing.

"What is it, Sir?"

"You don't see?"

"See what, Sir?"

The shadow warrior slowly lowered his bow and continued to smile at Jonathon.

They do not see what you see, Salal. They do not hear what you hear.

Jonathon breathed deeply. His eyes never left the warrior's as he slowly sheathed his saber. "Who are you?" he asked softly, after a brief moment. "Are you a ghost?"

The shadow warrior stepped up to Jonathon's horse and placed his hand reassuringly on the animal's nose. The horse jerked, then calmly settled.

I am not a ghost. I am he who is not yet seen, but will be—he who is not yet known, but is known . . . by you, Salal.

"I'll ask you again. What is your name? Why do you block my way?"

The warrior removed his hand from Jonathon's horse and stepped aside.

It was not your destiny to die that day, Salal.

The warrior turned and walked back toward the river.

"What? Die *what* day? Who are you?" Jonathon demanded, standing in his stirrups. The soldiers nearest him glanced nervously at one another, then back at their captain.

We will meet again, Salal. The shadow warrior's voice rang clear and sharp across the field, although his back was still turned to Jonathon. *In the Valley of the Utes.*

"Where?"

Come quickly, Squirrel. Hurry!

Shadow Warrior had disappeared, but his voice echoed and danced on the wind.

#

Jonathon jolted himself awake. He had been dreaming the same old nightmare—or had he? Something had been different this time. He rubbed his eyes, trying to recall the rapidly fading details of the dream. Suddenly he sat upright, breathing hard, remembering a strange Indian warrior who had never come to his dreams before—strange, but very familiar.

"Walking Elk?" *But that's impossible.*

He tossed his sweat-soaked bedcovers aside and sat on the edge of his bed, trying to remember more details. For a Cherokee, even a half-blood like Jonathon, dreams were nothing to trifle with and were to be taken quite seriously. If spirits spoke to you in your sleep, there was an important reason that could not be ignored. To do so was at your own peril.

So for his new friend, the elderly Ute called Walking Elk—even a much younger version of him—to appear to him in a dream was now a mystery that had to be explored and deciphered very soon.

Hurry, the dream walker had said.

The small upstairs room that Jonathon lived in at the St. James Hotel, provided by his gracious friend Henri Lambert in exchange for on-site security when Jonathon wasn't performing his duties as a deputy, was not soundproof. But right now, everything seemed oddly quiet. He stood and looked out the window. A distant dog barked in the night, but all else was still. He cocked his head and listened for telltale sounds from the saloon downstairs but heard nothing, which only indicated that it was late enough for the bar to have closed but still too early for sunup.

Even so, Jonathon decided that it was not too early for coffee. He pulled on his clothes, strapped on his gun, and went downstairs in search for it. He was immediately rewarded as the smell of fresh brew wafted up before he set foot on the first step of the stairway, which creaked softly under his boots as he made his way down.

Ever vigilant, even at this early hour, he let his eyes wander over the room. A movement caught his eye in the dim corner where a lone figure sat sipping from a china cup. The man smiled up at Jonathon and raised the cup in greeting. Jonathon thought he recognized him but he couldn't place him. He nodded in response, moved down the stairs, and threaded his way among the empty tables with upturned chairs on them.

"Deputy," the man said in a clear and strong voice as Jonathon approached his table, and as he did so, Jonathon suddenly recognized the man as one he had met briefly a few years ago at Tom Stockton's Clifton House hotel—a man who had appeared in a photograph with him, his old boss Charles Goodnight, Clay Allison, and Stockton. "It's very good to see you again."

Jonathon finally remembered the man's name. "Mr. Springer, I believe. Isn't it?"

The man set his cup down, stood up, and extended his hand. "Well, I am impressed that you remembered. But please, call me Frank. I thought I might catch you early today."

Jonathon cautiously shook Springer's hand, which had a grip that was firm and assured.

"Jonathon Carter," he offered.

"Yes, I remember—Charlie Goodnight's top hand. Half Indian, too, as I recall. You have done well for yourself."

Jonathon pulled his hand back, now doubly cautious. Springer noticed the look and attempted to wave it away. "Oh please, Mr. Carter. I meant no insult. I meant it as a compliment, actually."

"Most men don't."

Springer appraised Jonathon again, then sat down. "Well hopefully you will find that I am not 'most men.'" He gestured at a chair. "Won't you please join me, Mr. Carter—Jonathon, if I may call you that? Breakfast is on me."

Jonathon stood for a moment longer, and then sat down.

"I know it's a mite early, Bob," Springer said to the bartender who had materialized to refill coffee cups, "but do you think you could rustle us up a little breakfast?"

"Sure thing, Mr. Springer. What'll it be?"

Springer wiped a knuckle against both sides of his large walrus mustache and looked at Jonathon. "Eggs over easy, bacon crisp, not burnt, biscuits swimming in gravy? Sound good to you, Deputy Carter?"

"Sure, why not?" Jonathon sipped slowly at the hot coffee, letting it work its early morning magic while he kept a cool eye on the man he was about to share a meal with, a man whom Bob, the bartender, evidently already knew, at least by name. But Frank Springer was still a man of mystery to Jonathon, especially when the man had obviously been waiting for him since early in the morning for some reason. Springer caught him peering at him and chuckled.

"I can read your mind, Jonathon. Let me put you at your ease. I am, indeed, new to town. Only been here a few weeks. Brought out here by an old school buddy of mine from Iowa—you probably know him—Bill Morley?"

Jonathon took another long sip of coffee and nodded. "Yes, most folks around here are acquainted with William Morley," he answered, not mentioning that Morley had managed to make as many enemies as friends in the few short years since he had taken up residence in Cimarrón as President of The Maxwell Land Grant and Railroad Company.

"Anyhow," continued Springer, "it was Bill who brought me out for a brief visit the first time you and I met at that party at Stockton's place, near Otero, a few years back. Tried to get me to come out then, but I was still involved in my studies back East."

Jonathon sipped his coffee and let Frank Springer talk.

"Bill asked me to come back out and help him with some legal work with his company, and so here I am. Little did I know that the job would also include editing and publishing the *Cimarrón Chronicle News,* which actually is what takes up the majority of my time anymore, what with all the hooliganism going on around here."

Jonathon nodded. "Now I recall seeing you there at the newspaper office." He lifted his coffee cup in a brief salute. "Welcome to New Mexico."

Springer continued to talk and enlighten him on his background: he had not only obtained a degree in philosophy and practiced law in Iowa, where he had been born and raised, but he had also pursued a passion for the natural science of paleontology. He freely admitted that his fascination with the fossil record and geology of the western United States had been the primary enticement for him finally to accept Morley's offer and head west.

"You would not believe the magnificent specimens I have already collected here!" he exclaimed like an excited boy.

As he continued to speak, Jonathon continued to size him up. Springer appeared to be in his mid- to late twenties—roughly his own age. He was of good stature, had pleasant enough features, was quick to smile (especially at his own jokes), was self-assured, and had a ruddy complexion that confirmed his love of the outdoors—something unexpected for an attorney or a newspaperman fresh from the East. Most importantly, Jonathon's sixth sense detected neither guile nor subterfuge in the man. He began to relax his wariness.

Their food arrived and Springer stopped talking long enough for them to attack their eggs and biscuits, appreciating how hungry they had been. Jonathon finally washed a mouthful of food down with fresh coffee and decided to ask the question that had been on his mind for several minutes.

"Mr. Springer, it appears to me that, unless you are in the habit of buying breakfast for strangers, there must be something else in particular that you believe I might help you with." He waited patiently while Springer dabbed gravy from his ample mustaches before answering.

"Well said, Jonathon. Well said." Springer continued to chew heartily. He paused, fork and knife poised on either side of his plate, and studied Jonathon, appearing for the first time to be choosing his next words carefully.

"Deputy Carter, I could not help but witness a brief altercation in the street yesterday, across from my office, between some ne'er-do-wells and a certain prominent Mexican family." He paused as Jonathon's eyes narrowed warily once more.

"Yes," Jonathon said. "Please continue." The relaxed atmosphere at the table had grown thick again and they both sensed it.

Springer laid his silverware down, cleared his throat, and continued on a slightly different tack. He pointed up above their heads. "Jonathon, I surmise that you have surely noted those holes up there before—maybe you were even present when some of them were put there?"

Jonathon glanced up to where several bullet holes were plainly visible in the pressed tin ceiling of the saloon, stark reminders of past incidents of gunplay. He turned back to Springer without answering. After a pause, Springer continued.

"I would not want to conjecture how much of that ended in actual bloodshed, but I would hazard a guess that it would be a fair percentage." He picked up his coffee again, slurped, made a face, and gestured to the waiter for a refill.

"Are you trying to make some point, Mr. Springer?"

"Please—it's Frank. And no, Deputy, the only point I am trying to make is that even after my short time here, you and I both know that a certain, shall we say, *rogue* element seems to have pervaded this community—a certain type of person for whom a quick solution to any relatively innocent problem is too often found at the business end of a gun, if you get my meaning."

Jonathon continued to study Springer. Even though a certain tension had entered their conversation, he still felt no duplicity in the man and now told him as much.

"Mr. Springer, for all your fancy words, which on the surface might sound like a threat to any other person, I do not think that you are trying to intimidate me—or else this conversation would have ended shortly after it began." He stopped as Bob arrived and refilled their cups and waited until the man retreated back behind his bar. During the pause, he noticed that daylight was now peeking through the windows and that other patrons had begun arriving for breakfast and had already taken nearby tables.

Jonathon leaned over and lowered his voice. "Mr. Springer, I believe the incident you witnessed in the street involved some friends of mine, Señor Delgado and his daughter. If that's what you're referring to, I must ask of you just what specific business it is of yours, Sir."

Jonathon sat back and waited patiently for an explanation.

"Deputy Carter—Jonathon—I fear you have misunderstood my meaning in bringing up the matter at all. As a recent newcomer, I find myself sitting back, biding my time, and observing. As both an attorney *and* a newspaperman, it is part and parcel of what I do for a living—observing folks. Far be it from me to question your actions in defending the good people of this county. On the contrary, it is refreshing for me to find someone of your caliber in our fair town. After even these few short weeks, and seeing some of the absolute lawlessness roaming our streets and countryside, I was beginning to despair of any good souls in our midst at all." He spread his hands figuratively. "My hands are already full with the heavy legal responsibilities of trying to negotiate workable deals with the homesteaders who are now at odds with my friend's company." Springer leaned even closer to Jonathon, and glanced around to check on eavesdroppers.

"Jonathon, there are other forces at work here—political entities and interferences that are threatening to derail my lawful efforts and threaten the very lives of the settlers I am genuinely trying to help here. Several local citizens who feel that they have been victimized have already approached me for representation, but that would be a real conflict of interest. I fear that the tentacles of this beast may go all the way to Santa Fe, where nefarious minds even now plot against us all." Springer paused for a long gulp of coffee, followed by a dab of his napkin. "Now, don't get me wrong. That's a fight that I am not afraid to take on, and I feel it's one that is looming, but it is also one that will certainly take up the majority of my time from now on."

"So again I ask," interjected Jonathon in the pause. "How may I possibly be of help to you, Mr. Springer?"

Frank Springer dropped his hands in his lap, looked down at his plate thoughtfully, and looked up again.

"I suppose I was simply intrigued and wanted to sit nose to nose with you—get to know you better. I know you can punch cows, I have heard that you fought honorably in the late war, and I've seen you roust a bunch of bullies in short order. But what I really need right now is an ally—and one of integrity who can be counted on, if and when the time comes—and it will."

Springer pointed again at the bullet holes above them. Jonathon nodded slowly, his gaze unwavering. He took a final sip of coffee, wiped his lip, slipped his chair back from the table, and stood up. After a moment, he put his hand forward and Springer grasped it and asked, "Is it safe to say that we now understand one another?"

Jonathon continued to grip Springer's hand, peering at him thoughtfully.

"Thank you kindly for breakfast, Mr. Springer, and welcome to Colfax County. I think you will do very well and prosper here, so long as you find out who your real friends are."

"Please. Call me Frank."

Jonathon looked around the room, now filled with the low murmur and tinkling sounds of diners enjoying a quiet breakfast. He started toward the door, thought of something else, and turned.

"Oh, and Mr. Springer—you might not want to turn your back to those folks you work for at the land grant company, speaking of tentacles. Just a word to the wise—between friends."

#

February 24, 1873

The Cimarrón schoolhouse also served as the town hall and as a church on Sundays. It was now only Saturday evening, but the building was already filled to overflowing with townspeople, nearby homesteaders, and a few shadowy figures occupying seats in the back of the room.

A tall, lanky bearded man in a well-worn long, black tailcoat stood up and walked to a rough-hewn podium at the front of the room and laid a large well-read black Bible on it. He glared around the room with fiery eyes as he slowly buttoned the long coat across his chest. His smoldering gaze eventually quieted the loud sea of conversation as all eyes gradually and expectantly turned his way.

"My friends, my neighbors," his high but clear voice resonated around the room, "and some of you others. . . ." He let his voice fade as he glared into the shadows at those he knew were there to try to intimidate him.

They didn't.

Reverend Franklin J. Tolby did not intimidate easily. The 32-year-old Methodist minister had recently come to New Mexico Territory from back East, feeling the call to minister to the godless settlers as well as the Ute and Arapahoe who made their homes in the area. He had become a circuit rider, bringing the Gospel to folks from Elizabethtown to Cimarrón and all points in between.

His zeal had quickly turned political, however, with the realization that a group of underhanded Santa Fe attorneys, in conjunction with some of the less reputable railroad companies in the territory, were vying to snatch up Maxwell Land Grant land illegally in the wake of the Maxwell family's sale of the company to a financially troubled group of Dutch and English investors. This nefarious group, dubbed The Santa Fe Ring, was suspected of increasingly being behind several related murders and lynchings in Colfax County, and had been aggressively feeding the fires of fear.

Reverend Tolby was just warming to his topic.

"I am heartened tonight at such a fine turnout. In my travels around this great county and beyond, I have seen such promise in our fine lands and in our fine people who live on them, work them, and draw their sustenance from them . . . and I have, unfortunately, also seen great evil at work and rearing its monstrous head to dissuade you fine folks. I am here to give you some help!"

Reverend Tolby let a swell of concurring shouts and amens rise for a moment, and he stepped back from the podium, surveying the room again before raising his hands to call for an abatement of the noise.

"My friends, this is your land—properly settled on in agreement with Lucien B. Maxwell, and worked for years now by you and your friends, who understood it to be a binding agreement of sharing the produce of your labors in exchange for eventual full ownership. . . ."

The shouts once again threatened to disrupt the meeting, but once again Tolby knew the uproar was friendly to him, and he basked in the glory of it.

"The work of the homesteaders here is nothing less than the work of God Almighty!"

More loud amens.

"And we all know that the Lord may have rested on Sunday, but He labored all the rest of the week to see that all the land of His creation could be pronounced *good and holy.*"

Tolby continued to speak over the shouts, his voice now riding upon them like a ship on swelling seas, his fist now punctuating his words by pounding the top of his Bible on the podium. "And I am here to tell you that tomorrow may be Sunday and our own ordained day of rest, but that on Monday and every designated day of work after that, we shall all rise up against the devil himself—those culprits in Santa Fe who work iniquity in violation of the rightful contracts you all have on this land with the Maxwell Land Grant. I tell you, it is time for you all to rise up, to give the devil his due, and not bow down to him or his demons when they come knocking in the night! Do not fear him! God is on your side, *and so am I!*"

The shouts now rose to drown out any of Tolby's final remarks. Tolby raised his fists above his head and stepped back as the applause swelled even louder. His eye caught movement in the back of the room as several men in dark clothes and hats pulled low over their faces rose slowly from their seats and slipped out the door during the uproar. The smile on the reverend's face turned into a troubled frown as he watched the men leave.

#

Jonathon was leaning against the doorjamb of the town hall, staying just far enough outside the stifling press of bodies to get some fresh air but near enough to hear Reverend Tolby's comments. He suddenly had to step aside to allow a sullen group of four or five men to pass through the door. He watched through the doorway as they stepped off the sidewalk and into the shadows of the street. Their heads came together and they muttered to one another as they went. He didn't care for the sudden twinge in his spirit, but the darkness swallowed up the men, and his feeling soon passed with them.

Jonathon had attended a few of the good reverend's lectures over the weeks and months and was intrigued by the power his words had over the crowds—power to sway, power to incite. In his short life, Jonathon had already known similar men with similar power to mesmerize with their words: Stand Watie, Oliver Loving, Charles Goodnight, and possibly even his new friend, the attorney Frank Springer, who certainly had a way with his written newspaper editorials, some of which he understood to have been picked up and reprinted in the larger newspapers back East.

And Walking Elk, the elderly Ute warrior whom Jonathon now tried to go visit at least once a week in the Valley of the Utes, also had this gift to sway with his words. He and Jonathon had begun to take long treks together up into the sacred mountains just west of the valley, up to the frost line beneath Mount Baldy. This mountain, Walking Elk had told Jonathon, was a very holy mountain. He said that the *Mexicano* settlers who had come before had always respected that fact; but now the gold and silver seekers had come and torn into the bowels of the sacred peaks and valleys, ripping out the yellow and white rocks, raping the land and its people, and dishonoring its holiness.

In his own way, Reverend Tolby was delivering the same message as the old Indian, but with a different language and imagery. Each man spoke to dual sides of Jonathon's blood nature, the Cherokee and the White.

As Jonathon stepped back to the door to listen, his breath almost stopped as he suddenly came face to face with María, her father, and Don Gaspar de León, her new fiancé. He wanted to turn and flee but felt completely unable to move. Instead, they all stopped and looked at one another uncomfortably. Finally, Jonathon took a step back, removed his hat, and broke the ice.

"Señor Delgado . . . Señorita," he said in greeting, lowering his eyes. "I—I didn't see you there."

"Deputy Carter," nodded Delgado. His polite smile disappeared as he moved quickly past Jonathon and out to the sidewalk. María and Don Gaspar followed. Jonathon almost swooned when he looked to see María's dark eyes peering sweetly at him, and then he almost fell over when she suddenly stopped in front of him.

"Jonathon, I would like to introduce you to Don Gaspar de León. Don Gaspar, this is Jonathon Carter. Deputy Carter is my . . ." Her voice caught just slightly. ". . . my friend."

De León clicked his heels, bowed slightly without smiling, and then turned to María. "Come, my dear, we must be going."

Jonathon felt like the complete fool that he knew he was, but when his troublesome intuition tingled again, he felt compelled to follow them for a few steps down the sidewalk.

"Señorita . . . Señores," he called out. The three of them turned and looked at him inquiringly.

"Yes, Jonathon," María called back, almost expectantly.

"María, I—I didn't realize you were going to be here, listening to Reverend Tolby."

"Well, Mr. Tolby makes a lot of good sense," de León interrupted. "More people should take note of what he says—particular the law." Jonathon could almost feel de León giving him the once-over. "Come, María. We are late going home."

Jonathon glanced nervously up the dark street that had swallowed up the men he had seen earlier.

"María, please. I don't mean to be rude…"

"Well, you are indeed being rude, Señor!" Gaspar De León let go of María's arm and advanced on Jonathon, now inches from his face. "I believe you no longer have a right to accost Señor Delgado—or his daughter. So you will please let us pass on unmolested." He reached out his hand as if to restrain Jonathon.

"Don't," Jonathon said, his voice dropping suddenly to a menacing whisper. De León hesitated.

Jonathon felt a sudden calm descend upon him, the same calm that enveloped him before battle, a mantle of serenity and focus that lifted him out of whatever emotional state he happened to find himself in at the time.

He no longer felt like the fool here.

"Señor Delgado, María," he said softly, his eyes locked steadily on de León's but not acknowledging him in any other way. "You must listen to me, for only a minute. I believe your lives may be in grave danger. There are men who go to these meetings, enemies of Tolby—enemies of the settlers. I think they go just to see who else is there."

Señor Delgado had stepped up and assumed a protective position between Jonathon and María. He gave Jonathon a smug smile. "Deputy Carter—Jonathon—I do appreciate your concern for us. You have proven yourself a true gentleman and advocate for the settler's causes, and certainly have come to our aid before, for which I am eternally grateful. But surely you cannot believe any real harm will come from these—these political discussions, can you?" He placed a hand on Jonathon's shoulder and squeezed it lightly. "And I would hate to think that you fabricate such problems only to be able to approach my family for . . . other reasons, such as those you and I have already discussed."

Delgado smiled again and patted Jonathon's shoulder before turning away. "Please don't concern yourself any longer, Señor. Come, María . . . Señor de León."

Jonathon's vision swam from vertigo. His lower legs felt like rubber. Emotions welled inside of him—embarrassment at Delgado's abrupt dismissal, anger at the situation, and frustration with himself for feeling overwhelmed now with these waves of unknown warnings coursing through him. These intuitions were stronger than he had felt in a long time. Jonathon turned to María, almost in desperation.

"María, please. You of all people must know how serious I am. You know that I have not interfered with your life until this moment. . . ." He glanced at de León then continued. "Your life now is your own business. But I must speak because it is that very life that I must now try and protect!"

"That is quite enough!" De León gripped Jonathon's upper arm to pull him away from María.

Jonathon was not clear what happened next, but what he later remembered was a flash of red behind his eyes and a tremendous, almost grateful, release of pressure from somewhere within himself. When he came to his senses, he was straddling de

León's chest, his left hand on the man's throat, and his right hand pressing the barrel of his pistol against de León's teeth. María was in her father's arms, her hand up to her mouth, her eyes wide with fright.

"I told you not to touch me," Jonathon growled, his thumb tightening on de León's windpipe.

"Jonathon!" María's frightened shout brought him the remainder of the way back to reality. He slowly and incredulously loosened his grip on de León's throat and removed the pistol barrel from his mouth. He stood up, and de León rose shakily, rubbing his raw neck, touching his bloody lip, and glaring hatefully at Jonathon.

"This is not over," said de León, pulling María down the street and glowering back at Jonathon. "I will have your badge for this, Señor!"

"María . . . please. . . ."

Jonathon realized he had nothing else reasonable to say at all. He could only watch helplessly as the person he most desperately wanted to protect—most desperately wanted to be with—was sucked up by the darkness.

CHAPTER 12
Icarus Down

(Present Day – Sangre de Cristo Mountains)

Trent gave Angel the rein and allowed the horse to pick its own way down the ravine where he had seen the Ute warrior disappear. Ben followed closely behind.

"So, you're saying you saw some ghost dressed up as an Indian, you had a conversation with him, and he's now leading us to the chopper."

"No, he's not leading us. He just pointed and told us to hurry."

"And it was like I'm talking to you now, right? I mean, he was that real to you, was he?"

"Yes, he was that real to me, Ben."

Trent was weary of trying to explain to people the reality or unreality of his sporadic ability to hear or see things—things they would just label as supernatural. To him, it was something much more than that. Since the accident years ago on Cordova Pass in Colorado when his and Vicky's jeep crashed down the side of the mountain, seriously injuring Trent, and where a sniper murdered Vicky, he had given up trying to explain the visions he saw, even to himself. So far now, the apparitions had turned out to be dead people—like his wife—who had appeared with warnings and clues, but only at critical times, and completely out of his control.

"It was as real as Vicky was, Ben, when it happened with her."

Ben grew quiet for a while at that. Trent felt a little sorry for his former boss, his friend. He had already noticed a big change in Ben's personality over the months and completely sympathized with him: a loss of his usual dry sense of humor in any situation, his worries over parenthood issues with Jennifer, his increased drinking. And now Ben was in this situation where his only child's life was at stake, and Trent knew that his friend felt completely helpless to do anything about it. He glanced back and saw Ben looking worriedly at the sun as it dipped nearer the rim of the mountains behind them.

"We're running out of daylight," Ben said. "I want to believe we're going to get there—in time." He glanced at Trent. "You were right, of course. We should have gotten Search and Rescue involved. I don't know what I was thinking."

"You were thinking like a worried father."

"That's for damn sure."

Trent sighed, hearing and feeling the underlying desperation in his friend's voice. He pulled Angel up at the bottom of the ravine, letting Ben catch up to him.

"Ben, you have always been able to trust me before, haven't you? I know how different it is for you this time, with Jennifer being the one we need to find. I promise you: I am as sure of this as anything else I have ever been sure of. I can't explain it beyond that—this vision of an Indian. But I wouldn't lead you on if I felt at all otherwise." He leaned over in the saddle, put his hand on Ben's shoulder, and gave it a squeeze. "Whoever that guy was—is, he was as real to me as you are. We're going to find them, Ben. I feel it deep down, and that's all I can truthfully tell you."

Ben nodded and then dropped his eyes. It seemed to Trent that he was moving his lips in a silent prayer. "Now that's the most positive thing I've seen you do all day," Trent said with a smile, and nudged Angel on. As he moved away, he mumbled his own prayer.

An hour later, the sun disappeared behind Touch-Me-Not Mountain and the clouds began to spit snow. A half-mile further east and over the next rise, they suddenly came upon the crashed Huey helicopter, still smoldering in the fading light.

Bodies were strewn all around.

#

"What do you mean you didn't find it?"

"I mean it wasn't on them. Any of them." The agent rubbed a hand over a sweaty brow. The voice at the other end of the satellite phone was quiet for a moment.

"You checked them all—all the bodies?"

"Yes, and even interrogated the survivors."

"Survivors? What survivors?"

"Nothing to be concerned about—two were still alive when I got there. They couldn't tell me anything, so they didn't survive the interrogation—just as you instructed."

Silence again.

"So, just what are you not telling me?"

The agent pulled the phone away and stifled a nervous cough before continuing.

"There may have been other survivors—ones that may have left the crash site before I got there."

More silence.

"I'm on top of it. I've called in some additional help to track them down."

"Do you have any idea who these 'other survivors' are?"

"Yes. I do. I think they were hiding nearby. If so, they may have witnessed what I did."

"Then why are you wasting time talking to me? Get your people, go back, and take care of them, once and for all!"

#

Ben galloped his horse up to the crash site, jumped off, and ran from body to body, frantically pulling each one over and peering into the dead, staring faces. There were four bodies in all. One was the pilot, still at the controls inside what was left of the crumpled fuselage, and who by all appearances had died instantly. The other three were strewn at various distances among the debris field of the chopper. One body was burned badly, but Trent thought that he recognized him as one of Bouwmeester's bodyguards. The other was an older female, another of the aides whom Trent recognized from the reception. The third body was Minister Bouwmeester himself.

The most disconcerting thing was that in addition to their crash injuries, both the female aide and Bouwmeester had been shot in the back of the head at close range, execution style, which indicated they had both been alive after the crash.

The most hopeful sign was that neither Jennifer Ferguson nor Ilsa Bouwmeester was anywhere to be seen, which meant that they must have survived the crash.

"But where the hell are they?" cried Ben, after tearing through the larger pieces of wreckage, trying to find his daughter and her friend. "Where are the girls? Who shot these people?" Ben's voice grew thin with consternation and he clenched his fists at the side of his head. "Do you think they took them—that they have my daughter with them now?"

Trent had dismounted, tied Angel to a nearby bush, caught Ben's horse, and done the same for her. He then walked over to Ben and handed him a canteen of water. He did all of this calmly and methodically, and spoke softly as if dealing with a trauma victim—which he knew that he now was.

"Here. Drink something. We're no good getting dehydrated. And calm yourself. It's going to be a long night." The snow was still light but falling steadily. Trent knew they needed to begin investigating the scene before it blanketed the area and the victims. "We need to work the facts, Ben. Remember? You're a cop—so let's do the cop thing. The answers are here somewhere. We just have to find them." He pulled out his cell phone again but still had no signal. He glanced back up at the low clouds that continued to sprinkle snow on them. "But first, we need to make camp. Come on. Give me a hand."

Ben calmed himself enough to help set up a tent shelter and gather firewood while Trent fed and watered the horses, clipped their lead lines to a makeshift rope corral nearby, and put turnout blankets on them for the night. He then broke out some stew and sandwiches that Maggie had packed for them.

While the stew was heating up over a small fire, they finally began the grim task of searching the bodies while the weather still permitted. Trent took a few wide photos of the area from different angles with his phone camera. They then put latex gloves on, gently pulled the pilot from the wreckage, and laid him next to the others. Trent crawled back into the ruined cockpit and found the radio, or what was left of it. He crossed his fingers, flipped a few switches, and caught his breath when a couple of indicator lights suddenly came on; but his hopes were almost immediately dashed when he saw that the radio was smashed beyond repair. He wondered briefly if it had been done deliberately. Still, he picked up the hand held microphone and flicked the talk switch. The radio unit spluttered for a second. The lights flickered, then faded, and died out.

"Radio's kaput," he called out.

"Maybe we can use smoke signals," Ben answered, nodding back at their meager campfire. Trent smiled to himself at the welcome return of his friend's dry sense of humor.

They moved back to the bodies and carefully searched the victims' pockets for identification and any other clues, placing wallets and other personal items in protective bags for processing later. Trent then took out a small flashlight, carefully pulled aside clothing where he could without disturbing the victims too much, and examined their bodies up close—as much of a cursory exam as was possible under the conditions—looking for unusual bruising, other wounds or evidence of the crime. He continued to snap photographs.

"Shouldn't we be careful about touching them before the medical examiner looks at them?" Ben asked.

"That would be nice," Trent answered, "if she were here right now—or if we could get hold of her at all. But if we don't look at them now, they're either going to be frozen solid by morning, or else animals will get to them."

They completed their brief examination of the bodies, and then widened the search for anything else of interest.

"What are we looking for, do you suppose?" Ben asked.

"Well, for one thing, shell casings, since we know those two there were shot. Small caliber, by the looks of it. But if the shooter is as professional as I think he is, that's the last thing he would have forgotten to take with him." He stooped briefly. "A couple of footprints here, though. I'm betting they belong to the killer." He trained the light on them. The prints were poor, probably from an attempt to scuff them out, but they appeared to have been made by a military-style boot.

He stood up and swung the beam of light in a slow arc around the area. "I'm also curious how he travelled in and out of here. Cleaned up after himself fairly well, but I'm guessing a search of the other side of these nearby ravines will turn up some type of four-wheeler tire tracks. But we're not going to find them tonight. Got more important things to examine right here, before the weather shuts us down completely."

Something caught his eye and Trent moved back over to the rear of the helicopter fuselage, where the burned-out engine was located. He had heard and now saw a slow, steady drip of liquid from the remains of a fuel tank. He glanced around nervously but ascertained that other than a smoldering patch of ground here and there, the fire had burned itself out in the gathering snowfall. He removed one glove, touched the drip to his fingers, and smelled it. He frowned, and then stuck out the tip of his tongue to taste the liquid. He spat it back out.

"You were in the Air Force, Ben, right?"

"Yeah, I was. Why?"

"What do you know about these old choppers? They run on standard aviation fuel? Or something else?"

"Standard JP-4 or JP-5, I believe. Why? What are you thinking?"

"Well, as if I knew what it was you just said . . . but come smell this stuff."

Ben came over and smelled Trent's fingers. "Smells like kerosene."

"That's what I thought too."

"Why would someone spike the punch on this rig with kerosene? Why not just clip a cable or a fuel line, or water down the fuel?"

"I'm guessing it's because if you water it down, it's probably going to crash just a few hundred feet off the runway, or else not start at all. No, whoever pulled this stunt wanted the chopper to get far enough away to be isolated like this. Kerosene will burn just enough to mess things up, but at least the chopper would still be able to fly for a while, until the engine seized up."

Trent remembered something and went to retrieve the dead woman's purse. When he returned, he held a small prescription bottle with a few migraine pills in it. "I don't think these are going to help her anymore," he said as he dumped the pills out. He then let several drops of the kerosene fill a third of the small bottle, recapped it, and sealed it into an evidence baggie.

Trent stood up, looked around, and sighed. "Well, now we know how they did it. We just need to find out why." He caught Ben's worried expression. "And just where our missing girls are."

Trent turned his light back on and took his search wider around the perimeter of the crash site. He occasionally stopped and stooped down to examine pieces of the wreckage. Of particular interest was a large, flat piece of the fuselage skin that lay upturned. Something was odd about it. It appeared to have been moved after the crash, according to scrape marks on the ground. A small depression was underneath it, large enough for a small person or two to hide in if they pulled the wreckage panel over themselves. He frowned as he also spied spots of blood in the dirt here, as well as a faint bloody handprint on the underside of the panel. He hesitated, and then called Ben over, not wanting to keep this finding from him. "What do you make of this, Sheriff?"

Ben came over, stooped down, and squinted before his face went slack and pale. "What the hell? That's a small handprint . . . . Oh, my lord, no . . . !" He dropped to his knees, tracing the bloody stains with a gloved finger. "Jennifer," he moaned.

"Let's not get too anxious, yet. We don't know whose it is."

Trent stood up and shined his light along the ground. There were footprints here, starting to fill in with the spitting snow but still visible and slightly smaller than the other footprint he had found earlier. "Do you remember what type of shoes Jennifer was wearing, or perhaps the other girl, when they boarded the chopper?"

Ben rubbed his face and thought back for a moment, then answered almost immediately. "Jenn was wearing Nike walking shoes. White. I remember them specifically, because I bought them for her. And I'm pretty sure the other girl, Ilsa, had on something similar."

"Well, that's one bit of positive evidence we have, then. Look at this." Ben walked over and looked down where Trent had trained his light on a sneaker pattern featuring the distinctive Nike "swish" mark.

"Two sets of these sneaker prints lead over there for a ways, to the northeast. Looks like both girls were at least healthy enough to walk away." He retraced his steps, shining the light here and there. Something else was bothering him. "Why only two sets, though? The killer—or killers—would certainly have seen those footprints and followed them . . . unless . . . ."

Trent and Ben looked at each other, coming to the same conclusion, which Ben blurted out: "Because they waited until the killer left? They must have been hiding under here the whole time!"

"That would explain the prints and bloodstains in this hole. One or both of them was, maybe, hurt in the crash, but they were able to hide underneath this piece of wreckage here until the killers left; then they climbed out and took off." Trent shined his flashlight back up the trail, thinking. "More importantly, that means they witnessed the murders, which is going to make it even more critical for us to find them before someone else does."

Ben jumped up and strode toward the horses. "Then what are waiting for . . . let's get going!"

"No, we can't, Ben."

"Why not? We know they're alive, for now. We've got to go find them. Find out how badly they're hurt." Ben had switched blankets on his horse and was preparing to saddle her but stopped when he noticed Trent had not moved. "Well, what the hell are you waiting for? We've got to get going!"

Trent looked up at the snow falling more thickly now, shook his head, took off his latex gloves, and walked toward the tent. "We're not going anywhere tonight, Ben. It would serve no purpose at all. It's going to be completely dark soon, at least until moonrise later; snow's already covering everything, including their tracks; horses are tired, and so are we. I don't know about you, but I'm not any good at night navigation, even if I could see the stars. We'll be no use to those girls if we get turned around in the dark out there and freeze to death ourselves."

"Well, what if I go myself, then? You can stay here if you want, and I'll try and find them tonight, then you can come in the morning, in case I get in trouble."

"No, Ben, that won't work either. I'll just find you dead out there and have to face Jennifer with that news, too, when I find her."

Later, after they had eaten, they sat just inside their tent flap, watching their small fire sizzle when the wet snow hit the glowing coals. Between here and the wrecked chopper lay the four bodies. The snow had completely shrouded them, making them look indistinct and strangely normal, as if they were merely sleeping beneath white sleeping bags. Trent had hoped to dig temporary graves for them, but that would have to wait. For now, they were simply shapeless mounds on the ground, gruesome reminders of the evil that some people do to others.

What little evidence they had seen thus far indicated that, for whatever reasons, this particular evil person, or these persons, had set in motion a series of events here, having sabotaged the chopper beforehand and followed up their actions by getting here first and murdering the survivors—well, maybe not all of them.

Ben fidgeted. He had barely touched his food. "Still think we should go after them," he mumbled sullenly.

"We can't go anywhere in this stuff."

"Why not? Those girls are helpless out there."

"Those girls are going to be fine. Didn't you tell me you used to take Jennifer out camping when she was younger? She's not going to forget those skills. And Ilsa didn't strike me as helpless. Looked like the outdoors type to me. I'll bet they're cozied up somewhere safe, under a tarp, with a nice fire going." Trent hoped his total lack of conviction wasn't coming through in his voice.

"Anyway," he continued, "we need to survive ourselves, or else those girls don't have any chance. We know which direction they went. So let's get some sleep and we'll head out at first light."

#

At some point well before dawn Trent was startled awake by the sound of the horses nickering and stamping the ground nervously. He sat up and immediately froze.

The Ute shadow warrior, as he now referred to him, was sitting cross-legged at the open flap of their tent, quietly watching them sleep. He put a finger to his lips, motioning to Trent to stay quiet. His mouth then moved, and Trent again heard words, but only in his spirit.

Brother of the Moon is here. You must remain very quiet.

"Brother of the Moon? Who is that?" Trent whispered.

Shhhh.

The shadow warrior slowly pulled the flap back and pointed outside. Trent looked past him and went numb as he saw a large cinnamon-colored bear huffing, pawing, and tearing at one of the frozen bodies, not twenty yards away. The bear stopped suddenly, sniffed, turned, and looked straight at Trent. He reared up on his hind legs, swatted the air in anger with one massive paw, and let out a huge roar.

At that moment the horses began screaming in fear, rearing, and pulling at their tethers. This distracted the bear for a second. He dropped to all fours and then began loping toward the terrified animals as if just now noticing the fresh prey. Trent began to emerge from the tent but was bowled over by Ben charging out past him, a .357 magnum pistol in his hand, firing while he shouted at the top of his lungs. The horses continued to scream, finally broke the leads on their halters, and scrambled wildly over each other to escape both the approaching monster and the explosion of the gun.

"Ben, wait!"

But Ben continued to move forward, the pistol extended at arm's length, firing twice more in the direction of the rushing beast. Whether any of the bullets were hitting their mark or not, the bear was seemingly impervious to them as it crashed through the makeshift rope corral as if it weren't there and wrapped itself around the neck of the nearest horse, whose screams were suddenly cut off by slashing claws against its throat.

"Oh lord, no," whispered Trent, head swimming from a combination of fear and adrenaline. In the half-light of the rising moon, he couldn't tell whose horse it was. For some reason he prayed it wasn't Angel, not because he was his horse, but because the gelding had already gone through a similarly vicious attack not quite a couple of years before.

Whichever animal it was, the other horse was able to take advantage of the bear's attack and make a break for it, and the thunder of its escaping hooves soon faded into the night.

Ben stopped about ten yards from the horrific scene, took one more steady aim in a classic shooter's stance, and fired once. This time the shot definitely connected and the bear reared up, howled in obvious pain, shaking its head fiercely and swatting at its neck before glowering at Ben and lumbering off to disappear into the juniper and pines, yowling as it went.

Ben fell to his knees, breathing hard as if he had just run a marathon. Trent stumbled over and stood beside him, staring at their mortally wounded horse that now lay in a pool of its own blood that still pumped out of severed arteries. Trent, almost in a trance, reached down and gently took the pistol from Ben's hands, shuffled over to the dying animal, cocked the gun, and put the horse out of its misery. He could now see that it was Ben's mare, not Angel, which was only a small relief to him at this point.

As the echo of the gunshot bounced off the surrounding hills and ravines, Trent heard the distant answering howl of a wounded, hungry bear, somewhere off in the night—somewhere out in the same rugged country where two vulnerable, frightened girls were hopefully well hidden and still alive.

And of course, Shadow Warrior was long gone.

CHAPTER 13
This Bloodied Soil

(Letter from María Consuelo Delgado)

June 5, 1873

Jonathon S. Carter
Deputy Sheriff
Colfax County
Territory of New Mexico

Dear Jonathon,

I trust that this letter finds you well. I have continued to think about what you may have been trying to tell us that night, after Reverend Tolby's lecture. You seemed so troubled and serious, and . . . well, when you and Gaspar had that altercation, I wasn't at all sure about the person you had become. But now, I wonder. . . .

Oh, dear Jonathon, who am I fooling? Myself, I suppose. The truth is that it was such a relief for me to once again gaze on your handsome face and hear your wonderful voice and my heart raced to be in such close proximity to you again! Oh, why has custom and decorum conspired to keep us apart, my darling? And why, oh why can we not follow our hearts where love is concerned?

Listen to me prattle. You must think me an awful trollop of a woman, for alas, I am betrothed to another now. I no longer doubt you and your concern for my family and me. You have always been the consummate gentleman I know you to be. I just could not go on with the path my life is now on, without once more expressing my true feelings to you, pointless as it may be.

Please forgive me, my darling. I promise this will be the last time I speak of it, for I fear it causes you pain, or worse, disgust for me. I apologize for the tears that stain this page.

The next time we meet, I shall be Señora Gaspar de León, and you will be . . . I don't know what you will be, my dearest, but I know you will not be mine.

I remain, with love, your devoted María.

#

(August 20, 1873 – Cimarron, New Mexico)

Clay Allison sauntered into the St. James Hotel saloon. It was a sweltering evening and he had just spent the hot afternoon riding from Elizabethtown through the canyons. It had been several months now since his escapade involving Charles Kennedy's severed head, and he felt at ease once again showing his face in Cimarrón. Indeed, no one else dared bring the incident up in Allison's presence as his reputation for sudden, explosive anger and violence now preceded him wherever he set foot.

Allison stood in the doorway for a minute, surveying the smoke-filled room where the noise now dropped to a whisper as people became aware of his presence. He relished the attention, taking his good, sweet time lighting with a flourish the cheroot he held between his teeth and flicked the used match into the beer belonging to the man sitting nearest the door. The man did nothing but laugh nervously.

Allison's attention was drawn to a table in the back corner filled with rough-looking men drinking heavily and playing cards noisily—miners, probably. They appeared to be the only ones in the room who had completely ignored Allison, and that bothered him. He took a puff of his cigar, adjusted his gun belt that carried matching pearl-handled Colt .45s, and moved slowly through the saloon. Chairs scraped and slid out of his way as if by a magical will of their own. He ignored the *Mister Allisons* that were nervously tossed his way, his eyes fixed on the table in the corner. When he arrived, he stopped behind the chair of one of the men and stared in turn at the faces of the other three. He vaguely recognized one of them, a lowlife by the name of Cruz Vega—an occasional deputy town marshal, occasional mail carrier between the towns, and a full-time drunk—and then studied their respective piles of winnings. The table was full of chips, bills, and coins of several denominations, and the man with the fewest chips happened to be the one in front of Allison with his back to him. He now put his hands lightly on the man's shoulders.

"Friend, you seem to be having an unlucky time of it. What say you call it a night?"

The table at last grew quiet as the other three looked up and recognized the gunfighter. The fourth man obviously did not know yet who was speaking to him. He shrugged Allison's hands off him.

"And just who the hell do you think you are, asshole?" The man stopped short when he saw his friend across from him nervously shake his head in warning. Then he turned around to look up at Clay. "Oh, it's you, Mr. Allison. I didn't recognize you."

"Well, of course you didn't, Sir. That would have required you to have eyes in the back of your head. So far as I am aware," he chuckled, and then continued, "I am the only one present who has that particular feature." His chuckle turned to a growl. "I believe you are sitting in my chair. Now git!"

Allison kicked the legs of the chair and simultaneously jerked it out from under the unfortunate man, who tumbled unceremoniously onto the floor. The man forgot himself for a moment; a snarl crossed his lips and he reached for the pistol on his hip. But Clay Allison was faster and had the barrel of his own gun pushed painfully into the man's left eyeball. Allison cocked the big pistol and breathed heavily, a madness entering his eyes and giving him tunnel vision. A complete hush had fallen over the room, with only the sound of an occasional chair scraping as someone tried to get a better view of the forthcoming carnage.

"That'll be enough, Clay."

All heads swiveled as one to look up in surprise at the source of the voice. On the landing of the staircase leading up to the hotel rooms stood Jonathon Carter, his hands relaxed at his sides but a bit too close to his own weapons for Clay Allison's liking. Allison's face was a storm of emotion, which gradually subsided as he calmed down. "Why look, gentlemen—if it isn't my old friend, Deputy Carter!" He straightened up, letting his victim slide to the floor in a puddle of his own urine. Allison looked down at the man again, disgusted, and then nudged him hard with his boot as he slowly holstered his weapon. The vanquished card player scrambled away on all fours like a crab.

Allison picked up the chair, righted it, and sat down, his back now to the staircase as he pointedly ignored his old friend standing there. He looked at the meager pile of chips in from of him, reached into his pocket, deposited an additional stack of coins with them, and looked around the table at the other three remaining players.

"You gentlemen don't mind, of course, if I join your friendly game. It seems you are now one short."

"Them ain't yore chips," growled the most unkempt of the three, glaring across the table at Allison.

"Chunk, leave him be," said the man named Vega, clearly drunk but not relishing another confrontation with the famous gunfighter who had just joined them.

"Chunk?" repeated Allison thoughtfully, studying the man's face closely. "Chunk . . . oh my, surely not *the* Chunk Colbert, feared scourge of the territories, and third best gunman in Colfax County?"

The man called Chunk snorted derisively. "*Third!* Hmmf. Who's first then? You, I suppose?"

Clay Allison took a long puff of his cigar and blew the smoke indiscriminately into the faces of his new card partners. At this point, they all became aware that Deputy Carter had made his way down the stairs, across the room, and now stood at Allison's elbow.

"Well," began Allison, "let's just say that I am either the first *or* second best," jerking his head toward Jonathon, "and that my good friend Deputy Squirrel here may also be the first or second. It has, unfortunately, never been put to the test—yet."

"Like the man said, Clay," Jonathon said evenly, "those aren't your chips." He leaned over and scooped the markers into his hand, leaving Clay's coins behind. "And I've told you before—don't call me Squirrel." He turned and walked over and gave the chips to their owner, who stood now slumped over the bar, pressing a wet bar towel up to his sore eye socket.

Jonathon bought the man another beer, got one for himself, and then made his way across the room to an empty table in the opposite corner, from where he could keep a quiet eye on things, as was his agreed-upon job for his friend Mr. Lambert.

An hour or so passed, and the room had returned to its usual boisterous level of laughter, conversation, and clinking glassware but was otherwise uneventful. Jonathon found himself almost dozing off when a sudden burst of angry voices erupted from across the room. He moved his feet from where they were propped on the table and stood up.

Across the room, Clay Allison, Chunk Colbert, and Cruz Vega were at an angry standoff. Allison's fist gripped Vega's collar and shook him, while Colbert pushed himself belligerently between them, shouting in Allison's face.

"Leave him alone, you son-of-a-bitch!" Colbert yelled.

Allison shouted at Vega, but Jonathon could make out only something about a drawing on a piece of paper that Clay was brandishing in the man's face. Jonathon was halfway across the room when Colbert suddenly backed off a couple of steps and reached for his holster.

"Hey!" Jonathon shouted, shoving now past other patrons who were getting in his way, trying to see for themselves what was going on; and before he could get any nearer, Clay pulled one of his Colt .45s lightning fast and leveled it at Colbert's face before he got his own gun up.

Several things happened at the same time: Colbert froze as the sound of two pistols being cocked filled the otherwise silent room—Allison's aimed at Colbert, and Jonathon's pointing at the side of Allison's head. Clay's eyes darted sideways at Jonathon, and he slowly grinned like a lunatic.

"Well, Mr. Chunk Colbert, it appears we now have a real contest. We may find out the answer to your question after all."

"Wha—what question?" Colbert stuttered, staring at the huge pistol barrel in his face.

"Why, who is the best and who is the second-best gunman, of course." He nodded down at Colbert's half-drawn weapon. "We evidently already have the evidence right there that you are, indeed, the third. So, unfortunately you are out of the running." He lined his pistol up squarely between Colbert's eyes, put his other hand on his hip, licked his lips in anticipation, and shrugged. "And also unfortunately, you won't be around to see who here *is* the fastest."

"You don't want to do that, Clay. What's this all about?" Jonathon asked.

"Oh, this is about answering an important point of discussion, Deputy Carter—Sir."

"No it ain't," blurted Colbert. "Sum bitch was trying to get Vega there to draw him some kind of map, to some old gold mine. Vega wasn't fallin' for it, so's he roughed him up for it. Besides, Vega's too stupid to know if he's got a gold mine or not—which I seriously doubt." Jonathon glanced at Cruz Vega, who had now collapsed back into his chair, passed out, drunk, and unable to object either way.

Colbert's voice trailed off, and his eyes crossed as he stared back into A barrel. "You're not gonna just let him shoot me, are ya, Mister?"

"No, I do not believe I will, Mr. Colbert. Clay, put it down. You know works—you shoot, I shoot."

"Nah, I don't believe you would shoot me, Squirrel. I mean, after all we'v through together?"

"Clay," Jonathon's voice dropped to almost a whisper, and repeated s "You know me. You shoot—I shoot. Not a threat. Promise."

Allison hesitated, took a step back, then uncocked his pistol and lower "Yeah, you are probably right, Squirrel. And if that happened, how on earth w I ever know the answer myself?"

"You mean, who's fastest?"

"Exactly."

"Well, I would say you would be the very first to know, Clay." Jonathon his pistol aimed squarely at Allison, knowing not to take a chance.

Allison made as if to holster his pistol, then suddenly whipped the barrel l across Colbert's face and nose, breaking it wide open in a torrent of blood. Colb grabbed his face in both hands and sat down hard on the floor. Allison turned Jonathon, his pistol uncocked and now dangling from one finger through trigger guard, indicating surrender. He bowed slightly at the waist.

"What's the charge, then, Deputy Squirrel? Drunk and disorderly? Attempt murder? Mistreating miscreants? Whatever the case, you may now take me to jail.'

At that exact moment the saloon door burst open and Sheriff Rinehart ran i out of breath, eyes wide, and unsure of what was happening. When he spoke, i became clear that he was here for something else entirely.

"Ute and Arapaho war party just attacked a homesteader's settlement north of town. Burned the house and killed the settlers, from what I've been told so far." He glanced around the room. "I need a posse right now to go after the bastards. Who's with me? Jonathon, I'll need you of course."

A chorus of a few voices around the room called out, "I'll go, "Count me in," "Me too." Allison slowly holstered his weapon, still carefully holding Jonathon's eye, and nodded at him. "You can count on me, Sheriff," he said, moving cautiously past Jonathon, who followed him with his gun until he walked out the door. Jonathon let out a breath, and only then holstered his weapon.

Rinehart moved quickly up to his deputy, took him by the arm, and led him away from the others. "What the hell was that all about?"

"Clay just being Clay. And I'm afraid he's getting a bit more unpredictable by the day."

"Never mind all that right now," Rinehart said. He leaned in closer to speak quietly to him.

"Jonathon, you should brace yourself—it's the Delgado place!"

#

Delgado Rancho, Ponil River Valley)

The posse numbered fourteen men, including Rinehart, Jonathon, and Clay Allison. No one had expected Town Marshal Cruz Vega to come along, which he didn't, being still passed out in the St. James, drunk. But surprisingly, Jonathon noticed that Chunk Colbert had joined them, still holding a filthy handkerchief to his ruptured nose.

They rode hard, pushing their horses almost to their endurance as they frothed and coughed. Half an hour later, they swung off the main road and headed north into a wide verdant canyon. A mile further, they rounded a bend and could now see the flames that still dotted the horizon where the rancho should be. As they neared, Jonathon felt the lump in his throat sink to his belly, recognizing what was left of the Delgado house and barn, now just smoldering timbers, and the odd flame here or there burning itself out.

As they got within hailing distance, Trent could see nondescript lumps lying in various places out around the yards, and one in the corral area. Ominously, arrow shafts could be seen protruding from some of the lumps, which in the moonlight soon materialized into bodies lying motionless, dead.

A sob escaped Jonathon's throat involuntarily as he leapt from his still loping horse and ran to the nearest corpse, a small one, and rolled it over in trepidation. It was Pepé, María's youngest brother. His surprised eyes were frozen open and staring at nothing, his face white and drained of color, the top of his head bloody and missing his scalp. Two arrows had pierced his back, as if he had been running for his life when he was cut down.

The other visible bodies were quickly identified as those of the other brother, Antonio, and of Señor Delgado, who had been scalped and had his throat slashed.

"Two others in the barn—burned down around them, looks like," said one of the riders.

"No," Jonathon whispered to himself, and ran to the burned-out building, pushing the men there aside and plowing into the space that had been roughly cleared around the half-burned bodies. He knelt down slowly, gingerly pushing aside whatever smoking clothing remained, feeling lurid and obscene as he did so but needing to identify the person, if possible. He sat back on his heels and blew his breath out. Whoever these unfortunates were, they were not female, and therefore not María. Jonathon surmised that they might be hired Utes or other hands, who would have routinely slept in the barn.

"Anybody check the house?" he shouted.

"Nobody in there that I could see," Rinehart answered, coughing from the latent smoke as he came around from behind what remained of the home.

Jonathon ran around the property, making ever-widening circles, trying to locate María's body in the light of the moon, but to no avail.

"She's not here," he puffed as he came back to the others near the empty corral. "They might have taken her." Sheriff Rinehart and Clay Allison were now both down on one knee, studying the ground, tracing out prints with their fingers.

"These horses were wearing shoes," mumbled Rinehart. He squinted up at

Jonathon who stood over him. "Reckon these were really Indians, Jonathon?"

Jonathon wondered if the sheriff's quiet question was directed at him because of his racial mix, as if he would be quicker to shift the blame to white men from an Indian raiding party. Jonathon made a show of dropping down, licking his finger, and touching it to the hoof print. He brought the damp dirt up to his tongue and tasted it before spitting it back out.

"Yep. White men," he answered, matter-of-factly before standing up and straightening his clothes. The men standing near stared at him incredulously.

"You can really tell by tasting a hoof-print like that?" one of them asked. Jonathon remained expressionless.

"Of course he can't," laughed Allison. "But it's sure clear that you idiots thought he could. Let's just hope you geniuses are smarter than the bunch we're after."

Jonathon turned on his heel and headed to the corral. "Whoever it was, doesn't really matter. María's gone. I'm going to go find her."

"Well, let's get mounted up then," shouted Rinehart.

"You go ahead, Sheriff," said Jonathon over his shoulder. "I'm not going with you." He pulled his horse out of the remuda and tended to cinching the saddle.

"Not going with us? Why?"

"She's not with them, that's why."

Rinehart scratched his head under his hat. "But you just said. . . ."

"I just said that it doesn't matter if it was Indians or Santa Fe Ring regulators. Frankly, I think it was the Santa Fe bunch. They're the ones behind everything else around here." He put his foot in the stirrup and mounted his horse. "But she's not with them, either way. And I'm going to find her. Up there somewhere, I figure." He nodded toward the foothills beyond the Ponil River, which ran a hundred yards or so to the northeast.

"Well, you do what you need to, Jonathon," said Rinehart, pushing impatiently past the rump of Jonathon's horse to find his own in the corral. "We're following the trail of these bastards, white or Indian. You coming, Clay, or going with Carter?"

Allison stood peering into the distance, toward Mt. Baldy and the Valley of the Utes. He nodded in that direction. "That's where they're headed, looks like to me—back toward the Indian settlement." He looked over at Jonathon, who could see a hint of his old friend in his eyes. "And you reckon they were white men, Jonathon?"

Jonathon nodded.

Allison lit a new cigar, and then shook his head. "Then the bastards will definitely swing for this."

"Nah! They was obviously Injuns," blurted Chunk Colbert nearby. "Why would Whites shoot people full of arrows, torture and burn 'em, and take their scalps like that?" A chorus of *yeah* and *let's go* answered him as he moved past Jonathon so closely that the latter could smell his stench. "You gonna miss out on all the fun, Deputy," Chunk muttered as he jumped on his own horse, wheeled it around, and trotted out the gate. "It'll be like shootin' fish in a barrel."

Jonathon felt a core of anger seething up inside him, urging him to jump Chunk Colbert and take him down hard, right now. Instead, he pushed it all back down, saving the anger for when he might need it most.

"You should have let me put my bullet between his eyes when I had the chance," Allison said.

Jonathon breathed slowly and steadily, centering himself again. "Colbert can wait, Clay. Right now, my first and only priority is María." He looked over at his erstwhile friend. "I'm headed out on my own, but I need you to ride along with that posse, Clay—you try and stop them from doing anything crazy tonight. Can you do that, without making it any worse?"

Clay Allison puffed his cigar as his madman's smile slowly blossomed on his mouth. He turned and mounted his horse. "I shall surely try my best, Deputy Squirrel."

#

The posse whistled and shouted at their horses as they loped out across the meadow behind the burned-out ranch, making for the nearby trail that threaded its way through the foothills of the Cimarron Range and eventually spilled into the Valley of the Utes some fifteen miles distant. Jonathon sat on a small hillock near the stream that ran from the same foothills, watching their dust cloud diminish and evaporate in the moonlit breeze.

His heart had stopped pounding and he closed his eyes and breathed in the brisk early morning air to drive the oxygen deep into his body, calming him further. He willed his senses to reach out and communicate something to him, anything, that he could use to find María. The only impression he got was that she couldn't be too far, which is why he didn't ride with the posse. He knew she was not with the raiders, whoever they were.

But where was she? And what exactly would he find once he found her?

He pushed that last question firmly aside and concentrated. A pearly pink light quickened on the eastern horizon, a signal of the pre-dawn's arrival and gradually revealing the silhouettes of ancient volcanoes there. He nudged his horse forward, turned upstream, and headed uphill for a hundred yards before stopping his horse again. He closed his eyes, breathed deeply, and calmed himself. He sat this way for several minutes; listening to the awakening day, before finally turning the animal back to the east. He coaxed it up a steeper embankment toward a large pile of rocks that had rolled down from higher up in some prehistoric cataclysm. He couldn't have explained it to anyone, but he had learned long ago that following these internal signals was akin to following a magnetic lodestone—turn one way, and then another, as the feeling grew stronger.

The rocks formed a natural passageway large enough for horse and rider to pass through. Once inside, the massive stones rose on all sides like a natural fortress. He stopped suddenly in the center clearing formed by the circle of stones.

He had just walked into a trap.

"Don't you move," a strong but familiar voice growled shakily from behind him. "I have a shotgun pointed at the back of your head and believe me, after what you did down there, I will gladly blow it off."

"Easy there. Can I just raise my hands, to show that I mean you no harm?"

"*Jonathon?*"

Behind him he heard the clattering of feet scrambling down a rocky path, running around his horse at a wide berth, and finally someone coming into view.

It was María, still holding the double-barreled shotgun on him.

"Jonathon? But how did you find me? What . . . ?" She stumbled over her words, moving closer to him, the rifle still unwavering. Jonathon kept his hands raised.

"Um, I would really feel a whole lot better if you pointed that thing somewhere else."

María stopped, looked incredulously at the gun in her hands, and then lowered it. She immediately sobbed and ran to him, burying her face into his thigh as she clung to his leg. Jonathon timidly reached down from the saddle, touched the top of her head, and then gently stroked her black hair back behind her ears. He nudged her momentarily with his knee so that he could dismount, and when he did so, she fell into his arms, still sobbing. He felt he would be damned forever, but he couldn't help returning her embrace and wrapped her tight in his arms. She raised her face to him and he melted into her dark eyes, right before his lips melted into hers, praying that time would stop completely and they could remain this way forever, safe from all else.

But time did not stop, and eventually they pulled apart, reluctantly, but inevitably.

"I thought you were dead," he said quietly, gazing down at her dirt-streaked, but still lovely face.

"And for a moment there, when I saw you just now, I thought you were one of them—the attackers."

He shook his head at her, frowning. "How could you think such a thing?"

"That's just it. I wasn't thinking. After all that happened—after they, they. . . ." She couldn't finish and stifled a sob. "I was down here, near the river, when they arrived. All I heard was all the laughter, and cursing, taunting. Then, when they dragged my father and brothers out and began to. . . ." She paused, turning away as a vacant, haunted look invaded her eyes. "I crossed the river upstream and hid there, in the trees. But I saw everything they did to them. And heard their screams. I threw myself onto the ground and stuffed my skirt into my mouth, to muffle my own screams. Oh, Jonathon . . . they were Anglos, acting like Indians. How could they do such things? And to my little brothers. . . ." Her voice failed and choked in her throat as she stared down at her smoldering homestead, now clearly visible in the dawn that spilled across the landscape below.

Jonathon came up slowly behind and put his arms gently around her. She sagged against him.

"Afterwards, when they set the fires and rode away with our stock and horses, I waited for the longest time before daring to move. But when I finally did, I ran down there. I had to see what they had done to them. See it with my own eyes, so that it would be real—so that I would remember it all, every detail, seared into my mind." Her voice became ragged, and filled with muted rage; she twisted the loose hem of her blouse tightly as she continued. "And so that one day, someday, I could find them and do the same thing to them! Or pay someone else to do it, while I watch."

Jonathon started to caution her, to warn her not to say things like that, knowing that going down that path would lead to madness. But instead, he let her rant for now. Perhaps it would be good, for the moment, to let it out.

They stood there for the longest while, Jonathon's arms around her protectively, until he felt the sunbeams warming the air around them.

"Let's go, María. We have some work to do down there. We need to go care for your family."

She turned to him suddenly. "Wait!" She broke away and quickly ran back in the direction she had come from moments ago. She stopped and looked back at him when he didn't immediately follow. "Over here. You need to help me. He needs attention."

Jonathon shrugged his shoulders, not comprehending. "Who needs attention?"

Instead of answering, she turned and scrambled back up the rocky path between boulders before disappearing into the oak bushes. "Up here," she called back.

Jonathon followed her uncertainly, pushing through the bushes and into a small hidden clearing shaded by the trees. There, he found María kneeling down, bathing the fevered forehead of a man whose face was severely burned and who lay semiconscious and moaning on the ground. His shirt and the ground beneath him were wet with blood, and an arrow protruded from the left side of his chest.

It was María's fiancé, Don Gaspar de León.

CHAPTER 14
Bad Moon Rising

(Present Day – Sangre de Cristo Mountains)

A quarter mile north of the crash site, just as dawn began to spill its light onto the crests of the mountain peaks above them, Trent and Ben found their next sign of the missing girls.

The two men had risen from a fitful sleep at 4:30, gathered whatever emergency supplies—food, water, first aid, sleeping bags, and ammunition—they could carry, and loaded them into their backpacks. Thankfully, the snow had stopped sometime in the night, leaving behind only six to eight inches in most places, so that hiking out proved to be only moderately difficult with the multipurpose boots they were wearing. One of the last things they had done was to cover the four bodies with their dismantled tent and stake it down with heavy rocks, providing some semblance of protection from the elements—and a little dignity. As the dawn sky had lightened to a pearly gray, they had stood and prayed over the bodies for a few minutes before shouldering their packs and rifles and trudging out of the basin, following the directions the girls' footprints had indicated the night before.

Trent led as the two men walked in single file, and though they were wearing layers of clothing and heavy winter jackets, the crisp morning air cut through them like blades of ice, setting his teeth to chatter.

"'Darkest hour is just before dawn,'" mused Ben, his voice quivering.

"Actually some truth to that," Trent said. "Sorta like a microwave oven heating up a frozen dinner. There's an exchange of heat. The ground absorbs the sun's rays all day, then at night the heat escapes again. When dawn comes around, you would think it would heat things up right away, but that's not true. The sun's rays are very weak at first, at that angle, and the heat continues to leave the earth even faster, actually cooling things down even more for an hour or so."

Ben was silent for a moment, and then chuckled. "You know, I wasn't thinking about science. I was just quoting that old Crosby, Stills, and Nash song 'Long Time Gone.'"

They topped a rise and Trent held his hand up, signaling a stop. Below was a clearing that was several yards wide. He pulled a small pair of binoculars from his jacket and looked into the distance, then lowered them, chewing his bottom lip.

"Somebody has been there," he pointed, "just under the lip of that ridge over there, under those trees." He handed the field glasses to Ben. "See it, how the ground there is kicked up? Looks like a fairly recent campsite of sorts."

"Yeah, I see it. Looks like they maybe had a campfire?" Ben handed the glasses back to Trent, who suddenly felt exposed. He knelt down on one knee and trained the glasses on the ground all around the site. "Looks like some tracks leading away, on up the draw there. Can't tell whose they are from here, but they were made recently—after the snow stopped. Could be good news."

"Yeah. And the bad news could be that anyone else tracking them is smart and staying hidden within the trees, not leaving tracks so easy to see."

"Your rifle ready?"

"Locked and loaded."

"Well, keep it handy. Don't want any stupid mistakes. We already know there's a murderer loose out here somewhere."

Trent led them in a circling pattern just below the edge of the ridge so that their silhouette wouldn't be readily seen by anyone watching. He slowed as they approached the primitive campsite tucked into the hillside and searched for any other sign of footprints nearby, besides the two pair they were following. A small juniper tree sheltered one side of the campsite and the ground beneath it was disturbed. Someone had clearly rested here recently. A small circle of stones had been placed to contain a recent fire. Trent knelt, took off a glove, and touched the ashes. "A little warm. A few hours old, though, I'm guessing."

Ben looked around, walked behind the tree, and then stiffened. "What's this?"

Trent came over to join him. Just behind the tree trunk was a small mound of trash. He moved it around with the toe of his boot, revealing a couple of candy bar wrappers, an empty plastic water bottle, and, more disturbingly, some bloody tissues and discarded wrappings from bandages.

"Shit," Ben blurted, stooping and picking up one of the latter. It had held a five-by-five inch sterile gauze bandage that came in a standard first aid kit.

"Must've taken the kit from the chopper," Trent said. "Looks like they had time and forethought to scrounge some water and a little food, too, before heading out," he added, trying to remain positive.

"Yeah, but looks like they needed the first aid kit right away, judging by all the blood here and back at the crash."

"It would explain why they had stopped for the night within such a short distance."

Ben tossed the trash aside in exasperation and frowned up at Trent. "If we'd only set out last night, like I wanted, we would've found them right away."

"Oh, come on, Ben. Like I said, it was snowing heavy, visibility was bad, and we were exhausted—doesn't take long to get turned around in those conditions."

"Say what you will, you made a mistake. Don't know why you just can't admit it." Ben stood up, adjusted his load, and slung his rifle back on his shoulder. He glared at Trent, and then turned to walk away. "I just hope it hasn't cost us one of their lives—or both."

Trent started to reply, then thought better of it. He let Ben take the lead this time, now that they had actual prints to follow. The trail led them back up onto a small ridge, where it followed the top for a while. The ridge was cloaked with pine trees and ran generally northeast. They continued to climb steadily uphill. Their breathing grew ragged, and after another mile of steady climbing they stopped to take a water break. Ben wondered aloud about the terrain.

"Why do you suppose they're continuing uphill," he nodded, "instead of making for the valley? If I were them, I'd be headed to low country, maybe find a ranch and some help, or a road."

"I don't know," Trent answered. He looked back uphill and thought for a moment. "You know, for one thing, I think we haven't given these girls much credit so far. We've been thinking of them like lost kids, when they're young adults now."

Ben looked at him with a puzzled look. "Yeah? So?"

"Well, think about it. They both have been in the world for a while, so to speak, away from home at college, starting to make their own decisions. Then they get up here and survive a terrible crash, witness some horrible murders, and were able to successfully hide from the killer—or killers. At some point, one or both of those girls stopped and began to think rationally."

"Still doesn't explain why they're headed up instead of down."

"I think it does, Ben. First of all, they would have stayed put, underneath that wreckage, until they were sure the killers were gone. That would mean listening for the four-wheeler, or whatever they were driving, to fade off into the distance— probably downhill. And when the girls thought it was safe to leave, they sure weren't going to go in the same direction the murderers went, not at first. No, I think they did the smart thing, for now, anyway. They circled up here to put some distance between them and the bad guys, probably knowing they might return to look for them."

Ben listened for a moment, took another swig of water, and then put the canteen away. "Well that doesn't exactly leave me warm and fuzzy, either."

"Why not?"

"Because if you are right," Ben answered, nodding back downhill, "then those guys are probably headed back out here this morning themselves, and possibly with backup."

Trent straightened his load and stood up. "Well, that's one point we are in agreement on, and a good argument to keep going. The girls can't be too far ahead. So let's be the first to find them."

This time, Trent took the lead. The terrain became even steeper and within ten minutes they both were feeling the effects of the higher altitude. Ten minutes later Trent suddenly stopped. Ben came up next to him as Trent pointed slowly a few feet ahead of them, where the girls' footprints disappeared over the edge of a short embankment before leading into a ravine. But that was not what concerned him. He pointed again to where their relatively small prints were now dwarfed by a set of much larger ones—animal paw tracks that were tipped by the unmistakable impressions of huge claws, and trailing drops of bright red blood against the stark white snow. Trent and Ben exchanged worried looks.

The wounded bear that had attacked their camp last night had cut the trail.

More than one predator was now hunting the girls.

#

Jennifer Ferguson and Ilsa Bouwmeester had at last reached shelter, in the form of the abandoned ruins of an old miner's shack, its roof partially caved in and its old doors and windows now only gaping openings. It was excellent timing, because they had needed to stop to change the bandage on Ilsa's leg, which was bleeding badly again. They were cold, exhausted, and hungry; and they had no idea exactly where they were. Ilsa had been leaning on Jennifer to take the weight off her badly torn upper thigh, and they feared her right arm was broken. They had fashioned a sling for it, but the arm continued to throb with each beat of her heart.

"I have to stop, Jennifer. I just have to. I'm sorry," Ilsa had repeated over and over for the past half hour.

And Jennifer had answered her patiently. "Just a little farther. We need to find a sheltered area first—where we can make a fire."

The mid-morning sun had gradually brought some increasing warmth, but the wind cut through their ski jackets, their night of exposure to the elements had left them chilled to the bone, and they were exhausted. Jennifer knew that if they didn't get to shelter or find help soon, they would be in real trouble, and the discovery of the old cabin had sent a thrill of hope through her.

They had been stopping periodically to try and get their bearings from the climbing sun and listen for the sound of anyone pursuing them. After what they had seen the day before, Jennifer had no doubt that the murderer would be back looking for them soon, and she doubted he would be alone. She also knew that her father would surely have been aware of the accident by now and would also have people out searching for them. She knew that soon they would need to circle around and go back downhill to find help—very soon, judging by Ilsa's worsening condition and by their dwindling supplies.

Jennifer cleared off some snow from the dirt floor of the cabin, carefully helped Ilsa sit down against one wall, and shrugged off the small backpack she was carrying. She rummaged until she found some water, and handed it to Ilsa, who gulped it down. They were down to their last two bottles, which she knew was no good. She had filled up two of their empties with snow, but with the brisk temperatures it had yet to melt.

She set about finding kindling from the collapsed house and starting a wonderful fire that caught the old wood immediately. Soon they began feeling the thaw and were able to shed a layer or two of wet clothes that they spread out, hoping that they would dry near the fire.

Jennifer pulled the first aid kit from her pack and worked on Ilsa's leg, removing the old bloody bandage, cleaning it with water, then spraying the wound with an antiseptic from the kit and re-bandaging it. It was the last big gauze bandage they had.

"Did you hear those gunshots?" Ilsa asked, now slurring her words feverishly.

"Yes, we heard them—but that was last night. Don't you remember?" Jennifer was concerned that her friend was starting to lose her sense of reality and would not be able to continue on much longer. They had indeed heard distant gunfire the previous night, after settling in around their small fire. They had originally decided they would not venture too far from the crash site, trusting that someone—hopefully her father—would surely be along to look for them soon. But after the gunshots had echoed away, Jennifer had quickly doused their fire with snow and they had huddled together, listening to what sounded like screaming animals. Those sounds had been followed by one or two more sporadic gunshots, some shouting, and then silence. They had waited, wondering if the killer had returned, until Jennifer couldn't stand it anymore. After the snow had stopped, and using a flashlight that they had also taken from the chopper, they had decided to keep moving under cover of the night to put more distance between them any possible pursuers.

But now, she feared, they had gone just about as far as they were going to.

"Ilsa, stay with me." She broke off half of their last candy bar and gently forced some between her friend's lips. "Here . . . you need to eat something."

"Just want . . . sleep—need some sleep. Just a little . . . nap . . . that's all . . . ." Ilsa's voice drifted in and out and her eyelids drooped. Jennifer rolled up one of the jackets and put it under her friend's head as a pillow. She felt her forehead. It was burning up with fever. She took a spare T-shirt from her knapsack, dampened it with water, and bathed Ilsa's face before laying it across her forehead. Jennifer then leaned back against the wall and closed her eyes. Maybe a little sleep wouldn't hurt her, either.

"Where are you, Dad?" she mumbled to herself.

She drifted off to sleep—or at least that condition of pre-sleep when one starts to see visions and dreamlike scenes while still aware of being not quite asleep yet—when she thought she heard her father's voice, calling her in the distance. In her trance-like state, she could see him walking toward her, across a sunny meadow full of wildflowers, smiling and waving to her, beautiful aspens framing him from behind with the glittering gold of their fall adornment.

"Jennifer!" he was calling out to her. He carried on one arm what looked like a picnic basket and on the other a red-checkered blanket, which he now dropped on the ground in front of him. As a little girl she had dearly loved going on picnics with her parents. Those had been the good times. Her father would make the most elaborate lunches, with wondrous sandwiches layered with all sorts of goodies—although her favorite was always the old faithful standby, peanut butter and grape jelly, which he had always made sure to include—and with her favorite soda, a huge bag of potato chips, and big pickles like the ones at the movie theater, topped off by an entire package of Oreo cookies. Her mother would pretend to be outraged by the unhealthy choices but would always laugh and participate anyway—at least, until she wouldn't. That was when the not-so-good times began, when her parents would shout at each other, sometimes throw things, and slam doors. They would never actually hit each other, but Jennifer would still hide under

her bed with her hands over her ears until the shouting died away or until she went to sleep.

Like now.

"Jennifer . . . ."

"Daddy?" she mumbled.

"Jennifer, where are you?"

"Here, Daddy . . . right here."

She could see him standing in the meadow, the picnic lunch all spread out on the blanket, waiting, his hands on his hips, looking around as though he couldn't see her. She waved her hands at him. Why couldn't he see her? She was right here.

"Here, Daddy. Right here . . . . Don't you see me?" She waved her hands again, but this time it was as if she were swatting away a cloud of flies or mosquitoes that buzzed irritatingly around her head.

"No, go away," she whined. Her eyelids wouldn't open. They felt glued shut and she strained to open them, just a little, but she could see only shadowy figures in front of her, figures of something—someone—who was bothering her, messing with her. She slapped at them again with her hands, which felt heavy and useless.

"Daddy, help me."

"I'm right here, Jenn. Wake up."

"Daddy, I can't see you." But her father had faded away in a cloud of irritation, along with the beautiful golden aspens and the wildflowers. All that was left were shadows and confusion and the flies buzzing around her.

Suddenly she was wide awake, and her fear leapt into her throat as she realized she was back in the old cabin with Ilsa passed out beside her, and someone was grabbing her shoulders. Her eyes wouldn't focus clearly; strong hands held her upper arms so that she couldn't move. She opened her mouth and screamed, but one of the big rough hands covered her lips, stifling the scream.

"Jennifer, stop!"

"No. . . . NO!" her muffled voice shouted against the hand.

"Jennifer . . . it's me. It's Dad!" She struggled for another second, then stopped, letting her eyes focus on the blurry face coming into view a few inches in front of hers—the face of her father. Behind her in the doorway stood another vaguely familiar figure, her father's friend, Mr. Carter. He was holding a rifle across his arms and smiling down at her.

"Hi, Jennifer," Mr. Carter said as he stepped into the cabin. His voice was soothing, and he had a kind, handsome face. He leaned his rifle against the wall and stooped down near Ilsa. "Let's have a look at your friend here, shall we?"

She stared, unbelieving at first, at her father's relieved face in front of her. She closed her eyes again, and as she collapsed into his warm, protecting arms, it occurred to her that it was the most wonderful place she had ever been.

\#

Two hours later, Jennifer awoke to find that the fire was built up and a delicious smell of cooking food filled the room. She had fallen asleep in her father's lap and his hand was stroking her hair. She rose up and looked around. Trent was sitting on a makeshift bench made from stones and old wood scavenged from the cabin's wreckage, drinking something hot, and stirring what looked like a container of stew bubbling on a rock by the fire. They had also unzipped a sleeping bag to make Ilsa a more comfortable bed, where she was now sleeping soundly.

"She was running a fever, I think," Jennifer mumbled, rubbing the sleep from her eyes as she looked from one of the men to the other.

"I gave her a strong dose of Tylenol," Trent said. "I think it finally broke the fever. She's been sleeping good for an hour now. Probably a good thing she was passed out, though. I had to set that broken arm of hers and splint it." He looked back at Jennifer and smiled. "You did a good job doctoring her, though, what with your lack of resources."

"What time is it?"

"Little past noon." Trent answered, checking his watch. He had checked his phone earlier, but still had no signal, so he kept it turned off to conserve the battery.

"You did real good, honey," Ben said, scooting over to sit next to his daughter. He put an arm gently around her shoulders and pulled her close. "I am very proud of you."

Jennifer put her head on his shoulder, and then squeezed her eyes shut as the tears started to flow. "Oh, Daddy, he shot those people! That woman first, then Ilsa's father . . . and he would've—would've. . . ."

"We know, honey, we know. We found them. We took care of them best we could. I'm just so thankful you guys are okay. I thought I had lost you forever. I don't know what I would have done if something had happened." Jennifer wrapped her arms tighter around his chest. He leaned down and kissed the top of his daughter's head. As he did so, he caught Trent looking at him, a smile playing at the corner of his mouth.

Trent nodded, winked at him, and mouthed, *"Good job, Daddy."*

In a little while, Ilsa also stirred. Trent dished them all up some of Maggie's stew and they ate hungrily in silence for a while. Afterwards, the girls filled them in on what had happened after the crash.

The survivors had all been thrown clear, with various injuries. Ilsa's father had suffered the worst ones—a couple of broken bones and possibly some internal bleeding, judging from how he had been coughing up blood. They had soon discovered that there was no cell service, had also tried the radio, and were trying to make each other as comfortable as possible while discussing what to do next, when they heard an approaching engine. Mr. Bouwmeester had grown strangely quiet and suspicious and for some reason had ordered the girls to hide, which they did. They had become ecstatic when they peeked out and Ilsa recognized one of her father's bodyguards walking up. They had almost come out of hiding then, until he started questioning Ilsa's father and his assistant, shouting at them angrily.

"He started beating them—torturing them," continued Ilsa. "Then he pulled out a gun, and . . . ." She couldn't finish. Jennifer reached over, took hold of Ilsa's hand, and finished telling the story for her. After the man had shot them, he stormed about, searching the bodies, their things; then tearing through the wreckage, cursing the whole while. It wasn't until he found Ilsa's flowered backpack that he stopped ranting.

"I think that's when he realized that we had also been on board—Ilsa and me— because he then started looking around a wider area, I think for our footprints. After he looked for awhile, though, his phone rang. . . ."

"His phone?" Ben asked. "Our phones didn't work there."

"I don't know. It was bigger than a cell phone. But he got some sort of call on it and answered it."

"Did it have sort of a large-looking antenna protruding from the top?" Trent asked.

Jennifer thought for a moment. "Yes. I think it did."

"Satellite phone," Trent said. He had thought once or twice today already how helpful it would have been for him and Ben to have brought one along. "Those work about anywhere on the planet."

"Anyway," Jennifer continued, "he talked for a minute, then abruptly gave up the search. For some reason, I think he had run out of time, or else whoever was on the phone ordered him somewhere else or something, because he just took off after that. We waited a very long time, even after we heard the engine fade away, before we dared come out of hiding."

"So, just what do you think he was looking for, when he was questioning them?" Trent asked.

Jennifer shook her head. "I don't know. Do you have any idea?" she asked Ilsa, who stared into the fire silently for a few seconds, and then just shook her head quickly.

"Hmm," said Trent, watching Ilsa. "Sure would be helpful to know."

The girls continued to talk, but from there on, the story was all pretty much as Trent had surmised earlier. They had gathered some gear and taken off, to get at least far enough away from the chopper and to find help.

They all sat quietly for a few minutes, gazing into the fire.

"Mr. Carter, we heard gunshots last night," Ilsa said after awhile.

"Yes. That was us."

Trent and Ben then told their story about finding the wreck, investigating it as best they could, and then about the bear showing up, and losing their horses.

"A bear?" Both girls' eyes grew wide and they stared at each other. "There's a bear out here?"

"Well, your dad hit it pretty good with a couple of those shots. I am fairly certain it's probably bled to death by now." Trent exchanged looks with Ben and shook his head just slightly, signaling him not to say anything further to alarm the girls.

They finished off the remainder of the stew, and then Trent stood up, stretched, and reached for his jacket. "We've got a long trek to get everyone back off this mountain, but given the time of day, plus the conditions of you ladies, I figure it isn't going to happen today." He stepped to the doorway and looked out. "We're in about as protected a place as we're going to find for now, so I'm suggesting we plan to stay the night. We have a little more food, lots of available firewood, and enough snow to melt if we run out of water."

He turned and looked at them. "Tomorrow, I'll get up early and hike out of here." Ben stood and began to protest. "I know, Ben, I know. But I can make better time alone. Everyone's better off if you stay here and take care of the girls, and I will get some help up here by the end of the day. Besides, the sun's back out, things should start to warm up nicely again, and the snow's melting." He turned around and grinned, attempting to put a good face on things. "You know . . . Indian summer!"

He stepped out the door, put his jacket on, sniffed the clean mountain air, and then stuck his head back in. "Ben, you want to come help me get some more firewood in for the night?"

Ben grabbed his jacket and joined him outside. They walked a few steps from the cabin and Trent stopped and turned to him. "Okay, Mr. Detective, did you pick up on anything in there just now?"

"Pick up on what? With the girls?"

"Yeah, when Ilsa was telling about her father being questioned, and when I asked her specifically what the killer may have been looking for?"

"No, I didn't notice anything."

"Well, something sure flicked across her eyes, and then she took just a half-second too long in answering me." Trent sucked on his teeth for a second and glanced back at the cabin. "She's hiding something. I know it."

Ben shrugged. "Maybe. Who knows? They have been through quite an ordeal, though. Maybe she's still a little loopy from the fever and all, you know?"

"Maybe. But I don't think so."

They split up and roamed the edges of the clearing, gathering armloads of scattered wood and kindling, bringing it back to the cabin and depositing it neatly outside the door. They made a few more trips like that and were about fifty yards apart, with Trent out in the middle of the clearing and Ben somewhere on the other side of the cabin, when Trent suddenly felt a flash of burning go through the scar on his forehead and sear into his brain. He doubled over in tremendous pain.

The seizure lasted only a few seconds, but Trent knew it was a portent of immediate, terrible danger.

"Brother of the Moon!" he heard a familiar voice shouting from somewhere above him. *It is Brother of the Moon!"*

He stood up again painfully, his head still reeling, and saw the silhouette of the Shadow Warrior on the rim of the ridge a few yards to the west and above him, pointing and shouting at him, then kneeling and pulling back his bow and aiming it off into the distance, somewhere beyond the cabin. Trent stared in puzzlement, then slowly turned to look where the Indian was aiming—right at a large cinnamon-colored bear that had just emerged from an arroyo that led into the cabin clearing. It was standing very still, except for its massive head that turned and looked from Ben to Trent and back again, as if making some decision.

It was the bear Ben had wounded last night and it had tracked them all down.

It panted deeply, staring now with its one good eye at Ben, not twenty feet away from him with his back to the animal, seemingly unaware of its presence and whistling something that sounded like "Long Time Gone."

Trent grabbed at himself, searching for a weapon—anything—and then cursed, remembering that he had left his rifle just inside the cabin door.

"Ben!" Trent shouted, dropping his firewood and waving his arms.

He glanced up again at Shadow Warrior who looked back at him and shouted, *"Run, Squirrel!"* and then fired his arrow. It flew on a downward angle straight into the bear's side but, of course, disappeared completely with no obvious effect. After all, Trent reasoned, it was a ghost's arrow.

Ben looked up in surprise as Trent began to run toward him. Trent's legs felt like they were encased in cement, as if this were a bad dream. He watched in horror as the massive bear also began to move forward and then broke into a lope, its tongue lolling out of its jaws hungrily. If he could only divert the bear from Ben, then one of them might at least have a chance to go for the rifle in the doorway.

Maybe.

Ben finally took a step or two, still unaware of the mass of fury descending on him, a puzzled look on his face as he watched Trent waving his arms and shouting like a madman. "Run, Ben!"

Too late, Ben began to turn, as if in slow motion; but the bear had already leapt and caught him full force on his back, slapping him to the ground as its momentum carried its body over him and past him. Ben was momentarily stunned and began to raise himself on his elbows when the bear stopped, turned, glancing first at Trent as he still ran toward them, still thirty yards away, and then ignoring him as if to return to its real enemy, the man who had shot him the night before, to exact its terrible revenge.

As the bear lumbered for him, Ben looked straight into Trent's eyes and almost seemed to laugh at the irony of it all, a look of understanding and resignation on his face, and then disappeared from view as the beast reared and pounced full force onto his back, tossing Ben like a limp rag doll, and then bounced him repeatedly on the ground, tearing and ripping him wildly with its massive claws and teeth

CHAPTER 15
Slaughter of Innocents

(August 23, 1873)

(Telegram from María Consuelo Delgado)

To:
Sr. Manuel Diego Delgado
El Rancho de las Golondrinas
Santa Fe,
Territorio de Nuevo Méjico

Darling Brother [STOP] Terrible news [STOP] Papa, brothers all murdered [STOP] House burned [STOP] I am unharmed [STOP] More later [STOP]

[SIGNED] María

#

(August 21, 1873 – Ute Valley, New Mexico)

A dog barking before dawn awakened Walking Elk from a sound sleep. He had been on a vision walk, communing with white men who wore odd clothing made of smooth hides of many colors he had never seen. These men lit their cooking fires with small magic wands that produced tiny flames, ate their food out of strange symmetrical containers, lived in huge villages of thousands of people, travelled in shiny wagons that required no horses to pull them over their hard trails of blackened stone, and flew around in large mechanical birds. They were often helpless and were not at all wise in the ways of living out in the real world, the natural world created by *Mowun,* God. They had no knowledge or respect as his own Muache people did; the fact that all living creatures contained supernatural powers seemed to elude these white men. In his visions, this short-sightedness always seemed to lead the strangers into one problem or danger after another, requiring Walking Elk's constant aid and intervention.

Right before he was pulled back to his awakening body, he had come to their aid in fighting a large *que auget,* a Brother of the Moon that was attacking them, due in great part to their foolishness in ignoring the supernatural powers of the beast, even after Walking Elk had warned them of it several times.

One of these men seemed strangely familiar to the old chieftain and reminded him of his young friend Salal, but he could not quite understand why.

Finding himself returned to his wickiup after his vision journey, he sat up with a start, needing to relieve himself greatly. He threw off his warm buffalo robe, rose from his bed of juniper bark, wrapped himself in the heavy woolen trade blanket that Salal had given him on one of his many visits, and stepped out into the chill morning air.

A few of the other Older Ones were up and out already, chopping firewood, stirring their cooking fires to life, or wandering down to the stream as he was, to make water. He passed the mangy cur that had awakened him and was still barking at something unseen up the hill, toward the main Muache village. He stooped to pick up a pebble and tossed it at the dog to try to silence it, but it merely glanced at him briefly before resuming its barking. Then it suddenly ran uphill toward its imagined nemesis.

Walking Elk hurried into the tree line of ponderosa and added his night water to that of the La Flecha that flowed down a few miles until it joined the Cimarron. It was considered civilized to make your water downstream of your village but ever since he was a young boy it had also been considered quite a good joke to let your piss flow down to where the Anglo and Spaniard settlers lived and made their towns.

As the old man finished, he felt much better and turned his attention to his growling stomach. He would now go tend to his own cooking fire and boil some of the salt pork that was left over from what Squirrel had brought to him last week. He turned and felt his way in the dim shadows of the pine woods when he suddenly stopped and listened. He thought he had heard an unusual shout in the distance, and the dog's barking had stopped with an abrupt yelp. He leaned against a tree trunk, quieted his breathing as his father had taught him decades ago, and listened with curiosity. However, his curiosity turned to dread as the shouts turned into screams—amid sudden gunfire.

Walking Elk dropped to his hands and knees so that he could listen to the earth speaking. He felt faint tremors in the ground beneath him, a sign of galloping beasts—horses, no doubt. It crossed his mind that it could be a Muache war party preparing to leave for battle. But it seemed unlikely, even to him, because all of the village, even the outcast Old Ones like him, would have been informed of a pending war.

No, these hoof-beats were heavier and more concentrated and were getting nearer. Over the nearest rise that divided the Old Ones' camp from the main Muache camp appeared ominous pillars of black smoke, which he knew did not come from the camp's cooking fires; in the dawn light a galloping group of Anglo horsemen suddenly spilled over the ridge, shouting and brandishing their pistols and rifles. They spurred their excited mounts downhill, yelling angrily as if in vengeance. They leveled off their weapons at the Old Ones who came stumbling from their wickiups to find out what the commotion was, then they gunned them down where they stood with eyes wide in surprise but with no fear—until the first bullets struck home. Some of the horsemen dismounted, stooped over the fallen ones, some not yet dead, and with long knives hacked off the grey and silver scalps of Walking Elk's helpless friends, an ignominious end to elderly widows and ancient war chiefs—even if their own people had segregated them here to fade away.

Walking Elk stood in shock as his eyes filled with tears and his ears filled with gunfire and the cries of his friends. He sat back hard on the tall grass that was damp with morning dew, part of him wanting to charge the attackers with outrage, but another part of him wanting to shrink smaller and slink deeper into the shadows. He ashamedly listened to this latter part of himself and scooted back farther into the trees.

One of the horsemen turned and squinted into the trees as if sensing him from even that distance. He detached himself from the group of attackers and loped his horse across the meadow toward Walking Elk's hiding place. Alarmed, the old warrior rolled over onto his belly and crawled snake-like, through the pine needle covered forest floor, so as not to show a silhouette. He finally rolled straight into the ice-cold water of the La Flecha River, clenching his teeth against the shock of cold, and floated downstream several yards until he bumped into a large rock in the middle of the stream. He grasped its slick sides, allowed the pull of the water to take his numb body around to the far side of the rock, and held on for dear life. The horseman ducked under branches as he rode his tall horse into the shadow of the trees, brandishing a large pistol like the ones Walking Elk had seen the blue soldiers carrying in his younger days when he had gone to war with them. The rider had a large mustache and chin whiskers, and the former war chief could smell the man's overwhelming stench from here. The man cursed in English with words that Walking Elk did not comprehend, and he squinted into the dimness as he moved his horse carefully down the riverbank, getting nearer to the old man's hiding place with each step.

"Hey Chunk!" came the distant shout of one of the other attackers, back near the Old Ones' camp. The foul-smelling rider turned in his saddle.

"Yeah?"

"We're about done here. You gonna get any of these scalps, or ain't ya?"

"Well, hold up! I would like me a couple more."

Walking Elk's breath came in painful, frigid gasps now, and his heart raced. He knew that the rider would hear him, but he was too exhausted from the icy waters and exertions. He was about to let go and prepare his death song, when the rider suddenly whipped his horse's head around and galloped away.

Walking Elk immediately pulled himself onto the bank, fell over on his back, lifted his eyes to the sunbeams filtering through the trees, and croaked out a prayer of thanks to Mowun.

#

(Delgado Rancho, Ponil River Valley)

Jonathon ended up digging six graves behind the remains of María's house. Digging the first five took him the better part of the day while María methodically busied herself in making her fiancé Gaspar as comfortable as she could on blankets within the scant shelter of what was left of the barn. Earlier, Jonathon had been able to wrench the arrow from his side and tended his wounds as best he could, but he feared that the process had caused even more damage.

After she had done everything she could for Don Gaspar, María then drew fresh water and tended to the bodies of her father, two brothers, and the Ute ranch hands that had also died in the attack on her rancho. She asked Jonathon to remove the horrid arrows from their bodies, and he apologized to her—and to them—when he finally had to break them off, the arrowheads being too deeply imbedded to pull out. He watched as she tenderly bathed their bodies and rearranged their torn clothing as best she could. Jonathon found the remainder of some blankets in the ruined house to wrap the bodies in, and together they carefully carried the remains one by one to the graves, where Jonathon covered them with soil and stones. After they had prayed over them, María finally allowed her emotions to spill over as she collapsed to her knees on her father's grave and wept.

Early the second morning, Jonathon dug the sixth grave after they awakened to find that Don Gaspar de León had expired of his wounds sometime during the night.

"He was a brave but misguided and foolish man," María said finally after they had buried her fiancé and prayed over him. "He thought his title and money were enough to impress people to do his will. Poor deluded man! Title and money mean nothing in the badlands of Nuevo México."

"Unless someone is trying to take it from you by force," said Jonathon, standing hat in hand and looking down at the new but growing cemetery.

They spent the remainder of that day sifting through the ashes of the house, retrieving whatever belongings were fit to be rescued, and storing them in the barn, which still had its roof and three walls and was where they had been sleeping at night. Jonathon had found some usable tools and spent the third day fabricating another wall to the single-story barn, as well as a makeshift door; María occupied her time with clearing the barn of debris, and cleaning up and repairing some of the items salvaged from the house. By the end of that day, the barn space was almost livable as a new home.

That night they sat outside the barn, stoking the fire they had been cooking on, and talking in hushed tones. Jonathon broached the subject that he knew they needed to discuss.

"Tomorrow, I need to head back to town."

"Yes. I knew you would need to go soon."

Jonathon hesitated, and then continued. "I would like you to come with me."

María sat in her father's smoke-smudged rocking chair that she had pulled outside. She pulled her woolen shawl around her, rocked a bit, and then nodded.

"Yes. I suppose I should go into town too, and restock some supplies. The Lord knows I will be needing them." She paused. "I only hope that I will still have some credit with the merchants, now that . . . all this. . . ."

Jonathon watched her, then reached over to tentatively take her hand.

"María, I meant that I would like you to come with me . . . for good, now that you have no one else, and Don de León is . . . well. . . ."

"You mean leave my land? My home?" She shook her head vigorously and pulled her hand away. "Oh, no. I would never do that! My place is here, forever. Most of my family is buried right over there. I will never leave them to live anywhere else." She looked at Jonathon with a touch of anger. "How could you expect me to do that?"

Jonathon frowned at the fire, attempting to get his mind around several things at once.

"María, you must know that these people attacked your family for a reason. They want your land. They will stop at nothing to get it. Which means they will be back someday and finish what they began here." He chanced a glance at her, but her eyes were fixed on the fire, a stony expression on her face. "And you must know my other reasons." He paused, took a breath, and continued. "You must know that my feelings for you have never changed."

María stopped rocking, but continued to stare blankly into the fire.

"I love you, María. I loved you before, I love you still—and I always will."

"I know," she finally said, her voice small and barely a murmur as she stared into the flames. He waited a long while for her to say something else—anything else—but, after the prolonged silence, he stood up abruptly to go make his bed in the barn in one of the abandoned horse stalls.

As he rolled over in his bedroll that night, Jonathon angrily vowed to himself never to tell her his true feelings again.

#

Two days later he was back to his duties in Cimarron. As planned, he had brought María into town to resupply. At the livery stable, he negotiated for her the purchase of an old but serviceable wagon and a pair of older but fit mares to pull it with. It was there that he overheard men talking about a raid on the Indian village at Valley of the Utes several days earlier in retaliation for the recent attacks on some of the ranchos recently.

"How many were killed?" he asked the blacksmith.

"How many settlers, ya mean?"

"No. The Muaches . . . the Utes?"

"Oh hell, I don't know. Quite a few, I reckon, judging from the number of Injun scalps we brought back." The blacksmith chuckled, then stopped abruptly at the look on the deputy's face.

"Brought back? That's right . . . you were in that posse, weren't you?"

"Yeah . . . so what of it?" The blacksmith stood up to his full height and folded his arms in defiance.

"Nothing," Jonathon answered, and then looked over to the corner of the stable barn where a young boy of fourteen or fifteen was sweeping out a stall. Jonathon knew the boy and knew him to be a hard worker of good reputation. "Hey, boy," he called over. "Jim, isn't it?"

"Yes, Sir," the boy answered, coming over with his rake still in his hand. "Jim Withers, Sir."

"Well, Jim Withers. Just how much you get paid for this?"

"Dollar a month."

"I'll pay you six a month, plus room and board, if you come to work for me."

The blacksmith unfolded his arms and took a step forward. "Now, wait a minute!" Jonathon looked at him and smiled, but his eyes did not.

"But you have to come right now, Jim. This minute."

Jim looked from Jonathon's unwavering smile to his employer's scowl. "Six dollars?"

"Yes. In advance."

Jonathon opened his wallet, pulled out some bills, and held them up.

"You can't do that!" exclaimed the blacksmith, balling his fists.

Jonathon pulled his duster back, revealing the edge of his badge, and his Army Colt .45 below it.

"Yes, I believe I can." His smile had disappeared and his eyes had retreated into storm clouds.

The blacksmith backed down, turned, and stomped out of the barn.

Jonathon handed the bills to the boy. "Now, Jim, you go and tell your Ma that Jonathon Carter has hired you to be the full-time foreman at the Delgado Ranch, just north of town, if it's all right with her. Tell her you will come to town once a week to visit her, and you give her half of this pay right now and promise her she'll get half every month. Then you give her a big kiss, gather all your personables, and a gun if you own one, and meet me back over at the mercantile store in thirty minutes. You got all that?"

"Y-yessir!" Jim exclaimed, dropped the rake, and raced out the door.

After going to some of the merchants with María to help ensure that her credit was still good, at least for the next season, they met up with Jim. All three went back to the rancho and unloaded her wares. Before leaving, Jonathon handed her a good, but used, .45 pistol, which he had bought, along with a large supply of ammunition for it and her Winchester rifle.

"I promise you I will come out weekly to check on things," he told María finally, as he stepped up to his horse. Before he was able to get back into his saddle, she came up and gave him a long kiss on the cheek.

"You had better," she said, then turned, leaving him standing speechless and with a puzzled look on his face.

#

When he walked back into the Sheriff's office later, Jonathon found Sheriff Rinehart and Clay Allison playing a game of blackjack at his desk. He removed his gun belt, hung it up on a peg, and stared at them without speaking for a good long while.

"Well, if it isn't Deputy Squirrel, back from saving forlorn damsels and such."

"Shut up, Clay," Jonathon said, his voice even but with a dangerous edge to it. He then walked up to the edge of the desk and leaned down, placing the palms of both hands down on their playing area and looking them both alternately in the face.

"I do believe you are interrupting our game, Deputy," murmured Allison, working the words around his cigar.

"When were either of you going to bother to tell me about the people you murdered up in Ute Valley?"

"People? What people?" asked Rinehart. "You don't mean those Indians, do you?"

"Exactly the people I was referring to," said Jonathon, slapping the cards out of Rinehart's hands.

"Hey, now, that was entirely uncalled for!"

"You promised me you would not let things get out of hand up there—both of you," Jonathon said through clenched teeth. "How many died?"

Clay Allison squinted at his old friend and leaned back on two legs of his chair. "Well, things just got a mite confused out there, Jonathon. You know how the bloodlust gets some of those fellas. They saw an opportunity for some justice, and they took it."

"Justice! What sort of justice was that? I saw some of those scalps, hanging down at the livery stable, like some sort of trophies. The majority looked to be from women and old people!"

Allison set his cards down, then played with a photograph lying on the edge of Jonathon's desk.

"Did you even try to go look for the white enforcers? You know—the ones that actually carried out the Delgado murders?" Jonathon had stood up and paced back across the room, his hand rubbing the back of his neck in exasperation.

"Nah, lost their trail soon after," answered Rinehart, who stood up. He looked at Jonathon for moment, then went over and put a hand on his shoulder. "I know how all this must look, Son. But you gotta understand. It was like Clay here said. Things got completely riled up and out of hand so quick, it was over before I knew it."

Jonathon turned and looked at his boss. "Don't call me 'Son,'" he whispered dangerously, and shrugged off Rinehart's hand. "Any of those gray-headed scalps end up on your wall by any chance, Sheriff?"

Rinehart spluttered and fumed, then grabbed his hat and made for the door. "Gawd dammit, that was completely uncalled for, Jonathon—completely unnecessary! I would demand an apology, if I thought one would be forthcoming.

You and I will finish this conversation another time!" He opened the door and left in a huff, leaving the door ajar behind him.

"Well," Allison said, standing up slowly and adjusting his belt. "Guess that's my cue to be going also." He looked down at the photo still in his hand. "Say, Jonathon. Where did you get this from, anyway?"

Jonathon glanced at the photo. It was the one taken that night, years ago, at the Clifton House at Otero. He paused, remembering that it was the same night he had first laid eyes on María. He frowned, then waved the thoughts away. He stepped back to the doorway, grabbed his gun belt from the wall, and cinched it on. "Tom Stockton sent me a copy, sometime after it was made. Why? Didn't he send you one?"

"Why, no. He did not." Allison answered with a little indignation. He continued to trace the photo with his finger as he gazed at the five faces there gazing back at him. "If he had, I surely would have treasured it."

"Well, feel free to take that one," blurted Jonathon as he headed back out the door. "I, for one, no longer need the memories that are associated with that night."

CHAPTER 16
Fallen Star

(Present Day – Sangre de Cristo Mountains)

The horrific bear attack seemed to move in slow motion as Trent tried to run to Ben's aid. His legs felt as though weights had been tied around his ankles. The bear continued to trounce on Ben's back, grabbed a mouthful of his parka hood, and shook Ben back and forth like a dog with a chew toy. Other than that movement, it was impossible at this distance for Trent to see if Ben were even still alive.

He stopped for the briefest moment in utter helplessness, wondering for a second just what he thought he would do once he reached Ben and the bear—pummel it with his fists? Kick it off of Ben? He suddenly became aware of the girls screaming nearby and turned to see Jennifer and Ilsa standing just inside the doorway of the old cabin, hands to their mouths and eyes wide with terror. Trent waved them away from the door.

"Get back inside," he yelled. The last thing any of them needed was to have the bear's attention drawn to them. But one more glance at Ben's predicament let him know the beast was concentrating entirely on its prey. The attack was not letting up and blood speckled the snow-covered ground around Ben's body.

Trent looked again at the girls framed in the doorway. *The doorway! Of course!*

He came to his senses, no longer feeling entirely helpless, and bolted toward the cabin door. He didn't look back but imagined the bear stopping momentarily and watching him run past; the hairs on the back of his neck stood up as he could almost feel the bear's hot breath, as if the animal had already turned from Ben and come after this new running prey. Trent planted his feet and slid through the open doorway, pivoting as he did so, and stretching with his left hand as far as he could—toward his rifle that he knew was propped up just inside the doorframe.

As he grabbed the barrel he slid to a stop and fell to his knees right at the feet of the girls, who stared down at him in shock and fear. In one motion, he waved them back again, pulled the bolt action back and forward, chambering a round in the rifle, swung his torso around 180 degrees until he faced the doorway, and brought the rifle up to his shoulder.

The bear had indeed stopped its attack on Ben and had turned to ponder this new challenge, but had not, as Trent had imagined, run after him—yet. Instead, it merely stood there and frowned at Trent with its angry good eye and had its injured paw suspended in midair in front of it, as if contemplating its next move.

It seemed to make its decision, and only fifteen yards away now, it slowly advanced toward the cabin. It smacked its jaws loudly and Trent could hear its massive teeth clattering. Trent drew a shuddering, fearful breath, but then blew it out, and the fear went along with it. There was only one thing left to do. He aimed his rifle at the bear's face and began to squeeze the trigger.

Out of the corner of his eye, Trent may have detected a slight impossible movement from Ben but couldn't be sure, because the bear now demanded his complete attention. It moved steadily toward him, bloody saliva drooling from its lips as it pulled them back to bare huge snarling teeth.

At least it was now ignoring Ben.

Trent knew he couldn't wait any longer. He blew his breath out once more, held it, and pulled the trigger.

Inside the small space, the explosion of the rifle was deafening. The acrid odor of gun smoke filled the room, almost like a blessing, and for a moment Trent couldn't focus from the stinging in his eyes. A roar from the bear echoed and Trent could only assume that his bullet had missed and that the monster was still advancing. All of this went through his mind in the instant it took for him to chamber a new round. As his eyesight finally cleared enough he could again see the bear's massive head, shaking back and forth as if the beast were trying to clear its mind. The bear then looked back over in Ben's direction, seeming confused now. It took an uncertain step back toward Ben, although Trent could no longer see his friend past the bulk of the animal.

Trent centered the sights on the side of bear's face and fired again. He suddenly cocked his head to listen. He thought he had heard the simultaneous reports of two or three gunshots, but knew that wasn't possible, and that he must be hearing the echoes of his own rifle. He quickly chambered a new bullet and sighted on the bear once more.

But this time he didn't need to fire.

The bear continue to look away, back in Ben's direction, and slapped at its head like shooing away flies. It then stumbled once, turned back to stare at Trent, a bloody hole where its bad eye used to be, and a puzzled expression on its face. It swayed, swatted drunkenly at its face once more, and then collapsed in a heap with a monstrous sigh. Blood spread in a steady pool beneath its head as it blew out a deep, slow breath, then grew still.

But Trent and the girls were no longer watching the animal. Trent slowly stood up, his mouth open and the rifle moving away from his cheek as he lowered it. Behind the bear, three or four feet away, was Ben Ferguson, face streaming blood, propped on his elbows, and breathing hard. Later, Trent could never be sure whose bullets had felled the beast, because Ben was also aiming his smoking .45 Glock semi-automatic at the dead bear.

#

(Present Day – Cimarron, New Mexico)

"You know that those survivors are still out there. Time is of the essence, Agent de Jaager."

"Yes Sir, I will contact you when we find them."

"Find them and you will find what we're looking for." The line disconnected.

Britt de Jaager, the head of security for Laird Bouwmeester, the Third Minister of the Netherlands for Education, Science, and History, put the satphone back into her pocket and sighed. It was tragic that the minister had lost his life in this insane endeavor. *None of this should have happened.*

She paced and rubbed her eyes. Her mind swam with all of the consequences that were unfolding all around her, from what had begun as a simple operation. *Septum had demanded too much, pushed too hard, and now this . . . this fiasco! People were dead and probably more were going to die out there. And for what?*

She washed her face at the sink in the gas station women's room where she had secluded herself while taking the call, patted it dry, and stared at herself in the mirror—willing her accustomed icy core to rise up again. She pulled her weapon from her shoulder holster, checked the clip, then re-holstered it and zipped up her black leather jacket before running her fingers through her short blonde hair and pulling the door open.

She stepped into the brilliant morning sunlight that streamed over the rangeland from the east.

"Time to move, people!" she barked at the knot of men, similarly dressed in black commando gear, standing beside two black SUVs pulling flatbed trailers, each loaded with two large four-wheel-drive ATVs. The agents moved into action as one, jumping into the SUVs, and reserving the passenger seat of the lead vehicle for their AIC—Agent in Charge—Britt de Jaager.

Their wheels spun gravel as they pulled out of the gas station and headed out on State Highway 64, past the Cimarron town limits, and west toward the canyons and Ute Park. De Jaager chewed the fingernail on a forefinger and absently watched the foothills roll up to greet them. The stark devastation of a recent forest fire was still evident on both sides of the two-lane highway as their vehicles began to roll through the hilly curves.

Right or wrong, this ends today, she thought to herself.

#

(Sangre de Cristo Mountains)

By the time Trent and Jennifer had gotten to Ben, he had collapsed again unconscious. Trent gently removed the pistol from Ben's clinched fingers and pocketed it.

"Daddy!" Jennifer cried out. She had dropped to her knees and was gently touching his face and head.

"Don't move him quite yet," said Trent. "Need to check the extent of his injuries." He regretted his authoritative tone, but knew it was for his own benefit as well as Jennifer's. He still had adrenaline pumping and was trying to calm himself down from crisis mode.

The back of Ben's parka was in blood-soaked shreds where the bear's massive claws had ripped through the layers of Gore-Tex, padding, and shirts to flay Ben's flesh on his back. Trent knew that, in addition to the bleeding, there could be broken ribs, or worse, spinal injury. Better to render emergency treatment to his friend here rather than try to move him inside first.

"Go get me the emergency kits," he instructed.

"Kits?"

"Yes. Mine, and the one you and Ilsa brought from the chopper. We're going to need everything we've got left." Jennifer went to the cabin and Trent called after her. "And bring me a couple of spare shirts, or anything I can cut up for large bandages."

Trent and Jennifer began working gently but methodically on her father, who thankfully remained unconscious; they had no way to deaden any of the pain for him. Trent was able to cut away the remainder of Ben's jacket and clothing around the wound areas, and their first sight of the actual wounds made them both suck in their breath in shock. Jennifer started weeping and shaking until Trent reached over and grasped her arm gently. "Just stay with me, Jenn. He's going to be okay, but I'm really going to need your help here."

Jennifer nodded and swiped away her tears.

At some point, Ilsa had walked up and was standing behind them, watching. She nudged Trent with the toe of her boot and he looked up to see her holding a shirt out to him—her shirt.

"Can you use this?" she asked. Trent took the shirt, then noticed she had pulled her jacket around her to try and hide the fact that she had removed the shirt she had been wearing. Trent smiled and nodded to her.

"Thank you, Ilsa. Yes, this will help."

By the time they were finished, they had stopped the major bleeding and Trent had managed, with Jennifer's help, to firmly wrap Ben's ribs with strips of fabric cut from shirts and sleeping bags. When he was certain they had done all they could for the time being, he found a long piece of board from inside the cabin that was straight enough to use as a back brace. With Jennifer's help, they tied the board to Ben's back and legs, and then carefully and slowly rolled him onto his back on top of the board. They were then finally able to take a chance on moving him into the cabin. As they gently dragged Ben inside, he stirred, groaned, and fluttered his eyelids a few times. He moved his mouth to speak and raised one arm but uttered only an unintelligible whisper.

Jennifer leaned over him and washed his face gently. "It's okay, Daddy. I'm here. You're safe."

"Can you swallow something?" Trent asked him. Ben glanced at his former deputy and managed a brief nod. "Think so," he rasped. "Water. Need water."

Trent gave him some sips of water, then pushed four or five ibuprofen tabs into Ben's mouth and gave him more water. "Swallow these. They'll help."

"Isn't that an overdose of those?" Jennifer asked, slightly alarmed.

"No. It's what you would call a 'therapeutic dose;' hospitals and medics do it all the time, to help fight immediate trauma."

Ben tried to talk some more, but it sounded very painful.

"Don't try to talk right now, buddy," Trent said. "Lots of time to talk later."

"Bear? Dead?"

"Yes, he sure is, Deadeye—thanks to you and me." Trent smiled.

"What do you mean, 'you?' Your shot missed," Ben mumbled, then moaned and twisted his head back and forth in pain.

Jennifer stayed by her father's side, and after awhile found a safe place on his forehead to kiss him. But when he passed out again her tears flowed once more. Trent rushed over and checked Ben's vital signs.

"It's fine," he said. "He's actually sleeping now. He'll be okay," which Trent prayed wasn't a lie.

In his mind, he had already formulated a plan, which he shared with the girls later as the three of them sat around the fire eating a meal of canned beans and saltine crackers.

"I'm going to go ahead and hike down and find some help."

"No!" protested Ilsa.

"You can't leave us now," added Jennifer, pointing over to her sleeping father. "I mean, under the circumstances."

"If I don't go for help, your father has no chance at all to survive."

"But you just said he would be all right."

"Yes, and he will be all right—if we can get him to a hospital and some proper medical care. He's probably in shock; those wounds are likely to fester and who knows what infections could set in? We're not prepared to handle that. We've used up all our medical supplies as it is, and soon our food and water will be gone." He nodded at Ilsa's arm. "And you, young lady, are going to need some more attention to that arm and leg. Soon."

The girls were silent as Trent began to gather his things for the hike. He packed only one bottle of water and few of the crackers, leaving the remainder of the food and water for them.

"When your dad wakes up, get him to eat a little something. The beans will be great for protein for him. And make sure he drinks a lot. I melted some snow and poured it into some of the empty water bottles. But now that the snow outside is mostly melted, once this is gone, that's it. So pace yourselves with it."

"How long are you going to be gone?" Jennifer asked.

"Well, it shouldn't take me long to get to where I can get a cell signal. Maybe three, four hours. Then another two or three to get down to a ranch or someplace I can meet up with the emergency responders. Be nice if we can get a medevac unit in here, too."

"What's that?" asked Ilsa.

"A medical evacuation helicopter. We need to airlift you and Ben out of here, ASAP."

"No! No more helicopters!" she protested, her eyes wide.

"Ilsa," Trent said, patting her knee. "Your chopper was sabotaged—somebody wanted it to go down. That wasn't normal. Trust me, please. A medevac is the best way out of here."

He stood in the doorway, donning his jacket and pack, and looked over at the dead bear, and then up at the mid-afternoon sun.

"That thing's going to start stinking pretty soon, I'm afraid. You might even get some scavengers in here—some buzzards circling, maybe a coyote, or wolf."

"Wolves?"

"Well, only if they're hungry enough. They actually don't like to be too close to humans, so just you being here may keep them away—at least till I get back."

"And what if they don't keep away?" asked Jennifer.

"Well, you have your dad's rifle over there, for long range." Trent nodded at Ben's assault weapon leaning in the corner. "And you'll also have this." Trent reached into his pocket and pulled out Ben's pistol. "Here's your father's Glock. I've reloaded it. Ten rounds, hollow point .45s. Maximum stopping power at short range. You know how to use it, right?"

Jennifer nodded, took the semi-automatic, and pulled back the rack before slipping it into her own jacket. "Yes. Daddy taught me long ago."

"Good. I figured he would have. And here's a box of ammo." He picked up his rifle and shouldered it. "Well, if I don't go now, I'm going to lose too much daylight."

He stepped out the door but was suddenly stopped when Ilsa ran out and hugged him tightly with her one good arm. He put his hand on the back of her head and stood still until she slowly released her grip and looked up at him. She glanced back at Jennifer, who was standing in the doorway, and then whispered up at him. "You know they will kill us if they find us."

"That's not going to happen, Ilsa. I won't let it happen. Why, right now my people are probably on their way already."

Ilsa shook her head. "You don't know these people. My father didn't even trust them."

Trent looked at her with a frown. "Why?"

Ilsa stepped back, reached into an inner pocket in her jacket, and held something out to him. "Here. Take this with you. It is the reason my father died."

She pressed something into his hand. Trent looked down and saw that it was a thumb drive for a computer.

"What is this, Ilsa?"

"Never mind. Just take it. You must keep it safe. Show no one, not even your own people. No one is to be trusted."

Trent looked at her and cocked his head. "Then, just who am I to give it to?"

"Me, if I am still alive." She looked down, then continued. "And if I am not, then you will be contacted."

"And if I am contacted, how will I know I can trust that person?"

"They will use the name *Septum*. That's all I know."

"Septum," Trent repeated. "What's that?"

Ilsa pointed back at the thumb drive, where a small emblem was engraved in white. Trent looked closely at it and saw it was a small shell-like design with a cross-section cut out of it—the same emblem that was tattooed on the wrist of the body found in the grave at the ruins of the Clifton House several nights ago.

He shook his head. "I don't understand."

"Just trust me," she repeated, "and protect it with your life." She walked back to the cabin to stand with Jennifer.

Trent shrugged and placed the device in his pants pocket.

"I'll be back before you know it. You'll see. Then you can have this back."

As he retraced the path Ben and he had come down earlier, he turned at the top of the ridge to see Jennifer and Ilsa standing in the middle of the clearing, shading their eyes to watch him go. He raised his hand and waved, waited for them to wave back, and then turned and walked away.

He headed southeast, grateful that now he was at least walking downhill instead of up. Instead of going back to the helicopter, he struck due south after a couple of miles, knowing there were ranch roads that way. Within two hours he topped a ridge and stopped for a quick rest and a drink of water. He pulled his cell phone out and found a weak signal. He flipped it open and hit speed dial for the Colfax County Sheriff's Office.

"Sheriff's Department," came the familiar voice of Molly Swindoll, the dispatcher.

"Molly, you are a voice for sore ears!"

"Trent Carter? That you? You feeling okay? Not like you to sweet-talk a gal like that."

"Never better, Molly."

"So just where the hell are you guys? Maggie called all worked up this morning, said she hasn't heard a peep out of you."

"I know, I know. But just listen now, okay? It's life or death and my phone battery is almost gone."

Trent proceeded to briefly fill Molly in on the most important details, calming her voiced concerns when he told her about the bear attack on Ben, and urging her to get the word out to the other appropriate agencies and first responders. He advised her to dispatch armed response teams as well as a search chopper to pinpoint coordinates of the girls and Ben. He also told her that they would need the medical examiner's people up to take custody of the bodies at the crash site.

"And Molly, the perpetrators are still out here somewhere—probably some para-military types, ready for action. So, give everybody a good heads-up to come locked and loaded appropriately. These guys probably won't go down without a firefight."

"Got it, Trent. I'm on it. Oh, and Trent—"

"Yes?"

"May I say how good it is to have you back in the saddle?"

"Say goodbye, Molly."

"Goodbye, Molly," she answered, a twinkle in her voice.

Trent's phone died just as she disconnected. He took another swig of water before pushing on. He figured another couple of miles before he hit a road, then a little further to some sort of civilization.

He cut off his thoughts as he climbed out of another arroyo and came face to face with Angel, his gelding that had run off during the bear attack last night. The horse stood idly grazing, just a few feet away. It raised its head and looked at Trent curiously, then nickered at him and stepped over, and nuzzled the crook of Trent's arm fondly.

"Hey there, sweet boy—where have you been?" He chuckled and scratched Angel's forelock between his ears. "Bet that's the same thing you're wondering, huh? *Where have you been, old man?*"

Angel suddenly jerked his head up and turned, his ears perked, and his eyes stared into the near distance. He coughed once and shook his head.

"He is indeed a fine horse," came another familiar voice.

Trent started and looked in the same direction, where Spirit Warrior stood a few yards away smiling at him, with his arms at his side and his bow slung across his shoulders. Trent had had no feeling in his gut, nor had the scar on his forehead burned as it usually did before he saw a ghost.

"It is good to see that you do some things well."

"What do you mean?"

Spirit Warrior shook his head. *"It is not important. Something I was thinking about earlier, in another world."* The Indian ghost lifted his head to the sun and closed his eyes, as if letting the sun bathe him in its warmth.

Trent thought for a moment, and then suddenly asked in alarm, "What do you mean, 'in another world?' Is it the girls? Ben? Something has happened to them!" He took a step forward, but Spirit Warrior ignored him, seemingly content to bask in the warmth of the sun.

Trent turned and grabbed Angel's reins trailing on the ground. He noticed that Angel, of course, had no saddle. He was going to have to try to mount without the aid of a stirrup.

"Calm yourself, Salal. You must learn patience if you are to mount and ride like my people—like the Muache."

The warrior opened his eyes again and looked at Trent. *"But today, I fear it will take you too long to learn."* He pointed to the other side of the ridge, toward a tree with a large rock at its base, and smiled.

Trent scoffed and led Angel over to the rock. "I am so glad you have a sense of humor today, Ghost Warrior, if that's your name."

"My people call me Nämpäry. That is what I would prefer."

"And why do you call me *Salal?* I would prefer Carter." He pulled Angel around, and then got up on the rock, precariously balancing himself.

"Ah, yes. That explains it, then."

"Explains what?" Angel wasn't giving him much help and kept moving away. Trent slipped back off the rock.

Nämpäry thought quietly for a moment before answering. *"It is simply because you look, and act, a lot like a 'Salal,' of course."*

Trent shrugged, pulled Angel back over, and stepped up on the rock again. This time he was successful in throwing his leg over the animal's back and sliding on bareback. Angel trembled and shifted his legs in response to this unfamiliar riding style.

"Shhhh," Trent soothed him.

"*Shhhhh,*" Spirit Warrior—*Nämpäry*—echoed, but Trent's scar suddenly tingled, and he knew that the Indian was referring to something else—something of imminent concern. He looked at the warrior and saw him frowning and pointing to the west. Angel also perked up his ears again and looked in the same direction.

"*Do you hear that?*"

Trent listened hard for a moment, hearing nothing but the horse's slow breathing and his own heartbeat.

Then he heard it—the not too distant roar and intermittent accelerations of four-wheeler engines. He turned to ask Nämpäry another question, but the Spirit Warrior had disappeared.

CHAPTER 17
No Weapon Formed Against Us

(Anonymous Letter to the Editor)

November 5, 1873

The New York Sun
Re: The Territory of Elkins: The Petty Despotism That is New Mexico

Dear Sirs:

Please let it be known to your loyal readership that the population of an entire territory of these United States is currently at the mercy of a firm of sharp lawyers, namely Mssrs. Stephen Benton Elkins, Esq.; Thomas B. Catron, Esq., former Territorial Attorney for New Mexico; the Honorable (sic) Judge Joseph Palen; and Mr. Melvin Mills, among other possible higher ups; otherwise better known as the Santa Fe Ring. These men have collectively manipulated elections and court proceedings to benefit themselves financially and politically by illegally apportioning for themselves large chunks of the former Beaubien-Miranda Spanish Land Grant (now known as The Maxwell Land Grant) in New Mexico and Colorado.

Let it also be known that this collusion was made possible by the blatant disregard of the 1860 act of Congress that had previously validated the Maxwell Land Grant's original boundaries at 1,714,764 acres, vs. the 92,000 acres stipulated as the maximum by law for the old Spanish and Mexican land grants. In so ignoring the act, the Department of the Interior has illegally declared the Maxwell Land Grant null and void and its lands, therefore, within Public Domain. The immediate result has been the illegal and forced eviction of the rightful settlers from their lands.

Furthermore, it has come to this writer's attention that upon the Maxwell Land Grant and Railway Company's recent default of property taxes, Mr. Melvin Mills did personally bid over $16,000 to acquire said acreage, at scant pennies on the dollar, and then illegally resold the real estate to Mr. Catron for $20,000!

The above nefarious events and actions have now culminated to defraud hundreds of bona fide land owners who originally settled the properties represented to them by the esteemed prior owners of the Maxwell Land Grant, Lucien B. Maxwell and his wife, Luz Beaubien, with their express invitation to occupy the lands in perpetuity. But now these legal settlers, many descended from generations of noble Spanish blood, are being forcibly moved, under pain of death, from their hard earned lands!

This writer demands an outcry, both public and in the courts of the land, up to and including the United States Supreme Court, if necessary, to reinstate the validity of the original Maxwell Land Grant, to reinstate ownership to the rightful settlers under legal agreement with the Maxwell family, and to exact punitive damages against Mssrs. Elkins, Catron, Palen, Mills, and whomever else lurks in the long shadows cast by the Santa Fe Ring over the Western Territories of this great country!

Sincerely,
A Most Concerned Citizen

#

(November 12, 1873—Deldago Rancho, Ponil River Valley)

"When are you going to make that girl your woman, Salal?" Walking Elk's eyes followed María Delgado appreciatively as she walked from the barn to the corral, carrying a bag of grain for the horses. "If you don't soon, she will be past her ability to lie with you and give you sons."

Jonathon Carter and the young hired hand, Jim Withers, had been caulking the logs that would eventually complete the new walls of María Delgado's rebuilt house. Jim was mixing buckets of caulk and handing them up a ladder to Jonathon. The teenaged boy giggled and almost dropped the bucket before he caught Jonathon glaring down at him with distinct disapproval.

Walking Elk squatted near a small fire they were using to melt pitch for the work. He was wrapped up in a coarse trade blanket and happily gnawing on a chunk of peppermint candy with his few remaining teeth. It had become one of his favorite treats. His eyes twinkled up at Jonathon as he rocked back and forth on his heels. "If you don't lie with her, maybe I should."

Jim guffawed out loud, with no attempt to stifle it.

"What are you laughing at, boy?" Jonathon scolded down at Jim. He then turned to his old Ute friend. "And you," he stammered with a quick glance toward the corral before lowering his voice. "You stop being crude and just mind your own business."

Walking Elk turned and watched María again, squinting his eyes for a better look. Jonathon looked, too, pausing in his work. María poured the grain into two buckets, set them on the ground in front of the horses, and then stood back with one hand on her hip and the other pushing a long strand of dark hair from her eyes. She had never looked lovelier to Jonathon. Rebuilding her family's ranch had been very hard work and it was clear to him that hard work agreed with her very much. She turned, caught his eye, and smiled up at him as he quickly looked away in embarrassment. Out of the corner of his eye he thought he saw her shake her head slowly as she turned back to her work.

The days had already turned brisk and shorter, but if they kept hard at their labors, they would have the house roughed in before bad weather set in. At least, that was the goal. Jonathon paused and touched the corner of his mouth where he could still feel the kiss María had planted there a couple of weeks earlier—the kiss that had only confused his understanding of her feelings. Nothing especially tender had been spoken between them since then—only the necessary conversations to get the work done around the place and the *hellos* and *goodbyes* that bracketed his coming and going between the ranch and his regular job as a deputy sheriff. In the meantime, the stolen glances and the occasional shock of the touch of her sleeve against his arm as they passed each other during the workday only heightened his imagination that there might be something more at play here.

In short, her constant proximity was driving him to distraction; and Jonathon Carter, war veteran, seasoned military tactician, leader of men, and experienced lawman, was flustered and not entirely sure what to do about it.

The dilemma was solved for him the next afternoon when he rounded the corner of the barn, unbuttoning his shirt as he headed to the well to wash the sweat off, and ran right into María. He instinctively grabbed her shoulders with both hands to keep her from tripping backwards, and there they both stood, frozen in place, staring at one another and barely daring to breathe. Jonathon was about to pull away from her with an embarrassed apology when she slipped her hands under his open shirt, up the back of his damp shoulders, and pulled herself tight against him, her face lifted to his. The mixed earthiness of both their days' honest work filled his nostrils like the perfume of some magical elixir, and he abandoned himself to her embrace, encircled her tightly with his arms, and lifted her half off the ground until their lips met and melted away all doubt.

\#

By the first of the New Year, the log cabin was weathered in to the extent that it could be considered a real home again, and the repairs to the barn were finished. In the late spring of 1874, Jonathon Salal Carter and María Consuelo Delgado became man and wife in a small private ceremony in front of Reverend Tolby. Frank Springer and Jim Withers' mother stood up for them.

The newlyweds would have another year of bliss and relative peace before the land conflict that had been smoldering for a while finally erupted into a full blaze that would become known as the Colfax County War and change their lives forever.

\#

(June 19, 1875—Cimarron, New Mexico Territory)

It was noon and the temperature hovered in the mid 90s—hot by the standards of northern New Mexico in the late spring. Henri Lambert lugged a box of beer from the cellar storeroom into his saloon upstairs. He set it on the edge of the bar, breathing hard, and wiping the perspiration from his face with his handkerchief.

He looked around. Just thirty minutes ago, Lambert's saloon had been practically empty. But now, with even the hardiest souls being driven indoors to seek a reprieve from the sweltering heat outside, the saloon was gradually filling up with early customers.

At a corner table nearest the bar sat some of his regulars. Cruz Vega, his uncle Juan Francisco Griego, and Clay Allison had been drinking and playing cards for the better part of an hour, and judging by their occasional outbursts Lambert could see that they were already promising to become troublesome.

"Dammit to hell, Clay!" Vega threw his cards on the table, folding his hand in disgust, sat back, and caught Lambert's eye. "Henri! If you please," he called over, spreading his hands magnanimously to indicate a new round of drinks for the table. Lambert frowned and then complied with the order, pouring the gamblers fresh whiskey.

"Thank you, my good man," slurred Vega, tossing Lambert a dollar coin dismissively. Lambert caught the coin, pocketed it, and went back to the bar. As bad a poker player as Cruz Vega was—and as much as he drank—at least he was paying in cash these days, although no one seemed to know exactly where he was getting his money. Some conjectured that the former vagrant and ne'er-do-well had struck it rich with some secret gold or silver mine over near E-town. Others gossiped that Vega had been dabbling in some of the political intrigue permeating the county lately—namely, selling names and information to the shysters and land speculators who made up the notorious Santa Fe Ring—a dangerous activity, to say the least, in Lambert's opinion. If it were true, it meant that Cruz Vega was playing both sides of the conflict. It was well known that Vega's family, the Griegos on his mother's side, were long-time staunch opponents of the Ring, standing against it whenever possible on the side of the colonos, the settlers, most of whom had made their land deals with Lucien B. Maxwell himself, and usually on a handshake. And therein lay the problem: lately, those handshakes were not standing up in the courts, which more often than not were controlled by the shady attorneys representing the interests of the Santa Fe Ring.

Lambert shrugged and got back to his work, pulling beer bottles from the box and lining them up on the shelf under the bar. He knew that they would soon be sold and he would be shuffling back down to the cool cellar to retrieve more—and smiled. This day was shaping up to be a busy and most profitable one.

Or so he believed.

#

Griego held his cards at table level and peered across the top of them at Clay Allison, trying to read him. Unlike Griego's nephew, Allison was a cautious card player, a prudent better, and a good bluffer. Griego was aching to know what cards Cruz had folded with, and he glanced over at his nephew, who slouched back in his chair, bored and slurping his whiskey. He kicked the side of his nephew's boot under the table. Vega just frowned without looking at him and moved his foot out of the way.

Worthless. At least he could have given me a clue.

"Well, Pancho," Clay murmured. "What's it going to be?"

Griego looked back to his hand. Two fives and two aces. He peered again at

Allison, who was impossible to read and just sat there, one arm slouched lazily over the back of his chair, staring back at him blankly.

Again, impossible to read. "Don't call me *Pancho*, Clay."

"As you wish—but then it's *Mister* Allison to you . . . and the bet is still five dollars," Allison continued. "Are you calling, or throwing in the proverbial towel? I mean, five dollars *is* a lot of money, except to some people, I suppose." Here he shifted his gaze over to Vega, who reacted as he expected.

"Ain't a lot of money," Vega scoffed, bleary-eyed and gulping down the remainder of his whiskey. "Always more where that come from."

"Well said, Mr. Vega. And that *is* something that does interest me no end. Just where does such a fine upstanding citizen as yourself come up with your finances?"

Cruz grew suddenly reticent and looked quickly away from Allison's scrutiny. Instead of answering, he turned back toward the bar. "Hey! More whiskey over here. Can't you see we're working up a thirst?"

Griego tried to catch his nephew's eye, but to no avail. He studied his cards one last time and kept his face passive. *Two fives, two aces. A hard hand to fold on.* But if Allison had three of anything, it was done. He looked at the pot. Two rounds of betting, including one wild raise from Vega, had increased it already to thirty-three dollars. He fingered his chips and made his decision. Allison had to be bluffing, and if so, two could play that game.

"Five—and I raise another five," he said, tossing in the appropriate chips.

Clay Allison's left mustache twitched, just slightly, and Griego allowed a brief smile to appear at the corner of his mouth. Allison leaned to the table slowly, his eyes not wavering from Griego's, and moved as if he were about to throw in his hand. He then paused, running his forefinger lightly along the upper edge of his cards, and pushed ten dollars worth of chips into the pile.

"Call," he said softly.

Griego's smile vanished. He slowly laid his cards face up on the table and sat back, waiting. Allison raised his eyebrows and whistled softly.

"Two pair, aces high," he said, and then began casually tossing cards on the table, one at a time: a ten of spades, a queen of hearts, and three twos. "Nice hand, Pancho. But here sit I, with my lonely little twos." He chuckled and pulled his winnings toward him.

Griego sat back, defeated. He finished his drink, straightened his tie, and stood up proudly. "That taps me out for now," he said, and turned to leave.

"Hey, *Tío*, . . . want me to loan you some money?"

Griego looked down at his drunken nephew. "You drink too much," he said in disgust.

"Shut up, *Viejo!* You are just jealous, now that I am richer than you."

Without warning, Griego swept his leg out and caught his nephew's chair by the nearest leg and kicked it out from under him. Vega hit the floor soundly on his butt like a sack of rotten potatoes. He shook his head, tried to find his legs, and fell down again.

"You disgust me," Griego growled, then reached a hand down to help his nephew up.

"Some trouble over here?" All three men turned to look incredulously at the U.S. Army sergeant who had materialized behind them. The soldier's thumbs were hooked into his gun belt. He was tall, his uniform smart and clean, and his boots freshly shined and black—just like the sergeant himself.

Allison and Griego—both Confederate veterans—stared in shock at the soldier's face, then at two more Negro cavalrymen who had just entered the saloon behind him. The saloon had grown deathly quiet, with only the swish and clatter of the swinging doors to break the silence.

Henri Lambert tried to intervene. "No—no trouble here, soldier," he stammered, moving from behind the bar, wiping his hands on an apron. "I believe these gentlemen were just having a . . . family disagreement. Isn't that right, Mr. Griego?"

Francisco Griego said nothing and stood staring at the colored soldiers. He had heard of the 9th Cavalry being stationed down at Fort Union, barely a day's ride from here, and that the 9th was rumored to be all Negro, save for their white officers, but he had barely believed it—until now.

Cruz Vega stumbled to his feet, still exasperated. He grabbed his hat, and slapped his thighs with it. "Yeah!" he spluttered. "Just a family discussion is all." He wiped his mouth with the back of his hand. "Nothin' for you boys to get in the middle of."

Clay Allison chuckled and sat back slowly. "That's right," he drawled, laying on his Tennessee accent a bit thicker than usual. "Ya'll *boys* best just go about your own business." He leaned back in his chair and smiled up at the soldiers. His face suddenly took on an element of surprise and he slapped his knee.

"Why, I just realized why you boys are here! Ya'll are here to celebrate!" Clay looked around the bar at everyone. "Folks, today is June 19th—*Juneteenth!*" There was a murmuring around the room, but no one seemed to understand what Allison was referring to—except for the three Negro soldiers, who exchanged uncomfortable looks.

"Sure!" Allison continued. "Juneteenth. I mean, that's what you people call it, isn't it? The day Abraham Lincoln freed you *darkies?*"

The black sergeant shifted from one leg to another, peered closely at Allison, and rubbed his jaw. "Say, aren't you Clay Allison?" he asked slowly.

Allison twitched his eyebrows remained silent. The sergeant glanced again at the two other soldiers.

"We've heard complaints about you, *Sir,*" the sergeant continued, cautiously. Allison rocked his chair back down fully onto the floor. The smile slowly left his face and his hands disappeared under the table.

Griego suddenly stepped forward. "I have had enough of all this. Stand aside, Son," he ordered, and attempted to push past the black soldiers. The sergeant placed one hand on the butt of his pistol and the other on Griego's forearm. The other two soldiers stepped apart, nervously.

"I'm afraid you won't be going anywhere, Sir . . . not until we clear this all up."

Griego looked slowly at the soldier's hand. "Remove your black hand from me . . . *boy!*" he muttered between clenched teeth, his voice low and menacing. A chair or two scraped in the background, but the room remained otherwise silent and focused on the three soldiers and three card players, all of whom stood momentarily frozen in place. Suddenly, one of the other soldiers hesitantly drew his pistol and cocked it. Griego saw the sergeant's eyes roll back in regret and felt the man's fingers tighten his grip on his arm.

Griego took one quick step back, pulled his pistol with his free hand, aimed it at the nervous soldier who had drawn his gun, and fired, putting a bullet squarely between the man's eyes. He flipped his other hand and grabbed the sergeant's forearm in turn as the man suddenly tried to jerk himself free. In the same fluid instant, Griego turned his pistol to the second soldier and shot him once in the throat. By this time, the sergeant was shouting and flailing desperately to get free, which Griego finally allowed by suddenly letting go of his arm and simultaneously firing three shots point blank into the man's belly and chest.

All of it happened within five seconds, and all three soldiers hit the floor at roughly the same moment.

Henri Lambert fell back against the bar in shock, wringing his apron. Cruz Vega stared at his uncle, his mouth working soundlessly. Clay Allison flopped back in his chair, tipped his hat back, and gave another low whistle.

"Damn, Pancho," he said, admiringly. "Couldn't have done better myself!"

Griego reholstered his weapon, straightened his hat, and headed out the double doors. "Well, I sure noticed you did nothing to help, Clay." He paused at the door, turned to look at Allison, and then nodded at the bodies on the floor. "Almost like you hoped that *I* would be the one lying there in a growing pool of my own blood."

Allison said nothing. He smiled and idly flipped silver coins from one hand to the other.

"Naw, I had your back, Pancho. But I knew you didn't need my help."

Griego snorted. "Well, then, when they come looking you can tell them they know where to find me." He turned to leave, and then stopped once again, his hand on the door.

"And Clay," he said softly. Allison stopped flipping his coins and looked up at him. This time, the smile was gone. "Stop calling me *Pancho*. That's for my friends."

#

(July 15, 1875—Santa Fe, New Mexico Territory)
"Gentlemen, I am so very pleased you could find time out of your busy schedules to meet with me today. Now would either of you care to enlighten me as to what the holy hell this means, exactly?"

The two attorneys glanced at the copy of the *New York Sun* that the governor had just picked up from the top of his desk, then quickly at one another and back up to the governor's frowning face.

Governor Samuel Beach Axtell had been in office for only a few weeks, having been appointed to the Territory of New Mexico by the executive order of President Ulysses S. Grant upon the untimely death of Governor Marsh Giddings in June. Attorneys Stephen Elkins and Thomas Catron (Elkins' brother-in-law) stood in front of Axtell's desk like errant schoolboys caught pilfering candy from a jar. Each of them had met the new governor in passing, but not officially, and certainly had not yet determined the man's position on the political issues—at least the ones they were personally interested in.

Catron pulled the newspaper cautiously over and picked it up. "Perhaps, Sir," he stammered. "If we could peruse the article in question . . ."

"The article in question, Mr. Catron, is the one centered on the page there in front of you. You should not be able to confuse it—Sir—as it is the only letter to the editor that mentions both of you gentlemen by name." Governor Axtell slowly sat down and flipped opened a nearby cedar box. "Cigar?" he offered magnanimously. When they both shook their heads, he removed a *cubano* for himself and lit it. "I am assuming you both have seen the article, but I will indulge you. So, please take your good, sweet time to refresh your memories before answering my question."

Elkins glanced over Catron's shoulder at the newspaper and cleared his throat. "Governor Axtell, I am sure this is what we in political circles call a disgruntled voter, and can be easily explained away as. . . ."

"Explained away, Mr. Elkins? Pray, how do you explain away a New York newspaper with a circulation of at least 200,000 readers? How do you explain away the tarnished reputation of this office I have unwittingly walked into? And how do you explain away this—this so-called Santa Fe Ring, which apparently operates with complete impunity, and evidently within earshot of this very office?"

Elkins opened his mouth to protest, but Axtell cut him off with a wave of his hand. "Mr. Elkins, I am well aware of your political background and expertise, your time as territorial district attorney, and your current tenure as territorial delegate to the United States Congress." Axtell paused and took a deep puff of his expensive cigar. "Quite a blossoming résumé, Sir. But do not, gentlemen, dare to misjudge my own tenure in politics, nor my experience in navigating the polluted streams of intrigue frequented by such smooth-tongued serpents as yourselves." He puffed his cigar, relishing his rhetoric, and then indicated the chairs behind them. Catron and Elkins stole glances at one another, and then slowly sat.

"Governor," said Catron cautiously, "territorial politics being what they are, I would not dare to question your astuteness in seeing through the vagaries of the problems we have been dealing with here, but I would hasten to suggest to you that a few of us here have hit upon a fair and lenient process of handling these squatters. . . ."

"Bullshit."

"Um, excuse me, Sir?"

"You heard me, Mr. Catron. I did not stutter or mince words, as you, on the other hand, are clearly fond of doing."

"Sir, I think what Mr. Catron was trying to say. . . . "

"What your brother-in-law is trying to say, Mr. Elkins—yes, I am well aware of the familial relationship between you—is that this previously quiet and questionable scheme that you two among others, I hazard to guess, have dreamt up to defraud the good citizens of Colfax County of some valuable real estate, is no longer quiet—I mean, 'territorial politics' being what they are."

The two attorneys stared at him, chagrined.

"Almost what we should call a 'family affair,' is it not?" Axtell continued into the void of their silence, "I mean, given your relationship?"

"Governor, I feel our family ties to each other have little bearing. . . ."

"Mincing words again, Counselor." Governor Axtell frowned and pantomimed cleaning the wax out of one of his ears. "And completely missing my point, which is that I am afraid I just can't understand what you're trying to say." He leaned forward and placed both hands flat on the desk. "So, please allow me to paraphrase your bullshit, won't you? You two, and god knows how many others, have stumbled upon an amazing opportunity dropped right into your laps by the misguided efforts of the Department of the Interior in ignoring federal law—of acquiring thousands, if not millions, of mineral-rich acres of the Maxwell Land Grant, which straddles northern New Mexico and southern Colorado; am I on track so far?"

Both the other men started to speak but were cut off again.

"And it seems that said land is currently occupied by, shall we dare say, *squatters*—your terminology, not mine?" Catron and Elkins both nodded slowly.

"Don't forget the miners," said Catron.

"And the Indians," Elkins hastened to add.

"Ah, yes—the Indians," said Axtell. "I shall get back to them momentarily. But you say that said squatters are in the process of being properly served and evicted?"

The two men nodded slowly, now suspicious of the governor's tone.

Axtell reached over, snatched the newspaper out of Catron's hand, and spread it open on his desk again.

"And it would appear, if my other sources are correct on this, that there are certain other parties involved who are, shall we say, in opposition to your questionable legal actions in these matters?"

"Er . . . what such actions would those be, Sir?"

"Such as your effective manipulation of territorial policies and partitioning of the Spanish and Mexican land grants—a direct violation, by the way, of the Treaty of Guadalupe Hidalgo—for the benefit of you and others, *Gentlemen!*"

The two attorneys squirmed in their seats.

"And are my sources also correct that these so-called opposition parties have proven difficult to deal with efficiently and, um . . . legally?"

"Well, Sir," began Catron, after thinking hard for a moment. "Your sources do seem to be well informed and somewhat accurate." He glanced at Elkins, then reached over and tapped the newspaper article with a forefinger. "We believe that a certain preacher by the name of Franklin Tolby, among others, has been inciting these settlers. . . . "

"Again . . . you mean *squatters,* do you not?"

"Um, yes. Squatters. If I may continue, Governor. . . ?"

"Oh, please do. I insist." Axtell sat back and steepled his fingers on his chest.

"Indeed, we believe Reverend Tolby is the author of this letter and many others written to the New York papers, to the utter embarrassment of our fair territory."

"Hmm, yes; and to the utter embarrassment of you and your cronies, too, no doubt."

"Governor, I don't see how. . . ."

"What you do and do not see, Mr. Elkins, is of little concern to me." The governor leaned forward slowly, pointing his cigar at them. "What is of interest to me is just how this so-called Santa Fe Ring of yours intends to continue to exploit this amazingly large loophole it has found while now under the scrutiny of the world press." Governor Axtell leaned back slowly in his chair and studied his cigar. "You mentioned the Indians earlier, Mr. Elkins."

"Indians, Sir?"

"Yes. Indians." Governor Axtell took a puff of his cigar and watched the smoke as it escaped his lips. "Do you happen to know, Gentlemen, exactly which tribes currently occupy which specific lands within the region we are discussing?"

"Sir," began Elkins, "I think you are referring to the Ute and the Arapaho tribes who live on some particularly choice properties in the valleys and foothills near Baldy Mountain."

"Baldy Mountain?"

"Yes, Sir."

"I have heard of it. Where the gold is?"

"Yes, Sir. I believe a good amount of precious ore is still being mined in and around there."

"Well, gentlemen," Axtell leaned forward and referred to another page of the newspaper. "Are you aware that Lucien B. Maxwell is reportedly not in very good health?"

Catron and Elkins exchanged looks, failing to see the connection.

"No, Sir. I had not heard this news," answered Catron.

"No, not in good health at all. In fact, not expected to live much longer, it seems."

"I am truly sorry to hear that," said Elkins.

"Bullshit, again, Mr. Elkins," said Axtell, leaning forward and punching the air with his cigar. "I am certain that you couldn't give a good doodley-squat over Maxwell's pending demise. But I am about to tell you why you, indeed, should— that is, if either of you are still interested in—how did we say it earlier? *Exploiting* the opportunity before us."

"I am still unsure what you mean. . . ."

"Shut up, Catron, and I shall enlighten you."

"Yes, Sir."

"Fortunately for us all, I do have my other sources." Axtell pulled open a desk drawer and retrieved a small notebook, which he now flipped open, thumbed a few pages, and squinted at some writing. "I suppose neither of you have ever heard of a special deed that is rumored to have been drawn up by Lucien B. Maxwell a few years back, granting to the Ute and Arapaho the lands that they currently occupy in Colfax County and part of Colorado Territory?"

Catron and Elkins looked at the governor with utter shock on their faces.

"A deed that was executed by the Maxwells' signatures, but that seems to have never been properly recorded?"

"Um, no . . . No, Sir," the two attorneys answered simultaneously.

"Of course not." Axtell sighed deeply, put his cigar out in an ashtray, and leaned forward.

"Gentlemen, as it appears that neither of you have exactly been the wealth of information I called you both here to learn—indeed, it has obviously been the other way around—might I suggest that one critical strategy you might consider, in carrying your plans forward, would be to pay Mr. Maxwell a timely visit to express your concerns for his health—and to, possibly, ferret out the whereabouts of this mysterious, and quite dangerous, 'Ute' deed?"

"Dangerous, Sir?"

"Yes, quite dangerous. Since I am now doing much of the thinking for the both of you, imagine, for a moment, how muddied the waters might be if someone, somewhere, were to produce such a deed to such valuable lands and the minerals they harbor, and bring it forth in the courts?"

Axtell looked from one to the other of them.

"Um, am I mistaken, gentlemen, that you *are* both attorneys?"

The brothers-in-law colored slightly.

"Yes," said Elkins. "We can see your concern quite clearly, Governor."

Axtell slapped his desk and leaned back. "Good! Now let's talk about the others before you leave."

"Others, Sir?"

"Others who have allegedly sided with this Reverend Tolby. Give me some names." Catron and Elkins looked at one another.

"Why, yes," answered Elkins. "We know of several names—Tolby, of course, then there's William Morley, the President of the land grant company; Mr. Frank Springer, an attorney and rancher from back east; a Señor Juan Francisco Griego. . . ."

"And a particularly nasty character by the name of Clay Allison," blurted Catron. "A notorious gunman, I might add."

"Robert Clay Allison? I have heard of him. A former Confederate officer, was he not?" Catron shrugged and Elkins nodded. Governor Axtell looked from one to the other, heaved a sigh, pushed back from his desk, and stood up. He walked to the window and drew a heavy drape aside, peering down to the busy market plaza of Santa Fe below, where merchants worked under the shade of massive cottonwoods that protected them from the hot afternoon sun, noisily hawking their wares of native jewelry and blankets, vegetables, and tools. He reflected that money was continuously trading hands, day in and day out, all day long—a time-honored activity carried on in one of the oldest marketplaces of the country.

"So, tell me, Gentlemen. Do you have plans to silence these detractors and continue to maximize the potential that seems to have presented itself in Colfax County?"

Elkins touched his brother-in-law's arm as if to caution him. Catron shook the hand away. "Yes, Governor," he said to Axtell, who continued to look out the window. "We intend to hire someone to. . . ."

Governor Axtell whirled around, shaking his head and wagging a finger. "I merely asked if you have a plan. I do not want to hear the particular nasty details you may have dreamed up, Mr. Catron!"

Elkins squeezed the bridge of his nose between his thumb and forefinger.

"Yes, of course, Sir," said Catron. "My apologies, Sir."

Axtell moved back to his desk. "What you do, gentlemen, is on your shoulders and yours alone. You will keep me fully informed, *but,*" he paused and mashed his cigar out in a decorative pottery ashtray, "you will also take great pains to keep this office, and my territorial government, entirely out of these highly questionable affairs of yours. Do I make myself clear, Gentlemen?"

"Yes. Very clear," answered Elkins. "Thank you, Governor Axtell." He stood to leave and touched Catron's shoulder, indicating that he should do the same. Axtell stopped them at the door.

"Concerning Mr. Allison and his friend, Señor Griego. I just may be of some help to you."

The two attorneys looked puzzled.

Axtell continued. "I have just recently learned that those two particular *gentlemen* were recently involved in the shooting deaths of some members of the 9th Cavalry from Fort Union?"

"Cavalry, Sir?"

"Not just any cavalry—the *9th.*"

Still no response.

"Surely even you gentlemen have heard of the *Buffalo Soldiers?*"

"Oh, yes. You mean the Negro cavalry, Governor. "

"Precisely."

"Yes, Sir. Well, I heard that these soldiers were provoked by Señor Griego into a gunfight—over a card game, I believe. Tragic incident, just tragic."

"And am I to understand that Señor Griego and his family have been, up until now, sympathetic to these squatters we have been discussing?"

Catron scratched his beard and nodded. "Yes, Governor, he surely has. He and his family have been most adversarial to our cause."

"I understand that Señor Griego is, even now, languishing in jail, awaiting trial for these murders. Now, what do you suppose his attitude might be toward your efforts if he were to, say, suddenly receive some sort of *benefit* in exchange for his shifting his allegiances, as it were?"

"*Benefit,* Sir?"

"Benefit—as in, say, a pardon for his crimes."

Elkins shrugged. "Hard to say, Sir."

"But it might be worth a shot," added Catron quickly, eager to agree with the Governor.

"Yes, *worth a shot;* an interesting turn of phrase there, Mr. Catron."

"My apologies, Governor. I did not presume to mean. . . ."

"Presume as much as you like, Mr. Catron. Allow me to ponder the matter for a while. It would be a simple formality of penning just the right letter. . . ." Governor Axtell fingered a sheaf of blank letterhead he kept available in a nearby basket on the corner of his desk. "If Griego could be turned, might he be put to good use for, say, whittling down your so-called Enemies List?"

Catron's and Elkins' cheeks colored. They continued to stand uncomfortably near the door.

"Good day, Gentlemen," Axtell said in dismissal, then looked up once more. "Oh, and of course, Gentlemen, whatever other successes you might enjoy from this point forward in this . . . enterprise, I trust you will remember your friends here in Santa Fe from time to time. The wheels of government do turn slowly, unless they are occasionally well greased."

CHAPTER 18
Greater Is He Within

(Present Day – Sangre de Cristo Mountains)

Britt de Jaager gunned her 4-wheeler and topped the ridge before braking to a stop. She stood up on the footboards, brought her field glasses up to her eyes, and swept the rugged ravines and pine-laden ridges that rose ever more precipitously to the north. Two other 4-wheelers slid to a stop, one on either side of her, their riders likewise scanning the area with binoculars. She had left a fourth man with their big SUVs at the end of the county road below, and it had been slow but steady going as they had ridden and climbed at least two thousand feet from there. The snow was several inches thick at this elevation, and they had cut the trail of several footprints a few miles back that were headed this way—footprints made by different people at different times, which concerned her.

De Jaager lowered her glasses, adjusted the assault rifle slung on her shoulder, and sighed. It shouldn't be long now, but she needed to find these girls quickly or there would be hell to pay.

And just who else were they about to find up here?

She glanced at her men, motioned them all forward, and gunned her engine.

#

Jennifer Ferguson tended to her father's wounds as best she could. He moaned as she washed his fevered face with a wet cloth and his eyelids fluttered.

"Daddy, drink this," she said, carefully tipping the mouth of a water bottle between his lips. He roused himself enough to take a few sips, coughed weakly, and lay back on his side with a groan.

"What happened? I feel like shit."

"Do you remember anything, Daddy?"

Ben thought for a moment, shook his head weakly, and then smiled up at his daughter. "Just remember finding you guys. Then everything's just a blur." He frowned and looked off in the distance. "But something really bad happened, didn't it?" He suddenly got a panicked look on his face and rose up again with a grimace of pain. "Trent! Where is he? He okay?"

"He's just fine, Daddy. He went for help. Remember? He's been gone a couple hours now."

"Oh, I should've gone with him." Ben tried to throw his blanket off, but excruciating pain tore through him so that he collapsed back on the ground. "What the hell?" he exclaimed.

"Daddy, you shouldn't move. You've lost too much blood."

Ben lay still, staring at the old cabin wall, trying to remember. His back felt as if it were on fire and every bone in his body felt cracked. "Was I shot? Attacked? By who?" He looked at Jennifer imploringly. She pulled the blanket back over him and nodded out the doorway. Ben followed her gesture and squinted until he saw a huge furry carcass lying a few yards outside.

"Bear?" he asked, still unsure of what he was seeing. Jennifer nodded, then tried to smile.

"Took both Mr. Carter and me to drag it off of you, after you both shot it."

"Shot it?"

Ben furrowed his eyebrows, confused, and then raised them as horrific memories came flooding back, such as that of the freight train he thought had barreled into him. He started at footsteps approaching and then relaxed as he recognized Laird Bouwmeester's daughter, Ilsa, at the doorway with a small armful of firewood. As she stooped to stoke the fire, he noticed that her other arm was in a sling and she herself sported a few bruises on her face and arms.

"Guess I'm not the only one who's a little worse for wear," he said evenly. She shrugged, looked into the fire, and adjusted the sling around her broken arm and clenched her teeth, as if needing to feel the pain for a moment.

Ben watched her, recalling that Trent had cautioned him about the girl. Then softened a little as he remembered the dead people they had found at the crash site, one of them being her father. "Ilsa," he croaked. "I'm so sorry about your dad."

"It certainly wasn't your fault, Mr. Ferguson. You did all that you could. I know."

"Coulda tried to find you both all the quicker. Maybe avoided him getting . . . well, you know."

"Yes. Getting shot—*murdered!*" She turned and gazed back into the fire. "Bastards," she whispered finally, under her breath.

Ben closed his eyes and lowered his head to the makeshift pillow Jennifer had made for him from a wadded-up jacket. The heat from the fire felt good as it soaked into his aching body and he tried to remain as still as he could with his throbbing wounds, willing himself to pass out again.

But it was not to be, as they all three suddenly raised their heads, eyes widened in alarm, as the distant whine of approaching engines drifted to them from somewhere nearby.

#

De Jaager slowed her 4–wheeler to a crawl as it spilled out of an arroyo and rounded a corner to reveal an old wreck of a cabin about a hundred yards away, its roof caved in and encroached upon by an overgrowth of scrub oak and other trees. She waved her arm at her side to signal the others to slow, then stopped entirely and cut the engine. She stepped from her vehicle and looked cautiously around, not seeing anyone at first. She trained her binoculars on the crumbling shack at the other end of the ravine, where afternoon shadows from the pine forest were just now beginning to throw shade over the ruins. A telltale finger of smoke meandered through the exposed roof openings, but nothing stirred. A few feet away from the door lay what looked to be the body of a bear. It wasn't moving. Several sets of tracks led to and from the area.

De Jaager surveyed the scene, trying to put two and two together, but the pieces didn't all fit. She didn't like what she saw. Too quiet. If it were just the two girls, they would be exhausted, maybe injured. That would explain the silence. But what of the dead bear? De Jaager was no avid hunter, but she could tell that the animal had not been dead that long; which meant someone had to have dispatched it, and in short order; which also meant someone had to have been adequately armed to do so.

And if so, that someone might have her in their gun-sights at this very moment.

She wet her lips, lowered the glasses to let them dangle from the strap around her neck, and knelt slowly behind the scant cover of her 4-wheeler. She unslung her weapon, checked the breech, chambered a round, and took it off safety.

"Hello," she finally called out, her voice echoing back at her after a second. "Anyone down there?"

Silence.

"We're here to help."

Nothing but the trail of campfire smoke and more silence.

"Want us to flank the cabin?" asked one of de Jaager's men. He clutched his rifle anxiously, ready for action. Britt shook her head and held out a hand to signal the agents to stay put. She didn't need bullets to start flying without having some answers first.

"Ilsa?" she called out, finally. "Are you in there? Are you okay?"

Britt waited a few more moments before taking a deep breath and standing up. "Ilsa, it's me, Britt. No need to be frightened. I'm coming down."

She held her weapon at port arms and stepped out, moving steadily forward. "Stay here," she cautioned her men.

"What if they start shooting?" asked the anxious one.

"Then I will probably be dead and you will then be in charge, won't you?" she snapped.

She turned and continued toward the cabin, crouching slightly into a military stance of advance, and called out once more as she shortened the distance to the cabin. "Ilsa, it's Britt. I'm coming in. It's going to be okay."

She crouched even lower as she came within just a few feet of the cabin wall, took a deep breath, then suddenly trotted forward until she could flatten herself against the wall. Her heart was now racing, more from the unaccustomed altitude than from anything else, and she held her weapon up to an aiming position, her finger steady against the trigger guard, ready to slip quickly onto the trigger if needed. She blew out three short breaths, held the last one, and lunged around the corner to the doorway, where she stopped and aimed into the dim interior—and straight into the muzzle of a Glock .45 semi-automatic pistol.

The muzzle was only two feet away from Britt's face and was being aimed by Jennifer Ferguson, that local sheriff's daughter whom Britt remembered from the governor's reception. By the way that she held the Glock, it was obvious that Jennifer was no stranger to firearms. Ilsa was standing behind the girl, as if for protection, with fear in her eyes. Britt likewise continued to point her weapon at Jennifer, ready for anything. It was a standoff, but de Jaager knew that, at this close proximity, if either one of them fired now, the other would get off at least one shot on reflex and they would probably both have their heads blown off.

Her eyes glanced quickly left and right, assessing the remaining scene; a man lay in the shadows, unconscious near a small fire. She couldn't identify him from here, but he seemed in a bad way. No one else was present. Britt kept her rifle trained on the girls, but uncurled the fingers of her left hand from the barrel and held it up slowly in a sign of caution.

"I think you need to lower your weapon," she said more calmly to Jennifer.

"You first *murderer!*"

#

Trent crossed a few more arroyos and climbed three long ridges on horseback, backtracking uphill before he crossed the trail of three 4-wheelers in the snow. He pulled Angel up short, reached over, and patted the animal's neck. It was warming up in the early afternoon sun but still cold enough at this altitude so that the gelding blew fog with his breath.

"You hear anything, boy?"

Angel tossed his head, eager to run some more, but Trent held him back. He held his own breath as he thought he heard the engines again, but there was now only silence.

Had they stopped? And if so, what did that mean?

Was he too late?

He forced back his thoughts and nudged Angel forward into a lope, following the four-wheelers' trail along the top of the ridge.

Twenty or thirty minutes later, he pulled up again. The tracks had disappeared back into a ravine, but the real reason he had stopped was that the warrior spirit, who now called himself Nämpäry, had suddenly appeared out of nowhere from out of the dark pine forest ahead, crouching and moving swiftly, looking down into the ravine. He held his bow ready with an arrow already strung and poised. He stopped and knelt, then turned to Trent and put a finger to his lips.

"The roaring wagons are nearby, Salal," he said softly but urgently. "You must be like a warrior now—stealthy and sharp as a knife!"

Trent dismounted and led Angel over until he stood next to the Indian. He peered into the shadows of the ravine where the warrior looked, but he saw nothing. "How close are they? How many of them?"

"I can only show you *where* to look." Nämpäry shook his head. "As I have tried to tell you before, I can only show you so much . . . only guide you so far." He stood and looked Trent up and down. "You have much of a Salal in you . . . but so much that remains untapped—in here." He put his palm lightly on Trent's chest and shook his head again sadly. "I fear it is the curse of your tainted white blood. You have forgotten so much, from the disuse of the powers of the *Jalagi*—of your people."

Nämpäry's eyes widened suddenly and he took a step back, in shock. He pressed his hand more firmly onto Trent's chest and cocked his head as if he could sense something there. "But you have another Power I did not realize until now," he whispered, incredulously. "You did not receive this power from any ordinary man's blood . . . or from any *tribe*." The warrior stepped back again and almost in reverence gazed deeply into Trent's eyes.

Trent felt as if Nämpäry were peering into his very soul.

"I'm not sure what you—"

"You have a great Power living in you . . . one that comes not of this world, but from the world of *Mowun!*"

"Mowun? Who is this *Mowun?*" Trent felt a quickening of his pulse, almost afraid to hear more.

Nämpäry stood still, and smiled. "Mowun," he repeated, nodding. "The Ancients called him *YHWH* . . . You Whites call Him Yeshua—the Nailed God—the Eater of *Death!*" The warrior nodded knowingly. "You have walked with Him through the dark valley before—and have come out scarred, but much stronger.

The warrior nodded again, greatly impressed, put a hand on Trent's shoulder, and squeezed it. "His Spirit lives within you. But you must learn to use it—*listen* to it."

Trent felt lightheaded but at the same time felt a surge of something rise through him, like fresh oxygen, a familiar strength, but one not his own.

Nämpäry turned again suddenly, raising his bow this time, and urgently stepped to the edge of the ravine. He looked at Trent, a frown on his face. "We must go, Salal. Now! No more time to spare!"

Nämpäry leapt over the edge without a sound and disappeared into the shadows below. Trent edged forward, clucked at Angel, and led the horse by foot after the spirit warrior. His lightheadedness had now been replaced by a fierce determination, and he stepped boldly into the deepening shadows below him.

As he finally gained the bottom of the ravine, he brought Angel up to him. He threw himself belly first over Angel's back and swung his leg over, pleased to have finally mounted the animal bareback on the first try. *Guess my Cherokee blood's coming to the fore after all,* he thought as he quickly urged the horse forward again.

The tracks of the 4-wheelers reappeared briefly here and there before following the incline up to the next ridge, this one very familiar. He dug his heels into Angel's flanks and trotted along the edge for several yards. Suddenly, the gelding snorted and planted his back legs, skidding to a sudden stop and rolling his eyes back in his head. Nämpäry had once again appeared out of nowhere and stood with his arms raised in front of horse and rider, again warning Trent to be quiet. He then pointed to the rim of the arroyo.

"They are there!"

Trent suddenly stiffened. At this vantage point he could just see a distant curl of smoke and the ruined roof of the miner's cabin he had left early that morning. He quickly climbed down, pulled his rifle from his shoulder, and crouched and scooted his way to the nearby line of pine trees. From here he had a clear view of the cabin's doorway, where there seemed to be some movement.

He knelt and put the telescopic sight up to his eye and focused in tighter. A knot of people squirmed in and out of focus. There seemed to be some sort of argument going on, people gesturing with their hands, and occasionally someone turning and moving away from the group. Trent recognized Ilsa, then Jennifer. Both were standing just inside the cabin and were visible through the broken walls as they moved about, their arms alternately folded across their chests and then flailing in animated conversation. The person standing nearest the doorway was dressed all in black and faced away from Trent, but then turned around—and he froze in recognition.

It was Britt de Jaager, the head of the late Laird Bouwmeester's security detail. She had a military-grade assault rifle slung on her shoulder, but the thing that concerned him was that in her right hand she brandished a large, semiautomatic pistol that she occasionally waved in the direction of the girls in a threatening manner.

It couldn't be, he thought to himself. *De Jaager is the mole? The assassin?* She was the last person he would have suspected.

Trent lowered his rifle for a moment and rubbed the sweat from his eyes. He suddenly heard distant shouting and raised the rifle back up to see what was happening. The scene jerked and swam in the telescopic sight until he locked in on yet another person in black, another bodyguard, this one running toward the cabin from some heretofore unseen place, waving his weapon, shouting excitedly, and pointing with his other hand back toward the ridge where Trent was located.

Crap! Had he been seen? He put the crosshairs onto the back of the running man, then shifted them onto de Jaager, who took several steps in the man's direction, whipped her own weapon off her shoulder, and aimed. Trent put his finger on the trigger and began to apply the slightest pressure. From here, his shot would take half of de Jaager's head off.

Suddenly, Trent's head burned like fire and his pulse pounded in his throat. He felt a presence and turned his head to see Nämpäry kneeling beside him, his hand on his shoulder.

"*Listen*, Salal."

"To what?"

"Listen to *Mowun*."

Trent shrugged away the surge he felt in his heart. "Enough of the mumbo jumbo," he growled. He raised the rifle again.

"Trent Carter," Nämpäry said softly. It was the first time he had used Carter's given name. "Things are not always as they seem."

Trent's mouth dropped, hearing the words he had heard so often when the spirit of Victoria, his slain wife, had visited him many times before. Nämpäry slowly turned his face to Trent, who gasped and pulled back. The young, strong features of a warrior were dissolving, like wax, crinkling and wrinkling until they solidified again into that of an ancient elderly man of wisdom. Nämpäry smiled and squeezed Trent's shoulder. "You remind me so much of someone else . . . always so eager to rush into battle before using your powers to instruct you." He pointed again down to the scene unfolding below them.

The running man shouted at de Jaager again, abruptly brought his rifle up, and fired off a wild burst of rounds, then yelped as several other gunshots rang out—but Trent could not immediately tell from where. Bullets slammed into the man and threw him up off his feet and momentarily up in the air before he crashed onto his back, no longer moving. More shots rang out in rapid succession from somewhere below, but he couldn't immediately see what was happening. Trent swung his gun sights around desperately until they lined up again on de Jaager, who now crouched halfway to the doorway, her own weapon raised and scanning the area.

Had she just shot her own man? Who else was she shooting at?

Trent froze as the muzzle of de Jaager's weapon stopped and came to rest . . . *on him!* His finger moved from the trigger guard to the trigger itself, ready to squeeze.

After several seconds, de Jaager slowly lowered her rifle. Through his sights Trent could see her blue eyes staring right at him, her face grim and her lips tight. He swallowed hard as he swore that he could see a thin smile nudge the corners of her mouth—and she nodded once in his direction, as if acknowledging that Trent was too far away to do anything now to stop her.

"What should I do?" Trent asked, lowering his weapon momentarily, but Nämpäry was nowhere to be seen. Trent kicked at the ground angrily. *Damned ghosts! Always disappearing at just the wrong time!*

Trent thought hard, his head swimming with uncertainty. What had the old Indian said? "*Things are not as they seem.*" What the hell was that supposed to mean?

He pulled the telescopic sight quickly back up to his eye.

There was sudden movement in the cabin and Trent watched helplessly as de Jaager swung around to confront Ilsa and Jennifer, who had appeared just behind her, gesturing wildly. De Jaager glanced around the open space once more, then pulled the pistol out of her belt and advanced on the girls, driving them in front of her back into the cabin doorway.

Trent was out of options. He had no time to readjust the crosshairs, only to hope for accuracy. The blood still pounded in his ears, and the scar on his forehead throbbed with a vengeance.

He let out his breath, held it, and squeezed the trigger.

The millisecond it took for the bullet to traverse the distance to the cabin door seemed longer to him than that, but Trent finally saw, with a degree of satisfaction, the round finally slammed into Britt de Jaager and propelled her through the cabin door and out of his sight.

CHAPTER 19
A War Broke Out In Heaven

(Letter from Rev. Franklin J. Tolby)

September 2, 1875

Editor
The New York Sun

Re: Judicial Failure and Further Outrage in New Mexico Territory

Dear Sir:

In the wake of the recent death of my old friend and confidante, Lucien Bonaparte Maxwell, on July 25 of this very year, I bring attention, once again, to the ongoing travesties of justice being carried out in our fair territory by known agents of corruption whose orders are being given out summarily from the highest offices in Santa Fe, contrary to the original contractual arrangements and desires of the late Mr. Maxwell himself, as alluded to in the Land Grant that continues to bear his name. I speak of none other than Governor Axtell and his cronies Stephen Elkins and Thomas Catron, those known members of the nefarious "Santa Fe Ring" whom I have brought to your attention before; and I now add to that ignoble list the name of Judge Joseph Palen.

Let it be known far and wide that the (less than) Honorable Justice Palen deserves nothing less than to be disbarred and to be stripped of his office and duties in the District of Cimarrón, due to his gross negligence and mishandling of the murder trial of notorious gunman Juan Francisco "Pancho" Griego!

Mr. Griego, in July of this year, and in broad daylight and unprovoked, I might add, did mercilessly gun down in cold blood three highly regarded soldiers of the United States Army as they enjoyed an evening of cards at Lambert's Inn in Cimarrón. Instead of the necessary guilty verdict being pronounced, Justice Palen allowed Mr. Griego his freedom upon payment of a meager and insulting fine.

It is more than evident to this humble servant of God that this shocking slap on the wrist was orchestrated and originated in none other than the headquarters of the aforementioned Santa Fe Ring, the office of the highest official in the territory, Governor Axtell himself, in an ongoing scheme to rob the good citizens of Colfax County of their God-given rights to property, life, and liberty!

And to all of this I cry, "Enough!"

181

Most sincerely,
Your humble servant,
Reverend Franklin J. Tolby
Cimarrón, Colfax County
New Mexico Territory.

P.S. Owing to my close relationship to the late Mr. Maxwell, I happen to be privy to the fact that, prior to his selling the Maxwell Land Grant to the current owners made up of a consortium of foreign and domestic investors, Mr. Maxwell had signed a document carving out a certain amount of land from the original Spanish grant and deeding said portion to the Ute and Arapaho Nations for the purpose of establishing a reservation in perpetuity. At one time, Mr. Maxwell proudly shared said Reservation Deed with me. But alas, this deed was never properly recorded, and I have confirmed with Maxwell's widow, Luz Beaubien Maxwell, that the deed had mysteriously disappeared from the estate and possessions of her late husband. Where is this document, I demand to know? I sense, once again, the long, dark arm of the Santa Fe Ring as such a deed would severely disrupt its underhanded attempts to acquire the rich and precious lands it certainly represents!

#

(September 14, 1875 – Upper Cimarrón River Canyon)

The cottonwoods threw their ample afternoon shade over the bubbling river in the upper Cimarrón Canyon. Their branches were bright with autumn gold and an occasional leaf detached itself and floated effortlessly to ride the water's current. Jonathon sniffed the crisp afternoon air. There would be an early snow this year.

He sat on the bank of the rushing waters, leaning back against one of the massive tree trunks, and lazily balanced on his knees the small branch he had whittled into a fishing pole. A line dangled from its end and disappeared into one of the less turbulent pools of water at his feet. The afternoon sun, the giggling flow of the stream, and the apparent lack of hungry trout conspired to lull Jonathon into a nap. His eyelids drooped and his breathing lengthened—until Walking Elk began to chuckle.

His old Indian friend had been squatting on his heels a few yards downstream, idly chewing a piece of dried buffalo meat that Jonathon had brought to him and enjoying the passing of the day. Jonathon jerked awake and frowned.

"What's so damned funny?"

"Do all white men fish in such a useless manner?" Walking Elk nodded at Jonathon's pole and shook his head. "No wonder you stay so thin, Salal."

"If I recall, *you* were the one who was starving when we first met."

"Well, at least I know how to fish properly."

"So, why weren't you fat and happy at the time, then?"

"Because I do not like to eat fish."

182

"Even when you're starving?"

"Perhaps it is more honorable to starve than to force yourself to eat something that is detestable to you."

"Hmm. Guess I'll have to ponder on that." Jonathon gave his line a few tugs and frowned. "Not that it matters much today, anyhow. No fish in this spot."

"Oh, there are plenty of fish here."

"Really?" Jonathon sat up, pulled his line out of the water, and offered the pole to his friend. He gestured at the river magnanimously. "So, why don't you show me how to *fish properly*?"

Walking Elk studied Jonathon for a moment, as if deciding whether or not this was a worthy challenge, and then seemed to decide. He stood up slowly and walked quietly toward Jonathon's fishing spot, where he took the pole carefully from him, looked it over suspiciously, and dropped it unceremoniously on the ground. Without a word, he carefully rolled up the sleeves of his shirt, gingerly lay down on his stomach, fully prone, and inched his way like a snake toward the stream. He raised his head just enough for his eyes to clear the edge of the bank, peered down into the water, slowly pushed his open hands out level over the still surface, and waited.

It didn't take long. Suddenly, water flashed as the Indian's hands sliced the water's surface like stabbing knives, then churned in a frenzy of splashes and noise as Walking Elk leapt to his knees, his hands clutching the throat and gills of a large, wriggling brown trout. He scooted backward on his knees a foot or two before turning and tossing the fish into the lap of a thoroughly surprised Jonathon, who scrambled and grabbed at the trout as it continued to twist and jump. He almost lost it back into the water before finally getting a good purchase on it. He glanced around, spied a nearby flat rock, and quickly slammed the fish's head against it. It finally grew still in his hands as he breathed heavily, stared at it in awe, and turned to look at his friend admiringly.

"Filthy creature," breathed Walking Elk, grimacing and looking as if he might get sick. He turned and plunged his hands back into the water, washing them vigorously before wiping them quickly on the nearby grass.

Jonathon laughed. "And here I thought you were a brave warrior!"

"It is a *wise* warrior who knows what he does and doesn't. . . ."

Walking Elk stood up suddenly and froze. He cocked his head to one side, listening, and held up one hand to signal silent caution. Jonathon rose to a crouch and also listened, hearing nothing at first, but then hearing the sound of approaching hoof beats on the nearby trail that ran just above them. Jonathon moved a few feet upriver to where both of their horses were tied, just as the animals' eyes rolled wide, their ears twitched, and their heads turned to the source of the sounds. He placed a hand on each of their noses and stroked lightly to calm them.

The hoof beats grew gradually louder and Jonathon could now feel the ground tremble beneath his boots. He glanced over at Walking Elk, who looked back at him and held up two fingers. Jonathon nodded as they both crouched lower behind the trees and made themselves small. In this remote area—and in these perilous times—it wasn't wise to reveal oneself too soon.

Jonathon could now make out two shapes racing from upstream, just beyond the rusted foliage of the scrub oaks that crowded the edge of the road as it ran eastward from the Moreno Valley, down into the canyons here, and on to Cimarrón and beyond. As the winded and frothing horses and their riders heaved into view in a break in the branches, Jonathon put his hand on the butt of his pistol, ready to pull it if necessary, and then suddenly recognized the two men. One was Manuel Cardenas, a part-time lawman and part-time outlaw; the other, close on his flank, was none other than the town drunk, Cruz Vega. Both men spurred their animals mercilessly and galloped on past, as if the devil himself were on their heels.

But Jonathon would soon learn that the devil had already been quite busy—and was about to get busier.

#

(Cimarrón, New Mexico Territory)

Later that evening, a growing buzz ran through town as the news spread slowly at first, then quickly—from one saloon to another, from the blacksmith's barn to the hardware store, from storekeepers to their shoppers to other storekeepers next door, and then door to door until it finally reached Frank Springer's office. As he jumped up from behind his desk and went out the door, Springer could see men and boys already running down the main street of Cimarrón toward the edge of town. Here they met the two riders who reportedly had been making their way slowly down the trail that led from the river canyon above.

Springer stepped out onto the porch, held up his hat to shade his eyes against the setting sun, and squinted up the street. A small dust cloud there, kicked up by the excited throng, boiled up from the road, and caused beams of sunlight to dance and flicker like wraiths, further obscuring his view. He moved slowly off the porch and walked toward the cloud of dust and the shouts and the knot of jockeying bodies that now suddenly parted like the Red Sea to allow the two men and three horses finally to come into view and pass into the outskirts of town. The crowd fell in quickly behind the riders. They excitedly pointed and called out to the other citizens, who had begun lining the street.

It was a macabre parade that made its way back toward Frank Springer, and he suddenly recognized the two men on horseback. Deputy Sheriff Jonathon Carter and his frequent companion, the old Ute Indian Walking Elk, both seemed road-weary and troubled as they led behind them what was clearly the body of a dead man draped across the third horse—the man about whom the news had spread through town like wildfire—the Reverend Franklin J. Tolby.

Clay Allison had appeared at Springer's side just as the men's tired horses had plodded their way slowly up to where Springer stood, his hands on his hips, and unbelieving; Jonathon Carter looked down at his two friends, shook his head sadly, and rode past.

#

"Where'd you find him, Jonathon?" "Who did it?" "Did you catch them?"

As he stepped out of the doctor's office, where he and Walking Elk had carefully deposited Tolby's body for further examination, Carter ignored the questions that arose anonymously from within the crowd that now ringed them and their tired mounts. He slapped the dust off his pants with his hat, forced his way silently through the crowd, and then he and Walking Elk led their horses back up the street toward the St. James Hotel.

In the past, when he had stopped by his friend Henri Lambert's saloon, he hadn't necessarily needed a drink. Today, he needed one. Badly. Today, Jonathon was sick at heart and troubled to the depths of his soul.

He started at the light touch of a hand on his shoulder and turned to find his hired hand, the young Jim Withers, smiling sympathetically.

"Here, Mr. Carter. Let me take them horses for you."

Jonathon smiled weakly, handed Jim the reins, and pushed at the doors of the St. James as the boy led the animals to the livery stable. Jonathon knew that Jim would properly care for them, just as he now counted on Henri to properly care for his own deep thirst—although he suspected that this thirst was not one that could be quenched by mere strong drink.

Walking Elk, Springer, and Allison, who brought up the rear, followed him. The crowd, which had tagged along, tried to push through behind them until Clay Allison turned and slammed the door in their faces. "Bar's closed!" he shouted.

Jonathon walked to his favorite table in the back corner and sat down wearily. The saloon was unusually empty for that time of the evening, due to the excitement out on the street. Henri Lambert came through a door behind the bar to see what the commotion was all about, hurried over to serve his friends, and then stopped in his tracks when he saw Walking Elk at the table.

"Jonathon, you know I can't serve him in here. . . ."

Jonathon cut him off with a glare and a raised, pointed finger. "Don't start, Henri. Just . . . don't."

Henri looked to be at a loss for words, then shrugged and walked back to the bar. "Beers all around, then," he muttered.

"Make mine a bourbon—double," said Jonathon.

"Make that two," said Springer.

"And three," added Allison as he finally took a seat after reassuring himself that the crowd outside wasn't coming in after all. He glanced across the table at Walking Elk, who was craning his neck and seemed to be counting the bullet holes in the pressed tin ceiling of the room. "How about you, Chief?"

The elderly Indian looked at Allison and slowly shook his head.

"I tried the Whites' firewater once, when I was much younger."

"Don't tell me—you didn't care for it, I suppose."

"Oh, no. I liked it very much. Too much. But I noticed that it kept my spirit from making its journeys at night. It always made me sleep very well, but I found that without my spirit being able to wander when I slept, I often awoke more exhausted than if I had not slept at all."

The drinks were served and Clay Allison raised his tumbler to the old man. "Henri," he said. "Bring our Indian friend here some sweet soda water, or some milk, or some such. I, for one, *do not* want his spirit to come wandering into *my* dreams later tonight."

Walking Elk smiled and nodded his head pleasantly at Allison. Then he looked at Jonathon and lost his smile. "I am afraid Salal will not rest well tonight, either."

Jonathon sat staring at nothing, his drink motionless in his hand. He sat that way for several minutes as the others left him to his thoughts and made small talk. Suddenly, Jonathon stirred, drained his glass in one gulp, wiped his mouth on his sleeve, and abruptly interrupted their conversation. He spoke in a monotone and barely above a whisper. Springer and Allison stopped talking and leaned forward intently.

Jonathon and Walking Elk had found Reverend Tolby with two bullet holes in his back in the upper Cimarrón Canyon after backtracking in the direction Cruz and Cardenas had ridden from. They had found Tolby's horse grazing peacefully nearby, and there appeared to be no sign of robbery—his pockets, wallet, and saddlebags were unmolested. Jonathon figured that the reverend had probably been returning from his biweekly trip to Elizabethtown, where he regularly preached fire and brimstone to the good citizens of the Moreno Valley and had probably thrown in his usual dose of damnation against the gang who ran the Santa Fe Ring.

"It's probably what got him killed, in the end."

There was a long silence in the saloon as Carter finished his story.

Springer sighed, took a sip of his whiskey, and then cleared his throat.

"I am certainly not one to cast aspersions before all the facts are in," he said, "and the good reverend and I certainly didn't always see eye to eye; but it does seem that our friend's fiery rhetoric finally caught up to him, does it not?"

"It would appear so, Mr. Springer," said Allison, studying his drink. "That, and his *penchant* for airing certain individuals' dirty laundry in the newspapers." He then stole a glance at Jonathon, who appeared to have retreated back to his silent shell for the moment. "So, Squirrel—Jonathon—you mentioned certain familiar names. Would those, by any chance, be the scoundrel Manuel Cardenas and our old friend Cruz Vega?" When Jonathon remained quiet, Allison scratched his bearded chin and continued. "And is there any chance in hell of those two ne'er-do-wells hanging around long enough to confess to anything?"

Allison looked around the room, then continued, warming to his topic. "And just where in the hell is Sheriff Rinehart during all this?

"He was called out this morning," said Henri from where he was wiping down the bar. "Something about another attack on settlers south of here."

"Well, that's very convenient, isn't it? But in light of the sheriff's absence, shouldn't we start thinking about some sort of posse to go find the scoundrels—

bring them to justice—that sort of thing?"

"Justice," Springer scoffed. "I'd like to see what sort of *justice* those boys would get from any posse—*or* any jury—from around here!"

"More's the point, Counselor," said Allison quietly. He leaned forward and lowered his voice. "Maybe some quick justice is what is actually called for, under these circumstances—or do we just sit and twiddle our thumbs until the return of our noble sheriff?"

Springer began to protest, but Allison continued. "I mean, for example, remember what sort of *justice* was given to our so-called friend Pancho Griego after he murdered those poor, innocent soldiers last month. For some odd reason, he got off with barely a warning. Why, I was sitting right over there and saw the whole thing. Oh, sure, they were just *darkies,* but still . . ."

Frank Springer suddenly slammed his glass down, pushed his chair back, and stood up. He pointed his finger at Allison, but for once seemed to be at a loss for words. He then turned abruptly to Jonathon.

"Deputy Carter, I apologize, but I must take my leave, Sir. I cannot, in all good conscience, remain here while such talk of . . . of *vigilantism* is bandied about! Good night to you all . . . *gentlemen.*"

Springer stormed across the saloon, opened the door to the sudden clamor of the people still crowded outside, and slammed it behind him.

"My," said Allison, holding his shot glass up to the light and examining its amber contents, "but it does seem that the counselor is a might testy tonight, is he not?"

Jonathon said nothing. The room grew quiet again, and Walking Elk resumed counting the bullet holes above his head.

"How many of those holes do you reckon are up there, Chief?" asked Allison after a long silence.

"I do not know. I keep losing count," answered the old Ute. He looked back at Clay and raised his eyebrows. "I was just wondering. How many of those holes are *you* responsible for, *Tumbioo Puckki?*"

"Tomb-by-oh . . . what was that, again, old man?" Allison squinted his eyes dangerously at Walking Elk.

Jonathon roused himself and laid his hand lightly on Allison's forearm. "Closest translation is *gunman, gunfighter* . . . 'one who does battle with a gun.' He meant no harm—it's a compliment, Clay."

"Well, that's all right, then, I suppose." He hesitated and then raised his glass once more to the Indian. "I think I'm starting to like you, Walking Elk. I'm beginning to see why Jonathon hangs around you so much."

Walking Elk smiled again. "Thank you," he said, and then shook his finger up at the ceiling. "But I do not know that I like you so much, yet, *Tumbioo Puckki.*"

#

An hour later, Henri Lambert had snuck Jonathon Carter and Walking Elk out the back door of the St. James to avoid the crowd of men who still lingered out front. From there, the two walked through the alleys until they got to the livery stable, where Jim Withers awaited them with fresh horses for the ride back home to the Delgado *rancho*.

In the meantime, Clay Allison exited through the front door, where he stood on the porch and lit a cigar while the men there, eager for news, shoved around him.

"What can you tell us, Mr. Allison?" "What happened?" "Who killed Tolby?"

The questions came at him all at once, spilling over one another. Allison took a long drag on his cigar and breathed its smoke out slowly.

"Well, boys," he began, "let's just say that it looks, to me, like it's time to get us a posse together."

#

(October 30, 1875 – Upper Ponil River Valley)

"Pass me that jug."

Oscar McMains passed the clay jug of liquor over the small fire to Cruz Vega, who tilted it expertly over his forearm and took several gulps. Vega suddenly lowered it and his eyes took on a fearful glint in the firelight.

"You hear that?

"I didn't hear anything."

"You sure? Sounded like a twig snapping." Vega stood up quickly and peered into the dark trees nearby.

They both listened for a moment longer. "You're jumping at ghosts, Mr. Vega. It's probably just the sheep. Calm yourself. Take another drink."

"Yeah, I suppose you're right. Just jumping at things." Vega sat down again and crossed his legs. He tossed more wood on the fire against the growing chill. He glanced across at McMains. "Boy, I can't tell you enough how grateful I am that you took me in, Reverend. I didn't think anybody was going to believe me. I mean, I was going crazy for a while there. That posse almost caught me a couple of times. I swear on a stack of Bibles I had nothin' to do with Mr. Tolby's killin'!"

"You mean *Reverend* Tolby."

"Yeah, yeah, *Reverend*. Anyway, I shoulda known that I could trust a man of God, like you, to believe me!" Vega hugged his upper arms and glanced around nervously once more. "I wonder where he is?"

"Where who is?"

"You know, the owner . . . the guy you said was supposed to meet us out here? The one you said wants to hire me to watch his sheep, while I hide out hereabouts for a while?"

Oscar McMains looked into the fire and poked it with a stick. He had been Tolby's assistant for a year now in the Methodist Church's defined area of ministry throughout three counties in the northern territory of New Mexico and had not always understood or agreed with his superior's stance on territorial politics and the so-called Santa Fe Ring. But over time, he had also grown to be concerned over the increasingly violent confrontations involving local settlers and those who wanted them evicted from their lands; and of course he was duly shocked at Tolby's murder and remained so at this moment.

He glanced up at the man across the fire from him—the man he knew to be one of the prime suspects of that murder, although that was not for McMains to decide. That would be for a jury and a judge to properly determine, and then for almighty God to deal with Vega's eternal soul.

"He'll be along shortly, I think."

#

The posse burst out of the tree line without warning—twenty men on horseback, some with kerchiefs drawn over the lower parts of their faces, some completely hooded, and almost all of them under the heavy influence of strong drink. It was a wonder that they had not been heard.

Cruz Vega jumped up from the campfire, ran a few feet in one direction and then changed course and charged the other way, but the riders had quickly encircled the two men so that there was no place to run. Even so, Vega continued to dart one way, then the other, like the frightened rabbit that he was.

"Run for it, Reverend!" Vega screamed breathlessly. He tried to shove his way between two horses, but they closed ranks on him quickly and penned him in. One of the masked men had loosened a lariat and was now twirling it above his head. The other horsemen jostled each other and laughed as the lasso floated out and over Vega, where it dropped down to his knees before tightening suddenly and tripping him. He fell heavily on the ground, where he rolled around and babbled incoherently.

Reverend McMains remained seated by the fire, staring absently into it as if nothing were amiss.

"Reverend," Vega screamed, his knees now pulled up to his chin. *"Don't let them kill me!"*

One of the riders pushed his bay gelding between the other horses and stepped it up slowly to where McMains sat. The man was wearing dark clothes covered by a long duster. His lower face was covered with a red bandanna, and the rest of his face was hidden in the shadow of a large black hat. The man stopped two feet away and pulled down his kerchief.

It was Clay Allison.

"Reverend McMains," Allison said in greeting.

McMains continued to stare into the fire. "You said you weren't going to hurt him," he said softly. He then turned his face to look up at the famed gunman. "Was that a lie?"

"Oh no, Sir. That was no lie." Allison turned and looked over at the prone Vega, who continued to chatter away in fear, rolling in the dirt and tugging on the numerous ropes that had now joined the first one and were tightening around his body. Allison spread the palm of his hand out and gestured. "As you can see—I am not personally laying a hand on Mr. Vega."

Reverend McMains stood up slowly and looked over at Vega, trussed up like a lamb for slaughter and now lying still, his eyes wide in terror and staring straight at the preacher. Understanding had finally seemed to dawn on Cruz Vega. McMains stepped over to the unfortunate prisoner and squatted down.

"I am so very sorry, Mr. Vega," McMains said softly. "They have promised me you will be well treated. We all want the same thing, do we not? The absolute truth and God's justice and mercy." He reached out a tentative hand and touched Vega's trembling shoulder. "I know that you want the same thing. If you are innocent, answer their questions truthfully. The truth shall set you free. But if you are guilty, admit it. And God *will* have mercy on your soul. Confession is a good thing."

The fear momentarily left Vega's eyes and was replaced by a look of vehement hatred. Vega puckered his lips and spat full into McMain's face. McMains recoiled and fell backward, just missing falling into the fire.

"You can go straight to hell, you Judas, you!" Vega screamed.

Clay Allison dismounted and walked over. "You all right, Reverend?" he asked, helping McMains to his feet.

"Yes—yes, I am not injured." He slowly took a handkerchief from his coat pocket and wiped the spittle from his cheek.

Allison looked up at the posse, then looked around, and spied a telegraph pole by the nearby road. He nodded to it, and then gestured toward Vega. "Get him to his feet—and take him over there. I'll be over directly." He stopped, glanced at McMains, and then continued. "And don't hurt him."

Several men jumped from their horses and moved to Vega, who began shouting and screaming again in earnest. Allison put a hand on McMain's shoulder and walked him away from the bustling activity behind them.

"Reverend, I think this would be an excellent time for you to be going."

"But . . . you promised he wouldn't be hurt."

"Oh, they aren't going to kill him. Just urge him to answer a few questions . . . truthfully."

"Yes. That's exactly what I am afraid of."

As McMains got on his horse and began to ride away, he paused and looked back over his shoulder. Two of the horsemen had lit torches from the campfire and their flickering pools of light danced bizarrely away from him, flaring up here and there, illuminating the knot of shouting men. He knew that somewhere in their midst, unseen for now, was their victim, Cruz Vega, the poor man—guilty or not—he had helped lead them to. Their forms diminished and became indistinguishable as the group moved toward the telegraph pole. In a distant splash of light now, McMains could see where someone had already thrown a rope over the cross tie of the pole at the top, and it now dangled and danced in the air like a long, writhing snake. Cruz Vega began screaming and begging for mercy.

#

"Let me have a few words with him, boys—if I may."

Clay Allison had been standing idly by, just outside the undulating circle of light thrown by the sputtering torches of the posse. Shadows danced and leapt like demented spirits against the cottonwoods that lined the road and spilled away into the darkness. The crowd of men, laughing and shouting and passing whiskey among themselves, didn't respond at first but continued to surround the prone figure of the unfortunate Cruz Vega, who lay jibbering and writhing at their feet. Vega's hands were free, but the noose of a rope that had been thrown over the nearby telegraph pole had been tightened around his neck. Between vicious kicks from the drunken mob that doubled him over into a fetal position, he alternately held his midsection and then clawed to loosen the rope at his throat.

"Boys," repeated Allison just a little louder, "I asked you to give me some space and a few moments with Mr. Vega, if you will." A couple of the men heeded Allison's request and stepped back from their prisoner; the remainder either did not seem to hear Clay or chose to ignore him.

One did not ignore Clay Allison without consequences.

He pulled his Army Colt .45 deftly from his holster, held it up high, and discharged it over the posse's heads. At this close proximity, the sudden clap of the gunshot deadened eardrums and caused some of the vigilantes to fall to the ground while slapping themselves all over, searching for wounds, and a few others to stumble back while fumbling with their own side-arms. At lease one startled man dropped his whiskey bottle to the ground in a shattering of glass. All eyes were soon glued on Clay Allison—all except those of one poor drunken soul who hovered yet over the trembling form of Cruz Vega, slapping him with the end of the hangman's rope that dangled over him. Allison stepped into the widening space that had now materialized between him and Vega and whacked the unsuspecting cowboy on the back of the head with the barrel of the pistol.

Chunk Colbert collapsed like a sack of flour at Allison's feet. Clay holstered his weapon, nudged Colbert with the toe of his boot, and looked around him. "Thank you, gentlemen," he said to the posse with a grateful smile. "Now, if you will be so kind as to step back just a mite further, I would appreciate a little privacy for a moment with our friend here." Allison turned back to Vega, who began to scoot himself away from this new threat. The mob muttered and cursed but obediently stepped back away several feet and resumed their passing of a bottle.

Allison squatted down, tipped his hat back from his forehead, and shrugged at Cruz Vega. "Now, Cruz," he said quietly. "You and I have spent more than a few hours together in the pleasure of each others' company, have we not?"

Cruz Vega nodded vigorously. "Please, Mr. Allison—don't let them do this. You know me—I may be a troublemaker, of sorts . . . but I *ain't* no killer!

"And Cruz, we both know that a liquored-up mob is no small thing to trifle with, don't we?"

"Yessir, Mr. Allison, I sure do know that to be true. Why, whiskey can do terrible things to a man—I myself just today have decided to swear off drinking, I truly have."

Vega's voice grew louder and more strident, fear driving his words. "Manuel Cardenas was the one pulled the trigger on the good reverend. They tried to get me to do it, but I ain't no killer. I swear! I didn't do it!"

"Shh—shh, now, Cruz. Calm yourself. That all may be as it may. But the truth is," Allison chuckled. "I really don't care who killed that damned preacher man."

Vega began to jabber and weep again. Allison shook his finger at him, then finally reached over and slapped him once, hard. Vega stopped making noise and stared at him with fear-filled eyes.

"Now, Mr. Vega, there is one small thing that I *am* most interested in and if you can help me understand it better. . . ." Allison had been steadily pulling the rope tied around Vega's neck, forcing the suspect up onto his knees, just a few inches away.

"Anything, Mr. Allison. Just ask me. . . . I'll tell you anything, if you'll just let me go!"

Allison dropped the rope, reached into his vest pocket, took out the stub end of a pencil, and then paused. "Now, let's see—something to write on," He patted his other pockets absently, finally producing the photograph he had taken from Jonathon Carter's office—the photo of himself and four other stern men posing in front of Tom Stockton's bar at the Clifton House. Allison looked at the photo fondly.

"Hmmm," he said, then looked up at Vega. "You don't happen to have any paper on you, do you?" He looked back down at the photo. "No, of course you wouldn't." Allison sighed, then turned the photo over on his knee and handed the pencil to Cruz Vega.

"Well then, how about you draw me a little map here to that gold claim of yours, before our friends back there lose the remainder of their patience?"

#

When he was a quarter mile away, tears streaming down his cheeks, Reverend Oscar McMains stopped his horse in the middle of the road as a gunshot suddenly rang out in the distance. He held his breath and listened intently. Several minutes later, the horrific screams began again, then mercifully stopped with an abruptness that could mean only one thing. McMains clinched his fists and held them tightly against his ears as if to block out the now deafening silence. After a few minutes, he composed himself, gritted his teeth, and nudged his horse forward into the darkness as he muttered a prayer over and over.

"Lord God, forgive me, chief among sinners!"

CHAPTER 20
Enemy Of My Enemy

(Present Day – Sangre de Cristo Mountains)

When Britt de Jaager had burst into the cabin she was not at all sure who—or what—she was going to find, other than a couple of frightened girls. The last thing she had expected was to come face to face with a determined Jennifer Ferguson, ready to shoot her in the face with her father's Glock .45. When she suggested to Jennifer that she lay down her weapon, she was almost certain that at least one of them was about to die—that is, until Jennifer called her a murderer.

"Murderer?" she responded, incredulous at first.

In an instant, the girl's outburst brought images from the prior days' events cart-wheeling through Britt's mind until suddenly it became quite clear to her what was wrong here.

"I said, *you first,* bitch!" yelled Jennifer. Britt could see the girl's finger tighten imperceptibly on the trigger.

"I think you had better do as she suggests, lady."

Britt jerked her head toward the voice, where a pale Ben Ferguson leaned on one elbow and pointed a .357 magnum Ruger revolver at her.

Britt slowly raised her left hand while holding up her assault rifle in her right in compliance.

"Okay," she said, keeping her voice even, looking back and forth between Ben and Jennifer. "Let's not make any more mistakes here, shall we?"

Ben coughed, grimaced in pain, but held his pistol steady. "Oh, I think there's only one person's made any mistakes here today." He motioned with his pistol for her to lay the rifle down. "Now slide it over here, near me, if you don't mind," he continued. "With all these guns waving around careless-like, I'd like to keep them all close by where I can keep count."

"Sheriff Ferguson," Britt said, her hands still held up at shoulder height. "I fear there has been a terrible misunderstanding. And if we don't sort this out very quickly, all of us are about to die here."

"Again—you first, *bitch!*" Jennifer interjected.

"Now, now, Jennifer," said Ben. "That is such an ugly word—effective, but not very pretty."

"*Sheriff,*" Britt continued, raising her voice urgently now. "I know what you are thinking, that I am somehow the one behind this tragedy. But you must listen to

193

me—"

"Ilsa," Ben called out, ignoring Britt's pleas. "Come over here and find my backpack. Inside you'll find a pair of handcuffs. Ms. de Jaager," he continued, turning back to Britt, "the only thing that I *must* do is secure this situation. Now, if you would please turn around and place your hands against the wall—oh, and then don't move a hair again until I tell you."

"No," Ilsa said, timidly at first.

"What was that, Ilsa?" asked Ferguson.

"I said, *no!*" she repeated, this time more insistently. "I won't get the handcuffs. Britt said she is not at fault here. I trust her, and so should you. You have to *listen* to her, Sheriff!"

"Fine, then. *Don't* get them. And no, I don't have to listen to what she says. If you hadn't noticed, *Ms.* Bouwmeester, I am the one trying to keep us all alive here, and for all we know, this agent here killed your father!"

"It's okay, Ilsa," said de Jaager. "Go ahead and get the handcuffs. I'll cooperate."

Ilsa shook her head, tears welling in her eyes, but Britt nodded again at the backpack near Ben. "Do as I tell you. I will find another way to convince them."

Ilsa wiped her nose, then moved across the room. As she knelt down to the backpack, Ben suddenly had a seizure of coughing, momentarily letting his pistol hand drop.

"Daddy?" Jennifer blurted, turning to look at her father with concern. In that moment, de Jaager whipped around, slammed a fist into the girl's gun arm, and with the other hand grasped the barrel of the Glock and twisted it away from her, all in one practiced move. Ben was still wracked with the fit of coughing but tried to raise his weapon again. In another swift move, de Jaager leapt across the short distance that separated them and deftly kicked the Ruger out of Ben's hand. It bounced off the backpack and landed harmlessly at Ilsa's feet.

"Ilsa, pick up the gun," Britt commanded. The girl reached out her trembling hand, and then hesitated. *"Do it now!"* de Jaager barked. Ilsa picked up the gun, stood up, and held it awkwardly at her side.

"Bring it to me."

Ilsa stepped over and handed her the Ruger.

"I'm sorry, Honey," Ben said, his coughing finally subsiding. Jennifer knelt down and gave him a sip of water.

"That's okay, Daddy," she said sadly, then glared up at de Jaager. "It was really my fault."

Britt stepped back until she could cover the room with Ben's Glock, took several breaths, and then slowly sat down on her haunches. "Why don't we all stop saying whose fault this all is." She lowered the Glock, then waved it idly. "Ilsa, you go on and have a seat there, too, next to the fire. I need to explain something to you all—now that I have your undivided attention." She paused and glanced toward the doorway. "And it won't take long, because we don't have much time."

\#

It took only a few minutes for Britt to tell them her story. There was silence in the ruined cabin, except for the occasional crackling of the fire. Ben was staring at the floor, and then he raised his head to look at Britt.

"So, we're just supposed to automatically believe what you've said is true? I mean, is it because that attractive little accent of yours is so convincing, or because European women never lie—unlike their American counterparts?" Ben quickly glanced at his daughter. "Present company, etcetera, Sweetie."

"Well if I were really lying," answered Britt, "why wouldn't I just shoot you all here and now and take what I want==since I do have all the guns?"

"Yeah, well, that is a very good question."

"And it wouldn't do her any good, anyway," said Ilsa, standing up and looking at them all in turn.

"Why not?" asked Britt, peering at Ilsa.

"Because I no longer have what you all are looking for." She hesitated before going on. "I . . . I gave it to Mr. Carter, right before he left this morning."

"You gave what to Mr. Carter, exactly?" asked Jennifer, suspiciously.

There was another awkward silence.

"She gave a thumb drive to your friend," said Britt, standing up slowly. They all looked at her with apprehension. "The evidence that I was instructed to retrieve."

"Instructed by who?" asked Ben. Britt started to answer, then thought better of it.

"So . . . what happens now?" continued Ben. "You call your other friends out there to come in and finish us off for you—keep you from getting your hands dirty?

"Not exactly. But you *do* have part of the answer to your question already: one or both of my *friends,* as you call them, are double agents. I've suspected them for a long time now." Britt looked over at Ilsa. "One or all of them are responsible for the crash of your helicopter and for your father's death. And those men are still out there, waiting for me to bring you all out, presumably to save you, but in fact they are waiting to kill us all as soon as we step out that door."

"Wait a minute. Let's say that's all true," said Ben. "It still doesn't fully answer my first question. I mean, why don't you just take out that fancy sat phone you say you have and call up your boss—get him to send in the cavalry?"

Britt looked at the Glock in her hand. She shifted it to her other hand, then reached into her jacket to pull her own SIG Sauer 9mm from her shoulder holster.

"Because right now, *I* am the cavalry."

She hefted both firearms in her hands, checked their magazines, and proceeded to walk over and hand them over, butts first, to each of them in turn: to Jennifer, the Glock; to Ilsa, her own pistol, the SIG Sauer; and to Ben, his Ruger. "Because if I meant you harm and were lying to you, why would I do this?"

Ben watched carefully as Britt moved back across the room and leaned against the wall, arms folded. Ilsa suddenly stepped quickly over and handed Britt's pistol back to her. "I don't want this," she said. "I hate guns!" She shoved the SIG Sauer back into Britt's hand and turned away. Britt looked at the gun in her hand and then moved toward Ilsa.

"I think I should insist that you take it, Ilsa. As I said, we are not out of here yet, and if anything happens to me, then. . . ." Britt stiffened suddenly as she heard a noise. She grabbed the rifle and moved to the door, the pistol still in her other hand. She turned at the doorway and looked at them all. "They're coming. Get ready!"

From somewhere outside came a voice, shouting from the middle distance and echoing around the draw. "*Lieutenant de Jaager?*"

"Yes?" Britt called out from just inside the doorway. "I am not finished here. Go back to your station."

"Oh, I think that you are quite finished, Lieutenant."

Britt stepped cautiously out of the cabin. She had shoved the pistol in her belt and held the rifle at the ready.

"What's the meaning of all this, Lars?"

The man had been approaching the cabin on foot and now stopped about twenty yards out. He held his own assault rifle at port arms, his finger on the trigger.

"We need you all to come out now Lieutenant. Bring the others out and this will be over very quickly."

"We, Lars? Who's *we?*"

"You know—Karl, me, and Gert."

Britt smirked to herself. She had suspected Karl, but Gert, the man she had left with the vehicles, was in on it too.

So I really am on my own, she thought.

The man called Lars turned and gestured back toward the trees, where the rogue agent Karl now stepped out, his rifle aimed at Britt, waiting for a further signal.

"Don't do this, Lars," Britt reasoned. "There is no point. *Septum* knows everything; your names—all of you."

"*Septum* knows nothing! Not everything. You and your sad excuse for an outdated *dark ops* group serve *no* purpose any longer—no earthly purpose whatsoever! So, hand the girls and the data over—right now!"

Britt stepped slowly forward to clear the doorway from any stray fire.

"You know I can't do that, Lars. I *won't* do it."

Lars raised his rifle and pointed it at her. "Drop your weapon, Britt. It's over."

Britt peered at him for a few seconds and then lowered her rifle slightly. She felt a sudden sadness play at the fringes of her wall—the one she had built around her emotions. She licked her lips and took a deep breath, forcing her feelings back down.

"Who murdered Cobus, Lars?"

"What?"

"You heard me. Who killed him? You?"

Lars pulled his eye from the gun sight and seemed to hesitate.

"Does it make any difference in what happens here?"

"No, not really." Britt took a deep breath but kept her countenance cold and unreadable. "But I need to know. Who killed Cobus and why did he have to die?"

Lars shrugged, looked back over his shoulder at Karl, and then back at Britt.

"All I can tell you is that I didn't kill him. But I probably would have if I had been the one to find him digging around where he shouldn't have."

Lars smiled and in that moment something clicked inside Britt's head.

"Good," she said, curtly. "That's all I needed to know."

Britt suddenly dropped to one knee and squeezed the trigger, unleashing a burst of rounds. Lars fired twice, but his shots went wild just as Britt's bullets stitched him up the thigh, stomach, and chest. The Kevlar vest protected his torso, but the leg wounds made him fall forward to his knees with a cry. Britt took quick, careful aim through her scope and placed one more bullet neatly through the middle of Lars's forehead. He slumped to the ground without a sound. Britt lunged to her feet and sprinted back to the cabin.

The second man, Karl, who stood just outside the distant tree line, fired a wild burst toward Britt and the cabin, but none of his shots connected. She fired a quick burst back at him, knowing that at that distance her automatic fire was also ineffective. She was now halfway to the cabin door. She rolled to the ground, making herself a smaller target, switched the weapon to single fire mode, and quickly scanned the area through her scope, hoping to glimpse her traitorous agent again and get a cleaner shot, but to no avail. Karl had disappeared back into the shadows of the forest.

Suddenly, Britt froze, the gun sight still up to her eye, as the image of yet another man swam into view along the rim on the far side, just above where Karl had disappeared. Her heart thudded as she realized that this man was also training a rifle on her. At that moment, he lowered his rifle until she could see the surprise on his face—and then she also slowly lowered her weapon in similar surprise as she recognized him.

It was Trent Carter.

She smiled knowingly, and then she nodded at him. At this distance, without the aid of the scope, it was impossible for her to see his reaction, if any.

But the immediate threat was still Karl.

Britt knew she couldn't remain exposed any longer. She twisted back to her feet and ran for the cabin door. She had to get these people out of here, and the only way to do it would be to leave them for a while and go make it safe for them all. She needed to hunt down the other turncoat, get around behind him, and dispatch him quickly or else he would pick them all off one by one.

But what about Trent Carter? Was he an ally or another obstacle? Had he looked at the data Ilsa had given him? And if so, whose side was he really on now? Could she count on him to help her get to Karl?

She shook the questions from her mind. She knew she couldn't take a chance on Carter either. Not now. If he got in her way, then. . . .

Britt de Jaager never finished the thought. She was crossing the threshold, absently pulling her pistol out of her belt to give to Ilsa, when out of nowhere something fierce slammed into her back and spun her around.

#

After he fired his rifle and saw Britt de Jaager fall into the cabin, Trent rolled away from the edge of the ravine until he was almost certain that he could stand up without being seen from below. He raced over to where he had tethered Angel to a scrub oak, climbed up, and dug his heels into the gelding's sides.

Angel leapt into action and obediently loped along the rim of the draw, wet snow flying from his hooves as they entered the relative obscurity of the nearby pines. Here, Trent pulled the horse to a stop and waited, listening to whatever he might hear other than the puffing of Angel's heavy breathing. He had seen de Jaager fall and just before that had witnessed her gunning down one of her own men, but he had no idea how many more of them might be lurking just below him, out of sight. He cursed himself for not paying closer attention to the 4-wheeler tracks in the snow to determine exactly how many of them had come this way.

He listened quietly for another few seconds. During those moments the thought even crossed his mind that the old Indian might reappear to give him just one more clue.

"Screw it," he muttered, knowing he could not chance waiting another moment. His friends were in mortal danger.

He looked around immediately below him to where the pine trees growing down this side of the draw offered additional shadows and a modicum of cover. He clucked softly at Angel and let him have his head a little as they picked their way downhill through the trees. Soon they came to the edge of the tree line and Trent pulled up, still in the shadows. From here he could see the cabin on the far side of the field. There seemed to be no activity there. He listened and looked a while longer, scanning the perimeter of the draw, looking along the rim above him, and finally back toward the cabin. In the middle of the draw lay a dark lump that Trent knew was the dead gunman. He had seen more than his share of bodies but it always amazed him how small and insignificant a man could look after he was dead. Maybe there had been only the two of them—this guy and de Jaager. He still couldn't understand why she had shot down her own man and then fired wildly in his direction up on the ridge. A warning shot, perhaps? A professional like de Jaager would know that her bullets wouldn't hit him that far away. Something just didn't ring true here.

He paused, suddenly aware that not only Nämpäry but also his reliable sixth sense had abandoned him. He reached up and idly touched the scar on his hairline.

"Well, big boy," Trent finally said softly, leaning over Angel's neck. "Guess it's just you and me now. Looks like we're on our own—a one-man cavalry."

Trent slung his rifle over his shoulder and reached into his jacket. Taking his semi-automatic pistol from his shoulder holster, he pulled the clip to check the load and then chambered a round. He took a deep breath and nudged Angel forward.

"Here we go . . ."

Angel loped forward as Trent held the reins loosely with his left hand and held the pistol in his right, aimed upward. He didn't want to shoot one of his own people by mistake if they came running out of the cabin. He scanned the area back and forth, keeping a careful eye peeled on the distant cabin. He had gone about twenty yards and was now completely exposed from all angles. He started to pull up on the reins again but suddenly felt the familiar tingle and a familiar phantom voice in his ear.

"*Run, Squirrel!*"

Angel, as if he had also heard the disembodied voice, jumped forward into almost a full gallop before Trent realized he had never touched the animal with his boots. He lost the reins, scrambled to grab a handful of Angel's mane to keep from falling off, and fumbled to keep hold of his pistol. But at the last moment he felt it also fly from his hand.

It was at that moment out of his peripheral vision that Trent saw yet another man, also dressed neck to toe in the black assault gear, run several steps out of the trees. The man raised his assault rifle to track Trent and his horse as they sped across the field. Like a bad dream, Trent saw fire spurt briefly from the muzzle again and again, followed immediately by bullet hits plowing up earth and snow in a steady line marching toward them, and then finally heard the flat thuds of lead hitting flesh.

Trent felt his left leg go immediately cold and numb; Angel reared, screaming in pain and terror; and horse and rider fell over as one in what seemed like the terrible and familiar slow motions of a nightmare.

#

"*Stront!*" cursed Britt de Jaager, slipping into her native Dutch as she spun through the cabin doorway. She stumbled and fell headlong into Jennifer Ferguson, who tried vainly to catch her but managed only to lose her own footing. They both hit the floor heavily. The steel-jacketed bullet had slammed into de Jaager's back, shattered her clavicle and scapula, continued its downward trajectory, and broken her humerus cleanly in half as it exited her upper arm. De Jaager had immediately dropped her assault rifle just inside the doorway and the pistol she had been holding had gone skittering across the floor as she fell.

"Verdomme, verdomme!" she moaned loudly, cursing and rolling to her uninjured left side while holding her shattered arm tightly with her good hand. She finally stopped rolling and stayed very still, tears of pain seeping out of tightly closed eyes, sucking her breath wetly through clenched teeth, and willing herself not to go into shock. "*Damn* me!" she exclaimed, reverting back to English and berating herself. "Shit, shit, *shit* . . . how could I have been so stupid?" Slowly, she opened her eyes and stared blankly at the sky through the rotted roof timbers, trying to calm herself. She began to slowly move her other extremities, testing them to assess the overall damage to her body. After a few seconds, she determined that aside from some possible heavy bruising and contusions from the fall, there were no other serious injuries—except, of course, for the bullet that had torn through her. But one glance at the blood seeping through her fingers that were clamped over the bullet's exit wound told her that she had better get the bleeding stopped and quickly. She attempted to sit up, but sharp pain exploded in her shoulder; and with another angry curse she collapsed again hard on the floor .

Jennifer, who had had the wind knocked out of her from her collision with de Jaager, rolled over and sat up. She suddenly realized what was happening and moved over to de Jaager, who was again writhing on the floor. Jennifer quickly looked the wounded woman over, took a deep breath, eased her arm under de Jaager's neck, and gently helped her to a sitting position. "Ilsa," Jennifer called over to her friend, who stood against the wall, fear etched on her face. "Find something to tie this arm off with. I have to get the bleeding stopped."

Ilsa shook herself, then looked around for something, anything that could be useful.

"What about this?" asked Ben, holding up the torn shirt Jennifer had taken off him earlier.

"Yes. Perfect. Bring it here . . . and whatever's left of the first aid kit!" Jennifer looked down at de Jaager, whose face was drawn and pale. "I'm going to have to move you, but you're going to need to help me, okay?"

De Jaager was leaning heavily against Jennifer but opened her eyes and nodded briefly. "You need to get my jacket off. . . ." she croaked through clinched teeth. "My knife," she added, gesturing with her eyes down to her feet. "I have a knife in my boot, just there. Use it to cut off the jacket."

"Get the knife," Jennifer said to Ilsa, who had brought the other items over to them. "I can't hold her and reach it at the same time."

Ilsa crouched down and fumbled at de Jaager's trouser leg.

"The other one," said de Jaager, and Ilsa finally found the knife and drew it out of its ankle scabbard by its heavy black handle. The black blade was a vicious-looking eight inches long with a serrated edge on the backside. It was razor sharp on the business side.

"Now," continued Jennifer. "Let's get you moved. . . . This is probably going to hurt like hell."

"I'm sure that it will," muttered Britt. "Let's just do it."

Britt held her breath and suddenly pulled a foot under her and pushed hard as Jennifer swiveled around on her knees, grasping Britt by the collar with one hand and clenching the sleeve of her good arm with the other. With Jennifer's help, Britt was able to get over to the wall, which she leaned against heavily. She blew her breath out hard. "You were right," Britt murmured, her face shining with perspiration.

"What?"

"That hurt like hell!" Her face had gone white and a trail of small blood spatters marked where she had slid across the floor.

Jennifer continued to take charge and lost no time. She nodded at Ilsa. "Start tearing up that shirt into bandages while I cut this jacket off her." She then turned back to de Jaager brandishing the knife. "You're going to have to help me some, and again, it's going to hurt like shit. But I have to get this jacket off you so I can stop that bleeding. First I'm going to have to try to cut that sleeve off."

Britt shook her head vigorously. "There's no more time for that now. Just wrap a tight sling around it for now to keep it from flopping around." She glanced again to the door, then nodded over to where her assault rifle had fallen. "And give me my rifle, will you? We're not out of this yet. Karl's still out there, and also—"

"But you could bleed to death!"

"Then I will just have to bleed to death. There's no more time!"

Jennifer retrieved the rifle and leaned it against the wall next to Britt. Ilsa brought the shirt over and together they fashioned a makeshift sling. They carefully worked it around Britt's shattered arm and tied it tightly around her torso. Britt grimaced, locked her teeth, and growled against the pain. She suddenly froze and cocked her head. "Too late," she said. "You hear that?"

They all stopped to listen but didn't hear anything.

"I thought I heard a horse," she explained.

"A horse?" asked Ilsa with surprise.

"It's Trent!" exclaimed Ben, realization joining the smile creasing his face. "He found his damned horse and came back."

"Yes," said Britt grimly. "I saw him out there just now, up on the ridge. I was just about to tell you." She frowned over at Ben. "He was aiming a rifle at me."

"What did you expect? You came charging up here like *Gunga Din,* guns blazing."

Britt gave him a wry smile. "Gunga Din was a pacifist. He carried water to the troops, not a gun."

"Ah, well at least you know your classical literature. That reassures me no end."

Britt suddenly raised her hand and listened again. Then they all heard it— distant hoof-beats this time, growing faster and louder, followed by the unmistakable sound of automatic gunfire, the terrified scream of a horse, and then silence.

"Help me up. Quickly!"

Jennifer and Ilsa grabbed Britt around her waist while she pushed herself up the wall with her legs. She leaned there for a moment, her face ashen, and wobbled. She reached a shaky hand for her rifle, then used it like a crutch to steady herself, and stumbled toward the door. There she stopped again, her legs unsure of themselves. She turned to say something but the words couldn't quite materialize. Her eyes rolled up and she collapsed in a heap in the doorway.

#

Trent came to and had no idea where he was. His cheek felt cold and wet but his face was growing numb. He groaned and raised himself up but something heavy held him down. His head throbbed, and he suddenly wanted nothing more than to lie back down and go to sleep. He was sure he could sleep forever.

But sleep was not to find him so easily. He heard the hard snow crunching underfoot nearby. The footsteps grew nearer and then stopped right out of sight somewhere beside him. He struggled to turn his head and saw a pair of feet come slowly into focus.

The feet were wearing moccasins.

Nämpäry knelt down and reached a hand out toward Trent. He poked him in the cheek and Trent flinched.

"You are not having such a good day, Squirrel." Trent watched out of the corner of his eye as Nämpäry shook his head at him. "You run straight into battle without a good plan; you do not even try to hear what *Mowun* has to say about it; and now. . . ." Nämpäry paused and looked sadly at the bleeding horse on top of Trent. "Now, you have gone and lost this fine horse of yours."

"Angel?" Trent mumbled groggily, trying to rise up again. "Angel's dead?"

"Angel?" came a gruff voice beside him. "Who the hell's *Angel?*"

It was no longer Nämpäry's voice that he heard, and Trent twisted his head up again to now see the black clothing of the rogue agent squatting beside him where the old Indian had been just seconds ago.

"Where'd he go?" wheezed Trent, glancing around weakly.

"Where did who go?"

The agent began to laugh, then spat on the ground just inches from Trent's face. Trent felt around behind his back with his one free arm, trying to locate his rifle, but it was no longer there. He realized that he must have lost it during the fall.

"You know what I think?" he continued, leaning farther down toward Trent, his hands on his knees. Trent suddenly saw the man bring a large Ka-Bar tactical knife up to his cheek. "I think that you're delirious and seeing things. I happen to have a great cure for that." He moved the knife and lightly touched the sharp tip to the soft skin under Trent's eye.

#

"Britt!" Ilsa screamed and ran over to kneel by her bodyguard's side.

"Quickly!" Ben yelled. "Get her out of the doorway." He pulled himself up from the floor, wincing and grimacing with every movement. He reached his arm out, his fingers grasping for Britt's assault rifle.

"Dad! You shouldn't try to move!"

Ben looked up at his daughter, his face crinkling into a wry smile. "Why? Do you think it might kill me?" His face then softened as he saw the hurt and fear in his daughter's eyes. "Honey, if we don't do something right now, then we'll all be dead in a few minutes anyway." He nodded toward the door. "Now, by the sound of it, either Trent has taken care of things out there . . . or else he's in bad trouble himself, and that trouble's now headed our way too. So help me up, will you?"

Ben grabbed the rifle while Jennifer moved quickly to help her father up, where he leaned on her shoulder and paused to catch his labored breath. He then shuffled forward, toward the door. Every bone in his body and every inch of shredded flesh screamed in protest. He made it to the doorway, where he leaned hard against the splintered framing and rested once more. He thought he heard voices and leaned his head slowly to peek out past the doorframe.

Halfway across the meadow, about fifty yards away, he saw the man Britt had called Karl kneeling down and gesturing—with a knife. Ben's breath caught suddenly as he realized what he was seeing: Trent was indeed in trouble, trapped on the ground underneath his dead horse while Karl seemed to be laughing and toying with him. Ben sucked in his breath and tried to raise the assault rifle but to no avail. It was impossible for him to raise the large weapon and steady himself against the doorframe at the same time.

"Here, Dad. Give me the rifle." Jennifer had moved around to face him and held her hand out.

"No. It's something I have to do."

"Dad! This is no time to try and play hero. Let me do it."

Ben gazed at his daughter lovingly. He reached over and moved a stray hair out of her face and placed it back over her ear. "Jennifer," he said, his voice soft with concern. "Have you ever killed a human being?"

Her mouth opened to speak, then closed again. "Um . . . no. Of course not. You know I haven't," she finally stammered. She hesitated, and then continued. "Have *you*?"

"Let's just say it's something I never ever thought you would have to experience." He licked his dry, cracked lips and glanced back outside. Trent's tormentor was still taunting him but was now standing up. Ben breathed a quick sigh of relief; at least his friend was still alive, though helpless underneath the horse. "And if this doesn't work," he continued, "you may still have to experience it before the end of the day. So, here—for once, let's try to accomplish something together, maybe like a real father and daughter." He paused again as Jennifer held his gaze for a moment. She then nodded, rose on her tiptoes, and kissed him lightly on the cheek.

"How do I help, then?"

"Stand right here," he said, moving her around until he had positioned her facing away from him, offset so that she was somewhat protected by the doorframe and the adobe wall, and so that he could peer over her left shoulder. "Here, now help me with this." Together, they swung the barrel of the assault rifle over her shoulder. Ben braced himself against the doorjamb and squinted into the rifle's scope. He paused, leaned over, and kissed his daughter on the back of her head. "You might want to plug your ears." He glanced at Ilsa. "You, too. It's going to be loud."

Jennifer put her fingers to her ears and closed her eyes.

"Steady . . . don't move now."

The scene appeared in much greater detail in the scope. Ben watched as Karl turned this way, seeming to look straight at him, sheathed his knife, and then stopped to turn back to say something to Trent. Ben took three deep breaths and held the last one. Karl chuckled, turned back toward the cabin, and started walking their way again, un-slinging his own rifle as he approached.

Ben squeezed the trigger.

There was a loud, deafening crack.

Jennifer flinched as the assault rifle bucked once.

#

"You know what else I think?" The man in black twisted the blade so closely that Trent could see it flash with the reflection of the late afternoon sun. "I think I can either slip this sweet blade cleanly across your throat—let you die quick, you won't feel a thing—or, I can walk away and let you bleed out underneath your dead horse there, nice and slow. Tell you what: I'll let you choose, eh?"

The man leaned in close again, this time putting his ear near Trent's mouth. "I can't quite hear you. . . . What's that again?" He stood up suddenly and put away his knife. "All right, then. Have it your way—nice and slow." He started to walk away, then stopped and turned his head. "You know, I think I would have chosen the blade. This way, you get to hear me kill your friends." He laughed and walked on.

Trent tried to call out a warning as he saw the man's black boots move away toward the cabin, but he couldn't get enough breath. He let his head drop back to the ground. He had screwed up badly and he knew it. Nämpäry was right: he just didn't take time to think—or to listen. All that was left for him to do now was to lie here helplessly and watch this . . . this terrorist murder his friends.

Trent squeezed his eyes shut and began to pray, hard.

Suddenly, he heard a strange, unfamiliar noise—a soft, sickening *whump* sound. He opened his eyes to see that the man in black hadn't taken too many steps away when he had stopped in his tracks, where he stood now, swaying strangely, still facing the cabin. He suddenly collapsed and sat down hard, his arms wide and his legs splayed out in front of him. Something looked very odd to Trent, and then he saw it: a large, vicious-looking arrow, dripping blood, protruded from the back of the man's neck. The man gurgled and his arms windmilled about, as if to balance himself. One hand then reached back, fingers fluttering as if trying to find the arrowhead behind his neck. After a few moments, however, the gurgling ceased, the arms stopped flailing, and the man in black slowly keeled over onto his side as blood pooled darkly red on the remaining white snow. He twitched a time or two, sighed, and then stopped moving.

Trent stared in disbelief, his forehead burning madly, as Nämpäry stepped into view, bow in hand, and stood over the dead man for a moment. Bending over, he pulled his arrow straight out of the man's neck in one fluid motion. It seemed to slide out effortlessly—unrealistically. Nämpäry knelt and wiped imaginary blood off the arrow in the snow and put it back into his quiver. He stood up and looked over at Trent.

The old Indian smiled, put a hand on his chest, and tapped it there, over his heart, in salute. He then turned and slowly disappeared, like a shimmering mist, into the trees.

CHAPTER 21
The Rocks Cry Out

October 25, 1875

Dear Sir(s):

A telegram that was previously delivered to you at Fort Union, outlining details of my "visit" to Cimarron, was intended to be leaked to our "friends" there, but the operator here says that he cannot raise the Cimarron office. If I were expected, our friends would probably be on hand, and I do not think your true and definite business would be suspected.

I have other agents in place who have been ready all along to assist you but they seem to doubt that you are willing. Their opinion is that you weakened and do not want to arrest the outlaw Allison. I must insist that you enlist whatever men you need to arrest or kill him and to kill all the men who resist you or stand with those who do resist you.

To that end, I have signed an invitation for the others of them to be on hand to greet me at Cimarron—including Mssrs. Morley, Springer, Carter, et al. Now, if they expect me on Monday the next, they will be on hand, and if any of these resist or attempt murder, bring them to swift justice too.

I am more anxious on our account than for any other reason. I clearly see that we have no friends in Colfax, and I have suspected all along that some of our pretended friends there are traitors.

Send me letters by messenger when it is done, and do not hesitate at extreme measures. I expect to hear from you quite soon. Your honor is at stake now, and a failure is fatal.

Yours. etc.,
S. B. Axtell, Governor

P.S. The above instructions are to be treated as proper warrant and authorization for all necessary actions alluded to therein.

*By direct order of this office, the bearer of this letter has lawfully done what has been done. --
S.B. Axtell.*

#

(November 1, 1875 – Cimarrón, New Mexico Territory)

Frank Springer took out his pocket watch and flipped it open. He checked the time, sighed, and put the watch back.

"I do believe you are about to wear that timepiece out, Counselor," said Clay Allison from across the office where he sat and played solitaire at the empty editorial desk of the *Cimarron News and Press*.

"And if I am, what of it?"

"Oh my, still a mite testy, I fear."

"I am not testy, Mr. Allison," argued Springer. "But you are correct to surmise that I am a touch fearful. Governor Axtell has yet to be a man of his word. And once again I am left to ponder the true meaning of his invitation to meet him here today. And by the way, the time, if anyone else cares to know, is 1:08 p.m., and our guest was supposed to arrive twenty-three minutes ago. Does anyone else find that already suspicious?"

"I, for one, certainly find it so," said Bill Morley, casting a glance around the office at the other men gathered there. "I mean, look at us—a more disparate group I have not seen in a long time: a distinguished lawyer and newspaper editor, a half-breed lawman—no offense meant, Jonathon."

"None taken, Mr. Morley, as usual." Jonathon called from where he leaned outside the open doorway, staring up the street and sipping coffee.

" . . . and a known gunman and killer," Morley continued.

"Offense taken, Mr. Morley," came Clay Allison's cold voice from across the room, which had grown suddenly quiet as all eyes turned his way. Allison threw another card down and then smiled, breaking the tension.

" . . . and me," Morley said finally, "a corporate president and railroad man. Now what, pray tell, do the four of us have in common."

"Well, given those descriptions," said Clay, "I would hazard the suggestion that each of us, in his own glaring way, is a scoundrel and a pirate, are we not?"

"No, we are not pirates," said Springer. "But we are *all* on Axtell's enemies list."

Morley snorted, stood up, and stepped over to the window to peer out. "My point, exactly. I mean, as dissimilar as we all are, we are often as not at odds with each other, politically. But we must collectively present some threat to the governor—and this so-called Santa Fe Ring." He turned back from the window and spread his hands. "And where the hell is Sheriff Rinehart? Is it bothersome to anyone else that when trouble arises, Isaiah Rinehart is always conveniently indisposed elsewhere?"

"It does give one pause to think, does it not?" said Allison, concentrating on his game. "Almost makes you wonder just whose side the good sheriff is on, after all."

"Well, no matter who's on whose side," said Springer, checking his watch yet again, "I am certain the governor is about to reveal his hand."

"Well, then let him reveal it," Allison said, dealing another card to himself. "I shall be more than happy to show him *my* hand in return."

Jonathon stepped into the room, set his coffee cup down on a table, and adjusted his gun belt. "Looks like you can show him right now." He jerked his thumb back to gesture outside. "Men coming up the street."

Frank Springer jumped up from his chair and joined Morley at the window, both craning their necks and squinting to see down the sun-drenched street. Clay Allison sighed, dealt himself a final card, shook his head, and then stood up slowly. "Well, this has sure not been a good hand anyway. Time to fold, I'd say." He followed Jonathon out the door onto the wooden porch.

"I don't think you're going to find this one to be much better, Clay," said Jonathon, nodding down the street.

Thirty yards away, three men walked steadily up the middle of the street. Their faces were shaded from the early afternoon sun, which beat almost directly down on their hats, but at twenty yards the men began to look familiar.

"Colbert," muttered Allison around the burnt-out stub of his cigar.

"And Pancho Griego on the right, there," added Jonathon. "But I don't know the third man, in the middle."

"That, my friend, is none other than David Crockett, from Tennessee. They must have hired him just for this little square dance."

Jonathon turned slowly and stared at Allison. "David Crockett?" he asked evenly. "Like *the* Davy Crockett, at the Alamo? I thought he was dead?"

"The great nephew of the dead one." Allison nodded. "This one's obviously alive and kicking. And he's a real son-of-a-bitch and as vicious as a bear, too. I knew him back before the war, back home in Tennessee. If you would like, I will shoot him now, and happily. It might take the others down a notch and make them a little more docile."

"Not yet, Clay. Let's see what they have to say first."

Allison shook his head and looked at the deputy. "Big mistake, Squirrel."

"*Clay?*" came a call from one of the men in the street. It was Pancho Griego.

"Might be. But like I said—best we hear them out," Jonathon turned and looked at Allison. "Then we'll probably have to shoot them."

Clay Allison pulled the cheroot from his mouth, dropped it on the ground, and stepped off the porch. "Ah, scrapping for a fight, are we, Deputy? Sometimes you do amaze me."

"I'm just ready to get this mess over with. But yes, sometimes I do amaze myself as well."

#

Chunk Colbert scratched his butt cheek nervously as the three of them walked slowly toward the newspaper office. Pancho had made their plan quite clear while they had been drinking the previous evening. He had even produced a letter and waved it in Chunk's face—something about it being from the governor of the territory, authorizing them to take out these four men. *Enemies*, he had called them. Later, Colbert had managed to slip the letter into his own pocket—insurance against a possible bad outcome. But as long as the whiskey had flowed, Pancho's plan had seemed quite plausible. They would attempt to mislead Allison with lots of friendly talk and would feign forgiveness for the lynching of his nephew, Cruz Vega; and when Allison and the half-breed deputy finally suspected that nothing was going to happen, they would all three open up on them before they were any the wiser. Once Allison and Carter lay dead, it would be no problem at all to execute the other two, Springer and Morley, on the spot—although Colbert sort of liked that Springer fellow. He had always been friendly and had a cordial word for Colbert, unlike most of those high-and-mighty-types. Of course, money was money, and the governor had paid them all very handsomely.

Like shooting fish in a barrel, Colbert reminded himself now as they marched down the street. He fingered the dried black-haired scalp he kept draped through his belt for good luck. *Or like shooting helpless Indians in their own camp.*

Chunk became suddenly aware that Pancho Griego had lifted two fingers just slightly. It was a prearranged signal for the three of them to begin to spread out across the width of the street, to make a more difficult target. Roughly fifteen yards from their adversaries, Pancho slowed his walk and the other two followed suit.

"Clay," Pancho called out as they finally came to a stop. Colbert narrowed his eyes and nervously moved his gun hand to finger the edge of his holster. He had moved himself to the very edge of the street and glanced now to his left, where that crazy Crockett fellow was standing with a silly grin plastered on his face. Crockett was clean-shaven, wore his long hair slicked straight back, and dressed like a dandy—all in fancy black clothing like some dime novel gunslinger. The man's fingers fluttered inches away from his sidearm. Colbert didn't like the guy and could still not figure out what he was doing here. There were so many other legitimate gunmen in New Mexico and Colorado territories capable of killing people that there was no need to import a rogue stranger. But it had something to do with putting *just the right finishing touches* on the day's grisly work—or some other such bullshit Griego had been spouting.

Colbert straightened up and tried to refocus. He sure could use a drink right now, but Griego had said they would drink when these men were dead. Allison and Carter had moved off the porch into the street and now faced them. Suddenly, the odds didn't feel so good to Chunk. Outnumbered or not, he had seen what both Clay Allison and Jonathon Carter could do with a gun; and now, sober and face to face with the two, Colbert was getting a queasy feeling in the pit of his stomach.

This might not end well at all.

#

"Pancho, how the hell are you?" answered Clay, smiling and nodding as if greeting an old friend.

"What can we do for you today, Señor Griego?" asked Jonathon, less friendly. He had moved to Allison's left and well into the middle of the street, positioning himself across from the gunman named Crockett.

Griego pushed his hat back and nodded. "I thought I should have a cordial word with Clay, here—clear the air between us, if we could."

"And you thought this *cordial* word could be best accomplished by bringing along your two friends here?" asked Jonathon.

"Yes, well, they feared for my safety, obviously." Griego removed his hat slowly and gestured with it toward Allison, who had casually moved one side of his coat back behind his holster. "I mean, after the arguments Mr. Allison and I have had," Griego dropped his voice a shade lower and fixed Allison with a steely look. "And after the part Mr. Allison played in the lynching of my nephew."

"Your nephew," interjected Allison, "that is, *the murderer*, Cruz Vega, was resisting arrest."

"I believe that is the way you have chosen to justify his death, Mr. Allison," continued Griego, darkly. He then seemed to catch himself and lightened his tone. He continued to hold his hat near his waist. "But that is not for you and me to decide here. Today, *Clay*, I would like for us to walk away as friends, once again—*amigos,* as we were before."

"How about your other friend here?" Jonathon asked, nodding toward Crockett. "You going to introduce us? Is he going to just walk away as an *amigo* today, too?"

David Crockett continued to grin, a somewhat mad look in his eyes, as if it were the only expression he had at his disposal. Despite the madness that crawled over his face, he looked surprisingly squeaky clean and was dressed in attire that could only be described as some easterner's idea of a western outfit: black duster over a tight vest with silver buttons, white shirt with starched collar, red silk kerchief drawn tight around his throat, and spit-shined cavalry-style riding boots over his canvas britches and up to his knees. He stared back at Jonathon as though he would just as soon devour him raw.

Jonathon moved his gaze over to Chunk Colbert. "How about you, Chunk? You here just to be friends?"

Chunk started to answer, but something flickered behind Jonathon's eye and the action seemed to slow down, a feeling he knew quite well and one he never ignored. Something was wrong—something about Griego's hat—and it was happening right now.

Jonathon saw the hat move just slightly but in an odd and unnatural way. He knew that Griego held his hat in his right hand while engaging Allison in conversation. But the hat was covering his holster and left hand, and Jonathon also knew that Griego was left-handed. Allison could not see Griego's gun hand moving in slow motion and now deftly gripping the butt of his pistol to draw it free of the holster.

"Clay! Gun!" Jonathon shouted, his own hand flying to his pistol as he instinctively dropped into a crouch.

Several things happened simultaneously. Pancho Griego flinched at Jonathon's shout and fired too quickly. The bullet passed through Pancho's hat, ripped through the fabric of the lower right arm of Allison's coat, shattered the window where Frank Springer and William Morley stood, passed between the two men, and buried itself in the back wall of the newspaper office. Clay Allison calmly and smoothly drew his Army Colt and in the same fluid motion pumped two bullets through Pancho Griego's heart. Griego slumped silently to the ground in a heap. The gunman David Crockett slapped the leather of his holster and whipped out his weapon but was able only to discharge three bullets blindly into the ground—one of them plowing through his right boot and blowing off his own big toe. Meanwhile, his eyes had crossed and the grin had left his face as Jonathon's quicker shot had already passed neatly between his eyes and blasted out the back of Crockett's head. Crockett had only begun to slump backward when Jonathon swung his .45 around to defend himself against Chunk Colbert, but he checked his next shot when he saw that Chunk now stood firmly rooted to the ground and had both hands raised above his shoulders. He was looking very pale and shaking his head slowly.

"Don't shoot, Mr. Carter—please don't."

Crockett's body finally hit the ground with a thud. Chunk Colbert glanced over at his two dead companions.

"What'll it be then, Chunk?" Jonathon's gun did not waiver and was pointed straight at Colbert's chest. "You joining your friends, or what?"

"Ain't my fight, Mr. Carter. Never was. Wasn't s'posed to come to this."

"Yes, I'll bet that it wasn't," snarled Allison. He stood up straight, stretched out his arm, and trained his pistol on Colbert's head. "Move aside, Jonathon, so's I can put the bastard out of our misery."

"Hold on, Clay," came a voice from the porch of the newspaper office, where Springer and Morley now stood, surveying the scene. "How much did they pay you to murder us, Colbert?"

Morley had gone white at the carnage, but Springer stood defiantly with his hands on his hips, his walrus mustache almost bristling with outrage. "I asked you a question, Mr. Colbert! And I expect a prompt answer." Springer stepped off the porch and now advanced on Chunk Colbert, as if he were already prosecuting a case here and now, stepping in front of the guns being aimed by Allison and Carter. "*Who* paid you, and how much?"

Colbert quickly sized up the situation as well as his good fortune at Springer's coming between him and imminent destruction. He twisted, ducked, and sprang away down the dark alley between two buildings to his immediate right.

"Damn it, Springer!" yelled Allison as Colbert's running footsteps echoed away from them. "Get the hell out of the way!" He shoved Frank Springer and leveled off his pistol again, but it was too late.

Chunk Colbert had disappeared.

#

Several hours later, a shadow disengaged itself from behind the newspaper office building, moved to the corner of the porch, and stopped. Chunk Colbert held his breath and listened, then continued into the silent street, bent over, and peered closely at the ground. Suddenly, he stopped, squatted down, and picked up a small rectangular piece of paper that was lying there. Somehow, throughout all the turmoil and horrific action of the afternoon's gun battle, Chunk had seen something fall from the coat pocket of his long-time enemy, Clay Allison—something that might have had some value to Allison, and if so, could be turned against him.

Colbert stuffed the document into his pocket and ran back into the shadows. When he was far enough back down the alleys, he slipped into an old outhouse behind one of the buildings there. He took the stiff paper out of his pocket, lit a match, and eagerly studied it. After several disappointing seconds, he blew the match out.

The treasure that Chunk had hoped to blackmail Allison with was simply some meaningless old photograph of Allison, Carter, Springer, and a couple of others he didn't recognize. He started to wad it up and throw it through the seat hole and into the filth of the outhouse, but then stopped himself, thinking for a minute.

Colbert unfolded the photo, peered at it once again, and then slipped it back into his shirt pocket before exiting the outhouse. Had he bothered to turn the photograph over, he would have seen Cruz Vega's crudely drawn map to the most valuable treasure a man like Chunk Colbert ever could have hoped for in his life.

#

(November 9, 1875 – Elizabethtown, New Mexico Territory)

"Who paid you, and how much did you get paid?"

Jonathon Carter sat across the small table inside the jailhouse in Elizabethtown. Across from him sat a small, wiry Mexican by the name of Manuel Cardenas—the second man Jonathon had seen racing along the Cimarron Canyon road with Cruz Vega the day Reverend Tolby was murdered, the man Cruz Vega later identified (right before he was lynched) as the real murderer of Reverend Tolby and the man who yesterday had turned himself in to the town marshal at E-Town on condition that he be further turned over to no one other than Jonathon Carter.

"Five hundred dollars," answered Cardenas finally. He grabbed the bottle of whiskey that sat between them on the table and upended it. Jonathon watched him for a moment before reaching out, taking the bottle away, and slapping the cork in it.

"I need you clear-headed, Manuel. First you answer, then you can drink. Who paid you the five hundred dollars?"

"Don't remember."

"You don't remember?"

"Nope."

"Someone gave me five hundred dollars, I sure as hell would remember who."

"Well, maybe if it was you, you wouldn't be afraid they'd kill ya."

"Someone threaten you, Manuel?"

Cardenas snorted. "Hmmph. You have Clay Allison and your crooked sheriff, Rinehart, to thank for that."

"Rinehart threatened you?"

"Let's just say the threat is implied."

"You saying Rinehart is part of the *Ring?*"

Cardenas just looked at Jonathon.

"Clay Allison threatened you, then?"

Cardenas rolled his eyes. "Allison's the one got Vega to point me out. Vega's now dead. So, how do you suppose *that* story's gonna end for me?"

"Vega only confirmed what we already knew."

"Which is?"

"Which is, Manuel . . . *I* personally saw you and Vega riding away from the murder scene. It was me, then, rode up and found Reverend Tolby's body, right after. We had you already, based solely on that."

"Well, doesn't help me sleep none at night, knowing that Allison got Vega to confess."

"Who else is part of the Santa Fe Ring, Manuel?*"

"You get me to a fair trial—and I mean where the jury isn't loaded with government sympathizers—then I'll give you those names." Cardenas grabbed the bottle back. "And not until then."

#

Early the next morning, Jonathon rousted Manuel Cardenas from his jail cell, shackled him and tied him to a spare horse, and led him the twenty-four miles from Elizabethtown to Cimarron. They paused briefly in the upper Cimarron Canyon at the spot where Reverend Tolby had been murdered.

"Feel like saying a few words, Manuel?" asked Jonathon.

"Just get me out of here."

"Why? Afraid of ghosts?"

"Maybe."

From there, they dropped into the Valley of the Utes, stopping briefly at Walking Elk's wickiup to check in on him, as Jonathon often did when passing this way. The old Indian greeted them and invited them inside to eat, but Jonathon declined.

"This man is my prisoner," he explained.

"Yes," answered Walking Elk, gazing up at Manuel as he sat on his horse and studying him closely. "Yes, I recognize him. And he certainly is a prisoner. But of himself, not of you." Walking Elk shook his head in disgust. "This man has many devils hanging off of his spirit. They are eating him alive, and he will die from them soon."

Manuel Cardenas stared in horror at the old Indian.

"Get me the hell out of here!" he cried to Jonathon. "Get me away from this old man's crazy talk!"

214

It was late afternoon as they entered Cimarron. Several people stopped what they were doing to greet Jonathon and his prisoner.

"That him, Jonathon? That the other son-of-a bitch killed the preacher?"

One grey-haired lady, dressed primly and carrying herself nobly, walked over to Manuel's horse, gathered herself up, and spat as far as she could manage, which happened to be only to the man's knee. This seemed to be satisfactory to her, though, and she nodded. "I hope the bastard burns in hell!" she blurted before turning and walking away.

"Crazy old bitch! You oughta be arresting nasty people like her!"

"Same sort of folk that will make up your *fair* jury, I reckon," said Jonathon as they turned a corner and were pulling their horses to a stop in front of the jail.

Jonathon dismounted, tied the reins of both animals to the hitching rail, and then dove for cover and drew his pistol as a single rifle shot suddenly rang out from somewhere behind them.

Manuel Cardenas's horse screamed and bucked against the hitching rail as Cardenas slumped over, still tied to the saddle, his blood and brains spilling down the animal's neck

CHAPTER 22
From Darkness To Light

(Present Day – Sangre de Cristo Mountains)

An insistent measured thumping drifted in and out of the darkness and then the darkness itself waivered with intermittent stabs of light. Distant voices echoed; Trent felt as if he were being asked questions, but he had no idea who was asking or how to answer. He tried to wake up but couldn't; his eyelids felt glued shut. He weakly raised a hand to block the lights that he felt more than saw. He tried to speak, but his mouth was as dry as cotton balls—and he tasted blood in his throat. He felt somehow constricted, and then he remembered that Angel, his horse, had pinned him down.

Angel, he thought to himself, a pang of remorse and extreme sadness welling up inside. He coughed once, trying to choke back the emotion. He felt tears forming in the corners of his eyes—the sadness was overwhelming and now faded back to a dream.

He suddenly felt jarred, jostled about, freed suddenly from the earlier constriction, but vaguely aware of dull throbbing pain everywhere. The heavy thumping sound was back and more pronounced, like some powerful engine washing out the echoing voices. He was just on the verge of waking and turned his head to see where he was. His eyelids finally opened into slits, just enough to make out a bit of shadow and light. There seemed to be something—someone—moving around him. He tried to sit up, to pull himself free, but he found that he was strapped down, immobile, trapped. The wind began to howl more loudly around him, and Trent felt a sudden rush of vertigo seize him. He sucked in his breath, but felt that he couldn't get enough oxygen, and he struggled vainly. He was being lifted slowly into the air, higher and higher, by some great noisy beast.

"Easy there—easy," shouted the nearby shadowy figure. "We'll be there soon. . .." But some of the words were lost in the wind. Trent was able to open his eyelids a fraction more but still couldn't focus. The hazy figure seemed to be messing with him, prodding him uncomfortably. He squeezed his eyes shut and fell back into blessed darkness.

#

(Raton, New Mexico)

Trent awakened into a dim stillness. The thumping noise and wind were gone, and he now seemed to be lying in a room where he could just make out colored lights dancing in the periphery of his vision. He again heard the distant voices, but this time not so . . . *echo-y*, just . . . distant. He wondered how long he had been trapped under the horse. He wondered what that overwhelming thumping noise had been earlier, and what these colored lights were, and just whose voices he was now hearing. And just *where was he?*

And then he wondered to himself if he were dead.

He was suddenly aware of someone standing near him and looked that way to see an angelic being, dressed all in white, who leaned in close with some sort of a wand—or maybe a sword—and Trent flinched as it was swiped across his forehead. The spirit being then turned away and Trent heard a rapid clattering noise. It was annoying and interfered with his reasoning.

He tried to move, but as he did so tremendous stabs of pain went through his left side, arm, and leg.

"No," chuckled the figure in white. "You aren't dead—not yet."

How had the spirit heard his thoughts? *Or could this be Nämpäry*, his Indian spirit friend, in yet another guise? He knew that Nämpäry could read his mind. Squinting in the dim light for recognition, Trent looked again at the white angel. After all, Trent had seen the Indian ghost transform in appearance from a young, vibrant warrior to a wrinkled and grizzled elder.

Yes, that must be it. This must be the spirit warrior, *Nämpäry*, come to help him again.

"My horse," he croaked, the dryness in his throat taking control. "*Nämpäry*, *w*here is Angel?"

"Oh, so *now* you're seeing angels. No wonder you think you're dead."

There was the sound of liquid pouring, and then the white spirit leaned over again.

"Here. Drink this. It should help."

A straw found its way between Trent's parched lips, and he gratefully slurped the cool water. It was the best water he had ever tasted. His head fell back against a soft cloud, and his heavy eyes sealed shut again. Soon, the clattering faded, the beeping subsided, and the lights dimmed again to darkness.

When Trent awoke again, the room was much lighter. He was suddenly aware of the most wonderful aroma—someone was cooking nearby and the smell of the food was incredible, overwhelming his senses. His stomach growled and he realized that he was ravenous. He tried to move, more slowly this time as he remembered the pains throughout his body. He realized that he was no longer trapped underneath his horse but was lying in some sort of bed—and still restricted somehow. He tried to raise himself and fell back on the bed with a painful groan.

Trent looked around and tried to examine his situation. His left arm was in a cast, his left leg was heavily bandaged and lay with a pillow propped underneath his knee. He was in a gown, but otherwise pantless and shirtless and could see—and feel—that his chest was tightly wrapped. *Broken ribs, probably.*

He looked back over at the angelic being in white who was checking the bandages, who, as he could now clearly see, was not the old Indian spirit, but a young female nurse—younger than his daughter Sophie and just as pretty.

When she saw that her patient was finally awake, the nurse turned the lights up a degree brighter.

"Good morning," she said cheerfully.

"You're no angel," Trent said matter-of-factly.

The young nurse feigned a pout and put her hands on her hips. "Well, thanks a lot! You're no saint, either."

"No, I meant that . . . oh, never mind."

Trent lay still for a few moments, frowning and taking stock again. He tried to remember how he had gotten here. Last he knew, he had been up in the Sangre de Cristos, having just shot and killed a woman—a foreign agent—and wondering whether his friends in that cabin were still alive or dead, and then finally having his favorite horse shot out from under him. And the man who did it was about to kill him but instead fell dead with an arrow through his neck.

Or at least that's what I think happened.

That was about all he remembered. Instead, he found his mind now going back a few years earlier, to another time he had awakened in a hospital, bandaged from head to toe, memory half gone, and being visited by ghosts.

Not much had changed since then, he thought. *Except for Maggie.*

Trent suddenly panicked.

"Where's my wife? Where's Maggie?"

"I think they said Mrs. Carter finally went home late last night to get some rest. She was just exhausted—had been here since they brought you in. Said she'd be back early today, so I'm guessing that she should be here any time now."

The enticing smell of food again asserted itself, and Trent finally decided that if he was this hungry for hospital food, then his injuries—and his memories and everything else—could just wait.

"So, just who is *Nämpäry?*" asked the nurse, typing some more notes into the bedside computer.

"Nämpäry? Why?"

"You were calling out that name earlier—at least that's what it sounded like—in your sleep."

Trent suddenly felt embarrassed. "Oh, just an . . . old friend of mine."

"Interesting name. Native American?"

"Um . . . yes, I suppose so."

"What's it mean?"

"Pardon?"

"You know. Indian names have cool meanings. What's your friend's name mean?"

"I, uh . . . I really have no idea."

Trent suddenly didn't feel like talking to this woman about ghosts. He decided to change the subject.

"I smell food. You think some of that may be for me?"

"Let me go see what we can find for you, Mr. Carter." The nurse smiled as she took off her gloves, washed her hands, and headed for the door. She stopped, turned back, and nodded toward a shadowy corner of the room. "And I'm betting that she'll want something to eat, too."

Trent raised his eyebrows in a questioning look, then turned his head just far enough not to hurt his ribs, and peered into the shadows there.

Not three feet away from him sat a visitor's lounge chair—a small recliner. Someone was lying asleep on the chair, facing away from Trent, a thin hospital blanket pulled up over her shoulders. The slumbering form snored softly, then rolled this way, moaned once, and slept on.

The sleeper was Ilsa Boewmeester.

#

"How long has *she* been here?" Trent asked around a mouthful of hospital eggs and bacon, which, right now, was the best food he had ever tasted.

"She's another one that's been here ever since they brought you in," answered the nurse, who was again making notes on the computer. "Can't get her to budge. She won't leave your side. Something about you saving her life."

"And when was that, exactly—when did they bring me in?"

"You've been here for three days. Search and Rescue choppered you in. You've been out like a light for most of that. Doctor had to sedate you pretty heavily until we got that fluid off your lung." She turned and nodded down at his bandaged body, then referred back to his chart on the computer screen. "Gunshot wound to the calf, arm broken in two places, badly sprained knee, concussion, three cracked or bruised ribs, and a slight puncture of your left lung. Had to keep you immobile." She looked him over once more and shook her head. "And it looks to me like you have been through the ringer more than once, judging by that roadmap of scars you're wearing."

"Three *days?*" Trent was almost afraid to ask but finally forced himself to continue. "They bring anybody else in with me?"

The nurse turned from her computer, looked over at the sleeping Ilsa, and then went back to work. "Other than her, I assume you mean? I'm afraid I can't talk about other patients with you, Mr. Carter. Privacy laws—I'm sure you can understand."

"Oh, come on now! There was my friend, Ben—*Sheriff* Ferguson, and his daughter, Jennifer—and more than a few other folks who were injured and shot up."

The nurse remained silent and ignored him. Trent stared at her for a moment in frustration, sighed, and returned to his breakfast. "What's your name?"

"I'm Patricia—call me Pat. I believe the name means *She Who Hunts Down*

Breakfast."

Trent stopped chewing and looked at her blankly. He thought he detected a smirk on her face as she continued to type.

"Well, Pat, tell me this: Here I almost die trying to save some peoples' lives, and you can't even tell me if I succeeded or not?"

Pat glanced at Trent for a moment, her eyes seeming to flicker as if giving him a quick once-over. "Are you law enforcement?"

"Retired law enforcement."

"Then what can I say? It appears to me you succeeded okay—*you're* not dead." She nodded again toward Ilsa. "She's alive. Other than that, again I'm not at liberty to talk about it."

Trent looked at her, laughed, and grimaced as his bruised ribs grabbed his attention. The nurse's tone actually reminded him of Ben Ferguson's dry sense of humor. And it also reminded him that he really needed to find out if Ben was okay. It was obvious that Nurse Patricia here was going to be of no help in that regard.

He took another bite of his breakfast and then washed it down with hot coffee. "I think you and I are going to get along just fine, Pat. Just fine. So just keep your damn secrets, for all I care."

There was a soft stirring to Trent's right.

"Mr. Carter?" Ilsa groaned as she threw the blanket off with one hand and struggled to sit upright. Her other right arm was in a sling and encased in a cast.

"Well, good morning, Sleeping Beauty," said Trent, watching her carefully.

She got up and shuffled groggily over to his bedside, where she wrapped her good arm around his neck and hugged him gently for a long while, her cheek nestled warmly at his neck.

Trent was surprised at the familiarity and was speechless for several moments. He cautiously returned the hug. It reminded him of when Sophie was a little girl, dragging herself into his and Vicky's bedroom early in the morning. "Like I said," said the nurse with an understanding smile. "She hasn't left your side."

Ilsa finally disengaged herself and smiled sweetly at Trent. "I am so happy you're awake, finally," she said still grasping his hand tightly.

He smiled tentatively back at her, still somewhat ill at ease. "Ready for breakfast?" he finally stammered.

"In a moment," Ilsa murmured, then made her way to the bathroom, and shut the door.

Trent stared at the door for a minute.

"Are . . . are visitors allowed to use my toilet?" he pointed and asked, at a loss for anything else to say.

"Why not?" quipped Pat, as she reached down to check the catheter bag clipped to the side of Trent's bed. "You sure aren't using it yet."

"Funny. Real funny."

At that moment there was a light knock at the door and it swung slowly open. Trent grinned as Maggie stepped through the doorway. She was a sight for his tired eyes; dressed in fashionable jeans and a cream-colored long-sleeve blouse open to the second button. Her shoulder length auburn hair was tousled but charming, as if she had just brushed it out quickly upon getting out of bed.

"Oh, Sweetie, they said you might finally be awake." Maggie came quickly over and sat on the edge of the bed, leaned over, took Trent's face gently in both hands, and kissed him forever on the mouth. He closed his eyes and felt all the stress and tension drain from his body and mind.

She finally let him come up for air and sat back, her beautiful blue-gray eyes gazing at him with just a hint of tears welling up. Trent reached his good hand up and stroked the corner of her mouth lightly with the back of his forefinger.

"I told you I'd come back to you," he said softly. She nodded and grasped his hand in hers, then kissed his fingertips. "Yes you did. But when I saw them take you off that helicopter. . . ." She choked and couldn't finish.

The door to the bathroom opened and Ilsa stepped out. She smiled when she saw Maggie and rushed over to join the reunion at Trent's bedside. "I wondered where you got off to," Maggie said, putting an arm around Ilsa's shoulders and giving her a squeeze.

"I'm going to go now—give you all a little alone time," said Nurse Pat, signing off the computer and stepping out of the room. Trent overheard her excuse herself to someone standing just outside the door.

"Oh, that reminds me," Maggie continued, wiping her eyes, standing up, and moving back to the door. "Look who I found wandering the halls just now. Said she's been waiting until you came around to say 'Hi.' Wanted to give us a little privacy, first, though."

Trent had just taken another sip of coffee but choked on it when Maggie opened the door. Britt de Jaager, the rogue agent he had shot and supposedly killed, stepped into the room, alive and well and with her right arm in a sling. She shut the door firmly behind her and stood almost at attention at the foot of the bed, staring down at Trent.

All the tension and stress came flooding back to him with a vengeance.

"So good to see you looking well again, Mr. Carter. We need to talk."

#

"Grandpa, are you ready to go? Hector's planning on meeting us at the hospital soon. Maggie says Daddy's finally awake."

Sophie Carter-Armijo glanced once more at the text message on her phone, put it into her coat pocket, and then walked up next to Walter. She slipped her arm through his and leaned her head on his shoulder. Clouds were scudding in from the north, over Raton Peak, and the temperature had dropped noticeably. She shivered and pulled closer to her grandfather for some warmth.

"Just a few more minutes, Baby Girl," Walter murmured, kissing the top of his granddaughter's head. He glanced down at the small bouquet of red roses he held in his hands, then bent down slowly and placed them against the headstone. The grave was one of four—five, if you counted Tim's—occupying the same family plot, with room for a couple more. He touched a finger to the stone and traced the name, his lips moving as he did so. *"Elizabeth Sophia Carter."* He kissed his fingertips and then lovingly patted the headstone. "Here you are, my love . . . some fresh ones."

"I sure do miss them," said Sophie, giving her grandfather's arm a soft squeeze as her eyes wandered to the grave next to her grandmother's. "I'm glad we put Mom next to Grandma," she said. "She would've liked that." She pulled gently away from Walter, stepped over, and knelt down, brushing some dead leaves and a small pinecone from the top of the stone that adorned the grave of her mother, Victoria Ann Carter.

"I like it, too," said Walter. He looked to his right where his own mother, Penelope Ann Carter, lay at rest in a much older grave, with a smaller, worn grave marker near her feet engraved with the name of his little brother, Timothy Peter Carter. Walter sighed, knowing that not much lay in the latter two graves. Not much had been found to bury—other than the odd shoe or some other article of clothing—after the train had exploded on Raton Pass in 1945. "I miss them all," he added, wiping at his nose with his handkerchief. "You know, Timmy would have been 81 now. Imagine that." He paused for a moment, touched his brother's name, and continued. "Seems the older I get, the more I realize just how much I miss them."

Sophie finished tidying up her mother's grave, and then pulled a single, long-stemmed rose out of the bouquet Walter had laid on his wife's grave. She laid it gently across the top of the headstone. "Hope you don't mind, Grandpa."

"It'll just blow off of there," muttered Walter gruffly.

"I know. But until it does, it will look just right."

"Hardheaded as your daddy," Walter scoffed, then caught her eye, and smiled. "But pretty as your mama!" He was proud of his only grandchild; proud that she had landed on her feet following such tragic losses in her, as yet, short 36 years of life; and proud that she had finally found some happiness in her marriage to Hector Armijo—even though this gave the family one more law enforcement officer to worry about.

Sophie stood up, blew her mom a kiss, and then stepped around to the other graves. She stopped in front of the one that lay to the right of Penelope's, and was the last in the family plot, for now.

"Tell me about my great-grandfather," she said, kneeling down and brushing away the many dead twigs, leaves, and dirt that almost obscured the name carved in stone. She looked up at her grandfather, but he was frowning. "Grandpa . . . tell me about Walter Senior, your dad. Please? You never talk about him."

Walter wiped at his nose again and looked away. He let the late fall afternoon breeze cool his upturned face as it whispered through the large blue spruce pine trees that filled the air above them year round with a beautiful shaded canopy. The cemetery lay on a plateau in the north part of the City of Raton that carried the earlier distinction of having been the first stop where, in 1846, Lieutenant (later General) Philip Kearny encamped his troops after crossing Raton Pass and entering New Mexico. From here, he led them to liberate Santa Fe for the United States, and finally on to Mexico where he further distinguished himself in the Mexican-American War.

The ghosts of those particular soldiers melted away, and Walter finally forced himself to turn back and look down at the grave he had always managed to ignore each time he visited this place: the simple military monument of yet another warrior, his father, Sgt. Robert Walter Carter, Sr., a United States Marine who had suffered horrific wounds in the Pacific during World War II; the man who Walter, as a child, never felt close to, and who, upon his return from the war, had further alienated his only surviving son; and a man Walter had grown to despise for the remainder of his life for his complete lack of caring. Walter had come to terms with the loss of his mother and brother in a senseless act of what would now be called terrorism, but evidently his father had not. And despite the atrocities and senselessness the Japanese must have visited upon Walter, Sr. (which he never spoke of), giving him his physical as well as mental battle wounds—what today would be diagnosed as post traumatic stress disorder—Walter, Jr., had never come to terms with, nor been able to forgive, the ultimate act of betrayal by the man whom he still refused to think of as *father*.

Three years following the death of his wife and youngest son, Robert Walter Carter, Sr., at age 35, had hung himself from a large elm tree in the middle of the back yard, where 15 year-old Walter, Jr., found him early the next morning.

Walter was breathing hard and he wiped the sweat from his face—or was it tears? He suddenly realized he was on his hands and knees in front his father's grave, his teeth tightly clenched, and his heart racing. His fingers were sore and torn where they had dug into the grass and hard dirt in front of him, as if trying to unearth something—or someone. Sophie was on her knees beside him, her arms around his neck, and was weeping.

"Wha—what just happened?" Walter said, rising up and grasping his granddaughter's hand. Sophie shook her head quickly and traced the back of her fingers down her grandfather's face, wiping away tears.

"Why have you never talked about this, Grandpa? How have you kept all that bottled up inside?"

Walter looked away, incredulous. He had no idea that he had just been verbalizing these feelings, these thoughts, this hurtful past that he had refused to deal with—or share with anyone—for over 70 years.

"I'm so sorry," he mumbled, choking up again and fighting back tears that still fell from down his cheeks and onto the grave of his father. "I am so, so very sorry."

"It's okay, Grandpa. It's really okay. You needed to get that out."

But it wasn't his granddaughter Walter was apologizing to, or to the man in the grave.

CHAPTER 23
Death Comes To Dine

(Letter from Governor Samuel Axtell)

November 12, 1875

The Honorable Isaiah Rinehart—Sheriff,
Colfax County,
Territory of New Mexico

Dear Sheriff Rinehart:
　I shall dispense with the usual amenities and get right to the point: I am greatly vexed to learn of your apparent inability to bring order from the chaos that is now being called, in the New York newspapers, The Colfax County War. I had presumed that you and I had a clear understanding of where your loyalties lie in this entire affair. Notwithstanding the recent silencing of the insurrectionist Tolby, as well as those responsible for his demise (I shall not second guess what your own role was in those unfortunate affairs), the recent fiasco in which our friend and supporter Francisco Griego and his ally David Crockett were gunned down in the streets of Cimarron in cold blood and in broad daylight by the outlaw Clay Allison leaves me at wits' end as to how to proceed. I now also have it on very good authority that none other than one of your own sworn deputies—a half-breed by the name of Jonathon Carter—was in on the shootings, taking up the part of Mssrs. Allison, Springer, and Morley, et al.
　Suffice it to say that "extreme disappointment" does not fully describe my opinion of your ability to properly protect the peace in your county. Therefore, I hereby inform you of my decision to send a troop of the 9th Cavalry from Fort Union to aid you in the apprehension of the murderers Clay Allison and your own Jonathon Carter. Let us pray that with the help of these Buffalo Soldiers you may restore the confidence of this office in your own. Far be it from me to assume that the Southern Gentleman Gunfighter, Allison, would rather go down in a hail of bullets than to go peaceably into the custody of Negro soldiers—but such an outcome might make all of us breathe much easier.

　Sincerely, etc.
　S. B. Axtell, Governor
　Santa Fe,
　Territory of New Mexico

　P.S. Please have the good grace to destroy this letter once you have fully digested it.

#

(November 19, 1875 – Cimarron, New Mexico Territory)

"Who do we think his source of information is?" asked Frank Springer.

"I can hazard one very good guess, Counselor," answered Clay Allison.

"Your old friend Chunk Colbert?" suggested Jonathon Carter.

"One and the same."

It was mid-morning, and the three men were meeting, along with Sheriff Isaiah Rinehart, in the back room of the *Cimarron News and Press*.

"*A clear understanding of where your loyalties lie.*" Frank Springer shook his head and handed the letter back to Rinehart. "So, if this is true, just why are you sharing this with us, Sheriff Rinehart?"

"Yes, I was beginning to wonder the same thing, Isaiah," added Allison. He lay on a small cot in the corner of the room that served as a place of respite for Springer when he was working too late in the office to return home to his ranch a few miles south of Cimarron. Allison's hat was pulled over his eyes and he raised it now to peer up at Rinehart. "And I might add that up until now, most of us in this room *have* noticed how often you have been, shall we say, somewhat conveniently absent at crucial times."

"Gentlemen, rest assured I have always been about the business of my office. You will admit that this county is a large place to cover, and my jurisdiction spans a huge area, not just the town of Cimarron."

Rinehart took a deep breath and studied the letter again. "But now that things have escalated to this point—and to think that Governor Axtell and his cronies believe I can be swayed in my duties to allow . . . *this* . . ." Rinehart's voice trailed off and he angrily wadded up the governor's letter.

"Hold on, Isaiah," said Jonathon, who leaned in the back corner chewing on a stick of peppermint. "Don't destroy that yet." He stepped over and took the wadded letter from the sheriff, straightened it out on the small table in the middle of the room, read it again silently, and then looked around the room. "So what's to be done now?" he asked. "Mr. Springer? The rest of us are just . . . tools. We just react—and sometimes very badly." He handed the letter across the table to Springer. "This, I believe, will need your touch. You are the influential one in the room—the legal mind. You're the one that can properly act on these matters."

"I say we gather some men, hole up here somewhere, and ambush those dark-skinned soldier boys the minute they arrive."

"Shut up, Clay," said Jonathon. "That's exactly what they expect of us. Mr. Springer? What are your thoughts, Sir?"

Frank Springer sat down, rubbed his head, and glanced at the letter one more time. He then folded it and slipped it into his jacket pocket. Isaiah Rinehart waved his hand in protest. "I—I need to destroy that letter! There's too much in it that implicates me, if any of this ever gets out . . ."

"Don't worry, Isaiah," said Springer. "I don't intend to let this out—not just yet, anyway. When the time comes, it could prove very useful in getting our friend Axtell removed from office—properly and legally."

"Speaking of which, Rinehart said, glaring over at Allison, "I should really be *properly and legally* arresting you, regardless."

"I would love to see you try, Isaiah," said Allison, dropping his voice ominously, "but will leave it, of course, to your discretion."

"*When the time comes,* you said," reflected Jonathon. "And until then, Mr. Springer?"

"Until then, my young Deputy Carter, some of us will continue to go about our business as usual, and some of us will need to lay low for a season."

"Let me take a guess who is who," drawled Allison from the bed.

"Not a hard guess," said Jonathon. "I'll take Clay out to the ranch. We'll be protected enough out there. If we have to light out, there are plenty of nearby canyons where we can disappear fairly quickly." He paused and gave Clay a pointed look. "And Clay . . . from now on, you shoot so much as a coyote, I'll be the one who properly and legally throws your ass in jail."

Clay sat up on the edge of the bed, a smile creasing his mouth but his eyes smoldering. "Fair enough, Squirrel. If nothing else, I would surely enjoy some of María's fine home cooking."

"Yes, well, Jonathon will make sure that's *all* you do too," said Springer. "At least until you hear back from me. In the meantime, Isaiah here will await the arrival of the 9th Cavalry."

"Yes, but then what?" asked Rinehart nervously. "What do I tell them?"

"Why, absolutely nothing, Sheriff. You will have no idea where the suspects Allison and Carter are. You will, of course, have checked all their normal haunts, even gone out to the Carter Ranch—"

"*Delgado Ranch*," corrected Jonathon. "We carry the original name out of respect for my wife's family."

"Of course, Jonathon. Only proper. Anyway, the sheriff here will be the absolute model of propriety and cooperation with our army friends. At some point, though, they will tire of the waiting game and return to their post at Fort Union."

"And what if they demand to go back out to Jonathon's . . . I mean, the Delgado place? What do I tell them then?"

"I doubt that will come up. After all, Sheriff Rinehart, you are a fine ally of Governor Axtell's. Why would your word be doubted? But if necessary, we'll just get word to Jonathon so they can, as he said, head for the hills."

Rinehart looked doubtful but nodded his head. "It could work—maybe."

"And just what will *you* be up to all this time, Counselor?" asked Allison, rising finally from the bed and clapping a hand on Springer's shoulder. "Writing more pointed letters to the editor? Pounding your fist on the table down at Henry Lambert's restaurant?"

Frank Springer held Allison's eye, then smiled. "Yes, exactly that, Clay. Except the pounding-on-the-table part will be in the governor's own office in Santa Fe.

Samuel B. Axtell needs to be confronted; and he will want no part of continuing this charade when confronted with this." He patted the pocket of his jacket that contained the governor's letter. "Barring that, I shall begin legal petitions for his removal from office, up to and including the President of the United States himself!"

"Axtell will kill you first," smirked Allison, stepping to the door and peeking out.

The room grew quiet, except for the distant sounds of horse and wagon traffic on the busy streets outside and occasional shouts and laughter from citizens going about the daily business of a thriving town.

"Well, Clay," said Springer. "If it comes to that, then we shall already have lost this so-called *war*."

#

(January 11, 1876 – The Clifton House)

Tom Stockton stepped his mare gingerly across the shallow narrows of the Canadian River, topped a short rise, and reined her in. The mare stamped a hoof anxiously and snorted, her breath visible in the late afternoon winter air.

Stockton pulled his fur-collared overcoat tighter around his neck and looked to the west, where the skies were lowering over the Raton Range, threatening snow tonight. He looked back down the ridge to the Clifton House, which sat a quarter mile away. With its smoking chimneys and cheerfully lit windows, it was a welcome sight and a much-needed stop for the wagon trains, stagecoaches, military patrols, and anyone else who travelled the Santa Fe Trail these days. Located just a few miles south of the historic watering holes at Willow Springs, where the trail dropped off the rugged Raton Pass, the famed stage stop sat at the perfect location.

Stockton had wisely seen the opportunity to meet these obvious needs. After coming out West from Tennessee following the late War of Northern Aggression, he had overseen the building of the stage stop on his ranch, where the Canadian River crossed the Santa Fe Trail. Since then, the enterprise had grown to a full-blown two-story hotel, surrounded by covered porches on both levels, a formal restaurant, a bar, parlors, and full-service livery stables. He had modeled the project after his favorite hotels in Dallas, Denver, and Santa Fe; had spared no expense; and was now making a handsome profit from what was generally considered—along with Henry Lambert's nearby St. James Hotel in Cimarron—one of the finest establishments of its type in the Southwest.

He squinted downhill at the busy facility and smiled, knowing that he was now making more money on this venture than he ever could have on a mere cattle ranch. The hotel and restaurant were busy tonight, as expected for a Friday. Several horses were tied at the hitching posts out front, a couple of buggies were parked near the steps, and the corral hosted what looked like at least two teams of draft horses. One set of the teams had just now been unhitched from a stagecoach that was parked near the barn and was being led away. He couldn't quite make it out from here, but he knew that the name Barlow and Sanderson Stage Line was engraved on the side of the coach. Grooms were scurrying about, filling the feed troughs with grain and forage, and rubbing down the tired sweating beasts that had just hauled the heavy stage more than two thousand feet up and back down the Raton Pass that day from Colorado. He knew that the drivers and their passengers were right now enjoying the hospitality of hot baths, drinks in the bar, and a hot meal in the best restaurant they'd eaten in for days. Early tomorrow, after a wonderful night's sleep in a real feather bed and a great breakfast, they would gratefully pay a fair-sized bill, and continue on their route via Cimarron, Kit Carson's old fortress at Rayado for provisions and repairs, on through Fort Union and Las Vegas, and would hopefully pull into Santa Fe within a week—provided that they weren't waylaid by bandits or scalped by Comanches.

He clucked at his mare and stepped her downhill toward the sounds of distant laughter and the commerce it represented. He pulled up to the side porch, dismounted, and handed the reins to a scruffy-looking Mexican boy who had jumped off the porch and come running when he saw Stockton.

"Pablo," Stockton said as he nodded to the boy while pulling his pipe and a leather tobacco pouch from the inner pocket of his fur-lined overcoat.

"Good evening, Señor Tom."

Stockton squinted at the boy and scrutinized him as he expertly packed his pipe.

"Pablo, that shirt and them britches could sure use a good laundering," he said, leaning over next to the porch to shelter his match from the gusting winter breeze that sneaked around the back of the building.

"Si, Señor Tom," agreed Pablo sheepishly.

Stockton got his tobacco lit and raised himself again to full height, towering over the small boy. Billows of fragrant tobacco smoke escaped his mouth. The big man looked like a locomotive at temporary rest, harboring its strength. He stared at the boy, took the pipe out of his mouth, and leaned over to sniff the boy's hair.

"Whew-wee!" he exclaimed. "And I reckon it's been at least ten days since you had yourself a proper bath, ain't it?"

The small brown-skinned boy lowered his head, embarrassed. Stockton sighed, tousled the boy's uncombed hair, reached into his pants pocket, and tossed him a couple of coins.

"Here, Pablo. You know I can't abide filthy help. You get done with your chores this evenin', you go tell your *mamasita* I said give you the royal treatment. One of them coins there is for her, so you tell her from me to take that good soap, the stuff for the customers, and scrub you down good, you hear? Head to toe— with a big stiff brush!"

Pablo pulled at the front of his hair in respect. "Si, Señor Tom," he mumbled, none too excitedly. He finished tying Stockton's mare to a hitch and turned to walk slowly away.

"And Pablo," Stockton called after him. "You tell her I said to save me a big scoop of that peach cobbler that I know I can smell baking back there—and tell her I said to give you one too!"

Pablo now grinned from ear to ear and nodded. "Sí, Señor Tom!" he exclaimed and then ran toward the back of the building, where the kitchen and servants' entrance was located.

Stockton walked in the other direction, around to the front entrance, put one booted foot on the wide steps leading to the porch, and stopped to peer at two of the other horses tied there. One was a muscular little paint pony, similar to what he knew the Comanche liked to ride, and the other was a larger bay gelding, what he called a "gentleman's horse." They both appeared to have been ridden hard recently and were practically nodding off at the hitch, exhausted. He frowned and shook his head. He narrowed his eyes to look across the yard toward the corrals, put two fingers to his mouth, and whistled shrilly.

"Pepé," he yelled, and gestured when one of the groomers handling the stage team looked up from his work. The man dropped the armful of reins and bits he was carrying and sprinted straight over.

"Señor Tom," he said, breathing hard from his run. He tipped his broad straw plantation hat as he spoke, then slid his fingers into the waist of his dungarees. "I did not see you arrive, Señor. My apologies."

"No need, Pepé. You was busy doin' what I pay you for. 'S all I ask." Stockton waved the back of his hand toward the two tired horses. "These animals is spent. You seen them come in?"

"Sí. Came galloping in about half an hour ago." He hesitated, glanced at the horses, then shrugged and continued. "I tried to offer to Señor Clay to let me take the horses and care for them. But the other one, that bad *hombre*—you know, that one they call 'Chunk'—he just pushed me out of the way and told me mind my own business."

Stockton looked down at his hand for a moment, as if examining it for something interesting. "And Clay—uh, Señor Allison? He didn't say nothing to you about it? "

Pepé thought for a quick moment. "No, Señor Tom. He didn't say a word to me. Seems like he didn't even know I was there. He just looked angry, to me." He thought for another minute. "The way they galloped in here—horses foaming and everything—they looked like the devil himself had been chasing them!" Pepé shuddered and crossed himself.

Stockton looked up at the hotel entrance, pulled back his overcoat, and touched the walnut butt of the Colt Dragoon .44 caliber pistol he wore, cavalry-style, at the front of his left thigh. He then reached over, took another coin from his pocket, and turned back to the groom.

"Well, Pepé, you know how I hate to see horses improperly cared for. So I want you to go ahead and take these animals over, get their saddles off 'em, check 'em for sores, and rub 'em down good. Let 'em water, but not too fast or they'll founder. Give 'em a little hay feed and a handful of oats while you're at it." Pepé opened his mouth to say something and Stockton stopped him with an upraised hand and tossed the coin to him. "I know, I know. It'll be on my say-so; I'm going in right now to meet up with these gentlemen, and they ain't gonna quibble about you taking care of their horses. Bueno?"

Pepé nodded, tipped his hat, promptly untied the two mounts, and walked them away. Stockton pulled his overcoat shut again and ascended the remainder of the steps with a sigh. He nodded to a man seated on a wooden rocker, enjoying a cigar and the evening air; then he opened the door and entered the small lobby of the hotel.

A welcoming wave of warmth and the smell of burning pine longs greeted him from a nearby fireplace. A small man with huge walrus moustaches ambled across the room to meet him halfway. He was dressed in a spiffy black suit, white shirt with starched collar, and black string tie. He grimaced and stuck two fingers into the neck of his collar, showing his discomfort in the fancy clothing.

"May I take your coat, Mr. Stockton?" the small man growled, his voice like a heavy rasp on an iron horseshoe. He may have been dressed to the nines, short, and a little long in the tooth, but Stockton knew that Samuel Farnsworth, a grizzled old cowboy and one of his oldest hands, was still a scrapper and could be hell in a fight. It was one reason he had hired him to manage his hotel, once Farnsworth had gotten a little too old to sit a saddle all day, and a sign of Stockton's loyalty toward his employees—and they to him.

"Evenin', Farnsworth," he answered, shedding his overcoat quickly in the warmth of the room, his eyes squinting again to scan what he could see of the dining room through the big open doors ahead of him.

"And are you dining tonight, Sir?"

"Prob'ly. Maybe," he muttered, then shrugged. "Depends on what else may come up. Never know what might throw a man off of his feed."

Stockton straightened his suit jacket, reached down and felt once again for the comfort of his pistol butt, and continued to search the room.

"Allison's in his usual spot, I reckon?"

Farnsworth glanced sideways up at Stockton's face and then turned away again before muttering, "If you'd bother to wear them new spectacles your wife ordered for ya a while back, you'd be able to see for yourself right quick—*Sir.*"

"Shut up, Samuel, and quit your mumbling. It's my eyes that are going bad, not my hearing. Just answer my question."

"Yes, Sir. Mr. Allison and his—er—friend, are sitting in the back corner as usual."

"Humph," Stockton grunted. "Thanks, Farnsworth." As his manager began to walk away, he continued to mutter to himself. "And Samuel, speaking of eyes—you keep yours good and clear this evening. I may need you and that scattergun you keep behind the counter there, old friend."

Farnsworth answered over his shoulder as he quickly sidled away with the overcoat. "Oh, believe me, Mr. Stockton, both my eyes been peeled way back since them two busted in here!"

Stockton stepped into the sounds of tinkling cutlery, gurgling glassware, and the low murmur of merry conversations that blanketed the dining room. "As usual," he repeated to himself, spying the dark forms of two men in the far corner who were attacking platefuls of steaks with knives and forks.

From this distance, Clay Allison and Chunk Colbert looked like two good friends enjoying an evening out, a great meal, and a few shots of whiskey to mellow things out. But as Stockton meandered through the dining room, getting nearer to their table, he could see a dangerous scowl more or less permanently pasted on Clay Allison's face. He sat with his back firmly against the corner, where he could see everything and everyone at all times in the big high-ceilinged room.

Stockton sucked on his pipe and chuckled to himself knowingly: trust the *Gentleman Gunfighter* to always take the proverbial gunfighter's chair. He caught Clay's eye, moved on over to their table, and nodded.

"Clay," he greeted him evenly.

Clay Allison's scowl momentarily abandoned his face as he smiled up at Stockton and raised his glass of bourbon. "Why, Tom Stockton. This is indeed a surprise and a distinct pleasure," Allison beamed and gestured toward an empty chair. "Won't you please join us?" Allison's companion didn't look up or otherwise acknowledge Stockton but continued slurping and gnawing at his sirloin steak, occasionally using his utensils.

"Don't know why it's such a surprise, seeing as how I own the place," Stockton answered smoothly, removing his pipe stem from his mouth. "But don't mind if I do." He pulled out the proffered chair and sat, making a point of opening his coat and allowing his Colt Dragoon to be visible. At this, Chunk stopped chewing, glanced over at the pistol, then up at Stockton's face.

"Tom, have you met my, um, friend here, Mr. Colbert?"

"I am sorry that I have not had the honor."

"Well, then, might I introduce you to Chunk Colbert himself—infamous Indian fighter, mediocre military scout, indiscriminate dispatcher of redskins, disparager of all men, despoiler of women, self-professed shootist, lout, card sharp, cheat, and general ne'er-do-well—er, those last two or three epithets I came up with myself from general observation, as they are most probably the only words that he just now understood."

Chunk Colbert's mouth was full of meat and his chin shone with its juices. He had yet to speak a word but stopped chewing and scowled at the other two men in turn.

"Chunk," Allison continued, addressing his companion, "I would like to introduce you to the landlord of this very fine establishment and a very dear old friend of mine, Mr. Tom Stockton."

Stockton stuck his right hand out tentatively and just left it hanging there as Colbert simply stared down at it. Chunk then grunted and went back to tormenting the meat on his plate. After a moment, Stockton pulled back his hand and frowned.

"Oh, excuse his manners, Tom. I am not at all surprised. I don't believe he gets out amongst—shall we say—decent folk much. And just what are we to expect from someone with a name such as 'Chunk?'"

"Now, Chunk," continued Allison, turning back to chastise his dinner

231

companion, "you should watch yourself. You are in the presence of the man who, along with that big Colt .44 you've been eyeballing, single-handedly saved my life at Chickamauga by rousing up a decisive counterassault on those Yankee yellow bellies before they knew what hit them."

Stockton didn't take as much note that Colbert continued to ignore them both as he did that a nearby table of four army officers, probably from Fort Union, had suddenly stopped talking and were glaring in their direction. He attempted an apologetic smile and nod at the officers before turning back to Allison.

"What are you two doing here? Clay," Stockton asked, leaning close and lowering his voice to a murmur, hoping Allison would do likewise. He glanced back at Colbert, then continued. "It's common knowledge that you two well-heeled gentlemen have a profound dislike for one other. So just what is this dinner here? Some sorta joke?"

"No, not at all, Tom. You know me. I rarely joke about serious matters. Why, what this is is nothing less than the payment of a bet."

"A bet?"

"Yes—a small wager, if you will, between the illustrious Mr. Colbert and myself—a wager that, I admit to my chagrin, I lost and am now in the process of settling up by buying dear Chunk here a steak dinner, which I can see he, for one, is enjoying no end."

"But, what are you doing out in public, Clay?" Stockton glanced again at the nearby table of Army officers. "I had heard through the grapevine that you were in hiding—from the military."

"Very true, Tom. I have been cooling my heels for almost two months now out at the Delgado Ranch—Jonathon Carter's place—let's just say to avoid any . . . unpleasantness that might arise from some misunderstandings with our illustrious men in blue. Anyway, I developed quite a serious case of cabin fever and just had to get away from there for a while. I thought if I steered clear of Cimarron, and instead headed east toward your fine establishment, I would be safe enough. So imagine my surprise and delight when I ran into my old pal Chunk here on the same road. I was worried for a moment, due to some of our—er—more personal political differences and lively history, that we might have to resort to a brutal confrontation. But seeing that I may have been warned recently against any more rash gunplay, cooler heads prevailed, and we came up with the idea of settling our differences by way of a horse race. Of course, being the incurable wagerer that you know me to be, Tom, I couldn't resist the opportunity to bet on the outcome of our little race. Well, Mr. Colbert's spirited Indian pony out there did, indeed, lead my stately mount on a merry chase.

"And so," Allison spread his hands to indicate the table, "here we are, enjoying your fine hospitality, at my expense."

"Well, that would certainly explain the poor condition of your mounts out there," Stockton said, scolding a bit. "I hope you don't mind that I had one of my men take care of them for you."

"Take care of them?" Allison replied, a jovial smirk on his face. "As in put them out of their misery?" He chortled. "Well, I certainly wouldn't mind if you were to put that four-legged Comanche mongrel of Chunk's down."

Colbert reached over abruptly, grabbed the bottle of cheap bourbon from the middle of the table, emptied what was left into his glass, and drained it noisily. He wiped his dripping mouth with the back of a filthy hand, glared across the table at Allison, reached over to take what was left of Allison's drink, and drained that one also before throwing the tumbler against the wall so hard that it shattered two feet from Allison's head.

Stockton sat back, his mouth wide in surprise, but Allison didn't move a muscle.

"Well now, that was just plain rude," Allison said as he flicked small pieces of glass from the shoulder of his dark coat while his smoldering eyes remained locked on Chunk's. He leaned back, his left arm dangling lazily over the back of the chair, his right hand somewhere in his lap. "I simply cannot abide blatant rudeness, Chunk. I believe that you must know that about me by now." Allison waved his left hand generally toward the table. "And, if you must know, I will not be paying for the damages you caused here. Our wager was for the meal, only."

"Screw you," growled Chunk, wiping his greasy mouth on a dirty shirtsleeve. "And you can just go get me another bottle. That be part of the meal, ain't it?"

"Well, will you listen to that?" Allison remarked, turning back to Stockton with an air of offense. "He finally speaks, and all we get is rudeness and presumption, both at the same time."

Colbert scrunched up his face, revealing rotten front teeth. "Screw you and your bitch whore of a mother, you silver-tongued, satin-mouthed pimp." Chunk pushed back his chair and abruptly pulled his pistol and slammed it on the table, clattering the dishes. He jabbed a finger at Allison. "Now, you get your pansy ass up and go get me another bottle, or we can finish this fight right now!"

"Oh, I see," Allison replied, his words coming very smoothly and even more slowly now, his face impassive. "So that I understand—because it's very important that I do—I can either *get my pansy ass up and get you a bottle,* or I can *finish this fight now.* My choice, then, is it? Isn't that how you understood the question, Tom?" Allison glanced over at Stockton, whose senses were immediately heightened by what he knew was coming and what he suddenly felt was an urgent need to create space between himself and the table.

Stockton awkwardly pushed his chair backward, regretting the scraping sounds the legs made on the hardwood floor. At the same moment, he spied Colbert's hand dart quickly to grab the pistol again. Before Stockton had time to think of anything else, the table exploded in front of them all. Shards of wood and pieces of imported bone china splintered upward, imbedding themselves into the massive wound that had been Chunk Colbert's upper lip and nose. Instantaneously, a spray of blood and matter erupted from the back of his head. Clay Allison's bullet had travelled through table, dinnerware, and leftover food to find its specific target after being fired from the unseen pistol he had been holding in his lap.

Chunk Colbert's chair had tipped back on two legs and he balanced there for what seemed a long while, his arms splayed wide, his head flung back, and his mouth and eyes wide open in shock.

Tom Stockton was rooted in place. He didn't remember having moved at all, but somehow he was now standing right beside Clay Allison, his Colt Dragoon .44 drawn, cocked, and pulled in tight to his side as he watched the scene unfold.

Pandemonium ensued as chairs, tables, and dishes went clattering and smashing, and the other diners either hit the floor or ran for the exits. The table of nearby army officers had been pulled onto its side, and two of the officers crouched behind it for cover, their side arms drawn and ready.

Only at this moment did Chunk Colbert's chair finally tip all the way back to deposit him full force on the floor with a crash. The room grew eerily quiet for the next several seconds, everyone's eyes flicking back and forth, trying to guess what would happen next.

Clay Allison slowly lifted his pistol in the air for all to see, deliberately uncocked it, gently laid it on the table, and stood up, keeping his hands elevated and visible.

"Now, everyone, just breathe easy," Allison said, spacing the words evenly, as if calming a spooked horse. "I believe everyone could see this was purely self-defense." He pointed down to Colbert's body, the man's hand still gripping his unfired pistol.

After a few moments, the room became alive again with activity as the other patrons began standing back up, pointing over to the corner, and excitedly talking among themselves. The army officers moved slowly, giving Allison sidelong glances, finally holstering their weapons as they drew closer. They stared down at the ruin that had been Chunk Colbert. One of them whistled low.

"Boy, that's quite a mess there," the officer noted, pointing at Colbert's head.

Clay Allison nodded, a serious and concerned look on his face now as he met the officer's eyes.

"Yes," he agreed, surveying the dining room. "Quite a mess, indeed. And Tom," he turned back to Stockton and put a reassuring hand on his friend's wrist, forcing him to finally lower his pistol, "please ignore what I said earlier. I will, of course, pay for all the damages."

#

Snow had begun falling again as Tom Stockton instructed his man Pepé to hammer together a rough-shod casket while two other hands hastily carved a grave out of the frigid ground behind the Clifton House. Chunk Colbert's body was unceremoniously dragged out the back door of the hotel, down the steps, and across the yard for several feet before it was laid in the casket. A crowd of onlookers stood by, huddled in coats, rubbing their shoulders, and exhaling foggy breath in the frosty night air.

"Terrible time for a funeral, if you ask me," muttered Farnsworth to Stockton. "Shoulda waited 'til it was warmer."

Stockton gazed into the shrouded night sky and then nodded at the grave.

"Yeah, well, it isn't likely to get warmer anytime soon, Samuel. Tomorrow the ground will be frozen solid—and that body sure won't be smelling any nicer. Best get it done right now."

Before the lid was hammered down, Clay Allison appeared out of the cold darkness.

"Hold on a minute," he ordered as he pushed past the crowd and squatted by the casket. He gazed for a moment at the ruined visage of his old nemesis and wondered why dead men immediately looked like such shrunken versions of their former selves, as though something of substance had actually left the body—as if the soul actually possessed physical mass.

He sighed. Then he reached down and patted Chunk's pockets. His search produced some silver dollars, a small paper packet, and a letter. He stood up as Stockton moved over to him.

"Here," he said, handing the coins to the men who had dug the grave.

"*Muchísimas gracias, Señor,*" they said, gratefully touching their hats.

Allison unwrapped the paper packet and smirked. He removed three gold teeth from the packet and bounced them in the palm of his hand. "Well, I figured old Chunk was worth something." He looked at Stockton. "Wonder whose smartass mouths he took these out of? More gold than I saw in all those years hunting for it at Elizabethtown."

He pocketed the teeth and turned his attention to the letter, which he slowly unfolded, and studied. He whistled low. "Well, would you take a look at this!" He held the letter up to catch some light from the windows of the hotel. People crowded close to look, several asking what the letter said.

"Looks like a warrant of some sort," Allison said, handing it to Stockton to read, "ordering my death—among others." Allison smiled, almost proudly, and shook his head. "Never has anyone so illustrious signed a death warrant for me before."

Stockton looked around, self-consciously fished his eyeglasses from an inner pocket, and put them on. Allison looked over his shoulder as Stockton finished reading aloud the list of names that appeared there:

F. J. Tolby,
Robert Clay Allison,
Frank J. Springer,
William Morley,
Thomas Stockton,
Jonathon S. Carter.

"Well hell, Tom, I am very humbled to be in such highly regarded company," Allison laughed, pointing over Stockton's shoulder. "And I particularly like this last part: *'By direct order of this office, the bearer of this letter has lawfully done what has been done.'*"

The letter ended with a flourished signature that wouldn't have meant much to most of the others present, had it not been for the printed letterhead at the top of the page:

Office of the Governor

New Mexico Territory

Stockton stared incredulously at the list of names for several seconds. Then he looked around.

"You folks clear on out, now," he ordered gruffly, removing his glasses and refolding the letter quickly. "Go on, time to call it a night. We'll take care of things from here."

In a few minutes the crowd had disappeared, most of the people having wandered off to find a warm bed in the hotel, leaving only Stockton, Allison, Farnsworth, and the two gravediggers standing nearby.

Stockton handed the disturbing letter back to Allison.

"If I were you, Clay, I'd burn that damned thing before it causes any more trouble." He and Farnsworth wandered slowly back inside.

Allison gazed down at the body of the hired gunman sent by a corrupt governor to assassinate him, then folded the letter and put it in his coat pocket. "I have a much better idea," he said.

A few minutes later the Mexican gravediggers were finally shoveling dirt into the grave, where it hit the top of the plain casket and splattered. They were grateful for the physical activity that warmed them up in the sputtering snowstorm. The men had no idea that, beneath their feet, tucked deeply into an inner pocket of the oilskin duster wrapped tightly around the gunman's corpse (a pocket that Allison had somehow missed in his search) was hidden a treasure map, scribbled on the back of a photo, that was worth thousands of times more than the few silver coins they had just received from Señor Allison, or of the trouble that map would cause for the next hundred and fifty years.

#

It was mid-morning the next day before the cold sun finally broke free of its shroud of clouds. Although there was still only a dusting of snow, the sun's attempt to thaw out the frozen ground was in vain. Clay Allison stamped his feet on the porch of the Clifton House, pulled his fur-lined overcoat tighter around him, and cinched it up tight. He pulled his hat snug as he looked across the yard toward the stables. He raised two fingers to his teeth and whistled impatiently, waited a moment, and started to whistle again but saw Pepé and another ranch hand finally step out of the barn door, leading Chunk Colbert's paint pony and his own bay gelding. Allison figured that it was now up to him to take the dead man's horse in tow and find someone in Cimarron to buy the mongrel animal—perhaps a friend, because to his knowledge, Chunk had no family in the area. Both the wranglers were bundled heavily against the cold, and the other ranch hand had his head down and his slouch hat pulled low over his face to block the icy breeze. They brought the animals across the yard at a brisk walk, and the horses blew fog with each breath. As they tied them to the hitch rail, the animals stamped their hooves and snorted in protest against the cold winter air.

"They did not want to leave their warm stalls this morning, Señor Allison,"

Pepé quipped nervously, as though anticipating Allison's impatience.

"I can surely sympathize with them," muttered Allison as he looked slowly around the place, taking in the usual activity that accompanied a typical morning at a busy stage stop and resting place on the Santa Fe Trail. Across the way, men were busy hitching up the stagecoach with a fresh team of horses as other guests—passengers, presumably—dutifully filed out of the hotel lobby, where they had just reluctantly paid their bills. They stopped now on the wide veranda next to Allison, stretched, and braced themselves for the prospect of a cold ride. Most of them recognized the famed gunfighter from the shootout in the hotel restaurant the previous evening and gave him a wide berth as they finally made their way down the steps while he, for his part, merely ignored them all.

He scanned his surroundings once more. *Typical activity*, he repeated to himself, but something else nagged him; something was not quite right.

As the other travelers filed their way past him, he shrugged off the feeling and stepped off of the veranda and turned to his horse, beginning to adjust the saddle and secure his gear. He glanced across the neck of his horse and watched curiously as Pepé smiled but backed nervously away before turning and sprinting back toward the stables, looking once or twice over his shoulder. Nearby a few of the stage passengers had stopped their movements toward the coach and were also staring his way.

Too late, he heard the unmistakable cocking of a firearm behind him and froze, his hands lifting slowly away from his horse and up to shoulder height.

"I do believe you have the drop on me, Sir. Please show some restraint." Allison's words, honey-smooth as usual, reflected calm and were meant to play for time while his mind raced and considered options; but options were not immediately evident.

Instead, he heard two quick steps come up behind him and felt the cold steel of a pistol press into the base of his skull. Next, a heavy boot kicked his feet apart so that he could barely keep his balance, and a practiced hand reached around to search him expertly and quickly, pulling Clay's coat open and finding his two matching pistols and, surprisingly, the hideaway derringer that he kept hidden in a vest pocket—a small but deadly companion that very few others knew about.

"Easy, friend," Clay said softly. "No need to get too familiar. If it's money you want, I will certainly accommodate you."

There was a clatter of metal, and then the unknown gunman's hand draped a pair of handcuffs on their long chains over Clay's left shoulder. "You know what to do," growled a voice, barely above a whisper. *Something about that voice.* The gun immediately pressed harder into Clay's back, forcing his head forward painfully. Anger burned now in Clay's throat, but he choked it down. No need to do anything rash—yet. He did as he was instructed and snapped the cuffs on one wrist, then the other. No sooner was he finished than his assailant's hand reached over and draped the handcuffs' connecting chain over Allison's saddle horn, then looped it around two more times to tighten it in place, effectively immobilizing him. Only then did the man step around where Clay could finally see him.

Clay now recognized the stable hand who had brought his pony around with Pepé, but this was no ordinary wrangler. The man who held his gun on Clay now tipped his slouch hat up off his forehead with the tip of his gun barrel and nodded grimly.

"Clay," the man said familiarly.

It was Deputy Sheriff Jonathon Carter.

#

They rode out east and an hour and a half later pulled up near a small stream that flowed along the southern slope of Johnson Mesa. The massive formation was so named for a settlement of homesteaders who had recently moved in on top of the rugged tableland and were attempting to scrape out a living as farmers up there. Jonathon dismounted and led both of their animals over to drink. He glanced up at Clay as he checked the shackles wrapped to the saddle horn, then bent down to fill both of their canteens with fresh water.

"You recognize this place, don't you?" Jonathon asked, looking around and nodding at the landscape.

Allison had ceased talking about thirty minutes into their ride from the Clifton House, having pressed Jonathon unsuccessfully for the reasons for his actions. He now looked around sullenly. "Should I?" he responded.

"One of the last times we were together with Mr. Goodnight, working the herd up over the pass and into Colorado." Jonathon looked around wistfully. "First time we ever laid eyes on this country. Man, that was eight, ten, years ago, wasn't it? Were we ever really that young and foolish? Running off from such a sure thing to hunt gold, of all the damned things!"

Allison stared down at it his former friend with no emotion in his face. "You are still that young—and foolish. Get me out of these chains and I'll show you just how much."

Jonathon sighed, stoppered the canteens, and stood up. "You see, Clay, that's the one thing that always puzzles me about you. No matter how tough you make life for yourself, somehow God always intervenes and pulls you out of the fire; yet you don't even realize it."

"That's because I don't believe in God," muttered Clay, looking away.

"Okay, so call it blind luck then—which *I* don't believe in, by the way. Anyway, you never seem to fully appreciate it."

"What should I appreciate—that my best friend has betrayed me? You will forgive me, Sir, if I fail to see the logic of it all."

Jonathon stepped over to Clay's horse and stowed both canteens into a saddlebag. He then went to his own saddle and pulled out a packet wrapped in cheesecloth and also packed that into Clay's bags. "You see, that's the puzzlement, right there. I warned you not to get into any more gunplay, until all this mess settles down some. And by all rights, as an officer of the law, I should be taking you into Cimarron, to jail, to stand trial and hang for murder. But yet here we are, riding in the exact opposite direction of jail."

Jonathon went back to his horse, retrieved something more from his bag, and then stepped away downhill several yards. "And you still don't appreciate at all that I am actually saving your life." Jonathon took a step back and heaved Clay's pistols one at a time into a stand of tall grama grass. Next, he reached into his coat pocket, produced all the bullets he had removed from the guns, and threw them away. He then turned to face Clay and held up the key to the handcuffs so that Clay could see it before he tossed it over into the grass also.

He nodded at Clay's handcuffs. "By the time you get untangled from that saddle horn, get off your horse, find that key, and load your guns, I will be up over that ridge yonder, and you will be square in my rifle sights."

Jonathon walked over slowly, placed a hand on the neck of Clay's horse, and looked up at his old friend. "When I told her what I was doing, María was kind enough to pack you some fresh bread and a side of bacon, which you now have in your bags. And you have plenty of water. Now, as I see it, you can do one of two things, Clay, once you free yourself: you can turn this horse around and head northeast—I would strongly suggest Oklahoma or even Kansas. If you head to Texas, well, they're liable to string you up just based on your reputation. Or, you can come riding straight at me, hell bent for leather, to try to take some misguided retribution, and we can both go out in a blaze of glory." Jonathon stroked the horse's mane and looked off into the distance. "Frankly, I might prefer the latter, as it would take the worry out of what happens later."

"Later? What do you mean by that exactly—Old Friend?" Clay said through gritted teeth.

Jonathon looked back at Clay, his face suddenly dark.

"It means, Clay, that if I ever see you again in New Mexico, I will hunt you down and put you out of my misery, once and for all."

Thirty minutes later, Jonathon topped the rise of the ridge to the west, turned his horse around, and looked through his binoculars. He sighted a plume of dust raised by a distant rider galloping away eastward. Near the horizon, perhaps two miles away, Jonathon watched Clay Allison pull his horse up and around, looking back his way. Clay drew a pistol, aimed it straight up, and fired two shots silently into the frigid winter sky before pulling back around and disappearing over the ridge. The delayed reports of those shots echoed off the surrounding mesas and finally reached Jonathon's ears.

But he wasn't sure if they were meant as a farewell or as a warning.

CHAPTER 24
Phoenix From Ashes

(Present Day – Raton, New Mexico)

"What the hell is *she* doing here?" Trent exclaimed, shifting in the bed as if he could get away from Agent Britt de Jaager, the former head of security for the late Dutch Minister of Whatever-It-Was and the person who now blocked the doorway to his hospital room. Trent winced as excruciating pain shot through his ribs. Then he glared again at the assassin across the room. "I saw you get shot," he growled through clenched teeth. "You're supposed to be dead!"

"Oh, I got shot, all right," said Britt de Jaager, matter-of-factly. "But as you can see, I'm definitely not dead—yet." She stepped slowly over to Trent's bedside, grimacing and shifting the sling on her right arm as she went. "And I suppose I have you to thank for that, Deputy Carter."

"I'm not a deputy any more. And thank me for what?" asked Trent, peering at de Jaager suspiciously.

"Why, for taking him—Karl—out of action, of course. Or else we would all probably be dead right now."

Trent pursed his lips and continued to glare at de Jaager for a moment. "I'm more than a little confused. Who the hell's Karl?" He thought for moment, his memory still fuzzy. "Was that the guy who shot me up? Threatened to cut my eye out? And why aren't you in handcuffs . . . or dead?"

Ilsa Bouwmeester had appeared at de Jaager's side and slipped her hand inside the bodyguard's arm. "Please just listen to her, Mr. Carter. She's the reason we are all alive right now. . . ." She bowed her head sheepishly. "Well . . . and, of course, *you.*"

"*She's* the reason. . . !" Trent sputtered, then winced again. He bit off his pain.

"Hush up, Cowboy, and just listen," ordered Maggie from the end of the bed, reaching over and pinching the big toe of his uninjured foot.

"Ow! Do I have a choice?"

"None at all." Maggie raised her eyebrows at him, put a finger to her lips, and directed his attention back to Britt.

"As I was about to tell you: I found out only a few days ago that my security team, Minister Bouwmeester's detail, might have been compromised; that it might have included an agent—or agents—who had gone rogue. I had identified one of them already—a former marine from my country, who. . . ." Britt paused in her story, as if carefully choosing her words. "He was an agent by the name of Cobus

240

de Groot. I believe you found him dead a few days ago, outside of Raton."

Trent searched his memory, remembering the bodies found at the ruins but not any particular name. Then he recalled something Ben Ferguson had told him about the coroner's report—something about a former UN Peacekeeping soldier who had supposedly died years ago in Kosovo.

"Yes," he nodded slowly. "I was at the crime scene. Someone put the business end of a pickaxe through that poor guy's chest and threw him on top of a skeleton in an old grave outside of town. Handy piece of work, that." Trent narrowed his eyes as he studied Britt's face. He felt sure that she was hiding something. "And mighty convenient, I might add. You kill him?"

Britt de Jaager's tongue briefly touched her lips, but otherwise she betrayed no emotion. "No, I did not kill him," she answered flatly. Trent watched her pause and take a deep breath before she continued. "I am not entirely surprised that he was killed. He was misguided, but he didn't deserve what he got. We believe that whatever it was that Agent de Groot was after out there in that grave is what got him killed." She looked down and adjusted her sling again. "No, one of the others murdered him. I came along too late that night to stop it."

Trent narrowed his eyes at her, and started to speak, but Britt quickly continued. "Yes, Mr. Carter, I got to the crime scene first, and yes, I tampered with the evidence. And yes, I left the scene without notifying the authorities." She allowed herself a brief smile. "But I suppose that little confession is irrelevant, isn't it, since you were so quick to point out that you are no longer with law enforcement?"

Trent shrugged his shoulders, then sucked in his breath in pain again. He looked back at de Jaager. "Well, I did think that something seemed odd with that grave when I was there. I figured it had been searched, but too meticulously—too precise—to have been done by someone in a hurry. That part would have been your doing, I imagine."

"Yes. I was thorough but didn't want to disturb it more than I had too. I needed to be careful. I am impressed, though, that you suspected something." Trent started to shrug again, then thought better of it.

"Compliment taken. Let's just say that I have some sort of a sixth sense about some of these things." He shifted uncomfortably in the bed, still feeling a little trapped, figuratively and literally. "But tell me: just what were you and the killer—and de Groot—looking for in an old gunfighter's grave?"

It was Britt's turn to shrug. "I am still not at all sure. We were only sure that there was some sort of conspiracy; something that could be very beneficial to some people in certain positions of authority, if certain information were found—beneficial to some but very dangerous to others. But I know that they found something there. I'm not sure exactly what, but they found it quickly and left. When I finally got there, I did a more careful search and satisfied myself that, whatever it was, the murderer already found it." Britt paused as she pushed a strand of blond hair out of her eyes. "And Cobus was killed for it."

Trent thought some more. "Cobus sure dug a lot of other holes out there that night, almost as if he was obsessed over it. Seems to me that with such a big undertaking, he would have had some help—maybe from you, since you were evidently partners—before going out there all alone."

Britt looked out the window. "Cobus—Agent de Groot—got to the point where he trusted no one, not even me anymore. The last time that he shared his thoughts at all on the subject, he would only tell me that they were closing in on him; that if he weren't careful from now on, his life would be in danger."

"This from a trained agent and a seasoned former marine? A marine, I might add, who was apparently operating under an assumed identity of a soldier who supposedly died years ago, in Kosovo?"

"I know nothing of this," de Jaager said abruptly. Trent watched her closely as she pushed at her bangs again, the sleeve of her dark blue jacket slipping away from her wrist. She still wasn't telling him everything.

"Agent de Jaager, earlier, you said *we believe*. Who's we?"

"My . . . associates in the Netherlands and me."

"Your man Cobus—he had a strange tattoo on his wrist."

"Yes," said de Jaager, after a pause.

"Similar to the one I just caught sight of on your own arm?"

De Jaager held her arm up slowly and pulled the sleeve back, revealing a stylized tattoo of some sort of shell. She looked at it and then back at Trent proudly, as if she were happy to talk about a slightly different subject.

"It's called, Mr. Carter, a nautilus." She held it out so that he could study it. "It is a fossilized shellfish that, in this example—if you look more closely—contains a cutaway cross section that exposes its inner construction . . . walls within its outer shell creating separate chambers—a protective device for the shellfish, to prevent contamination, illness, and the like, from spreading."

Trent squinted and even dared trace his forefinger over the tattoo. He glanced up at Britt.

"That's an awful lot of scientific detail to describe a mere tattoo. Any real significance—that would matter to me?"

"Its significance, Mr. Carter, is that the protective chambers within the nautilus are called *septums*. . . ." She paused, as if wondering whether to continue. "Which also happens to be the name of a . . . shall we say . . . certain organization that I belong to—*Septum*."

Trent took his hand away from her wrist and looked back up at de Jaager. "Why are you telling me all of this?"

"My organization is a very old one, more than 100 years old now—one that exists to serve, to protect—to insulate—against certain rogue elements in society. This we often do in . . . *unorthodox* ways."

"*Rogue* elements, huh. Like your *rogue* agents. So, again I ask: why tell me, if it's such a secret group?"

"It's not that it's such a secret; far from it. We have operated in Europe for over a century." De Jaager shrugged, then offered the slightest smile. "And after all you have gone through now. . . ." She paused and looked at Ilsa. "After you risked your life for hers—and the others, well, we felt you deserved a little transparency."

"There's that mysterious *we* again ."

De Jaager shrugged, smiled, but said nothing more.

"And yet, Agent Britt de Jaager of Septum, why do I still feel as though you're not telling me everything?"

Her slight smile disappeared, replaced by her usual reticence. After a moment's pause, she responded. "There is always more to tell, isn't there, Mr. Carter? Just as I am sure I do not know all of your own secrets. Do I?

"*Touché*, Agent de Jaager. But this organization—this Septum—your man de Groot also belonged to it?"

"Yes, he did." Britt paused and looked down before continuing. "I don't suppose, Mr. Carter, that you have learned anything about the identity of the murderer—the one who actually killed Cobus . . . um, Agent de Groot?"

Trent shook his head. "No, I haven't. But then again, I am no longer a member of active law enforcement, remember? I am not privy to a lot of information." Trent noticed that Britt bit her lower lip for a second before she looked back at him, nodded, and smiled. *Another slip of the mask.*

Trent watched her carefully. "Agent de Jaager—Britt—your man de Groot, Cobus. Were you two close, by any chance?"

Another pause. *The mask went back up.* "Let's just say that he was one of my oldest colleagues, from way back."

"Hence the similar tattoo. And your other men—the ones on your security detail? Did they sport the same tattoo? Also members of Septum?"

De Jaager turned back to Ilsa and gave her a brief smile and a squeeze on the hand before continuing. "You are indeed persistent, Mr. Carter. Let us just say that it turns out that there *was* more than one traitor on my team. In fact, all of them had turned on us: Lars and Karl, whom you know about; another former marine named Gert Vos, who stayed behind with our vehicles that day in the mountains— a very straightforward, by-the-book agent who I thought I could always count on; and a few others we are still uncovering as we speak, both here and abroad." Britt looked away and out the window again for a few seconds. "I had hand-picked my team here, Mr. Carter, with Minister Bouwmeester's concurrence, of course. After all, . . ." She paused, catching Ilsa's eye again. "We were all supposed to be his— and Ilsa's—personal bodyguards for this trip. Instead, they became his. . . ." Her voice trailed off as she patted Ilsa's hand.

"His assassins," finished Ilsa, very directly, her eyes fixed on Trent's. "And almost ours."

"And so, here we are," said Britt wryly, pointing at Trent's bandages and her own. "They killed Cobus, then arranged for the helicopter to crash; and when that didn't kill everyone, they executed the Minister and his secretary, and chased down the girls—with your unintentional help, Mr. Carter, I might add."

"*My* help?"

"Yes. Your fumbling tracks in the snow were like a roadmap for me and my team."

"Well, we didn't really have much choice," Trent rebutted. "We knew you would be coming soon, and we knew we just had to get there first—which we did." Trent looked away, thought hard for a moment, and then turned back to her.

"About your gunshot wound. . . ."

"Yes," Britt answered, looking down at her shoulder and shaking her head in disbelief. "After Lars came after me at the cabin and confessed that he and the others were traitors, I couldn't take any more chances—and shot him. . . ."

"Yes, I saw you kill him."

Britt was silent for a moment.

"I had to. It was either him or me at that point."

Trent saw out of the corner of his eye as she clenched her fist against his bedrail. It was the first real sign of emotion he had seen from her today.

"But I don't understand something," Trent said. "After you shot . . . Lars, is it? Anyway, after you shot him, you shot up towards me, on the ridge. Why?"

Britt shook her head. "No, I was shooting at Karl, just below you, in the trees. He immediately opened fire as soon as I shot Lars. He was so far away, I knew it would do no good to shoot at him, but I also knew I had to get back to the cabin, to protect the girls and the other man, the sheriff. I mean, at that distance, I never dreamed that son-of-a-bitch Karl could even come close—but he sure did." She glanced down at her arm in the sling. "Nailed me right when I reached the door. And then, of course, thank God you shot him, before he could come finish the job."

"No," Trent said quietly.

"What was that?" asked Britt.

"I said, *no*. That's not how it happened at all."

"Then, you didn't shoot Karl?"

"No, I didn't shoot Karl, and. . . ." Trent paused, then looked Britt in the face. "And it wasn't *that* son-of-a-bitch, as you called him, who shot you, either."

"I don't understand."

Trent pointed at his own chest. "It was *this* son-of-a-bitch," he continued, sheepishly. "I'm the one who shot you—from the ridge, using my rifle with a scope. Then I rode down, and Karl shot me—*and* my horse. . . ." Trent paused again and caught Maggie's eye. "Damn good horse," he said quietly.

Britt's mouth and eyes opened in surprise. "*You?* Shot me? But why?"

"Because I watched you through the scope. I couldn't figure out who was shooting at who, at first, but then you shot your own man; and then I thought you were shooting at me; and then I saw you run to the cabin and begin to wave that pistol around at the girls. I thought for sure you were about to do something to them, and so I. . . ."

"You thought *I* was the killer, then?"

"Oh no, Mr. Carter," said Ilsa, coming to de Jaager's defense. "Britt has been guarding me and my family since before I can remember—since I was a little girl. She could never harm me. She was there to warn us of the danger we were in."

"But what about the pistol? Why did I see her threatening you with it?"

"She wasn't threatening me. She was trying to get me to take it—to defend myself with it if something happened to her, which . . . which, it turns out, it did. Didn't it?" Ilsa narrowed her eyes at Trent accusingly.

Trent looked away, thought for a minute, and then looked up at Maggie again. "Sorry about Angel," he muttered.

Maggie mouthed, "I know. Me too," and then patted him gently on his good leg.

Trent suddenly thought of something. He remembered being trapped under Angel's body as the assassin Karl walked slowly toward the cabin, his oily laughter cut short by what Trent only remembered as a bloody arrow through Karl's neck, shot by a ghostly warrior, who had immediately disappeared. Trent shook his head quickly. It was a part of the story that he knew he could never make any of the others here even begin to understand.

"So, if I shot you," he said finally, trying to sort it all out, "and Karl shot me, then . . . who the hell shot Karl?"

"*I* did, you poor excuse for a bear killer!" came another voice from the half-open door as Sheriff Ben Ferguson's wheelchair banged its way inside. Deputy Hector Armijo was clumsily pushing it from behind and was followed closely by Jennifer, Sophie, and Walter.

#

Thirty minutes later, Nurse Patricia—*She Who Hunts Down Breakfast*—came in, checked Trent's vitals, and clicked her fingers rapidly on the computer keyboard to update his chart. Finishing up that part of her work, she looked around the room at them all. "Looks like this has been quite a party," she smirked, folding her arms. "Standing room only."

Walter and Sophie had pulled up chairs to Trent's bedside, Ben's wheelchair was parked near the foot of the bed, and the remainder of them, including Maggie, had moved back to find whatever space they could crowd into around the room.

"I suppose now you're going to lecture us on too many visitors in here," growled Ben. "But I'm not leaving. I just got here and I'm the sheriff."

"Well, that is a good point *Sheriff* Ferguson. But yes there are rules; and yes they do apply to you, too. But no I don't really care if you all stay or not." Nurse Patricia moved back to Trent and began pulling aside bedcovers. "But my patient here just might. I'm about to help him go to the bathroom, give him a sponge bath, change the dressings on his wounds, and change his gown. So, if you all want to stay for that show. . . ."

At that, almost everyone started making moves toward the door.

"Well, I just got here, too," groused Walter, not budging from his chair. "And I'm not going anywhere yet. Besides, I've seen his naked butt several times before!"

"Walter. . . ." said Trent, embarrassed.

"And I've seen it, too," interrupted Maggie, walking over behind her father-in-law and placing her hands gently on his shoulders. "But we are *all* leaving; that means you too, Walter. Come on, folks," she continued as she dutifully ushered everyone from the room. "Let's leave Trent and his pretty young nurse to play bath time." She turned back at the doorway, blew Trent a kiss, winked, and left.

#

Afterward, the nurse helped Trent to a chair and stuffed pillows around him to wedge him in securely before she left. He was still hooked up to IVs and a small monitor that hung on a wheeled stand next to his chair but he felt much more human now that he had bathed, changed gowns, and was sitting up for a while. An orderly brought him his lunch tray, and he ate gratefully. Even though it was hospital food, he was still hungry. Probably, anything would have tasted wonderful. He also noted that for the first time since he had awakened in this place, he was alone.

He finished eating and sat back with his thoughts while he sipped at weak, lukewarm coffee. He looked down and surveyed his bandaged body, wondering just how much cumulative damage a person could sustain in one lifetime before it took a complete toll. He thought back to all the battles, accidents, and shootouts he had gone through: from old sports injuries, to skirmishes in Afghanistan, to gunfights with criminals as a cop, to the so-called accident on Cordova Pass in Colorado, which took his first wife's life and almost left him a disabled husk with no memories. And now . . . this: more bullet wounds and broken bones—more than he could count anymore, when added to the total. And for what? *Most people run away from conflicts. But not you. No, you have to run right smack into them; no matter that you now have your life back again.*

He thought of Maggie and smiled. He still had no idea how a man could be so blessed in one life. If Victoria Ann Carter had been the love of his life, Margot Van Ryan was surely his true soul mate. At first he had felt some guilt—that he was somehow betraying Vicky. Over the last two years, though—and in God's infinite grace and wisdom and perfect timing—he had come to realize that the gifts of these two strong women in his life were not something he had earned, much less deserved. But like all perfect blessings, they had been brought into Trent's life at just the right moments and for just the right purposes.

What he did know for a fact was that in this one life he had loved them both dearly and had been loved by them both dearly, and he would continue to do whatever was necessary to protect and live up to those gifts.

A light tap on the door brought him back to the here and now. The door swung gently open and a wheelchair quietly rolled in.

"Thought we would make a more dignified entrance this time," said Ben as Hector once again pushed him into the room. The door shut softly behind them.

"Where's everyone else?"

Hector stepped over and helped himself to some leftover French fries on Trent's tray. He chewed them eagerly and noisily. "Walter got hungry. Maggie and the girls were sick of hospital food. . . ." He paused, grabbing another fry and wolfing it down. "So they all left to go eat in town."

"Where's Agent de Jaager?"

"Don't know. Last I saw her, she was standing outside on the sidewalk, talking on her phone. Acted like she didn't want to be bothered anymore."

Ben turned to Trent. "I thought you was dead," he deadpanned, citing an old John Wayne movie joke between the two of them.

"Not hardly," Trent said, smiling and quoting the required response. Then he got serious. "Matter of fact, I was beginning to worry that *you* were the one no longer amongst the living. I couldn't get any information whatsoever from anyone around here."

"Yeah, I know," muttered Ben. "Damned Hippo laws."

"Um, I think that's *HIPAA,* Sheriff," offered Hector. "Stands for Health Insurance Portability and Accountability Act." Ben and Trent both turned slowly and stared at Hector, who had now opened Trent's untouched carton of milk and was washing down his fries. "1996, I believe." Hector suddenly noticed them looking at him oddly. "I was just, um, studying up on it in the lobby. They have this poster. . . ."

"Thank you, David Webster," Ben interrupted, snidely.

"I believe that it was Daniel," said Hector. "*Daniel* Webster. Not David."

"You're both wrong," said Trent. "It was Noah Webster."

Ben furrowed his brow and glared at them both. "Real funny. Nice to see things are almost back to normal around here, after all the excitement."

Trent smiled and reached for a cup of water on his tray. He took a sip, cleared his throat, and winced as he adjusted himself in his chair. "Well, speaking of excitement, Agent de Jaager and I were having a fairly lively chat just before you all burst in earlier. But after we compared notes, it seems we still have a few gaps left in our stories." He looked back at Hector.

"Go find her," he ordered.

"What? Why?"

"Since you are the proverbial Last Man Standing in the room, Hector—that is, the only one of us not banged up, still out there doing his day job—I think you need to enlighten us with what you know right now, I mean, other than your knowledge of current medical privacy laws."

Ben studied Trent for a moment. "And you think Britt can shed some more light on the investigation?"

"I think that Agent de Jaager is not telling us the whole story, Ben. I don't know what she's trying to hide, or that she will tell us any more than she has already said. But I want to look her in the eyes as young Deputy Armijo here fills us all in on the latest—to see her reaction. That might tell us a lot more than anything else she might have to say." Trent stared at his son-in-law again. "So why are you still here?"

Hector raised his eyebrows questioningly and continued to chew on Trent's leftovers. "Oh! Yeah, right," he said and left the room.

Trent watched the door and waited for it to swing silently shut. The clicks and dripping noises of his attached equipment filled the sudden void of silence. "All kidding aside, Ben," he finally said softly. "For a while there, I really thought we were both dead."

Ben held Trent's eyes soberly. "For a while there . . . we were." He looked away, then continued after a moment. "You ever wonder why we keep doing this to ourselves, Trent?"

"You mean, chasing the bad guys?"

"That too. But more than that, why we get so tied up and wrung out emotionally about everything—about everyone—that it starts to affect our thinking, our reactions . . . our better judgment?"

"Are you talking about Jennifer? Ben, you did what any normal father would have done. Your precious daughter was in harm's way, and you went to fix it. Don't start beating yourself up about this."

"I damned near got her killed."

"You damned near *didn't!* You are the reason she and that Bouwmeester girl are alive right now. Hell! You're the reason we're all alive! If it wasn't for you and that lucky shot. . . ."

Ben looked at Trent sheepishly, then grinned. "What the hell to do you mean by *lucky?*"

Ben's wheelchair had been parked at a close angle to Trent's chair so that their knees almost touched. Trent grimaced as he slowly leaned forward until he could grasp Ben's forearm with his good hand and squeeze it. "Thank you, my friend. Nothing more I can say."

Ben's eyes opened in mock horror and he leaned away. "You're not going to try and kiss me now, are you?"

The door suddenly opened again and Britt de Jaager came in, followed by a breathless Hector. "What did I miss?" he asked.

"Oh, nothing. Trent was just expressing his undying love for me." Hector looked incredulously from one to the other of them, the expression on his face like a confused child's.

Britt rolled her eyes, crossed her arms, and shook her head. She then took a step toward the door. "Gentlemen, I don't wish to intrude on your fun. Neither do I wish to waste any more of my time."

"Hold on, Agent de Jaager," said Trent. "My apologies. Just blowing off a little steam. No more fun and games, I promise. Please. Have a seat. Deputy Armijo was just going to catch us up on the investigation, and I wanted you here to stay in the loop." Britt stood with her hand on the door for a moment, then turned and sat down.

"Very well then. In that case . . . please proceed, Deputy."

Hector's countenance suddenly brightened again, as he realized he now had an audience. He began by telling them that everyone from the State Police to the Attorney General's Office to the FBI had now gotten involved and how most of the evidence so far has been sent down to Santa Fe for further analysis. This included the memory stick drive that Ilsa had given to Trent; all the weapons, vehicles, and ATVs recovered at the cabin shoot-out site; the wreckage of the helicopter and the bodies recovered there; the bodies of the dead Dutch agents; the pickaxe from the murder site at the grave; and even the 140 some-odd-year-old gunfighter's body found there.

"Everything but the grave itself, I guess." Hector beamed at the completeness of his report.

Trent looked at him wryly. "How about my horse and the bear?" he asked. "They drag their carcasses down to Santa Fe, too?"

"No, I don't recall that being on the list," Hector answered, rubbing his chin thoughtfully.

Trent took note of Britt's exasperation. "Never mind, Hector. Go on."

Hector shrugged. "Not much else, really."

"Where's Vos?" asked Britt, after a few seconds. "I assume they must have taken him into custody too—for questioning." Her voice was calm and steady. Trent watched her carefully as she sat upright in her chair, both feet flat on the floor, her chin up, and her face passive as she looked at Hector. Everything about her posture suggested calm and professionalism, but he had the inexplicable feeling that Britt de Jaager was anything but calm right now—inside.

"Oh, you bet we did," said Hector. "He's over in county lockup as we speak. But you know, that's the funny thing," Hector said, rubbing the back of his neck. "They never even asked to see Agent Vos. Not that he has cooperated any, so far."

"You questioned him, then?" asked Ben.

"Yep, sure did. He's not saying much at all."

"I hope you at least remembered to Mirandize him."

"Well, of course, Sheriff. I'm not a fool."

Ben looked at Trent and rolled his eyes.

Britt looked down at her hand and examined it. "What did he say about Cobus' murder?" she asked softly. "Agent de Groot? Did he say which of them did it?"

"Which of who?" asked Hector.

"Which of my other agents—it had to be one of them. Either Lars or Karl or Gert Vos."

"Well, whoever it was, Vos is not talking. Doesn't admit to anything and doesn't even seem worried. Almost like he knows we can't charge him with anything much. I mean, all we caught him doing was sitting in an SUV, waiting for the rest of you up at the cabin. Guess I could charge him with trespass, or loitering."

"How about an accessory to murder, to start with?" asked Ben, straightening up in his wheelchair, then hugging his ribs and clenching his teeth in pain at the overexertion. He caught his breath and continued. "Sounds like we have plenty of dead bodies piled up to be able to toss at least some of the blame his way."

"Well, you're still the boss, so you let me know exactly what. It's going on 48 hours and I either need to charge him or release him." Trent saw Britt look up at Hector, then just as quickly look away again, her face still blank.

Hector was moving from one foot to another, and then finally stepped over to the restroom door. "Okay if I use your restroom, Trent?"

Trent waved him on. "Sure. Why not? I've been told it's now a public facility."

Hector unfastened his gun-and-utility belt and draped it over a chair. As he did so, he seemed to remember something and patted his uniform shirt pocket. "Oh, I almost forgot." He unbuttoned his pocket flap and pulled out a small plastic evidence bag. He reached over and tossed it onto Trent's lap. "Some type of old photograph. We found it on Agent Vos when we arrested him. He tried to get rid of it, but I saw him toss it away in the bushes. Must be something important, don't you think?"

Trent stared at the plastic bag on his lap, then picked it up very carefully. It contained a faded, old photograph, the sepia-colored images now washed out to subtle light browns and whites, smudged here and there, and speckled where the silver base had worn off the paper with the passing of a great amount of time inside a corpse's coat pocket. Even so, Trent was intimately familiar with the images. Though the photo was much smaller, it was an exact duplicate of the one that had hung in the hallway of his childhood home for as far back as he could remember and now hung in Walter's room at Montaño del Sol Ranch; the one with the eyes of five stalwart-looking men of the 19th century staring back at him. Their names now came quickly to mind: Stockton, Goodnight, Springer, Allison, and Jonathon Salal Carter—Trent's great-great grandfather himself, one of the original sheriffs of Colfax County.

"Got some sort of map or something on the back," Hector called out as he finally stepped into the restroom and shut the door quickly, unable to hold it any longer.

Trent gently turned the bag over, revealing the back of the photo where there was indeed a faded drawing. He held it up to the florescent light. Roughly drawn lines and barely legible words came into view, along with small, crude drawings that seemed to indicate a mountain here, a river there, and a building with some faint words underneath. About halfway between the mountain and the river was what looked to be a faded *X*, and near it a small word that was only three or four letters long.

"Well, it's a map, all right. But I can't quite make any of this out," said Trent. "Like this little word right here—*Use?*"

"It says *Ute*," said Britt suddenly. Then she grew quiet just as quickly.

Trent realized that at some point, Agent de Jaager had gotten up from her chair and was now leaning over his shoulder, peering intently at the map. Her face had gone slack and she looked as if she were seeing a holy relic of some kind—or a ghost. She seemed to suddenly realize that Trent was looking at her intently. She immediately straightened up and composed herself.

"Yes," she continued matter-of-factly and turned to gather her things. "I would say that is definitely a map. Very interesting. Now, if you gentlemen will excuse me, I am very tired and should go to my hotel. I need to contact my agency and get further instructions. . . ."

Britt's voice trailed away as she moved to the door, exited, and shut it quickly behind her. Trent and Ben exchanged looks as the sound of her footsteps faded away down the hall.

#

Britt de Jaager walked purposefully down the hall, the hard soles of her shoes echoing off the tile floor and institutional walls. She passed a nurse's station and nodded and smiled tightly. She turned a corner into yet another long and empty corridor, looked around, stopped, and leaned back heavily against the wall. Only then did she lose any composure, but only slightly. She allowed herself to slouch as she braced herself with her good arm and hand against the wall, and let her chin sag to her chest as she gasped for air. She felt as if she were hyperventilating.

Blood pounded through her temples as the image of the old photograph and the worn map came roaring to the fore of her mind. It was the one missing piece of the puzzle, the one clue that Septum had yet to uncover, and the one piece of evidence that pointed directly to the man who had murdered Cobus de Groot that night as he dug holes and left him to die alone behind the ruins of an old hotel in northern New Mexico—Agent Gert Vos.

CHAPTER 25
Wars And Rumors

(Letter from Governor Lew Wallace)

October 5, 1878

Mr. Jonathon S. Carter
Cimarron
Territory of New Mexico

Dear Mr. Carter:

I hereby inform you that (at my urging) Mr. Isaiah Rinehart has resigned his appointment as Sheriff of Colfax County; whereupon, I am pleased and honored to inform you that, after much consideration, I am offering you the position in his vacancy.

I have it on very good authority from several sources (including our mutual friend, Mr. Frank Springer, Esq.) that you are just the right man for the job, with much hard-earned experience during these present difficult times.

I pray that you accept, and if so, I hereby pledge to you my full and unfailing support that we might all, with combined effort, bring about a lasting solution and peace to your troubled jurisdiction.

I await your decision by return endorsement, via Mr. Frank Angell, who represents our firm and fair interests on the federal level.

Sincerely,
Lew Wallace, Acting Governor
Territory of New Mexico

#

(October 10, 1878 – Delgado Rancho, Ponil River Valley)
"**R**ider comin'."

Jim Watkins stood in the bed of a wagon that was backed up to the hay barn. He had been tossing hay bales down through the double doors of the barn, where Jonathon Carter waited on the ground to receive them and drag them into place along one wall. Jonathan wiped the sweat from his eyes with the back of a sleeve and looked up at his young hired hand. Jim was shading his eyes and peering into the distance.

"Alone?"

"Yep. Appears so."

Jonathon squeezed between the wagon and the barn door, pulling his gloves off as he went, and walked to the corner where he could get a view down the lane. It had been sweltering inside the closed building, but out here the autumn afternoon had ushered in a refreshing breeze. From here Jonathon could see the gold- and rust-colored leaves, glittering and shimmering through the oak and cottonwood trees that lined the creek below him and heralding the inevitable change in seasons. He leaned against the wall of the barn, held his hat up to shade his face, and squinted until he spied a dark speck that seemed to wiggle as it emerged from the creek bottom, maybe half a mile down the road, headed slowly his way.

"Well, your eyesight is some better than mine these days, Jim. But I see him now. Recognize him?"

"No, Sir. I sure don't. Not yet, anyhow."

"Well then," said Jonathon with a deep sigh, pushing back from the side of the barn and slapping the dust from his pants leg with his gloves. "Best get on down here—and find your weapon. Can't be too cautious."

Jonathon turned and walked to the house. As he neared, the aroma of freshly baked apple pie wafted out the open windows, and his stomach made an involuntary growl. He stopped at the hand pump located just outside the door, where he removed the kerchief from his neck, held it underneath the spigot, and doused it down with cold well water. He gratefully wiped his face and neck, allowing the cool wetness to drain down the front of his shirt. Then he unhooked the ladle hanging there, filled it, and gulped the refreshing water until he coughed when it went down wrong.

The door opened and Jonathon turned to see María standing there, wiping her hands on her apron. Smiles lit up both their faces at the same time, and after a brief moment she stepped out the door and off the stoop to bring hers up to his until their lips met. The sleeves of her blouse were rolled up and she wrapped her bare forearms around his neck, pulling him tighter to her.

"Sweaty," he warned, whispering through the soft kiss.

"Me too," she murmured back. "And I don't care."

Jonathon pulled his eyes away from María's and took a sidelong look down the road again toward the approaching rider, who had cut the distance in half since he had first appeared. María turned and looked too. "Who is it?" she asked.

"Not sure."

María turned and peered back up at her husband. "Where are your new eyeglasses?"

Jonathon scoffed and moved past her, into the house.

"Don't *hmmph* me," she scolded, following him into the front room, where he was removing his gun belt from a peg near the door. "We paid good money for those. Maybe if you would wear them, you could recognize people when they come to visit—before shooting them."

"I'm not going to shoot anybody," he said, raising his eyebrows for emphasis. In the meantime, María found his spectacles on a side table and stepped in front of him, holding them out to him. Jonathon finished buckling his gun belt and then folded his arms, glaring at her. "Fine, then!" He took the silver wire-rimmed eyeglasses, made a show of cleaning them on the tail of his shirt, slid them up his nose, and uncomfortably worked them around his ears.

"Happy?"

"Yes. Much better."

They both looked back out the door as the sound of softly approaching hoof beats now reached them. Jonathon kept his eyes locked on the rider who, as he could now clearly see, was about a hundred yards away; but he pointed toward the shotgun that leaned in the corner behind the door and addressed his wife with an even voice. "Guess you'd better grab that—and stay in here. Can't be—"

"Yes, I know," María interrupted. "Can't be too cautious." It was an all too familiar litany they had adopted ever since the attack a few years earlier had left her family dead and her home all but burnt out.

As the stranger neared, Jonathon knew without a doubt that he did not recognize the man, and he began to size him up. The man was well dressed in a dark duster over a nice suit, topped with a black wide-brimmed fedora with a fancy crease down the middle. He rode comfortably enough on a nicely groomed black Arabian that loped easily up the trail and seemed hardly winded. At this closer distance, Jonathon spotted a nicely trimmed mustache on an otherwise clean-shaven face. He could also see, as the unbuttoned duster flapped in the breeze, that the man was well heeled; the butt of a large revolver—perhaps a Navy Colt—protruded from his waist.

Jonathon stole a quick glance across the yard to where Jim was slowly walking to the corner of the barn, his rifle in hand. "Why don't you move back to the wagon, Jim. You'll be on his blind side and will also have a bit of cover there." Jonathon moved past María again, but not before he noticed her face darken with a frown at his comment. "Only if needed," he explained to her as he went on out the door. "Besides. I have these on now." He tapped the corner of his eyeglasses and winked at her. "And I have you, guarding my back through the window." He nodded down at the double-barreled shotgun cradled familiarly in his wife's arms, then leaned down and kissed her forehead. "Shut the door behind me. I'll be right back."

Jonathon pulled his old cavalry hat on, tucked his shirt in, stepped down from the stoop, and walked to the middle of the yard, scattering a few chickens that had been feeding there. He faced due south down the road, the rider now approaching him dead on as he neared the far corner of the barn. The big Arabian stallion bucked his head, snorted, and bounced on his feet as he sensed the end of their journey, but the tall stranger easily reined the spirited animal back under control and guided him into the alley between the barn and the corrals. Jonathon stood where he was with his left thumb hooked in his front pocket and his right hand dangling free, two or three inches from the butt of his gun. He watched the man's eyes and couldn't mistake the quick flicker that he saw there. Jonathon didn't take the look as either fear or danger, but rather that the stranger was at least wise enough to recognize the calm readiness of someone who was quite accustomed to, and comfortable with, armed confrontation.

"Howdy," said the rider, pulling his mount to a standstill twenty feet away. Peripherally, Jonathon could see Jim behind the wagon and satisfied himself that his hired hand was, indeed, positioned perfectly in the stranger's blind spot. He could also sense the twin barrels of María's shotgun protruding from the usual window near the corner of the house and to his immediate left. He was also confident that María knew the deadly blast pattern the gun would create, and that she would not fire unless Jonathon hit the ground—either on purpose or otherwise.

"Howdy, yourself," said Jonathon. The stranger adjusted himself in his stirrups and poked the brim of his hat back with a forefinger. His eyes moved down and back up again, seeming to size Jonathon up.

"I'm looking for a Jonathon Carter."

"You found him, I guess."

"You, uh, seem a mite younger than what I was led to believe."

"That would depend on what exactly you were led to believe, I reckon."

The man glanced to Jonathon's right and spied the water pump. "May I get down?" he asked, nodding at the well and starting to dismount.

"Nope. I'm thinking I like you right about where you are—until I find out exactly *who* you are, and what you might want." Jonathon let the fingertips of his right hand drum once against his holster, sounding a quiet tattoo against the leather. The stranger sat back slowly again in his saddle, stared down at Jonathon, and whistled low.

"Well, I had heard that you were not an individual to trifle with," the man said. "And I guess that looks are a bit deceiving these days, what with your youthful countenance and such." He shifted his weight slightly. "Speaking of which, I suppose you have heard of the doings of William H. Bonney to the south of you, in Lincoln County? A similar young genius with a gun."

Jonathon pursed his lips and shook his head once. "Can't say that I recall the name."

"Goes to calling himself Billy the Kid lately."

"Now that name I *have* heard of. So, you rode all this way north just to bring me news of Billy the Kid?"

The man chuckled and looked down. "No, Mr. Carter, that is not my business here." He pulled his duster open and put his hand inside. "My name is Frank Angell and I work for the—"

By the time Angell had said his name, Jonathon had his Army Colt drawn and leveled at the man's head. Angell froze and his face went limp. He threw his arms into the air and shook his head vigorously. The big stallion jerked and turned in a half circle until Angell was now facing Jim Watkin's old Henry repeater as the ranch hand stepped calmly from behind the wagon and took several steps toward them.

The corner of Jonathon's mouth twitched briefly in a half-smile as he heard the twin hammer clicks of María's shotgun behind him. "Mr. Angell," Jonathon said softly. "I would advise you strongly not to make another move—given the fact that I am not, as you say, an individual to trifle with."

"Oh, dear Lord in heaven!" exclaimed the frazzled Frank Angell, pulling his stallion's head back around to face Jonathon, one hand firmly on the reins and the other still held straight up to the autumn sky. "It's only a letter that I have been instructed to give you. Do you take me for a complete idiot, Mr. Carter?"

Jonathon paused for several seconds, lowered his pistol, and motioned for Jim to stand back. "No, Mr. Angell. At least, not a complete one." He then stepped toward the horse and motioned with his pistol. "Right- or left-handed?" he asked.

"Excuse me?"

"Are you right- or left-handed?"

"Er, right . . . handed, that is."

Jonathon motioned again. "Then take your left hand, if you please, and remove your weapon with two fingers and hand it to me—really easy."

Angell wavered for a moment, then lowered his left arm and did as he was told, gingerly handing the Navy Colt, butt first, over to Jonathon, who took a step back and handed it on to Jim.

"That the only one?"

"Of course it is! Well, except for my rifle, back here in a scabbard. You want it, also?"

"Can you remove it with just two fingers?" Jim said with an even, deadpan voice and continuing to point his own rifle. Jonathon glanced back at Jim and chuckled.

"No. Of course not!" exclaimed Angell.

"It's just fine where it is," said Jonathon.

"Well, then, Sir—now may I dismount? I have to pee something fierce."

"You can just hold your water for another minute or so. That is, until you tell me your business here. So, I suppose now would be a good time for you to get that letter out. But be really slow and cautious about it." Jonathon took another step back, raising the pistol up at his waist and pointing it back at Angell.

Angell peered back and forth at Jonathon and his hired man, distrust in his eyes.

"You won't shoot me?"

"Not unless you do something *completely* idiotic."

Angell hesitated, then slowly slipped a sealed envelope from his coat pocket. He held it up as if it were written in gold. "As I was saying," he began with a degree of self-importance. "My name is Frank Angell, and I work for the Secretary of State, Carl Schurz. . . ."

"Secretary of which state?" asked Jonathon.

"Why, the Secretary of State of the United States—the federal government?"

Jonathon nodded slowly. Behind him, the door creaked open and María stepped slowly out onto the stoop, her shotgun aimed somewhere in the vicinity of Frank Angell's head. Angell looked up at her and his face went even paler.

"Oh, good Lord!" he mumbled, thrusting his hands up again and twisting his face away protectively from this new, double-barreled threat to his life. The stallion jerked and stamped its foreleg as water suddenly trickled from the bottom of Angell's trousers leg and down the animal's side.

"Please continue, Mr. Angell," said María, sweetly. "And Jonathon," she added, nodding at the growing puddle on the ground, "I think you had better let Mr. Angell off of his horse so he can tend to his, um, personal needs."

#

The three of them sat around the table in María's kitchen, drinking coffee and eating one of the apple pies she had baked that afternoon. Now that guns were no longer pointed at his head, Frank Angell was cheerfully wolfing bites of pie and washing them down with copious amounts of coffee while talking with his mouth full. He had gratefully changed into an old pair of trousers and long underwear that had belonged to the late Don José Delgado, María's father, and was delighted that they were almost an exact fit. Maria had graciously offered to soak Angell's soiled garments outside in a tub of laundry soap. Jim Watkins had left to go back home to check on his mother in Cimarrón and María had given him the other pie to take with him.

Across the table, Jonathon absorbed little of what the government investigator was saying. He sat quietly back in his chair, one finger thoughtfully rubbing his lower lip as he adjusted his glasses to reread the letter that Angell had given to him.

"*Acting* Governor?" Jonathon finally looked up. "What happened to Axtell?"

"Fired," said Angell.

"How did that happen?"

Angell shrugged and slurped his coffee. "It happened because of me, I suppose. As I alluded to earlier, I was sent here by the State Department to investigate the various crimes and misdemeanors that have been perpetrated in your fair territory over the last few years. And I can, and did, report that the blame should be laid directly at the feet of former Governor Axtell." Angell threw his hands back and shook his head. "Why, I have never seen more corruption, fraud, mismanagement, plots and murders in any other governor's administration in the entire United States. And let me assure you, I have seen more than a few." He leaned back over his plate and stabbed another bite of pie. "So, upon my direct recommendation and report back to Secretary Schurz, the incompetent Mr. Axtell has been removed." He looked Jonathon in the eye. "I suppose you could say that in the area of investigations of corruption I too am an individual not to be trifled with."

"So, what happens to him now?"

"Oh, the usual, I suppose. I mean, what *should* happen to him and what will happen are probably two entirely different things. He should have the book thrown at him and be locked up, and the key should be thrown away. But, politics being what they are, he will probably be left to cool off for a period of time. Then, I wouldn't be at all surprised to see him thrown some bone, some position in some backwater area where he can do little harm—hopefully."

Jonathon tapped the letter on the table. "And this Wallace? What's he like?"

"Oh, Lew Wallace is as good as they come—prosecuting attorney, state senator in Indiana, Civil War veteran—Brigadier General. Union, of course."

"Of course," said Jonathon drily, slowly removing his glasses and staring flatly at Angell. The investigator sensed that he had said something wrong, and then he spied the faded gray cavalry hat hanging on the corner of a chair.

"Oh, yes. Sorry. I forgot that you're a veteran of the, uh—loyal opposition. No offense."

"None taken."

"Anyway, Forts Henry and Donaldson, Shiloh, the Valley Campaigns. Very distinguished service. After the war, he had built such a reputation that he almost even accepted a commission in the Mexican Army as a major general. In any event, he did not take it, and last month President Hayes pulled him out of his continuing law practice and offered him the onerous task of cleaning up these so-called wars here in New Mexico."

"Wars?"

"Why yes, Mr. Carter. This fracas that you have found yourself embroiled in around here has been dubbed *The Colfax County War*, at least in the eastern newspapers. And another similar one is festering down in Lincoln County. Believe you me, Wallace has his plate full. But I do believe he is the man to bring it all to an end." Angell stole a glance back at Jonathon. "And if you don't mind my saying so, I think he can do it, especially with the help of individuals such as yourself."

Jonathon smiled and looked down. "You mean, ones like you and me—that aren't to be trifled with?"

Angell raised his coffee mug in salute. "Hear, hear!" he toasted, and washed down the last bite of his apple pie.

"Why Jonathon?" asked Maria, who had remained quiet up until now.

"Excuse me, Ma'am?"

"What does a man of Governor Wallace's caliber see in my husband?" She glanced at Jonathon, placed her hand softly on top of his as it rested on the table, and looked back at the investigator. "Jonathon has no political aspirations. He does not seek the recognition or the glory. What he does seek in all things is justice." Maria looked back at her husband admiringly. "And he is possibly the bravest man I have ever known. But those are characteristics known not by war heroes and politicians, but by a very few people, actually—his friends, those who love him. . . ."

"Let's not forget a few enemies, too," added Jonathon. "Those that don't particularly love me."

Frank Angell set his cup down, wiped his mouth with the back of his hand, and leaning back in his chair, raised his eyebrows and looked back at Jonathon. "Well, I suppose it may be that last fact right there that has brought your name to light, Deputy Carter."

"*Former* Deputy Carter. And you can talk to her, Mr. Angell," Jonathon interrupted, nodding at his wife. "She's the one who asked you the question."

"Well, I just assumed. . . ."

"Assume nothing, Sir. That's what's gotten folks into trouble around here for a long time now." Jonathon turned his hand over on the table so that he could lock fingers with his wife. "I just lucked into this charmed life. She's the one owns the place. She's the one whose table our feet are under; the one with the real brains— and heart—of the outfit." Jonathon looked at María lovingly. "And she's the one you have to convince here. Not me."

Angell cleared his throat. "Yes. My apologies, Mrs. Carter. No offense."

"None taken once again, Mr. Angell."

"Now where was I? Oh yes. Bravery and justice. I think you will find, Mrs. Carter, that those very attributes in your husband are what has caught the eye of Governor Wallace. Deputy Carter's timely actions are not as unknown as he would like to think they are: his own exemplary record in the late war; the apprehension of and bringing to justice the killers of Reverend Tolby; the banishment of the gunman Clay Allison from the territory. These and many other fine examples of your ability to uphold the law have not gone unnoticed by those now in authority."

Jonathon sat unmoved by the litany of his accomplishments. "Mr. Angell, as much as I appreciate your opinion of any of my so-called successes, I assure you that I am merely an ordinary citizen performing my sworn duties as anyone else would who wishes to live an ordinary and peaceful life. And these timely actions you speak of are less than noteworthy. The war is something that any true soldier who lived those horrors would just as soon forget as to glorify; and Tolby's murderers were all, themselves, unceremoniously gunned down or lynched before any real justice could be meted out—lawfully, that is."

"And what of the outlaw Allison?"

"What of him?"

"Is it not true that, following the murder of one Chunk Colbert a few years back, you single-handedly confronted Clay Allison, bested him, and then chased him from New Mexico with his tail tucked between his legs?"

Jonathon looked at Frank Angell, then scooted his chair back, stood up, and walked to the window where he stared in silence out across the pastures and meadows that rolled gently down to the trees that lined the creek in the distance. The lowering sun cast a golden hue on their leaves, which shimmered now in the quickening breeze. Beyond them he could see that the wind had also blown a line of ominous squall clouds up on the southeast horizon. They were laced and torn with lightning.

"Clay Allison is one of my husband's oldest friends, Mr. Angell," said María. "They go way back, which has made their estrangement all the more difficult at times." She glanced at Jonathon. "It is something he is not willing to discuss with strangers. Suffice it to say, after their last confrontation, my husband resigned his position as Deputy Sheriff."

Frank Angell poked the tip of his tongue between his teeth and studied the coffee grounds in the bottom of his cup.

"So, what if I were to tell you both that was not destined to be your last confrontation with Clay Allison?"

Jonathon turned from the window and squinted his eyes at the man. "I would say you had best speak more plainly, Sir, and come directly to the point."

Angell set the mug back down and met Jonathon's eyes. "What if I were to tell you that Clay Allison has been seen back here in New Mexico?"

Jonathon started to respond, but then he glanced at María and waited until he composed himself. "And just where would this sighting have taken place, exactly?"

"Various places. He was reportedly seen down in Las Vegas and even Santa Fe, as recently as two weeks ago. Some rumors have him even back here in Colfax County, skulking about in the hills. Some say he's scouring the countryside for gold."

"That's absurd," Jonathon scoffed, crossing his arms and turning back to the window but no longer seeing anything of interest out there. His mind was working.

"If Clay were here—anywhere near here," said María, "we would have heard of it. I'm certain of it." She glanced at Jonathon, and from her look it was clear that she was anything but sure. "Jonathon?"

Her husband turned to her. He chewed his lip for a moment, then stepped over to the table and picked up Governor Wallace's letter and squinted at it once again. María stood up and brought him his glasses. She took his arm and looked at the letter over his shoulder as he put the glasses on to reread it. "You're sure Allison's back?" he finally asked.

Angell shrugged. "Mr. Carter, I consider myself a good investigator and a worthy judge of men. More than one supposed witness has sworn to me that they have seen Clay Allison, in several locations, and I do not get the sense from any of them that they are lying."

Jonathon exchanged a look with María, nodded grimly, and then handed the letter back to Angell.

"Then you tell Governor Lew Wallace to keep Billy the Kid down south in Lincoln where he belongs. I'm going to have enough problems dealing with my own damn war up here."

Frank Angell slapped the table and grinned. "Then I will take that as a 'yes' to the Governor's offer; and to celebrate. . . ." He looked once more into his coffee cup, then caught María's eye and smiled. "Might I trouble you for yet another round of coffee and another slice your most excellent apple pie?"

#

(May 13, 1881 - Santa Fe, New Mexico Territory)
The pearly gray light of predawn eased into the bedroom and mingled with the smell of freshly brewed coffee that had drifted enticingly upstairs from the kitchen

below. Former Governor Samuel Axtell stirred from a sound sleep; the coffee aroma had slipped into his dreams, gently at first and then more insistently, until he could no longer ignore it. His eyelids fluttered as dreams receded into the dark corners of the room and pulled themselves heavily and reluctantly open. He lay blinking and staring at the ornate ceiling that was just now visible in the dim light and wondering why he was smelling coffee. His wife was out of town, visiting her mother in Las Vegas, and the maid was off on Sundays. He raised himself on his elbows and squinted at the mantle clock that quietly ticked nearby: 4:50 a.m.

"What the hell," Axtell muttered, throwing back the bedclothes, scratching his head, and searching the floor with his feet for his slippers. He stumbled out of bed, went to the window, and tentatively pulled back a drape. The second-floor window looked out over the side yard, and from here he could see part of the brick-paved street and the corner of the back yard that sloped away down to an arroyo that was choked darkly with juniper and Russian olive. A sudden movement caught his eye and he sucked in his breath, then let it out with a thankful sigh. It was only his old coonhound, Bonaparte, snuffling around the corner of the house and finding places in his wife's decorative bushes to relieve himself. Axtell chuckled at what his wife would say about that, and then caught himself as he realized that the dog should not be out at this hour.

"What the hell?" he repeated, then stiffened as he thought he heard a sound from downstairs—as from a door softly opening and closing. His pulse thumped hard in his throat and he tiptoed to the bedside table, opened the drawer, and retrieved a small revolver that he kept there. He checked that it was loaded, then moved slowly to the door and eased himself down the stairs, pausing as they made a 45-degree turn at the first landing and listening once more. This time he thought that he could hear distant humming or singing. Axtell swallowed hard and looked cautiously over the banister to the first-floor entryway below. This early, it was still too dark to make out details—except for an inexplicable light that spilled from underneath the kitchen doorway at the rear of the hall. Beyond this, the back door stood open and Axtell could feel the chilly breeze of the predawn move delicately through the screen door and touch his warm face; through the same door he now heard again the mysterious humming.

"What the hell?" he said again, getting perturbed now. He glanced at the pistol in his hand and cocked the hammer before moving down the remainder of the stairs and into the hallway toward the kitchen door. "Josefita?" he called out in a hoarse whisper, the gun barrel touching a door panel. Maybe the maid had decided to come on in to work today, but there was no answer. He pushed the door slowly open with the gun and then stepped quickly inside. A lit hurricane lamp in the middle of the kitchen table flickered with the rush of air. Axtell quickly scanned the room with the gun and breathed in relief. No one was there, but he suddenly noticed the steaming coffee pot simmering on the wood burning stove in the corner. He gulped once and backed slowly out of the kitchen.

The back porch was actually a nicely designed covered veranda that stood an entire story off the ground, because of the slope of the ground the house was built on, and extended around both corners of the back of the house. Facing south, it provided shade from the hot sun in the summer and protection from the snow in the winter and from the sporadic rains of the high desert mountains at all times. It looked out on a grassy five-acre tract of land that sloped away to small stream that ran in the nearby arroyo. A small orchard of black walnut, crab apple, and choke cherry trees mostly shaded the yard, and it was one of the former governor's favorite spots to sit and relax.

Axtell pushed the screen door slowly and winced as it squeaked. The humming melody had stopped a few seconds ago, and he poked his head around the door and quickly looked both ways. Again, no one. He gently allowed the screen door to close softly, relieved that the squeaking had stopped, and moved slowly toward one corner of the veranda, his pistol extended at arm's length and leading the way. As he reached the corner of the house, he stopped and took deep breaths, collecting his thoughts. If he rounded the corner, whom would he come face to face with? A former enemy perhaps? Axtell racked his brain. He knew that he had not made too many friends while in office as governor—before he had been forced to resign by the President three years ago now. And he knew that some of the many land deals he had struck around the territory, while making him and his family a lot of money, had made him more than a few enemies in the process. The few serious attempts to sue him for damages in civil court had, thankfully, been unsuccessful. But those exonerations did not necessarily mean that anyone had forgiven him. Axtell took two or three more breaths, held the last one, and leapt around the corner, aiming his gun—at Bonaparte.

The coonhound sat next to Axtell's empty rocker, tongue lolling from its panting mouth, and grinning up at its master. Axtell quickly pointed the gun away from the dog. "Boney!" he exclaimed. "You almost gave me a heart attack!" The dog woofed once, then bolted past Axtell, and disappeared back around the corner and down the back steps to the yard. But Axtell was no longer interested in the dog. He stared in growing concern at the steaming mug of coffee that sat on the small wicker table beside the empty rocking chair.

Bonaparte barked again from nearby, and Axtell broke his gaze from the mysterious coffee cup and turned to follow his dog.

"Boney! Where'd you go, boy?"

He shuffled down the back steps to the yard, his nightshirt billowing like a cloud in the fresh early breeze. He stopped at the bottom and squinted into the shadows of the trees where he could just make out his dog's tail wagging in the middle of the orchard. "Come here, Bonaparte," he called, but the dog seemed to be preoccupied and ignored him. Axtell took several steps into the trees, then froze as he thought he saw the silhouette of someone kneeling down, petting the coonhound.

"Who's there?" Axtell demanded. "Show yourself, or I'll shoot." Almost as an afterthought, he raised his pistol up and aimed it into the shadows.

"Careful now, Governor. You might accidentally shoot your dog, or your foot." Bonaparte turned and trotted away as the ghostly shape stood and stepped out of the shadow of the tree trunk.

It was Clay Allison.

Samuel Axtell sucked in his breath and stumbled backward, almost tripping over his slippers on the uneven ground. "Allison!" he blurted, his eyes popping wide and his mouth open and slack.

Clay Allison smiled, removed his hat with a flourish, and gave an exaggerated, theatrical bow. "Why, I am honored and humbled that you would remember me, Governor Axtell; much less my name. And I must say you were quite the vision of purposeful leadership descending those stairs just now, your bare legs fairly floating down to earth on a billowing white cloud."

Axtell suddenly became aware of his attire and pulled his nightshirt protectively around him, quite forgetting the pistol in his hand as Allison walked toward him now, his hands upturned as he went to show that he meant no harm.

"What say we adjourn back to the veranda to finish our morning coffee and discuss whatever it is that may come up?" Allison said, placing his arm around Axtell's shoulders as if he were an old friend and guiding the former governor back to the porch steps. "And here," he added, reaching out and removing the small pistol with two fingers from Axtell's loose grip. "This is going to be a friendly conversation, so I do not believe we will be needing any of our artillery—just yet."

As they ascended to the veranda once again, former Governor Samuel Axtell felt as if he were indeed a child, in a dream, floating on a cloud, bewildered, just as Allison had suggested. He walked along compliantly, only a small part of his mind wondering what was going on and a larger part wondering if he were going to survive this so-called conversation.

After they turned the corner, Clay motioned to Axtell to sit in one of the rocking chairs and then he sat down in the other one. Clay crossed his legs, sighed deeply, picked up the coffee mug that was there, and took a sip.

"Ahh," he said, a peaceful smile on his face. "Still quite warm. And now, Governor Axtell, what shall we talk about this fine spring morning?" He took another sip of coffee and squinted thoughtfully into the distance.

Axtell glared at the famed gunman who had somehow reentered his life so unexpectedly. "Don't call me *governor*," he growled. "You and your pal Springer forced me out years ago."

"Oh, you mustn't be so melodramatic, Governor. I strongly imagine it was your own greed that got the better of your political aspirations." Clay took another appreciative sip. A clattering of small feet was suddenly heard on the steps and Bonaparte raced around the corner of the veranda before sliding to a stop to place his head in Allison's lap. Clay laughed and dutifully scratched behind the dog's ears.

"I must say, I really like your dog, Governor. A good dog, a rocking chair, and a fine cup of coffee on the veranda are some of the most satisfying ways to spend a Sunday morning, wouldn't you agree?"

Axtell hesitated, then answered. "Don't you hurt my dog, you bastard!"

Allison looked at Axtell with a pained expression on his face. "Oh, now that really hurts my feelings, Governor Axtell. I may be guilty of a lot of questionable acts, but abusing an innocent animal has never been one of them." He shifted to the other side of his chair as Bonaparte settled down to lie at Allison's feet. "But I am surprised to find that you are a dog lover. It occurs to me that you would be more of a cat man since, like a cat, you have always seemed to be able to land on your feet. Wouldn't you say so?" Allison rocked contentedly in his chair.

"I asked you not to call me *governor*. And just get to the point and get out of here, you son of a bitch! I'll give you just. . . ." Axtell paused to pat his clothes for a pocket watch, then was reminded that he was still in his nightshirt. Allison smiled and reached into his vest pocket and produced a shiny gold one. He held it out to Axtell.

"Here, borrow mine if you like," he offered playfully. Axtell slapped it away.

"If you don't get out of here, I will get up and go summon the police right now. I no longer believe you are going to shoot me. But I do believe that I still have some pull around here and I will have them string you up by your thumbs and give you a flogging within an inch of your life Sir! You are a trespassing, murderous fugitive from the law, and I will see justice served upon you for your crimes!"

"Oh, now there you go again, Governor, making threats that we both know will never happen. And I hardly think that sort of punishment is even legal anymore in this country. Is it? Public floggings?" He shook his head, then his eyes suddenly lit up and he sat forward in his chair. He reached into the inner pocket of his coat. "But I do know what *is* legal. Would you care to see it again?" Axtell glared at him.

"I have know idea what you're talking about."

Allison slowly pulled out a folded sheet of paper—expensive stationery by the look of it—and carefully unfolded it. He held it up for the former governor to see. Axtell's eyes went wide and the blood drained from his face as he recognized a letter he had signed more than five years ago, while still in office. It contained a list of names of prominent New Mexico citizens and a thinly veiled order to cause their demise. Axtell sat back heavily and slumped in the rocker.

"I particularly like this part, here at the end," said Allison with a touch of glee. "'By *direct order of this office, the bearer of this letter has lawfully done what has been done.'* Now, does that not have a nice ring to it? And look here, signed by Governor Samuel Axtell himself." Allison reached his boot over and tapped Axtell's foot with it. "I do believe that is you, is it not? And by the simple fact that I am now *the bearer of this letter*. . . . Well, I really don't see what all the fuss is, Governor—all this talk of stringing me up and floggings and such."

Samuel Axtell sat still, his head down and his hand covering his mouth. He stared dully at the plank flooring of the porch in front of him, a deflated man.

"So this is blackmail then. What is it that you want, Allison?" he finally asked quietly. "What will it take for you to tear up that thing."

"What is it that I want. . . ? Let's see now. Let me think on it a bit." Clay took his cup, drained the last of his coffee, and set the cup back on the table. He made a show of scratching his chin thoughtfully, then seemed to have an idea, and snapped his fingers.

"Oh, I know! Why don't we talk about trading for that old Ute Indian deed—

part of the Maxwell Land Grant—that you stole from Lucien Maxwell years ago, while he lay helpless on his deathbed, shall we?"

CHAPTER 26
The Fallen And The Brave

(Present Day – Raton, New Mexico)

Three days later, Gert Vos ate his breakfast of scrambled eggs, bacon, and pancakes alone in the mess hall of the county lockup. Since his arrest he had always eaten his meals last and today was no different. After the other prisoners had finished their breakfasts and filed out to the exercise area, one of the jailers brought him out of his cell and sat him at one of the stainless steel tables near the door to eat alone. He had been told that it was for his own safety, but he really didn't mind the privacy, which also allowed him to eat at a leisurely pace. The food was actually not too bad and there was enough of it to fill him up. He had learned the hard way, in the Dutch army, that although meals were not always timely and were often tasteless, you had better eat what was put in front of you when it was put in front of you, because you were never sure when you would eat again.

Vos was pouring some more syrup on his pancakes when he heard the door open and shut behind him. "Time to go, Vos." He looked up to see the deputy who had arrested him the other day and who had questioned him three times already, then sullenly turned back to his food.

"I am not finished eating."

"Take another couple of bites and wash it down with your coffee then, because that's all the time you've got."

Vos turned around, still chewing, a bite of pancake held up on the end of his fork, and peered up at the deputy. "More questions then, Deputy. . . ." He squinted at the officer's nameplate on his chest, "Armijo?"

Hector hooked his thumbs in his belt and took two or three steps toward Vos before stopping right in front of him. "Nah. No more questions," he said and reached over to pull the food off the prisoner's fork with his thumb and forefinger. He looked it over studiously, then dropped it into Vos' coffee mug and wiped his fingers off on the collar of Vos' orange jumpsuit. "You wouldn't answer them anyway, would you?"

Vos stopped chewing and watched warily as the deputy walked back to the door and tapped on it. There was an electronic buzz and the door clicked open. Armijo pushed it open, then held it as he waited.

"So, what's the big hurry, then?" asked Vos suspiciously.

Hector just smiled and waved his other hand graciously at the open door, indicating that Vos should come along. The prisoner stood up slowly, wiped his hands and mouth on a napkin, and followed Hector cautiously. "Where are you taking me? Another hearing?"

A week ago Vos had been standing in a clearing in the Sangre de Cristo mountains, nervously awaiting the return of his colleagues, who had left three hours earlier on four-wheelers to finish up the business of retrieving incriminating evidence from the girl and silencing the witnesses—including Agent de Jaager, who had no idea what was really going on. Why he had been left behind with the vehicles he really didn't know. Surely Kurt and Lars could have used his help. Maybe they hadn't trusted him. He would never know now. He had been glancing at his phone again for messages and checking and rechecking his semi-automatic pistol in his shoulder holster when suddenly and seemingly out of nowhere a state police helicopter and three other law enforcement vehicles had descended on him, surrounding him with guns bristling and loudspeakers blaring, demanding that he drop his weapons and surrender—which he had done immediately.

But Vos had remembered his training, and like a good soldier he had not said a word, even when this hick town deputy sheriff had grilled him for hours. Before the next 48 hours was up he had been arraigned and charged with second-degree murder and conspiracy. Vos still wasn't sure what had happened to the others, and it nagged him still as he dutifully followed Deputy Armijo down the hallway. Had Kurt and Lars been arrested too, and had they already sold him out? And what about de Jaager? Hopefully she was dead and no longer a problem.

His rubber-soled jailhouse sandals squeaked on the linoleum floor as they turned a corner and stopped in front of Vos' cell. Hector unlocked it and motioned him to enter. Vos stopped and raised his eyebrows as he saw a set of civilian clothes folded in the middle of his bunk and a pair of brown loafers neatly lined up on the floor. He looked up at Armijo questioningly.

"Where are my old clothes?"

"Can't have you roaming the streets dressed like a terrorist, can we? Just get changed.

"What's this all about?"

"You're leaving, that's what."

"Leaving? Where to?"

Hector shrugged, put his hand in the middle of the prisoner's back, and gave him a small nudge. "Anywhere you want. You've been released."

"Released? Why would I have been released?"

"Hell if I know. Order just came through. Way above my pay grade. Charges were suddenly dropped and you're free to go." Hector glanced at his watch and frowned. "So, if I were you, I'd get a move on, before whoever it was figures out they just made a big mistake and changes their mind."

Thirty minutes later, Gert Vos walked out the front door of the Colfax County Detention Center in his new clothes with his phone, wallet, and the ninety-eight dollars that he had arrived with. Slinging his new windbreaker over one shoulder, he turned and looked at Hector, who had escorted him outside and now stood with his arms folded.

"Where am I supposed to go now? Vos asked.

"Again, not my problem," Hector said, and disappeared back inside.

Vos shaded his eyes and blinked up at the bright mid-morning sky. He looked down at his expensive cowboy boots and wiped one of them on the back of his pants leg. At least they had saved these after getting rid of his other clothes. An autumn chill was still in the air and he slipped on the windbreaker, put his hands in the pockets, and began to walk, aimlessly at first, then finally east and out of the city limits.

Half a mile later a black Chevrolet Tahoe passed him slowly as he walked on the shoulder of the highway. Then it pulled to a stop and idled a few yards in front of him. Vos also slowed his walk and stared suspiciously at the vehicle, then stopped completely as its backup lights came on and it slowly moved in reverse toward him. As it came even, the passenger window whirred down and he recognized Britt de Jaager behind the wheel. She continued to look straight ahead as the door locks suddenly clicked.

"Get in," she said evenly, still not looking at him.

Vos looked nervously around him, first up the highway and then back down the way he had come. Ahead of him the massive outcropping of Johnson Mesa loomed across half the horizon, grey clouds scudding across its rim; and behind him was the town of Raton. A few cars and a couple of semi trucks zipped past from both directions but ignored the big SUV on the side of the road. A feeling of dread enveloped him. De Jaager was supposed to have been dead, taken out by Kurt and Lars. Yet here she was, alive and well. *And just what all did she know?* For a quick, desperate moment, he considered turning and heading back to town, hoping maybe to flag someone—anyone—down. No, that was crazy thinking. *Maybe it's okay,* he thought. *She probably doesn't know anything. Just wants to help out. Besides, what choice do I have? Just keep your head.*

Vos licked his lips and stepped to the window. "Hey there, Captain," he called out cheerfully. "Man, am I ever so glad to see you! I mean, I had no idea what happened to everyone." He laughed nervously. "Still don't!"

Britt turned an impassive face to her agent. "I said get in," she repeated again, coldly.

"Sure, Captain. Sure."

Vos climbed in and had barely slammed the door when the Tahoe lurched forward with a spin of its tires. He grappled quickly with the seatbelt, then sat back and blew out his breath.

"Whew! Like I said. Real glad you came along. I had no earthly idea where I was headed. And I am very happy you made it out of that mess." He glanced down to the sling on Britt's right arm. "Guess you didn't get out totally clean though, huh? You okay there?"

"I am quite fine, Agent Vos." She said, continuing to stare at the road as they sped east. The highway wound through the ancient volcanic lava flows and the intermittent lush grazing pastures that defined the landscape between here and

Union County. Occasional flurries of wildlife burst across the fields as the passing of the large SUV scared up small herds of pronghorn and flocks of birds that foraged the land. Britt finally turned to him with a steely look. "And how are you doing, Agent Vos?" she asked, peering at him intently for a moment before turning her attention back to the highway. "I trust you were well-treated by the authorities."

"Oh, I'm okay. Just fine." Vos laughed nervously. "Got a bit of a scare there when they swooped in on me like that, up there in the hills, waiting for you all to get back." He looked away and cleared his throat. "So, where are Kurt and Lars, anyway? They wouldn't tell me anything back in the lockup. They're waiting for us up here somewhere, I suppose?"

"No. Actually, they're both dead." Britt said quietly, matter-of-factly.

"D—dead?"

"Yes. Dead." She looked over at him blankly. "I killed them." He blinked at her two or three times and his heart thumped. *Hold it together, you idiot!*

The SUV suddenly slowed at an intersection and swerved south onto a narrower two-lane farm road, then sped up again. Vos braced himself against the door, swallowing hard again and rubbing his face, which had gone pale. He suddenly noticed that de Jaager was wearing black leather gloves as she drove. His mind was now racing. "*You* killed them? But . . . why in the world would you do that?"

Britt stared back out at the horizon. The rugged landscape of malpais and sagebrush rolled past them. "Why do you think I did it, Agent Vos?"

Vos grabbed his thighs and squeezed them nervously. It was getting harder to breath. He no longer wanted to look at Britt, for fear of giving anything else away. *She knows!* "Um . . . I think I'd just like to get out now. Anywhere here is fine."

"As you wish."

Obligingly, the Tahoe began to slow and Vos began to breath somewhat normally. The vehicle finally stopped and Britt put the transmission into park. She sat back against the door and stared at him. Vos pulled the door handle, but the door was locked. He found the locking mechanism but it didn't respond. He punched it nervously a couple more times with a finger, but nothing happened. He looked frantically at de Jaager. "What's going on, Britt?" Vos asked, fear choking his voice. "Open the door."

Britt continued to look at him, a look of curiosity crossing her face now, as if she were studying a strange new species. She reached across with her good arm and switched off the ignition. "Let's just sit and talk for a while, shall we, Gert?"

"Talk? About what? Why do we need to talk?" Vos' fingers continued nervously trying the door lock, to no avail.

"Why did you do it, Gert? After everything else . . . why?"

"Why what? I don't know what you're talking about! Just let me out."

Britt's eyes now took on a hint of pity. She shook her head slowly. "In a minute, Gert. Be patient."

Britt sighed, slipped a gloved hand inside her black suit jacket, and withdrew a

SIG Sauer 9mm semi-automatic pistol. She pulled the clip, checked it, blew on it to clear any lint or dust, and then reinserted it into the handle with a slap of her palm. She gently laid the weapon on the console between them. Vos followed her every move with eyes wide and stared at the pistol that lay within mere inches of his hand.

"Now, Agent Vos. I believe I asked you a simple question, which you haven't yet answered."

Vos continued to stare at the pistol, his lips working soundlessly. He quickly rubbed his mouth with the back of his hand. "Question? I . . . uh, don't remember exactly."

"I asked you why you did it."

"Did what?"

Britt leaned in a little closer and peered into Vos's eyes. She lowered her voice and enunciated her next words clearly. "Why did you murder my little brother? And who, exactly, ordered you to do it?"

Vos jerked his head back as if he had been slapped. "Your . . . your *brother*? I don't even know who that is! Are you crazy?"

Britt leaned even closer. "It was Cobus, Vos. Cobus was my brother."

"*De Groof?* How could that be?"

"Because his real name was de Jaager. Like mine." Britt leaned away again and turned to gaze out the side window. A small hawk sailed up to land on a mesquite fence post just on the other side of the road. It preened its feathers and looked over at the vehicle, tilting its head as if listening to them. "He always wanted to work with me. He begged me, mission after mission. I always knew it would be too dangerous, but he finally wore me down."

"Impossible. Septum would have never allowed it," Vos argued.

The little hawk turned its head backward on its shoulder and screeched once, but the window heavily muffled the sound. It turned back and watched Britt again.

"It was actually Septum's suggestion. Septum helped to find an alternate identity for Cobus—some unknown dead agent from years ago in Kosovo, with no family left. No one would miss him. This was supposed to have been a milk run—a simple operation, in and out, no one hurt. Just a fact-finding mission to expose a small group of people, and that should've been the end of it. But instead, you hunted him down like the coward you are and drove a pick through his heart."

There was a metallic noise from the passenger side, behind her, and Britt held her breath for several seconds as she recognized the sound of a pistol being cocked. She sighed and continued to exchange looks with the hawk. "You need to rack it, Vos. I didn't chamber the round." Vos pulled the rack back on the SIG Sauer and let it slap back in place, a bullet now securely chambered, and ready to fire.

"You look at me, you bitch! I want you to see this coming."

Britt turned her head slowly to him, her eyes vacant and unflinching. "All right. I'm looking at you now, you piece of shit. But you still haven't answered me. *Why did you do it?*" Vos grimaced at her, sweat rolling down his cheeks and hate in his eyes. The gun began to tremble slightly. He swiped the sweat from his eyes with his other hand and then shrugged.

"Because they paid me to do it."

"Kurt? Lars? Someone else?"

Vos giggled nervously, his eyes bright. "Someone with a lot more clout. But what does it matter? You were part of the deal too. They figured if I took out Cobus, I was in. Besides, it was more money than any of us had made in ten years. But then Boewmeester had to go and screw it all up. And that snot-nosed brat of his." He nodded once at Britt. "And Lars was supposed to take care of you. But we both can see how that went. So now I guess it's up to me." He lifted the pistol and aimed at her forehead.

"And so, where was all this money supposed to come from, Gert? Did they ever even tell you? Ever even really trust you?"

Vos hesitated and glanced away, thinking for a moment. "It was the map, I figure. Something scribbled on the back of that old photograph I found on that corpse Cobus dug up. Yeah, your sweet baby brother! He was looking for it too, so don't give me all that innocence bullshit! Why do you think he wanted in on this mission so badly? He knew what was really up!"

Britt shook her head sadly. "Maybe. But no one deserved what you did to him."

Vos bit his lip, straightened his arm out, and aimed the gun straight at Britt's face. "Yeah, well, maybe this will be more to your liking, huh? Don't worry. You won't feel a thing."

Britt remained passive. Vos pulled the trigger. There was a loud click but nothing else happened. He looked in shock at the weapon, then aimed and fired again. And again, nothing.

Britt cleared her throat, reached over slowly, and gently took the useless weapon from Vos' trembling hand. She pulled back the slide, caught the ejected shell as it flew out, and then turned it between her thumb and fingers until the back end of the bullet casing was visible. She held it up to the light where they could both plainly see a small dimple in the middle of the primer.

"You see, Gert," she began, as if lecturing a child, "a bullet is impossible to fire when the primer has already been used. Did you think I would really hand you a weapon with a real bullet in it? Especially when we haven't concluded our little chat yet? But now that I know where you really stand. . . ." Britt reached into her jacket pocket and pulled out a fresh 9mm bullet and held it up so that Vos could clearly see its unspoiled primer. "Now this one should work just fine." She pulled the empty clip, loaded the single bullet, replaced the clip, and chambered the new round. Then she again placed the gun gently on the console but this time kept her hand on top of it.

"Now, Agent Vos. I want you to consider your options."

"Options! What options? Are you just going to shoot me now?" he smirked.

She caught and held his eyes. "No. That's not one of the options—as much as I would love to. But one still always has options, yes? It's something you have never learned too well." She adjusted her body and turned to study him closely again. "I just now realized something. You really don't know why you were released from jail this morning, do you?"

A worried look clouded Vos's face, but he said nothing.

"Who do you think arranged for you to be released? Who do you think had all those charges just disappear?"

"I have no idea."

Britt shook her head at him, a pitying look in her eyes. "Poor, poor Vos," she murmured. "You really haven't a clue, then, have you? Just blinded by the money."

"Who was it?" he asked, truly curious now—and concerned.

"I guess you don't know Septum as well as you thought. You have no idea how much power they have, do you—how far-reaching their influence?"

"Septum did this?"

"Oh, Gert," she repeated. "Who else could have gotten you freed so quickly? You—a foreign national in the U.S., charged with murder and who knows what else. Someone very powerful was obviously pulling the strings." She looked down and removed her hand from the pistol. "And your choices are very simple. Option number one is that you can pick up that gun, shoot me in the head, and then just drive away."

"That's way too easy. What's the catch?"

Britt looked down, straightened her clothes, and touched a hand to her hair as if preparing herself. "Oh, there's no catch, Agent Vos. But don't be fooled." She paused and looked at him, her eyes now taking on a certain dark intensity. "Nothing is ever that easy. If you take that option, know that you will be hunted relentlessly by those who wanted you out in the open; that your life as you know it will change irrevocably; and that when they do find you—*when*, not *if*—the end, for you, will not come soon enough. When it finally does . . . well, you will simply vanish from the earth without a trace that you ever existed." Vos stared back at her as if she were insane, and he said as much.

"You're crazy!"

"Perhaps I am. Maybe we all are, just a little, hmm? Perhaps it's how we all survive." Britt put her hand on the door handle, opened it, and put one leg out. "But not crazy enough to go through what I just described, if it were my choice. I have seen Septum get their hands on traitors before. It never ends well, Gert. Never."

Britt stepped out of the vehicle. The little hawk squawked, loudly this time, and fluttered its wings at her. It spread them, leapt off the fence post, and lazily flapped away. She watched enviously as its silhouette gradually diminished and finally disappeared behind a volcanic mound in the distance. She turned and began to walk slowly back up the road, leaving the door wide open behind her. She was not yet entirely sure of what would happen.

"Wait!" came Vos' voice, shouting pathetically from within. "You never told me what option number two is!"

Britt continued to walk away as she called out. "Remember there's only one bullet—a real one this time. So, let's just say that option number two is to avoid option number one at all costs."

Britt walked faster, her shoes beating out a measured rhythm on the asphalt as she marched back north on the desolate, high-desert highway. Her step faltered just once when the muffled report of a single gunshot echoed from somewhere a quarter mile or so behind her. She then lifted her face to the fresh fall breeze, briefly closed her eyes, took a long, deep breath of the cleansing New Mexican air, and fell into a more relaxed pace.

#

(Present Day – Montaño del Sol Ranch)

It was Trent's favorite time of day. He sat on the veranda in the heavy wooden rocker that Walter had made decades ago. It made a satisfying creaking sound as rocked slowly. It was brisk out here and he shivered a bit, realizing that he should have grabbed a jacket. He had awakened just before sunup; pulled on a long-sleeved flannel shirt, jogging pants, and a pair of slip-on sneakers; made coffee; and hobbled out here with the help of his trusty cane, which had served him well years earlier while he was recuperating from his injuries in a car accident.

The sun was just peeking through a distant shadowy stand of tall pines that stood like sentinels to the east of the barns. Its first cold beams on this early winter morning spilled gold across the meadows that rolled gently into the distance. From here, the old settler's cabin was just visible on the edge of the woods a couple hundred yards away. He had repaired it after they were married and Maggie had fixed it up and redecorated it for him to use as a man cave when he just needed a place to be off by himself for an afternoon of quiet reading.

His three-legged cat, Jarhead, came around the corner, rubbed against his ankle, and purred loudly for attention. "Nope, you little bastard. I'm not falling for it anymore." Trent took his cane and poked the tip gently behind the ears of the old tomcat. "Here. Gnaw on this instead. Better than the back of my hand getting bloodied." Jarhead rolled to his back and grabbed at the cane, but he quickly tired of the game. Growling menacingly, he spat and disappeared off the edge of the deck in a sudden flash of mottled orange fur. "Crazy cat," Trent muttered, before he burned the tip of his tongue on his scalding coffee.

"Ouch!" He grimaced as the reflex sent a sharp pain coursing through the tightened muscles of his left calf. The rogue agent's bullet had fortunately gone through without hitting bone, but Trent's surgeon and therapist had both told him that it would be months before he regained full use of the leg, if that. At best, he was told, he might always walk with a slight limp. He leaned over and rubbed the leg and gazed again back up toward the old cabin. He told himself that soon he would feel up to hiking up there again. It was a goal he had set for himself. Soon, but not today. Or tomorrow either, probably.

Trent heard the heavy front door creak open, followed by familiar light footsteps of slippered feet coming up behind him.

"What's all the commotion out here so early?" Maggie set her steaming mug of coffee on the small wicker table beside him. He shivered as she slid the cool palm of her hand down the front of his shirt and planted a kiss on the back of his neck. "You cold?" she asked, stepping around to the matching rocker on the other side of the table. She was wearing flannel lounging pajamas underneath a brightly colored afghan that she had pulled around her shoulders.

"A little."

"Well, you should be, silly man. Where's your coat?"

"Inside. Where I left it."

"Your own fault then, is it?"

"Usually is."

"Well, I shouldn't take any pity on you then, but I love you. So here." Maggie tossed him a second afghan that she had with her. Trent caught it and draped it over his body, snuggling down into its welcome warmth. He looked down at himself and laughed.

"What's so funny?"

"Now I really do look like a decrepit old man, with my cane, my rocker, and my lap blanket."

Maggie blew on her coffee and then sipped it, gazing at her husband across the rim of the mug. "Keep talking like that and I'll have to drag your crippled butt back into bed and show you what I can get an old man to do."

"You think so, huh?"

"I know so."

They sat that way for several long minutes, drinking their coffee and rocking, listening to the sounds of the awakening world around them: a light breeze whispered through the tops of the trees; birds sang out greetings to one another; the horses moved slowly as they stamped their hooves and grazed the nearby pastures, their teeth pulling the last of the summer grass.

Trent began humming an old song. "You know," Trent finally said. "It's the coldest just before dawn."

"Where'd you hear that?"

"Just something Ben tried to tell me recently."

Time slowed to a crawl, and Trent watched as the color across the fields and in the trees morphed and the hues changed almost imperceptibly. He squinted at the sun rising on its inevitable journey during which it would traverse at a slight southern angle now that the seasons were changing once again. In a few weeks would come the winter solstice, and he found himself reflecting now on all that had transpired already this year, both for good and not so good.

Life was settling back into a quiet or at least less troublesome pace once again. They had all survived the aftermath of yet another series of unspeakable crimes, although Trent was still banged up and Ben Ferguson was in the midst of several surgeries and skin grafts to repair the horrific mauling he had received from the bear. His daughter, Jennifer, had gone back to school in Denver but was spending more of her weekends and holidays here with her dad. Sophie and Hector had announced that they were now expecting their first baby in the spring, and Walter actually seemed to want to spend more time with Trent these days, although he was still obsessed and secretive about his collection of old letters and photographs.

The Dutch mercenary, Gert Vos, who had been suspected of murdering Cobus de Groot and assassinating Laird Bouwmeester, had been found dead in a vehicle on a quiet county road. It appeared to have been caused by a self-inflicted gunshot through his mouth. For some inexplicable reason, all of the charges against Vos had been mysteriously dropped the day before he had been found dead. Hector had also reported that most of the physical evidence obtained in the entire Bouwmeester incident had all been shipped down to Santa Fe to the FBI's forensic labs for further analysis. But within hours of its arrival, a team of serious-looking mysterious federal types in black suits arrived in an unmarked black cargo plane at Kirtland Air Force Base. Armed with official-looking NSA credentials and warrants, they took immediate possession of all the evidence and records of the investigation, crated it all up, and flew it out, destination unknown. The evidence included the memory stick and the air-gapped computer it had been plugged into at the cyber crimes division, but not before an analyst had been able to pull off plans and specifications of what looked like a large industrial complex of some kind—possibly for mining, possibly for military purposes—apparently to have been located somewhere in the Sangre de Cristo Mountains, just north of Ute Valley. More importantly, the analyst shared confidentially that the drive held a description of a 140-year-old deed of land to the Ute and Arapaho nations, signed by Lucien B. Maxwell. A brief investigation of the public records showed that no such deed had ever been recorded, and no clue as to the actual deed's location had been found. Its real significance was undetermined, and the original copy was presumed to have been lost a long time ago.

In addition to all this business, the mysterious Agent Britt de Jaager had completely disappeared without another word or trace. Trent had wondered more than once if it would be her body that turned up next.

In short, all of the intrigue and violence and questions that had been visited upon their relatively calm and quiet lives in the past few weeks had suddenly and conveniently been swept away and seemingly out of existence. Now all that Trent was left with, besides his injuries, was the hope and prayer that the calm and quiet would remain again for a long while.

He winced as he flexed his leg back and forth as the therapist had instructed him to do regularly. He drained the remainder of his coffee and stretched, noticing that the sun had crawled a little higher and the color had brightened into full morning. He stood up slowly and groaned, twisting and stretching at the waist to loosen up. He felt time once again and unrelentingly passing by once again.

"Where are you going?" asked Maggie, a twinkle in her eye. "Ready to take me up on my offer?"

"Maybe. But first, I thought you could use some breakfast. Thought I'd better go rattle around in the kitchen, since it is about the only thing I know how to cook."

"Most important meal of the day, they say."

"Yeah. Whoever *they* are."

He picked up their empty coffee mugs, grabbed his cane, and started to hobble back inside. He stopped and frowned at the sound of an approaching vehicle, revving its engine harshly as it turned the corner around the back of the yard and finally arriving in a cloud of dust as it braked to a hard stop. It was Hector's police cruiser, and both doors flew open as Hector and Sophie got out and hurried up the flagstone walkway to the porch. Hector was frowning and Sophie was running ahead of him, in tears.

"What the hell is this?" demanded Trent as he and Maggie met Sophie at the top of the stairs. Sophie fell into Maggie's arms, sobbing. Hector stood at the bottom of the steps, his fingers worrying over the hat in his hands. Trent glared at him. "What the hell did you do? You guys fighting or something?"

Hector stammered, then looked away across the meadows, trying to find the words to continue. "Ben's dead, Trent," he finally said, his voice raw with emotion. He gazed up at Trent with bewilderment. "They had him back in surgery this morning, early." Hector's voice broke, and he could barely continue. "He never made it, Trent . . . never woke up again. They said his heart just gave out on him." Tears welled in his eyes.

Trent stumbled backward in shock and caught himself on the porch rail to keep from falling. He braced himself there for a while, and then sat down hard on the top step, his leg throbbing and his mind numb.

CHAPTER 27
War And Peace

(October 1885 – Cimarron, New Mexico Territory)

"Sheriff J. S. Carter... that certainly has a nice ring to it."

Jonathon Carter tipped his hat up from where it had been shading his eyes as he dozed on the porch, his chair leaning back on two legs against the adobe wall of the jailhouse. He squinted up through the afternoon sun to scrutinize the familiar silhouette of a man on horseback who had just ridden up and was quietly perusing the plank sign that hung above the porch awning.

"Yes, it does sort of just roll off the tongue, doesn't it?" Jonathon stood up and stepped to the edge of the porch, where he folded his arms and leaned against the wooden column and smiled. "How in the world are you, Mr. Springer?"

"Well, I am quite well in fact *Sheriff* Carter."

"We don't see you much around here any more. Word has it you have quit this country for more prosperous pursuits—Las Vegas and Santa Fe now, isn't it?"

"Word has it pretty much correctly, Sheriff." Springer dismounted with a groan, tied his horse to the rail, and stretched his back. "I have actually taken up residence in Las Vegas. My family enjoys it there; and frankly there is not much around here to pique my interests lately. My brother Charles has pretty much taken the lead in running our ranching affairs here. And since the troubles around Colfax County have subsided somewhat, and my legal work tends more toward the goings-on in state and federal courts as well as some international concerns with the new Dutch owners of the land grant company, I find it more conducive to live closer to Santa Fe and the available railroads."

Springer stepped up to the porch and grasped Jonathon's hand firmly. "Really good to see you again, Jonathon. You got anything resembling coffee simmering inside there, by chance? I've been riding for the better part of the day and could surely use a fresh cup and a soft chair with a back to lean on."

Jonathon smiled and grasped his old friend by the shoulder. "Right this way, Counselor." Inside, he warmed up the pot and tossed a small, embroidered pillow onto his desk chair. "Here. María made that. Best I can do for now as to that soft chair."

"Then I expect that it will be more than comfy."

They sat sipping their coffee with the door open hoping to entice a late afternoon breeze to come on in. They were quiet for a good long while, enjoying the respite of the day.

"Rather quiet for a Saturday evening," Springer finally commented. "I don't recollect it as such too often, back in the day."

"As you said earlier, the troubles have subsided some."

"Speaking of María, how are she and the kids doing?"

"She's good. And the boys are growing like weeds. Fat and sassy. And yours?"

"Josie is quite well. She has now given me a fourth daughter, Ada. I suppose I am destined to fill the house up with women. But that is just fine with me. The longer I am in this world, the more convinced I am that it is the women who shall rule it all one day. They are just biding their time until we men mess it all up to the point where they will have no choice but to step in and correct our grievous mistakes."

"I know my María would agree with you on that point, for damn sure." Jonathon sipped his coffee and then studied his friend for a moment. "I must say that I am surprised you have not set up housekeeping in that new town that bears your name. I don't think I have ever met anyone face-to-face who has had an entire town named after them. Who did you bribe to make that happen, Counselor?"

Springer's mustaches bristled as he puffed a breath out in embarrassment. "Damned Santa Fe Railroad; that's how that happened. I suppose I was a mite too helpful to them when they finally came south out of Colorado and over Raton Pass. Seems money was tight and business was light, so with my continued business connections with the Maxwell Land Grant board, I was able to negotiate handsome enough concessions for them as they built on across the grant lands and into our fair territory."

"So I heard. Free right-of-way, four station points through the county, one-half interest in two new town sites—Raton and Springer. I am quite impressed that you arranged all of that."

Frank Springer raised his cup in a salute. "And I must say that I am equally impressed that you know your facts so well, Sheriff."

"Only what I have read in the newspapers, which all seem to be touting your accomplishments lately."

"Well, I assure you, I did *not* solicit that town to be named after me. It was done without my permission and in spite of my objections. That was never part of the deal. But the railroad insisted. Even offered to build me a big new house there on a hill overlooking the valley."

"Now that would have been something, wouldn't it?"

"I refused, of course. I suppose I could take them to court—force them to change the name. But Josie tells me that would appear to be ungrateful. So the next best recompense I can think of is to refuse to ever set foot in their fancy town, name or no name." Springer frowned and drained his coffee. He looked Jonathon's office over. "I could ask you the same thing, you know."

Jonathon leaned over to refill his friend's cup. "What would that be, exactly?"

"Why have you not moved your office to Springer? It is the new county seat, after all. They just built a fine new courthouse, and everything. I would think the county sheriff would need to be available to conduct business nearby."

"I'm near enough—two or three hours away, if necessary. Pleasant enough ride. Besides, I don't like to be that far away from the ranch, and María's not keen on selling it." Jonathon glanced around the old office fondly. "And I admit I'm rather used to this setup right here." He leaned back in his chair and folded his arms. "So is that what this visit's really about?"

"Why, I'm not sure what you are getting at, Jonathon."

"Well, you have had some of my bad coffee and we have shared our pleasantries and complimented one another. So when are you going to get around to telling me the real reason you came all this way this afternoon, Mr. Springer?"

Springer smiled and set his coffee cup down on the desk between them. "You have learned my ways too well, Jonathon." He stroked his large mustache and swiveled the desk chair until he could gaze out the open door and watch a dust devil spin its way silently down the dirt street. His eyes gradually took on a distant, glassy look. "Did you hear of our old friend William Morley's tragic accident last year?"

"Yes. I did. And I was truly sorry to learn of Mr. Morley's untimely death. He was a fine man and will be sorely missed. I know he meant a lot to you. Down in Mexico, wasn't it?"

Springer's cup paused halfway to his mouth. "Yes. Some desolate place called Aguas Calientes. You know how Bill loved traipsing around God-forsaken countryside, mapping out potential railroads; this one was for the Mexican government. They said that somebody's rifle fell off the wagon and discharged. Blew poor Bill's head right off." Springer shook his head morosely as his cup found his lips again. "One of my oldest and dearest friends."

"You think it was really an accident? I mean, some of our old *friends* from the Ring still have long arms—possibly even reaching down to Old Mexico."

Springer glanced up at Jonathon, and then shrugged. "The thought had crossed my mind. Especially in light of our old pal Samuel Axtell having been named Chief Justice of the Territorial Supreme Court. Whatever in heaven's name possessed President Arthur to appoint the bastard, I'll never know! But I assure you—I will not rest until Axtell is removed and permanently put out to pasture."

"I would not be opposed to such an occurrence. But again, Mr. Springer . . . how does any of that concern me?"

Springer cleared his throat and leaned forward. "We have a delicate situation that has arisen, Sheriff Carter, which is going to require your expertise, I'm afraid." He pulled a folded piece of paper from his coat, opened it, and spread it on the table between them. "You recognize this?"

Jonathon patted his vest pocket, produced his glasses, and peered at the document. The paper was crumpled and bore a date almost ten years old. Written on the formal stationary of the office of the territorial governor with a clear, firm hand, it contained the names of several prominent Colfax County citizens and was signed by former Governor Axtell himself.

Jonathon looked up with surprise. "My name is on this list!"

"As are mine, Clay Allison's, and a few others, including Bill Morley's, if you'll notice."

"This looks like an order for our deaths."

"Indeed . . . a regular death warrant."

Footsteps sounded on the plank sidewalk outside the open office door, and Springer fell silent until they passed. He stood up, went to the window, and pulled aside the green-checkered curtain to look out. "Guess I should be more careful how loudly I speak. I sometimes forget that I'm not in a courtroom." He turned back, returned to the table, and picked up his coffee.

"So, how is Clay, anyway?" asked Springer. "Have you seen him lately?"

"Not for a while now. He and his brother John stopped by the ranch a couple of years back. They were headed out to Texas—had bought a place and were hankering to get back into the cattle business. I'm not at all sure where he got all the money to pay for it. Matter of fact, Clay said he was about to get married and wanted to have a passel of kids before he got himself too shot up to do so."

"Well, you know Clay. Once he gets his mind set regarding a particular subject, best not to get in his way." Springer rubbed his jaw. "Rumor has it that he struck it big—hit some gold up near Baldy somewhere. That was probably where he spent all that time, while folks were wondering where he had gotten himself to. Maybe that's where he got the money to buy that ranch in Texas, you think?"

"Could very well be. All I know is, he's long gone. Probably just as well. Said he may or may not be back through this country ever again. But I hope not."

"Why not?"

Jonathon thought hard before answering. "For a long time there I was all set to arrest him if he ever set foot here again. I probably would have if he and his brother hadn't been on their way to Texas this time. Guess I'm thinking if he'd stayed around much longer, friend or no friend, one of us would've probably killed the other by now."

Jonathon moved back over to the table, picked up the Axtell letter again, and frowned. "Speaking of which, what am I supposed to make of this damned thing? A death order? Where did this come from, and what can we do about it?"

Springer leaned forward and lowered his voice. "All I can tell you is that Governor Axtell was stupid enough to affix his name to an illegal warrant shortly after the dirt hit the wind out here years ago. I don't know how many of these letters he sent out, but this one was delivered to me anonymously last month, and I wasted no time in taking action. The fact is, I have just come from Santa Fe, where I confronted Chief Justice Axtell with this, to his face, to force his hand. I told him in no uncertain terms that unless he immediately and completely dissolves the activities and very existence of the Santa Fe Ring once and for all and sends his cronies running, I would have no alternative but to make this document public. Furthermore, he is to step down from his current undeserved office and never return to public life again."

Jonathon bent over the letter again, reading it completely this time. He looked up over the rim of his glasses at Springer. "And he agreed?"

"In principle, yes. But here's the rub. Last month an incident occurred between some land grant enforcers and a group of vigilante ranchers led by a Mr. George Curry from Raton. Do you recall?"

"Yes. Luckily there was no bloodshed, so no charges were filed, and that was the end of the matter."

"Well, now it's reared its head again. Axtell wants the ranchers brought up on charges of armed incitement to riot and conspiracy."

"Those charges won't stick."

"You know that and I know it. And I think Axtell knows it too. But he wants some kind of example made of these men, especially Curry. No matter how slight a slap on the wrists they may receive."

"And what does Axtell get out of it?"

"I think he saves some face—maybe a last hurrah before he steps down. I don't like it much, but I think it's a small price to pay to get the son of a bitch out of office."

"What do you know of Curry and his people?"

"Hard cases—stubborn, but honest. But I think if they're handled right, with kid gloves, they'll see reason and cooperate. They'll come out with a misdemeanor and small fine, is my guess. And more importantly, Axtell is then gone."

"So what could go wrong?"

Springer crossed his arms and sighed. "Everything. I think Axtell may think he has another ace up his sleeve. He could try anything to turn this into a fight. Send a gang of enforcers in at the last minute and confront everyone. At the very least, he would love to put egg on my face and discredit me. And at the worst, people could die. That's why it's vitally important that you handle this, Jonathon. I trust no one else in the territory right now." He leaned forward again and lowered his voice. "But I strongly advise that you deputize as many good men as you see fit to accompany you. If this thing turns ugly—and it just might—you need to be able to shut it down, and fast."

Jonathon stood up, took his glasses off, and stepped over to the door. The sun had dropped behind the trees and the day was fading. Down the street, the golden glow of lamplights had come up in the windows of Lambert's St. James Hotel and saloon and the tinkling of gleeful piano music lilted through the open doors.

The population of the Wild West frontier town of Cimarron had already dwindled now that the county seat had formally been relocated 25 miles to the southeast, to the burgeoning new town of Springer. The ugliness and violence of the last ten or twelve years was also, hopefully, finally dying down. Billy the Kid himself had been gunned down four years ago in Fort Sumner in the late Lucien Maxwell's house, of all places. But Jonathon knew that more land grabs and killings were always lurking just a gunshot or a lynching away, just beyond the shadows. So, perhaps this opportunity before them all now could stop all of that.

Perhaps it could be the final nail in the coffin of the Santa Fe Ring and bring an end to this hated war in Colfax County.

#

(Delgado Rancho, Ponil River Valley)

"I do not believe that you should do it, Salal. This will not be a good thing at all."

Walking Elk rocked back and forth in front of the fireplace, a blanket spread on his legs and a pipe in his mouth that he puffed happily. It was his favorite place on these shortened days and longer, colder nights. He watched as the fragrant smoke that escaped the corner of his mouth mingled with the wood smoke from the dancing flames in front of him, leaving the impression that he was receiving a message from the elements.

The old Ute chief had moved in with Jonathon and María three years ago, when the army had finally driven the last of the Southern Utes from their valley beneath Mt. Baldy and relocated them to a reservation in southwest Colorado. Walking Elk was then already much too old to survive the arduous journey. At first, he had refused Jonathon's offer of a home and had sat down in the cold ashes of his fire ring—all that was left after the Buffalo Soldiers had torn down his ragged wickiup—and begun to sing his death song. That is, until Jonathon informed him that he would have a real rocking chair permanently in front of a roaring fire to keep his old bones from freezing in the winters; that, and all of María's home cooking that he could eat.

"He's right," snapped María as she entered from one of the two back rooms, bouncing their crying nine-month-old son, James, in her arms. "You are going to go and get yourself killed this time." She nodded off into the distance, somewhere beyond the walls of the house. "And the ground is getting too cold and hard out there to dig a proper grave. Here, José! Give me that!"

María had stepped over to where their older son, three-year-old José Isaac, squatted on a pallet of furs and blankets near the old Indian's rocker and cheerfully sucked on a stick of peppermint candy. He pouted as his mother took the candy away. She stomped back to the table and frowned at Jonathon, who was sitting at the table cleaning his revolver. "Well?" she asked, holding the candy out accusingly. "He is just a toddler, Jonathon. He could choke on this!"

"Don't look at me," answered her husband as he blew through the open cylinder of his weapon and squinted into the barrel. Jonathon looked over and gave his scowling young son a smile and a wink. "Now, where on earth did you find that, Joe?"

Walking Elk chuckled and reached down to comfort the boy by gently tousling his dark hair. María shifted the baby to her other hip, then scowled back and forth between her husband the elderly Indian.

"So, I suppose you two think this is very funny." María scoffed. She stepped quickly around the table and deposited James in Jonathon's lap, then turned away to noisily attack the dinner dishes soaking in the nearby sink. "You are going off tomorrow to get yourself shot and killed, and all you can do is sit here and make jokes."

"I am not going to get killed," said Jonathon as he placed the revolver onto the table, out of reach of his son's curious, grasping hands. He held James up face to face and scrunched his nose at him, making the boy giggle.

"It is a good possibility, Salal," added Walking Elk, continuing to rock contentedly. He waved his pipe and fingered the silver cross he wore on a piece of rawhide around his neck. "The smoke allows me to talk to Jesus—and then He shows me the future."

"See?" exclaimed María. "He has seen something."

"You hush up, Nämpäry," Jonathon scolded, using the old Indian's Ute name which he now insisted on being called and which roughly translated to *Elk That Walks*, "or I will dig up no more peyote cactus for you to mix with your tobacco. Then you'll just have to talk to Jesus the same old way the rest of us do."

Later, as they lay under a large buffalo robe in the back bedroom of the cabin listening to the rustle of the breeze in the trees outside and the soft, steady breathing of their children in a small bed nearby, Jonathon pulled María close and wrapped his arms around her.

"Have I ever failed to come back to you?"

María pulled herself even closer to her husband, as if to make herself one with him and keep him with her forever. "There is more than one way for a husband to come home. You have always returned to me whole and safe, ready for my bed. But I refuse to welcome you home the other way, ready for the cold earth."

Jonathon reached down and tilted his wife's face up to his. Her black hair spilled down her shoulder and across his chest, and he could just make out her beautiful features in the pale light of the waning moon outside the window. He leaned in and kissed her. "María Delgado, I shall always return to you safe and whole, as I always have, and more than ready for your bed." He paused and smiled as he heard one of his sons roll over and coo softly in his sleep. "After all, we must make many more fine sons."

María suddenly rolled over on top of him and enveloped him completely in the warmth of her body. "And perhaps also a fine daughter or two," she breathed as her lips melted into his and they slowly moved as one.

#

(Springer, New Mexico Territory)

At noon the next day Jonathon stood in the vanguard of a group of five deputies on the lawn of the brand new, three-story county courthouse in the new railroad town of Springer, New Mexico. They were each heavily armed and ready to enforce the law, which in this case meant, among other things, that no one but sworn law enforcement officers were to be armed while court was in session.

Jonathon had handpicked his deputies from experienced men he had ridden with before, and he knew that they would all perform their assigned duties with the utmost professionalism. At least, he prayed so. Among the five was his faithful ranch foreman, Jim Watkins, who had worked for him now for more than twelve years and whose big Henry repeating rifle Jonathon knew could always be counted on, no matter what. His old friend Tom Stockton had also agreed to ride with him today, along with Tom's grizzled old hired hand, Sam Farnsworth, who could barely sit a saddle any more but who, Jonathon knew, could still shoot the fly off a man's nose at twenty paces.

The six lawmen stood now, spread at intervals across the lawn, their backs to the double doors of the courthouse, their long dusters open and trailing behind them to expose their loaded and primed sidearms. Each of them also held, either at port arms or with the stocks balanced on one hip, a repeater rifle or a shotgun, ready to swing into action if necessary. The county judge and jury had all just arrived and were settling themselves inside the second-floor courtroom. The attorneys for the defense and the plaintiffs—in this case, the owners of the Maxwell Land Grant and the Territory of New Mexico—were also inside, preparing themselves for the proceedings.

All they were awaiting was the arrival of the defendants—local rancher George Curry, his brother Jasper, and eight other local cattlemen and businessmen, who two months ago had aligned themselves with the Currys in an armed altercation with supposed land grant enforcers, who had tried to evict some of the Currys' friends and neighbors from their property. Fortunately, no blood was spilled, and the regulators were peacefully escorted across Raton Pass and allowed to depart into Colorado. But since former Governor and now Chief Justice Samuel Axtell had felt his feathers ruffled by Frank Springer and now demanded a show of his own power, Curry and his men had been duly charged and subpoenaed to have their day in court.

"Jonathon." Jim Watkins spoke softly as he nodded into the distance. Jonathon turned in the direction of the nod and without his glasses, which he was too vain to put on just yet, could barely make out a cloud of dust gathering on the ridge at the north edge of town. Soon, though, he could make out the riders on horseback who were creating the dust. He began counting heads and breathed a sigh of relief when he counted ten. "Well, at least they all decided to show up," he answered back to Jim before raising his voice. "That's them, boys. Let's just take things nice and easy. It should be a cakewalk, but keep a clear eye. Nobody gets in with their guns." Jonathon pointed at a box near the doorway. "Let them know they'll get them back soon as court's adjourned."

The riders cantered up to the hitching rails by the street, dismounted, and tied their mounts. They paused until they were all finished, then marched as a group up the flagstone walkway that crossed the expanse of lawn, and headed for the line of lawmen.

They were all visibly armed with holstered pistols. Two of the men carried rifles at their sides. Jonathon took two steps forward to meet them and held up a hand to George Curry.

"Mr. Curry, I am Jonathon Carter, Sheriff of Colfax County. These men here are duly sworn deputies and authorized by me under county ordinance to temporarily relieve you all of your weapons. They will be safeguarded for you, and you'll get them back immediately following court today."

Curry and his men traded looks and then stared back at the lawmen. Curry took a step forward, held his hands up non-threateningly, then held out his hand and shook hands with Jonathon. "Sheriff Carter. I am pleased to make your acquaintance."

"Likewise, Mr. Curry. And I'm sure you are just as eager as I am to get this matter over with and resolved so we can all resume our business elsewhere."

"I agree whole-heartedly, Sheriff Carter. Seems a complete waste of all of our time, does it not? But I am a little reluctant to surrender my weapons, as I'm concerned that my opponents in this case are loath to let the matter conclude amicably. I'm also doubtful, Sir, that, as honorable as you may be, you would be able to guaranty our safety inside these premises, unarmed and unable to properly defend ourselves. You see my point, do you not, Mr. Carter?"

"I do see your point, Mr. Curry, and regret that there is no real alternative, Sir. The rules are the rules, and neither of us made them. I'm afraid we both have no choice but to follow them to the letter, so as to show good faith on all sides. You can be assured that everyone who has already passed through these doors today was similarly disarmed and therefore has no way of bringing undue bodily harm to you and your friends, no matter the ultimate disposition of your case."

"Um, Jonathon. . . ." said Jim Watkins. "We may have another problem." Jonathon turned to Watkins, who nodded again toward the horizon, where another, larger cloud of dust billowed, and another, larger group of horsemen had appeared, this time riding in from the south—the road from Las Vegas and Santa Fe—and making straight for the courthouse.

Several of these riders had their rifles out and ready.

Sam Farnsworth leaned forward and spat a mouthful of tobacco juice on the ground. "Them's regulators," he pronounced, then cocked the twin hammers of his double-barreled shotgun.

Curry stepped back quickly, understandably alarmed. "I suppose you're going to politely ask for their guns, too?" He didn't wait for Jonathon to answer, but signaled to his men. "Take cover, boys! I don't believe they are here to donate to our defense fund today."

Jonathon whistled, motioned with his Winchester to his deputies, and began moving. "Spread out, men. Like the man said, take cover where you can. But don't fire unless fired upon first—any of you. We need to settle this thing down quick!"

Jonathon ran forward and parked himself squarely in the middle of the courthouse lawn, facing the oncoming riders. When they were half a block away, he made a large show of cocking his rifle and flipping his duster back to reveal his badge, as well as the big Army Colt .45 at his waist. Curry's men and the deputies had scattered and taken up defensive positions wherever they could find them among trees and behind a small section of an unfinished stone wall that stood along one side of the lawn.

As the riders loped within earshot Jonathon took one more step forward. "That's far enough, gentlemen," he called out. "I am Sheriff Carter, and these other men are either my sworn deputies or lawful defendants here to stand trial today, and I hereby order you to stand down and surrender your weapons."

One of the riders, apparently their leader, stepped his horse out of the line and advanced on Jonathon. "Well, we are here today for the same reason, Sheriff," he said amicably, "to see that justice is carried out in full." He stopped his horse a few feet away and gestured toward Curry. "Now, this here fella and his gang interfered with the due process of law here while back, and we don't believe we're going to just stand by passive-like and see them walk away scot-free." The man was nicely dressed and was clean-shaven, except for a trimmed mustache. He likewise pulled his jacket back to reveal a badge of some sort. "Now, as you can see, we are also duly sworn under the regulations, and as such," he paused and smiled at his men, for effect, "we politely decline your offer to disarm us—that is, unless you care to try. Then . . . well, then I guess we will be less polite." The regulator pulled his rifle from out of its saddle scabbard and deliberately cocked it. "Either way, Sheriff Carter, we are here at your pleasure."

No one could ever say who fired first, but what everyone agreed on was what happened next. The doors to the courthouse flew open, and the district judge stepped onto the porch with his hands firmly on his hips and a scowl firmly on his face.

"Now just what in the holy hell is going on out here? I have a case to try in there, and I intend to do so immediately—with everyone's permission, of course!"

A shot suddenly rang out and a bullet ricocheted off the whitewashed brick wall, only a couple of feet above the judge's head. As he jumped back inside and slammed the doors, more shots answered the first one, and within seconds the courthouse yard was filled with gunfire, smoke, screaming and running horses, and shouting men all diving for cover. For a moment it was impossible to tell who was who in the confusing mêlée. Here and there were screams and occasional shouts of "Over there!" and "I'm hit!"

Jonathon Carter had thrown himself forward, prone on the ground, almost underneath the hooves of the horse belonging to the regulator he had been talking to. His heart racing, Jonathon laughed at the incongruity that he might actually be trampled to death long before being shot. The man wheeled his horse around, however, and Jonathon was soon completely exposed on the ground. His rifle was inadvertently wedged under his body, so he pulled his revolver and began simultaneously searching for cover and targets, which he identified as anyone who would be pointing a weapon his way. One of the other regulators quickly obliged him and whipped around in his saddle to bring his rifle to bear on him, not ten yards away. "Don't do it!" Jonathon shouted at the man and aimed the Army Colt at him. A wide smile spread on the man's face and he squeezed the trigger to fire, but suddenly the man's arms flew wide as he dropped the rifle and was jerked backward from his saddle as if by an invisible force. Jonathon twisted and looked behind him, where he saw Jim Watkins rise up from behind the partial wall, his smoking Henry repeater in his hands. Jonathon had rarely seen what a .50 caliber bullet could do to a man and had forgotten how much of a wallop it packed.

He smiled and nodded once in gratitude as he jumped up, grabbed his own rifle, and ran back to join Watkins at the wall. As he ran the twenty or so yards, he heard a man cry out in pain to his right and saw George Curry twist and fall to the ground, grabbing his shoulder and writhing. Jonathon scanned the battlefield to try to ascertain what else was happening. He heard hoofbeats approaching behind him and spun around in time to see the lead regulator bearing down on him on horseback, his rifle leveled from his shoulder. Jonathon fired twice from the hip. Out of the corner of his eye, he spied Stockton and Farnsworth aiming and firing simultaneously from either side of a huge cottonwood trunk they were sheltered behind. The regulator and his horse fell sideways as three bullets and a chestful of buckshot hit them. Stockton gave Jonathon a quick wave. Farnsworth shucked his shells and was reloading when suddenly, a bullet glanced off the tree trunk, and he gave a big gasp. His eyes grew wide in disbelief, and he dropped his shotgun and grasped his throat with both hands before slowly crumpling to the ground. "No!" Jonathon heard himself shout. Then he turned and ran in that direction. His battlefield sense was kicking in madly, the vertigo of it grabbing him and making his head swim.

"Over here, Mr. Carter!" came Watkins' shout. Gunfire continued to erupt from everywhere. Jonathon suddenly stopped midstride and stumbled, feeling strangely confused. He was halfway between the tree and the wall and suddenly couldn't decide which way to run. His battle sense had never failed him like this before. He took another step and his feet tangled. He dropped his rifle from his suddenly numb fingers and looked down. Something was not quite right, and then he saw it. Right above his gun belt, a couple of inches up his right side, a neat round hole had appeared in his shirt where before there hadn't been one. As he continued to stare at it, the hole blossomed with a bright red flower that grew slowly and spread over his shirt. He touched it with unfeeling fingers, and then looked up incredulously at his friend Tom Stockton, who was staring back at him with open mouth and great concern on his face. Stockton was moving in slow motion from behind the tree and coming toward him with an outstretched arm, as if to catch him, but Jonathon couldn't wait for him. He had to lie down now and he did so. He felt the coolness of grass on his cheek and could see various feet running back and forth past his field of vision. He heard shouts and more gunfire echoing, but the noise of it all grew gradually fainter as the world grew dimmer. He felt himself being dragged across the ground. It was painful, and he was cold, and he wanted to call out to whoever it was to just leave him the hell alone.

Lastly, Jonathon felt a sudden, overwhelming sadness and guilt as he thought of María and his broken promise to her to come home safe and whole, just once more, to her warm bed.

CHAPTER 28
Sons And Daughters

(Letter from Robert Walter Carter, Sr.)

October 1, 1948

My Dear Son,

   As you read this I am probably dead, which means I have, once again, taken the coward's way out. I will not bore you with the "whys," other than to say this has nothing whatsoever to do with you. I don't expect that you would understand my reasons anyway.

   You are a survivor. I thought that I was one, too, but not anymore. We each in our own ways have gone through things no man nor boy should ever have to experience. The irony is that although still a child you are already twice the man I ever was. I guess a child can best handle some of life's chaos and horror before he grows into a person with too many expectations, too many broken dreams. The god-forsaken Japs took away most of mine, along with any strength or willpower or dignity I had left. And the rest of it died along with your mother and brother on that damned train. I suppose I should have shown more gratitude that at least you survived, but that's been hard to do when all I feel anymore is numb and powerless.

   Nothing left now but a shell, and for that I am truly sorry. A shell of a dad is not what you need, even if I knew how to be a good one. For that, it takes a good role model. In that regard you and I, unfortunately, are too much alike. Neither of us had one. My own father—your grandfather, James—died in a mining explosion when I was also just a boy, not much younger than you are now. I wish I had known more about him. Maybe it would have made some difference, but I doubt it. I barely remember him, except that he was supposedly named after some old gunfighter who used to live around here. Although there's an iron cross at the Dawson Cemetery with his name on it, his actual body was never found. He's still buried under that mountain of coal out there somewhere. At least they won't have too far to look to find mine.

   Do not think too unkindly of me, my son. All that I ask is that you see fit to have them bury me near your mother and brother. Their loss has been more than I can bear, and when I look in your eyes, all I see is your mother looking back at me in shame and disgust for what I have become. Perhaps when I see her soon face-to-face the indictment in those eyes will have faded back to love. That, in the end, is all I have left to look forward to.

   Be strong, Walter, as I know that you already are. You will also survive this. One day you may have a fine son of your own and my prayer is that you will then somehow break this curse that seems to have befallen us Carters and that you will become the kind and loving dad to him that I could not manage to be to you.

I know you won't believe this, but I do love you, Son. You are the best of what little is left of me. Go and make something of it.

Your Dad

#

(Present Day – Raton, New Mexico)

Trent, Hector, and the other men who made up the group of pallbearers walked over and solemnly placed their carnation boutonnières on top of Ben Ferguson's casket. A light rain had begun pattering on the canvas canopy that had been erected over the gravesite and the mourners. Jennifer, her mother, Ben's elderly father, and other distant family members sat huddled together in the cramped chairs that had been provided for them. Other mourners stood outside the awning's slight protection under hastily deployed umbrellas or were already making their retreat to nearby vehicles as the minister concluded his final prayer with an amen.

Silence descended on the scene as heaven itself seemed to shed tears and pull an appropriate veil of gray across the autumn sky. No one seemed to want to move, as if doing so would declare just one more finality upon the unbelievable and unexpected loss that had concluded this particular chapter of their lives. Trent stood just inside the edge of the canopy, partially protected but feeling the rain begin to spatter the back of his suit but not acknowledging or caring about it. He stared blankly at the silver casket shrouded with sprays of flowers and their now muted colors that had been meant to provide some semblance of beauty and hope to this event. He was grateful that he could not see through the hard material of the box that contained his friend's mortal remains, and he tried to un-see the waxen face that had been on display during the viewing at the church service—a face that no longer represented what Trent wanted to remember about his friend and colleague in life. No matter the skill of the embalmer, that was not Ben Ferguson lying there.

For entirely other reasons, Trent was also determined to commit to memory all the details of this sad and miserable occasion. He not only carefully studied the surrounding cemetery, the casket, the flowers, the officiating preacher, the pallbearers, and mourners but also peered along the bottom of the box where it carefully sat on support straps that held it in place above the dark and yawning abyss directly beneath it. By the end of this day, Ben's body would be lowered several feet into dark oblivion there—at least so far as his earthly remains were concerned. Trent had no memories of his late wife's funeral, not because of the damage his mind had incurred in the attack on them both but because he had not even been present for Vicky's services. Instead, he had been lying in a coma in the hospital. It was something that had haunted him since then, in addition to her occasional ghostly visits. Perhaps now, by allowing himself to pay close attention to these details, he could substitute and appropriate even a portion of Ben's funeral for hers, at least in his mind. They couldn't have been much different; a funeral was a funeral, right? He didn't think Ben would have minded in the least and probably would have made a joke about it.

Trent felt a warm arm slide in under his and turned to see his daughter Sophie's beautiful but sad face looking up at him. "You okay, Daddy?" she asked. "I've been worried about you."

Trent looked back at the casket and sighed. "Do you think God considers it a sin to be mourning the loss of a completely different person at someone else's funeral?"

Sophie was silent for a moment. "It's probably a sin not to," she finally said, looking at Ben Ferguson's flower-strewn casket. "To not mourn means you're numb inside; something festering there. Loss always finds its way in, but it's up to us to let it out again, before that happens. That's the healthy part of it. Either way, it's always going to become ingrained into the fabric of your heart—imbedded into your very life and spirit. You can choose to shove it down deeper, where it will eventually turn to poison, or you can allow yourself to be reminded of those losses—of any kind, for anyone—even beyond this particular one, and let it out in grief. That, at least, means you're alive and healing—still hurting, maybe, but moving on."

Trent looked at his daughter. "Who made you so wise, Darlin'?"

Sophie paused, leaned her head against his shoulder, squeezed his hand tightly, and took a soft, trembling breath. "You remember when Billy died?"

Trent squeezed her hand back. "Of course I remember." Bill Connor, a soldier in the U.S. Army, had been Sophie's fiancé a few years ago—an entire world ago. She had just graduated from the University of New Mexico and was putting her journalism degree to good use when the news had arrived that Billy had been killed by an IED in Afghanistan. It had been a year after Trent's mother's—Sophie's grandmother's—death from cancer, and then a little over a year later before Victoria, her mother, was murdered. The triple blow was something few people should have to endure.

Sophie blew her nose softly. "For me, and I think for you too, all losses are more than just cumulative; the sum of them is much greater than their parts: Grandma, Billy, Mom . . . and now Ben. But if a person is incapable of mourning their losses—all of them—then they will stagnate and soon become incapable of making room in their heart for any new love."

Trent turned, took Sophie by the shoulders, and looked admiringly at his daughter for a very long time. "Why do I always get the feeling when I'm around you that you're the real parent here, not me?"

Sophie stood on tiptoe, kissed her father's cheek, and beamed up at him. "Because I have too much of Mom in me . . . and she never let you get away with crap either!"

Hector, Maggie, and Walter walked up behind them, arm in arm. Walter rubbed his nose roughly with a handkerchief and jockeyed for a dry place underneath the canopy.

Hector opened his mouth to say something.

"Don't say it," Trent interrupted.

"Say what? How do you know what I was going to say?"

"You were going to say that Ben's in a better place."

Hector looked at Maggie, then at Sophie, then back at his father-in-law. "Well, he is, isn't he?"

"Yes. He is definitely that. I just don't need to hear it right now, okay?" Trent looked toward Ben's family still seated a few feet away, accepting condolences from others. He patted Maggie's hand. "I'll be right back."

Hector looked confused as he watched Trent limp away with his cane. "But I don't understand," continued Hector. "If someone's gone on to be in a better place, isn't that something to be happy about?"

"Sure," blurted Walter. "But some people just want to stay unhappy for a while." He gestured toward Trent. "And that boy does enjoy his unhappiness, it seems."

"Oh, I don't think he enjoys it, Walter," murmured Maggie as she gazed lovingly after her husband. "I just don't think he knows how to absorb it sometimes. But he's learning."

"Yes. He is," said Sophie. She glanced around at them all and smiled. "And that's what we're all here for, isn't it? To help each other through it as it happens? That's just life; the good and the bad."

Trent made his way down the line of seated family, expressing his condolences and shaking hands with Ben's father and his ex-wife in turn, and then finally coming to Jennifer, who leaned against her mother's shoulder. He leaned down, but before he could say anything, Jennifer opened her eyes, which were red from weeping. Her face brightened a little and she stood up, wrapping her arms around Trent's neck, almost bowling him over.

"Oh, Mr. Carter. Thank you!"

Trent recovered his balance, then gently put his arms around her, unsure of what to say.

"Thank me for what?" he asked. Jennifer squeezed him tightly for a long moment before eventually letting him go and stepping back, her hands grasping his. She peered into his face.

"For saving Daddy's life, of course—in more ways than one."

"Doesn't look like I did too good a job of it."

"Yes, you did. He told me how you were there for him when he needed it most." Jennifer cast her eyes down and bit her lip. She glanced at her mother, who was engaged in conversation with someone else, and lowered her voice. "When the rest of us had let him down so badly."

Trent patted her arm. "Oh, Jennifer. You can't blame yourself. You didn't let him down. It was just one of those periods we all go through sometimes. I think he had temporarily lost his way, his purpose." He squeezed her hands gently. "But then he found it again—in you. You were the one who saved him. I was just there to keep reminding him of it." He looked over where those in his own small family unit stood talking to one another. Something surged inside his chest. "And to keep reminding myself of it, too."

"Thank you anyway. Dad told me you were the best friend he had had in a very long time . . . and now that makes you family, too. Okay? Don't forget it."

"I won't if you won't."

Trent felt his heart rise up to his throat and his eyes started to sting. He hugged Jennifer once more, quickly, then turned and limped back to Maggie, his cane punching moist holes in the earth. The rain had begun in earnest now, and she had opened an umbrella, which she held out over Walter and him as they all walked away from the gravesite.

"Come on, boys. Let's get you both to the car before folks mistake this rain for tears. Wouldn't want you tough guys to be embarrassed."

As Trent opened the car doors for Walter and Maggie, he spotted the lone figure of a woman retreating quickly to a nearby vehicle. She looked vaguely familiar, but her light brown raincoat and the umbrella held low over her brown pony-tailed hair momentarily delayed his recognition of her. Then, when she lowered the umbrella to fumble for keys, he suddenly recognized her. It was Dr. Nancy Fortner, the young state medical examiner whom he had met at the Clifton House crime scene a few short weeks ago and with whom he had not parted on the best of terms.

"Just a minute," he said to Maggie as he helped her into the front passenger seat. "I'll be right back. Someone I need to say hello to."

Dr. Fortner had just settled behind the wheel of her car and was about to close her door when Trent called out to her. "Dr. Fortner . . . just a moment, please." She squinted, one hand poised on the door handle, and then frowned slightly when she recognized him.

"Mr. Carter," she answered evenly as she sat back in her seat and fixed Trent with an indecipherable look. Trent stopped a discreet distance from her car. He shoved his hands into his overcoat pockets, pulled it tighter around him against the cold, and shrugged his shoulders sheepishly.

"I, um . . . I didn't see you here earlier," he stammered, at a loss for words at the moment.

"Yes?" the young woman said simply.

"Well, I, uh. . . ." Trent glanced away and nodded toward Ben's gravesite across the road. "I don't suppose any of us expected to meet again, I mean, under these circumstances."

"No. I suppose not." Dr. Fortner looked away as she briefly dabbed some moisture from her upper lip with a tissue.

"Well, I'm very happy to see you here, Dr. Fortner—Nancy. I know you didn't know him well, but I think Ben would appreciate that you came. And frankly . . . it also impresses me that you came, not that that matters at all."

Dr. Fortner glanced into the visor mirror, touched a couple more damp places, and then looked down at her hands as she bit her lip. "To tell you the truth, Mr. Carter, I wasn't going to come at all. Oh, I was shocked, of course, when I heard the news. But I thought it wasn't my place to be here, and I had more than enough to keep me busy. . . ." She twisted the tissue in her hands and then looked up at Trent, her hazel eyes wide behind her glasses. "Sheriff Ferguson was the first colleague of mine whose death I have experienced. I . . . I didn't quite know what to do, how to respond to that. It's a feeling I've never quite known before—except for when my father passed." She shook her head quickly. "Anyway, when today finally arrived, I tried to ignore it. But finally, all I could do was just get in the car and drive here from Santa Fe." She looked over to Ben's casket and sighed. "And even then I was almost late. And I'm never late—anywhere."

Trent nodded and smiled, ignoring the drizzling rain that had now soaked his hair and ran in rivulets down the side of his face and down his neck. "It's more than enough that you're here. You did the right thing."

Dr. Fortner turned and looked back up at Trent for a long moment. "Do you know that I was ready to file a formal complaint against you, Mr. Carter? A harassment charge?"

Trent looked down and shuffled his feet. "I don't doubt it. And it's something I also wanted to apologize for, when I saw you just now. I was wrong to chastise you like I did, Dr. Fortner."

"No," she shook her head. "No, you weren't. You said what I needed to hear." She paused and glanced up at the quickening rain. Then she seemed to make a decision. She suddenly stepped out of the car and peered intently up at him.

As the rain began to soak her hair, Trent thought she no longer looked like the austere medical professional but instead now looked like a forlorn little girl. Her mascara began to run, but Trent couldn't tell whether it was from the rain or from tears.

"My father died when I was nine years old, Mr. Carter." Dr. Fortner paused and hugged herself against the cold. "He was my entire world up to that point. Since then, I have spent my whole life trying to be the best at everything—the best grades, the best at sports—everything, just to make him proud of me. And when I landed this job, I had beat out twelve other highly qualified candidates, most of them males. I mean, men have come to represent either obstacles or irrational authority figures, only bent on holding me back. And it's me who should be apologizing to you, Mr. Carter. I was insensitive and abrasive, when you were only trying to lend your valuable skills and experience."

Trent started to respond, but words failed him and he was only able to lift his arms in resignation. But it suddenly didn't matter any more because the rain-soaked young woman, young enough to be his daughter, unexpectedly took a quick step forward and embraced him tightly, burying her head against his chest. He instinctively started to raise his hand to stroke the back of her drenched hair protectively when she just as quickly broke away, got back into her car, and slammed the door. He stood there watching dumbly as the engine roared to life and she drove away into the rain.

#

(Montaño del Sol Ranch)

The thunderstorm had passed by the time they had driven home through Yankee Canyon. They pulled up the long driveway and eventually made their way slowly onto the porch, where they all stood and talked softly for a while. Trent looked around at the familiar surroundings, enjoying the silence of the mountains and the smell of wet pine and moist earth, as if willing time to make a leap and return their lives to normal—whatever that was. Walter, Trent, and Maggie finally went inside and upstairs to change clothes. Hector and Sophie sat down on the porch steps just as Jarhead came up, purring his loud greeting, and rubbing himself against Sophie's knee until she scratched his back and behind his ears. She slowly laid her head against her husband's shoulder and they both quietly watched the horses grazing lazily in the meadows beyond the barns.

Walter was the first back downstairs, after slipping on a warm sweater and house shoes, and he had brought with him the small bundle of old letters which he gently laid in the middle of Trent's big desk in the corner as he sat down. His eyes were bright as he thumbed the edge of the parcel gently, allowing his thoughts to wander.

Trent had changed into his favorite old jeans, a Dallas Cowboys sweatshirt, and a pair of old sneakers and had made his way quietly back onto the landing, where he now stopped and leaned against the railing, watching Walter below. He smiled to himself, reached into his back pocket, and produced the evidence bag containing the old photograph that Hector had given him a few days earlier at the hospital. He leaned heavily on the banister as he limped down the stairs. Walter looked up at him.

"You lost your cane."

"No, I didn't. I know exactly where it is."

"The women will be all over you for not using it."

"What women?"

"Maggie and Sophie."

"I ain't 'fraid of them," Trent quipped, but glanced upstairs quickly before continuing over to the desk, reaching over, and placing the photo in front of Walter.

"What's this?" Walter asked. Trent tapped the photo inside the bag, pointing at the young cowboy on the left, Jonathon Carter, his great-great grandfather.

"Handsome fellow there, isn't he? Looks a lot like me, if I do say so."

"Huh!" Walter scoffed, then allowed a smile to touch the corner of his mouth. He pushed a damp strand of hair back from his forehead. "Well, maybe. But I would have to say if that's the case, it runs in the family." He squinted down at the photo again. "But seriously, where'd you find this?"

Trent shrugged. "They found it on that body in the old grave out at the Clifton House ruins. But here's what I find really interesting." Trent turned the photo over gently to reveal the map on the back.

Walter's lips moved as he silently read the scribbled names on the back. "Yep, that's all o' them, all right. Same as the one I've got upstairs. Great-grandpa, Allison, Stockton, Springer, Goodnight. But what's all this?" His finger traced the faded lines and squiggles. "Appears to be a map of sorts—Baldy Mountain, Ute something or other, something here with the word *Vega* and marked with an X."

"I don't know. Another mystery, I guess," said Trent.

Walter looked up at his son. "A treasure map, maybe?"

Trent nodded, then laughed. "Maybe. Who knows? Maybe that's why it was hidden on an old corpse. Either way, I should've known. Just like every other murder case. In the end, the whole thing is usually about the oldest motive in the world—money and greed."

Walter hesitated, looked up at Trent, and then stood up.

"What's wrong?"

"Nothing. Just wait here a minute."

Walter disappeared upstairs. In a few minutes he was back, carrying the large framed photograph that had hung on his walls for decades, the larger duplicate of the one Trent had just showed him. He laid it face down on the desk, next to the smaller one. He was a little out of breath, but traced some writing on the back of the large frame. "You're the policeman. You see anything interesting?"

Trent leaned over and looked. "Something written there. Pretty faded, though."

Walter nodded, getting excited now. "Well, if you've looked at this thing for as long as I have, you can make some of it out. Right here." He pointed at some words and read them. "*To my* . . . something, something . . . *friend, Jonathon.* Then a couple of others I can't make out, but then this: *Robert* something *son.*" Trent squinted at the words, then shrugged.

"So, what does that mean, exactly?"

Walter hesitated. *Keep it safe.* That voice. He had almost forgotten it. "Um . . . not too sure, really." *Keep it safe, mi ardillocito—my little squirrel . . . but maybe show your own son one day.*

"Oh, come on Walter. You didn't drag this thing downstairs just to play games again, did you?"

Walter reached over and picked up the packet of letters. The voice in his head came again, from down through the distant years. *Don't show anyone . . . but maybe your own son one day, when you are old and tired, like me!*

"Walter? You okay?"

"I was given these letters, you know. Years ago. I was just a kid."

Trent watched his father. "Who?" he asked quietly. "Who gave you the letters, Walter?"

"Most were written by my great-gramma, María." He pulled one free and turned it over in his hand. "I don't remember her. She died right after I was born. But she supposedly gave me a nickname. It was a Spanish word, hard to pronounce—*ardillocito.* It meant *little squirrel.*"

Trent caught his breath. *Squirrel?* He searched his memory. "I've heard that before—recently, in fact." He leaned on the desk with both hands, thinking hard.

Walter hesitated once more, and then handed one of the letters to Trent. "Go ahead and read it, if you'd like."

Trent carefully unfolded the letter. It was written on two pages of fine stationery, the handwriting beautiful and elegant, as if from a more elegant time, when such written communicative skills were more highly valued than in today's digital age of cell phones and social media. In it, María Delgado Carter—Trent's great-great-grandmother—wrote to her brother Manuel of how their old friend Clay Allison had come to their rancho one day to say goodbye. He had been on his way to join his wife at their ranch in Pecos, Texas.

"Says here, before he left he gave them a large, beautifully framed photograph as a gift." Trent paused and nodded at the old framed photo on the desk. "This very one, I imagine."

"Yes, I know. I've read it a dozen times." Walter picked up the evidence bag and looked at the back of the small photo again. "A person might have drawn themselves a map to that mine, though, if it existed. But how was this one found in that grave?"

Trent peered closely at the map and the names scrawled at the top of small photo, then again at the writing on the larger one. He looked back and forth.

"Walter," he said softly. "You might be onto something. It's the same handwriting."

"What?"

"Here. He says, 'To Jonathon,' and on the other one the name has been written exactly the same way. See how he made the little curly thing on the *J*?"

"Okay. So who is Robert? Followed by *son*? Robertson? Or Robert, somebody's son?"

Trent examined the envelope Walter had handed him. He was burning with curiosity about the contents of this and all the other letters in the packet. He was also still confused about the nickname María had given her great-grandson. Why did it mean something to him? He thought some more about what Walter had just said about Clay Allison. "Walter, do you know anything else about this picture?"

"Just that I was cautioned to keep all of this very safe. To only share it with my own son—that would be you—someday, when the time seemed right."

Trent looked closely at the back of the photo again. *To Jonathon* . . . from somebody? From who? *Robert* . . . *son*. Trent's mouth dropped open and he abruptly walked across the room to a large set of bookshelves, where he searched until he found what he wanted—a small book entitled the *History of Colfax County*. He thumbed through it quickly and then stopped and stared down at a page. He looked up at Walter and brought the book over, pointing at an old photo there.

"*Robert Clay Allison!*" he exclaimed. "The *son* was the last part of his name. The rest of it got rubbed off through the years. He stabbed at the crude map again. "And the handwriting is the same here."

"Which means?"

"Which means this Robert Clay Allison who signed the back of the frame is the same *Clay* Allison who drew the map on the back of this one that was found in that grave."

"Okay. But what does that tell us, exactly?"

Trent rubbed the back of his neck. His head was beginning to swim with too much information and still too many questions. "Hell if I know, Walter. Not yet, anyway. Too much to think about."

Walter grew strangely quiet. He stared at his son, then thumbed through the old envelopes until he produced one more, and slowly handed it to Trent. The envelope was smeared with fingerprints and was dog-eared but was not quite as old as the others. It had obviously been handled often but remained completely sealed, as if it had never been opened.

"What's this?"

"Well, it's one more thing to think about—for both of us to think about, maybe."

Trent turned it over again. It had no return address but was addressed to *Robert Walter Carter, Jr.* "It's addressed to you, Walter."

"Yes. I know."

"But it's never been opened."

"I know it hasn't."

"Why not?"

Walter shrugged. "Maybe because I never wanted to know what that son of a bitch had to say."

"What son of a bitch, Walter?"

Walter rubbed his eyes, sat down heavily, then looked back at his son. "My father, that's who. Your grandfather, who you have always asked me about." He nodded again. "So open it, and let's see what he has to say—together."

Trent stared at his father for a few seconds and then pulled up another chair and sat down next to him. He took a letter opener from the corner of the desk, paused, and looked back at Walter. "You sure you want to do this right now? I mean, together? Seems rather private."

Walter rubbed his mouth. "Open it."

Trent slit the edge of the envelope, unfolded the two sheets of paper that fell out, and began to read it aloud.

#

Walter and Trent sat in stunned silence for a full minute. Both stared numbly somewhere into the space of the large living room, their eyes misting. Trent didn't react when the letter dropped from where it had been loosely held in his fingers.

"Suicide?" Trent whispered. "And you're the one who found him?"

Walter nodded. "In the backyard. Hanging from a tree."

Trent turned and stared at his father in shock. "And you decided to never tell me?"

Walter frowned. "Guess I'm telling you now, aren't I?"

Trent waved the rebuke away. "So just how old were you, Walter?"

"Fourteen—few months shy of fifteen, maybe. I don't really remember. Tried to block it all out, I guess. Until now. Like I said. Didn't want to have anything more to do with him. Anything he would have to say would be. . . ." He didn't finish, but he shrugged again. "I'm sorry, Trent."

"For what? Sounds like he's the one who should've been sorry."

Walter stood up suddenly, kicked his chair back, stepped to the window, and folded his arms. His voice began to break. "Because he was right, okay? What he said there in that . . . that damned letter!" He put a hand in his pocket and searched. "Where's my frickin' handkerchief?" Trent stepped over and handed him his own.

Walter continued. "There is a curse of some kind we seem to be carrying around with us in this family. You know? Generation to generation, maybe. It's poisoned us—poisoned *me*. And I know I've poisoned you, too."

"Walter. . . ." Trent began, and then stopped, suddenly thinking about something Sophie had said to him at Ben's funeral.

Walter's voice began to tremble as he continued softly. "I'm sorry I haven't been the father you needed, Trent. Just like your grandfather said there, you're also the best thing of what's left of me. But unlike him, I need to tell you that now, while there *is* something left of me—of us."

Trent placed a hand on his father's shoulder and squeezed tentatively. "So, what do we do about it . . . Dad?" he whispered.

"Can't say that I really know, for sure. Seems we've been practicing avoiding it for way too long now. It's become a habit."

Trent felt tears welling in his eyes as a sob caught in his throat. He cleared his throat. "Most habits can be broken, or so I hear."

Walter swiped at his eyes roughly and blew his nose. He turned around and looked at his son and nodded. "Well, there is one thing I do know that we do really well together."

"What's that?"

"Eat!" he said, and abruptly walked across the room toward the kitchen. "Let's go raid the refrigerator. I'm starving."

Trent shook his head, wiped his own eyes, and followed. "Nothing like hunger to make strong men forget about a day of raw emotions."

As he walked past the desk, he glanced down at the pile of documents and then stopped. He picked up the framed photograph and turned it over. His thumb wandered over to the corner where three or four inches of the backing paper had come unglued and hung loosely. He grasped it gently and the old brown paper peeled further still, exposing the inside back of the photograph—or what one would assume was the photograph. He sat down, picked up the letter opener, and began to work carefully at the old paper, not wanting to damage it. He loosened more of it from the old glue on the frame and finally peeled enough away to expose one complete edge, enough to reach his fingers inside and fumble carefully for a moment. He set the frame on its edge so he could hold it steadier. Biting his lip in concentration, he held his breath as his fingers dislodged something inside. Trent gingerly slipped out a large piece of heavy, yellowed paper from the frame and laid it carefully on the desk in front of him. He peered back inside the frame to find that the photograph still remained securely inside. The page he had found had been hidden behind the photograph and appeared to be at least as old as, or older than, the photo itself. He carefully unfolded the heavy paper to reveal an official-looking document of some sort, printed neatly in archaic typeface. But something else about it drew Trent's attention.

"Something's written on the back," he said. He pulled the page nearer, turned it over, and studied what seemed to be another map, a duplicate to the hastily scribbled one on the smaller photograph. But this one was more carefully drawn and in much greater detail. *"Everything but the grave itself,"* Trent mumbled.

"What's that?" asked Walter from the kitchen doorway, where he had returned with a cold chicken leg in his hand. "What are you looking at now?"

"Something Hector said at the hospital a couple days ago, when he was telling us about the Feds coming in and confiscating all the evidence. He said they took 'everything but the grave itself.'"

"Yeah. So, what?"

Trent stood up and paced for a moment. He picked up María's letter and read through it carefully again. Something was bothering him. "María said that Clay Allison left their place with a heavily loaded wagon."

"Yeah? And?"

"And that he was headed for the Clifton House, to pay his final respects, before leaving once and for all for Pecos, Texas."

"Okay. So?"

"So . . . why did he have such a heavily loaded wagon, if he was already married and had already set up his household onto a ranch in West Texas?"

Walter shrugged and took another bite of chicken. "Could mean that he married some demanding woman who insisted that he go buy her a new houseful of furniture." He smacked his lips and wiped them with the back of a hand. "Some women do that when you marry them," he said, lowering his voice and glancing upstairs sheepishly.

Trent turned his head slowly to stare at his father. "Final respects to whom?" He hurried back to the desk and pulled a magnifying glass from the drawer. "Clay Allison may have drawn a map to a gold mine, but for some reason he also felt it necessary to leave an updated version of it with his best friend Jonathon Carter, hidden in a frame that he told him to not look at, but to keep very safe. Because maybe, just maybe, he was also hinting at something else entirely."

"Like what?"

Trent trained the magnifying glass on the newly discovered map. "Like another X on this one; right by the name *Clifton House*. None of this was on the other map. And another word here, almost rubbed out." He looked up at Walter, his eyes wide with sudden revelation, and smiled. "It says *Chunk*."

"Chunk? What the hell does that mean?"

"It means Clay Allison left us one more puzzle—and it's a doozey; one that could answer a lot of questions."

"How?"

Trent suddenly went to the front door, jerked it open, and yelled outside.

"Hector! Go get some shovels and a couple of good flashlights!"

Walter walked to the middle of the room, scratching his head and gesturing with his chicken leg. "Can you tell me what the hell's going on now?"

"Finish your chicken and grab your coat! You're going, too. After all, you helped to figure this out."

"Figure what out?"

"That we didn't dig nearly deep enough in that grave!"

#

(Three miles south of Raton, New Mexico)

It was twilight when Hector swung his department SUV around the last bend in the rough ranch road, plunged across the shallows of the Canadian River that ran below the ruins of the old Clifton House, and parked where the headlights illuminated the slope to the old grave a few yards below them. In the cold evening breeze, weathered yellow crime scene tape still fluttered between stakes that had been driven into the ground around Chunk Colbert's old grave at intervals. Some of the other abandoned holes dug by the unfortunate Cobus de Groot had also been filled in, which Trent was grateful for as he led the way with Hector and Walter following closely, each of them carrying a high-powered flashlight and either a shovel or a pick.

"Mind telling us what we're supposed to be looking for?" asked Walter. He was already breathing hard and starting to regret coming along, as he zipped his heavy jacket more closely around his neck.

Trent stopped at the head of the old gunfighter's grave, kicked out a groove in the dirt to securely hold his flashlight, and leaned on his shovel as he pulled on a pair of work gloves. "One hundred and forty years ago, Robert Clay Allison shot a gunfighter named Chunk Colbert through the head while he was eating a steak dinner." He paused and nodded into the distance. "Right about over there, where the dining room of the Clifton House used to be. Not sure exactly what their fight was over, but afterwards they dragged poor old Chunk out here and buried him, along with all the possessions that he had on him, which included . . . this." Trent pulled the evidence bag containing the smaller photo and map out of his jacket. "Now, why exactly this ended up in Mr. Colbert's grave is anybody's guess. Maybe he stole it. Maybe Allison thought it was a fine joke to play on everyone else and hid it in there. Who knows?"

Trent put the map back in his pocket, took a deep breath, and started digging as he continued to talk. "Suffice it to say, Robert Clay Allison discovered a gold mine, or a silver mine, or whatever the hell sort of mine it was, somewhere up in the Cimarron Canyon/Ute Park area." He shoveled methodically and continued. "And that's what the late Mr. de Groot, the late Mr. Vos, the late Minister Bouwmeester, and all of them—and possibly even the mysterious and intriguing Ms. Britt de Jaager—were all out here looking for, all over our fair county, to begin with." Trent paused again to catch his breath. He leaned on his shovel and smiled at

Hector and Walter, took a big swig of water, and then gestured to them. "If you gentlemen would care to join me over here, it would go a whole lot faster, and the quicker we could find out what else Mr. Clay Allison, the Gentleman Gunfighter, wanted us to find out here; or rather, *didn't* want us, or anyone else, to find—I'm thinking his savings for a rainy day."

"Well, I'm confused," said Hector as he stepped over to wield his shovel.

"Me too," added Walter, scratching his head.

"Why, gold, Dad! Clay Allison's heavy wagonload of gold, to be precise."

At that, they all three began to dig faster. The ground proved to be soft; too soft for a grave that had been sitting undisturbed for more than a hundred years' worth of rain, snow, and compacted soil and rock. Thirty minutes and four more feet of exposed hole later, Trent was no longer curious why the work was relatively easy.

"Someone's already been here," he muttered, throwing his shovel aside and wiping the sweat from his eyes. He stood with his hands on his hips, breathing hard, and squinting into the dark hole. The grave was, of course, devoid of its previous occupant and bits of rotted casket, which had all been exhumed as evidence, along with the unfortunate Mr. de Groot, and shipped to the M.E.'s office in Santa Fe.

But it was not entirely empty.

"Something's down here, all right," said Hector as he stepped carefully into the hole and bent over, coming back up with a small black plastic trash bag. "And it sure isn't a hundred and forty years old." It was wrapped tightly and secured with duct tape.

"That's odd," said Hector, examining the parcel closely.

"What's odd?" asked Trent.

Hector looked puzzled as he handed the package up to Trent. "It looks like it's addressed to you."

Trent took the plastic bag and turned it over to reveal an envelope that had been neatly taped to the outside of bag. The envelope bore the name *Trent Carter* in bold black letters drawn with a heavy marker. Trent took out his pocketknife, sliced open the bag, and opened it cautiously. "Get me some light here."

Hector and Walter crowded close and pointed their flashlights into the bag. They all gasped as if on cue. Trent upended the bag and caught a heavy rock in his free hand as it spilled out. It was just smaller than a tennis ball and streaked with color that glittered and flashed as the light played over its surface.

"That what I think it is?" asked Walter.

"That, Gentlemen, is a piece of unrefined gold ore." Trent hefted it in his hand.

"Looks like a lot of gold in that rock," said Hector.

"It is a lot of gold."

"So, what's it doing here?" asked Walter. "And who put it there? And why did they want you to find it?"

"Excellent questions all. Let's find out." Trent then turned his attention to the envelope, which he slit open and reached inside to pull out a small card. It was an expensive-looking business card on high-grade stock, jet black on one side and plain on the other. On the plain side was a handwritten note.

"Who was it?" asked Hector. "The Feds?"

"No. It wasn't the Feds." Trent read silently for a moment, then aloud: *Dear Mr. Carter, Thank you for all of your hard work and help in finding this cache. In return, we have left you this small token of our thanks. The fact that you have found it means that we may now consider this entire matter closed, as should you."*

The message was unsigned. Trent turned the business card over. The matte black surface sported in the center a raised, stylized gray drawing of a fossilized shell, cut away to show its many interior chambers. Underneath was the single word *Septum* in a simple but stylized font, also in gray. There was no phone number or email address, but where an address should have been was simply the name of a city—*Amsterdam, The Netherlands.*

CHAPTER 29
Sojourn's End

(August 20, 1939 – Three miles south of Raton, New Mexico)

"Happy birthday, *mi ardillocito*," the old man said as he shuffled along the banks of the Canadian River that gurgled below. The water level was down but still rushed noisily along. "You're six years old now. Do you feel a year older today?"

The little boy and his great-grandfather walked hand in hand, enjoying the early morning breezes that whispered through the huge cottonwoods across the way. The boy looked up at the old man.

"I don't think so, Papaw," he replied thoughtfully. "No, I don't feel any different than yesterday . . . Am I s'posed to?"

The old man chuckled softly and gazed down lovingly at the boy. "No, mi ardillocito; of course not. You're only supposed to feel as old as your soul allows you to be." A small frown crossed his weathered, wrinkled, but still handsome face. "Your great-grandmother would have told you that God made you in His own image—that you were born with a certain amount of His greatness in you. But then she would also have said that it is up to you to make sure that greatness within you grows." He reached down and gently poked his grandson in the ribs, making the boy giggle.

He had brought the boy here to this place as a treat; it was a place he himself had not been back to in more than fifty years; a special place of many memories, many of which he had tried very hard to leave in the past. But now it was somehow important for him to share at least this particular memory—this place—with the boy, especially on the lad's birthday.

Time was growing short.

"And Great-gramma gave me that name that you call me, right? *Mi ardi . . . ardi-yo . . . see. . . .*"

The old man chuckled and bent down to the boy. "*Ard-ill-o-ci-to*. Here. Say it slowly after me. Ar-di. . . ."

"Ar-di . . ."

"Oh-see . . ."

"Oh-see . . ."

"Toe."

"Toe!"

"*Ardillocito.*

"*Ardee-yo-see-toe.*"

"Good! Yes. She called you that when she first held you as a baby. It's a nickname."

"What is a *nickname*, Papaw?"

"A nickname is a special name given to us by people who love us very much. And your nickname happens to be the same as my nickname."

"So, what does it mean, Papaw?"

"Well, it's a Spanish word. Another language. Your great-grandmother was from an important Mexican family—and her people spoke Spanish. She called you that, because it means *my little squirrel*."

A frown crossed the boy's face. "But, you told me once that was what *your* name meant—your Indian name. But it wasn't that word. Why isn't it the same?"

"Well, it is the same. At least, the meanings are the same. *Salal* is *squirrel* in the Cherokee language, from the people that I came from, and your nickname is from Spanish; but they're still the same name. And it's a very good name."

"Your father gave you that name, right?"

"Yes." The old man chuckled. "You remember your family history very well. That is a good thing."

They walked on in silence for a while.

"Why did Great-gramma have to die, Papaw?"

The old man thought for a moment. "Because her body became worn out. It couldn't keep up with her spirit any longer. And when that happens, the spirit has to leave the body and travel on."

"Because she got old?"

"Yes."

"But, aren't you old too, Papaw?"

The old man chuckled. "Yes. I suppose that's true, too."

"So, are you going to die now, like Great-gramma?"

The old man stopped walking and gestured at a nearby felled tree. "Here, *mi ardillocito*. Let's stop and sit for a minute. Rest our bones."

He sat down stiffly, and a grateful sigh escaped his lips. He smiled as the boy squatted near the log and began drawing in the dirt with a stick. Then he looked at his surroundings. The nearby Canadian River gurgled, and the sound of its waters blended with the whispered voices in the trees. It had been a warm day, but he looked toward the horizon beyond the Raton Range to the west and spied the burgeoning bulk of some late summer thunderheads and smiled at their promise of an evening rain. He knew that just above them lay a small plateau where the adobe ruins of an old hotel lie.

So many years ago. So many memories.

His old eyes squinted as he thought he caught a slight movement on the ridge, just beyond the old adobe ruins he had brought the boy to see. The smile left his face and he sucked in his breath and held it. The distant silhouette of a rider on horseback moved slowly into focus and stopped, gazing back at the old man. He sat erect on his horse, with no saddle, proud and assured; and now the old man saw that the rider was leading another riderless horse. The rider seemed to be waiting for something. *But for what?* Something about him was very familiar. *But from where?* Then the old man suddenly knew, and he gasped. The rider seemed much younger than he should have been.

Could it be? But that's impossible. He is long dead now!

Something feather-like seemed to adorn the rider's hair, which the old man could now see was long and braided as it hung down his shoulders. The figure raised his hand and beckoned, as if wanting him to join him.

The old man shivered, but not from cold. He forced himself to look away, but he couldn't for long. But when he looked again, the horse and rider had disappeared. An old feeling darted around his heart, almost like a sixth sense that he had had a long time ago, a warning of something important about to happen. His fingers absently touched his side, just a few inches above his belt, where the old wound still itched at times. He shook it all off and looked back down at his great-grandson.

Too many memories. Too many to carry. Too much of a burden.

Time to lay them down.

"Come, *mi ardillocito*. Let me show you something."

The old man stood up slowly, stretched his back, then moved away up toward the old ruins, where some of the oldest memories still lived, and still haunted him.

#

(Fifty-four years earlier; November 1885 – Delgado Rancho, Ponil River Valley)

"Wait just a minute, Jim."

María Delgado Carter stepped around Jim Watkins, who leaned now on his shovel where he had been about to scoop dirt back into the new grave. "He needs to have these with him."

She stooped down and carefully placed a single stick of peppermint candy, a well-used pipe, and a pouch of specially blended tobacco underneath the folded hands of the body in the grave. She paused and let her fingers rest gently on top of the gnarled fingers of the deceased, and smiled. "We wouldn't want him to be without his smoke. He always said that it helped him to talk to Mowun—to God."

"Yes. And with his vision walks, too," said Jonathon as he stepped up behind his wife and placed a hand lovingly on the back of her head. "Or so he said." He held James in his other arm, and smiled down at his older son, Joseph, who held onto his fathers pants leg.

"Come here, José," said María, still kneeling and now holding out her hands to her son. "Come and say goodbye to your Pa-pa Nämpäry. Come. . . ." Joseph glanced down at the old Indian in the grave, then buried his face shyly against his father's knee. María dropped her hands in her lap and shook her head.

María had insisted on observing as much of the Ute tribe traditions as they could remember, such as the duty of the female family members to clean and prepare the body for burial, and the inclusion of Walking Elk's most important personal possessions. Since it was taboo for anyone but the women to touch the body, Jonathon had María respectfully place the old warrior's bow and sheaf of arrows beside him in the grave. He knew that Walking Elk—Nämpäry—would want to be able to hunt buffalo in the afterlife.

Jonathon had thought about burying his old friend's body up in the Valley of the Utes, where he had lived. But the land was now private, and Jonathon liked the idea of him being in María's little family plot behind the cabin—right where family belonged.

"It's all right, Joseph," said Jonathon, kneeling down to join his wife at the grave. "We'll all say goodbye together—like a family."

María placed a square of tanned deer hide over Nämpäry's face, then reached over to hold hands with her husband for a few long minutes. Together, they gazed one last time at their old friend, the father figure who had, in essence, replaced both of their real fathers in their home. Jonathon finally nodded to Jim, who now put his hat back on and picked up the shovel to resume his work of filling in the grave as Jonathon and María stood to walk with their boys back to the house. Jonathon winced as he slowly stood.

"Are you going to be all right?" she asked him as she took James from him.

"Yes," Jonathon said, touching his side just above his belt, then slipping his arm around her waist as they walked. "I think the wound is healing a bit more each day."

"I'm glad to know that. But I was actually asking about today—about Walking Elk."

"His time had come, and he knew that it had."

"But he was like a father to you." Maria thought for a moment, then continued. "I don't think we lose our fathers without it affecting us deeply."

Jonathon stopped and turned to face her, holding both her hands in his. "You know, I've lost three fathers now. Perhaps I am getting used to it."

"I don't believe that for a minute. I think it's bothering you more than you let on. The loss of a father or a mother is one that you never get over." She started to turn away and then stopped. "What do you mean *three* fathers? I know of only two: Stand Watie and Walking Elk. Who was the third?"

Jonathon sighed. "The one who didn't mean anything at all to me—my real father—a no-good hunter, trapper, and drunkard named Daniel Carter, who took advantage of a young Cherokee girl and got her pregnant. After she died and I had to go live with him, he would come home drunk and beat me most every night." Jonathon and María rounded the corner of the house as they talked. "He was stabbed during a drunken brawl, and believe me when I say I shed not a single tear the day they brought his body home."

"Jonathon," said María, suddenly stopping him and staring off into the distance where a lone figure stood almost a hundred yards away beside a wagon being drawn by four mules. The man had his hat in his hands and his head bowed, as if he had been reverently observing the small funeral that had just taken place.

"Help you, Mister?" Jonathon called out, shading his eyes from the mid-morning sun and stepping forward to protectively keep María and the boys between himself and the stranger. He realized with regret that his pistol was hanging just inside the doorway. *Could he run to it in time?* The man donned his hat, held his duster open wide to show he was not wearing any guns, and climbed back aboard the wagon. He called out to his mules and drove the wagon toward their house. As he neared, he smiled and waved and Jonathon breathed a sigh of relief as he finally recognized the man.

It was Robert Clay Allison.

#

"Were we ever really that young, Captain Carter?" asked Allison, reverting back to Jonathon's honorific from when they had first met years ago in Fort Worth. He sat at the table, sipping María's after-dinner coffee, and studying the photo of five young men posed proudly in front of Tom Stockton's bar at the Clifton House. "That had to be, what . . . twelve years ago, now?"

"More like seventeen . . . eighteen, maybe." Jonathon stepped over to take another look at the brand new, professionally framed eight-by-ten photograph. It was a gift that Clay had brought back with him from Texas. He had tracked down the original photographer and ordered it especially for Jonathon to replace the smaller one he had had years ago.

"I always felt a little guilty, taking your only copy like that. Sent off all the way to Washington, D. C., where the fella's studio is, to have him fix this one up for you. Spared no expense." He paused, brushing some dust from his thigh. "Besides, I thought I'd better bring you a peace offering, seeing as how you had threatened to arrest me if you ever saw me in these parts again."

Jonathon ran a hand over the fine wooden frame. "Must've spent a lot on it. Too much, is all I can say." Jonathon glanced at Clay over the rim of his glasses. "And I didn't threaten to arrest you . . . I threatened to shoot you." They held each other's eyes coolly for several moments.

"It is very fine quality," interjected María. "And yes, very expensive, I am sure. We could not possibly accept it, Señor Allison . . . Clay."

"And I could not possibly accept it back, dear lady. It belongs here, adorning your fine home, as a memento of the past—of our pasts."

"What do you think?" Jonathon asked no one in particular, referring to the polished frame. "Walnut?"

"Hell if know. Fancy looking is all I can tell you. Just ordered the finest frame he had in stock."

Jonathon adjusted his glasses and studied each face in the photo in turn. "Were we ever really so young, indeed . . . or foolhardy?" He then turned it over and looked at the back. He ran his finger over the thick, brown paper that had been professionally glued to the back.

"Careful now," warned Clay. "Don't want that to come loose." He rubbed his chin thoughtfully, then reached over, and took the photograph carefully from Jonathon. He flipped it over in his hands and looked around the room, peering at each of the walls. "There," he pronounced finally, pointing, and then stood up and walked over to the mantle. He held the picture up to the stone chimney. "What do you think? Perfect place, I would say."

A few minutes later, after Jonathon had found a hammer and nails, the three of them sat thoughtfully sipping coffee, their chairs in a semicircle around the fireplace, admiring the newly hung picture. Jonathon looked over at Clay and smiled. José sat on Clay's lap and was playing with a carved wooden horse that Allison had given to him. Jonathon had never seen his oldest son warm up so quickly to anyone.

María held little James on her lap, where he giggled when the old gunman played peek-a-boo with him. "I cannot believe you named that little rascal after me," said Clay, reaching over and tousling the child's dark locks gently. "James *Allison* Carter. No child on earth should have to be saddled with that label."

"Why, I thought you said earlier that you and your missus are now expecting your second, Mr. Allison," said María. "You are surely accustomed to children bearing your name by now."

Clay laughed. "Well, Mrs. Carter, my children's names are merely an accident of their birth, and therefore they have no choice but to bear them." He gestured back at her baby. "But young Master James here is another matter altogether. He carries that name on purpose—I cannot believe that it was your husband's idea. He glanced over at Jonathon with a bemused look on his face. "Now that child will have to explain to everyone where that name came from, and the big bad man who shares it with him."

"Well, it's one sure way to keep your legend alive, Clay. And by the way, you're correct," Jonathon said, glancing with a quick smile at his wife. "It was María who insisted on naming him after you." He suddenly winced and adjusted himself in his chair. He touched his side.

Allison watched him closely and nodded. "How bad was it?"

"Oh, they nicked my liver pretty good. But the bullet went through and through—as clean as anyone would ever wish for. Doc says it's going to drain for a good long while yet and I will definitely feel it from now on. He says it will grab something fierce, maybe for the rest of my days."

María frowned and shook her head. "He's just fortunate that Jim Watkins was there to tend him—and bring him home alive."

"I am truly sorry that I was not present to be of aid to you that day at the courthouse," said Allison. "Perhaps I could have prevented you from being shot in the first place."

"Or more likely, you would have made it much worse, and we would both be dead! Besides, there was more than enough blood spilled that day."

Allison sipped his coffee thoughtfully, then shook his head. "I hear that poor old Sam Farnsworth met his end during the fight. Mean old cuss, but I did like him. Always reminded me of what I will most likely be like when I myself become old and toothless."

"Yes, it saddened me to see him fall like that. But to tell the truth, he probably would have had it no other way. I believe he was getting short-tempered and tired of his old age." Jonathon paused and gazed into the dancing flames in the fireplace. "I suspect that I will also feel much the same way, when my time comes."

"Say . . . did I hear correctly that the scoundrel Axtell and his cronies in the Santa Fe Ring have all finally cleared out and are no longer a big concern?"

"Yes, thanks be to God," answered María.

"It's what he actually promised Frank Springer before the courthouse fiasco didn't turn out his way," added Jonathon. "So President Cleveland himself was about to have him removed from office, except Axtell beat him to it by finally resigning."

Clay raised his coffee cup in salute. "Well, may your days now be long, peaceful, uneventful, and prosperous." He coaxed Joseph from his lap, drained his coffee mug, stood up, and set it on the table. "Mrs. Carter, I thank you profusely for the most delicious luncheon I have had since I left my own darling Dora's table at home in Texas. But if I don't make tracks back to her soon, she will make sure I have the devil to pay once I get home." He turned and gestured again at the photograph above the mantle.

"Make sure you take damn good care of that picture, Jonathon. There's more value there than might meet the eye."

"Yes. Good friends all," Jonathon said as he looked wistfully from one face to another in the photograph. "I may never know the likes of them again." He stood up, went over to Allison, and extended a hand. "Especially you, Clay."

They shook hands slowly. Then Jonathon walked him out to the wagon.

"Why Jonathon—I am deeply touched. Does this mean we are finally best friends?"

Jonathon hooked his thumbs in his belt and smiled back. "Don't flatter yourself too much. You know, when you showed up here earlier I really did entertain the notion of arresting you."

"So, what, pray tell, has changed your mind?"

"Mainly, it was the fact that you were unarmed. But then also, the way that your wagon here is evidently loaded to the axles with the remainder of your worldly goods, and that you have now said more than once that you were only here to say your final goodbyes before heading back to Pecos—back home."

"Home," Allison sighed, then looked around. "I can only hope and pray that I can make a home half as decent as this one—with the peace and love that permeates yours."

"Word of advice, then, Clay. When you get there, hang up your guns—for good, will you? Peace will follow. I am certain of it."

Allison smiled and clapped the lawman on the shoulder. "Spoken like a true warrior. Wise words, my young Squirrel. Wise words, indeed, and ones that I shall seriously ponder on my long journey home."

Clay paused for a moment to close his eyes and take a deep breath of the cool mountain air, as if savoring something he would never have again.

"I shall truly miss this life," he murmured, more to himself than to Jonathon.

María came out of the house with baby James balanced on one hip. Joseph

309

stood in the doorway holding his wooden horse tightly. María held out a small parcel that had been wrapped carefully in a dishtowel. "Some leftover goat's meat and tortillas for later. You will get hungry on your trip." She then stood on tiptoe and kissed him lightly on the cheek. Baby James cooed and reached out to play with one of the silver buttons on his namesake's vest.

Allison looked down self-consciously at the unexpected gift, suddenly overcome with emotion, and stammered. "I—I shall savor each and every bite of your kindness, Ma'am." He quickly donned his hat, mounted his wagon, and took the reins in his hands. He looked down at Jonathon and María with a fondness laced with what seemed to be a bit of sadness. He finally clucked to his mules. "Vaya con Dios, my friends. I must go pay my last respects to one more old amigo."

He clucked once more to the team and then called out over his shoulder as they lurched and pulled the heavy wagon away. "We may have taken all the wildness out of this here country, Squirrel, but it's going to take better men than us—like young Masters James Allison and José Isaac there—to finally settle it down completely."

Jonathon put his arm around María's shoulder. He had the distinct feeling he would never see his old friend again.

#

(Clifton House, three miles south of Otero [Raton], New Mexico)

Clay Allison drove his wagon northeastward through the fall afternoon. The sun was about set behind him, and the sliver of the waxing half moon was just rising in front of him over the familiar big mesa to the east—now called Johnson Mesa after some settler named Elijah Johnson had built a cattle ranch on top. He pulled up behind the abandoned two-story hotel, restaurant, and stage stop rising up before him in stark silhouette and jumped down stiffly from the wagon. After unhitching his mules and hobbling them to graze, he pulled his woolen scarf more snuggly around his neck, looked around and listened for a moment, and reached under the seat to grab a shovel and a pint of whiskey. He picked his way cautiously across the uneven ground, kicking at small stones and searching in the fading sunlight until he found what he was looking for—a single weathered wooden cross, which leaned over precariously where it had been long forgotten.

He squatted down beside the cross, uncorked the whiskey bottle, and held it up in brief salute. "Here's to you, mi amigo," he toasted. He took a long swig and then poured out a dollop onto the grave. "May all my secrets now also be yours—well, most of them, anyway."

Two hours later, Clay Allison, sweaty and breathing hard from his exertions, tamped the last of the dirt back onto Chunk Colbert's grave and readjusted the cross so that it was now upright again. He put his heavy coat back on, attached a shelter half of canvas to form a makeshift lean-to against the side of his wagon, and then built a small campfire, where he heated up one of María's goat meat tortilla sandwiches. He ate while he listened to the lonely song of a nearby coyote and

310

watched the climbing moon bathe the surrounding volcanoes and mesas with stark grays and whites.

He awoke well before dawn to frost on his bedroll, stoked the campfire, made some coffee, and finished the last of María's food. He then fed and watered his mules before breaking camp. When he finally climbed into the wagon, he sat still for several minutes watching the pearly predawn light wash some pink and light orange back into the landscape. He closed his eyes, breathed the crisp northern New Mexican dawn for the last time, and took the reins and slapped them against the backs of the mules. This time the wagon jumped forward lightly, happily freed from its previous heavy weight of gold ore, which now lay safe and secure six feet under the earth with the ghost of a dangerous gunfighter to guard it—maybe for a year, maybe for a lifetime, maybe an eternity. In any event, Clay knew it should still be there whenever he needed it. Or, if not by him, at least the whereabouts of the gold would always be available in the detailed map tucked safely away in the fancy picture frame he had just given to his friends, for them to perhaps find someday— that, and a mysterious old land deed from Lucien B. Maxwell.

These were, then, Robert clay Allison's secrets; and they were now safer than in any bank.

Allison made his way down to the Canadian River crossing and then followed the old Santa Fe Trail wagon ruts which now paralleled the newly laid Santa Fe Railroad tracks. A couple miles or so farther south, he waved at the engineer as a southbound train fresh from the yards at the new railroad town of Raton churned and roared past him, causing his mules to rear and bray. He quickly got them under control and waited to allow the locomotive pulling its freight and passenger cars to slide on by.

As he pushed his team forward once again, Clay Allison did not notice the two men on horseback who had pulled out of a draw several hundred yards behind him and began to shadow him; nor would he notice that they would continue to stalk him silently all the way to South Texas. And none of the three of them ever noticed the smoke that now billowed up over a ridge two or three miles further back from where they had come, where sparks from the locomotive's smokestack had ignited a fire on the roof of the old, abandoned Clifton House, which was now burning out of control in the cold dawn.

#

(October 28, 1940 – Raton, New Mexico)

In the latter part of the 19th century, the railroad company had built a big roundhouse and service yards at the new town of Willow Springs for the locomotives that labored to and fro over Raton Pass. The town had soon also taken its permanent name from the mountain pass itself and had eventually grown to just under 9,000 in population with a thriving economy centered around not only the railroad, but also coal mining as represented by several large mining camps scattered throughout the nearby canyons.

Jonathon lay in his bed, gazing out the window of his second-story bedroom of the house he and María had built just after the turn of the century. Jonathon sighed, the ghosts of his past parading in front of him. "Too many memories," he whispered. "Too many to carry anymore."

It was noon and his grandson's wife, Penelope, had just taken away his half-eaten bowl of stew, which tasted very good, though he could no longer enjoy food the way he once did. His weakened system could not handle it. Penny, along with her two young sons, had come to live with and care for him when her husband, Robert, had left to enlist in the army, believing that war was about to come and wanting to be in the action when it did.

Jonathon coughed weakly and frowned. He had tried to convince his grandson that in his own long, futile experiences of fighting Yankees, Comanches, outlaws, land regulators, and now death itself, war in any of its forms never brought the glory that men so desperately sought. But Jonathon could not really fault his grandson. He knew too well the seductive pull that battle and the smell of gunpowder could have on a young man.

In fact, it was his old Muache Indian mentor Nämpäry who had finally taught Jonathon that, although there was indeed honor in being a warrior, there was seldom glory in it; and that only God—Mowun—could bring a man fully to grace and glory, and then only if the man would humble himself before Mowun's nailed son, Jesus.

The frenetic noise of the town's activity happening beyond his windows now faded and was replaced by more memories, flooding in on him now, one after the other, until they slowed and finally settled on one particular vision. Jonathon gestured with his hand feebly toward the near distance, where he now saw a young Indian warrior ride bareback onto his manicured lawn, his bronze features handsome as he sat straight-backed on his painted pony.

"Get off of my lawn," Jonathon croaked, his voice barely above a whisper. The young warrior looked up, smiled broadly at Jonathon, and gestured at another fine pony that he led behind him.

"Come, Squirrel. It is time."

Jonathon raised his eyebrows in sudden recognition and tried to smile and wave back, but he was much too weak. "Nämpäry?" he asked, incredulous. "But you are so young!"

"Yes! And you are so old now," the young warrior chuckled. *"Remember when we first met? It was the other way around."*

Jonathon coughed again and closed his eyes. *Yes, perhaps he's right—a long time ago, now. And too many others long gone.* They paraded now behind his closed eyes.

Not too long after Jonathon and María had said farewell to him, Clay Allison had been found dead on his ranch near Pecos, Texas, after having fallen off a wagon full of supplies he was bringing back home. One of the wheels had rolled over him and broken his neck; or at least that was what some folks said had happened. Jonathon believed otherwise. It had been widely reported that Clay had, indeed, hung up his guns for good. Jonathon chose to believe that had Clay been armed that day, his story might have ended differently.

His old friend Frank Springer had died in 1927 at his daughter Ada's home in Overbrook, Pennsylvania, where he had lived since his health had begun to fail him. The accomplishments of the last part of his life, after he left Colfax County, had been astounding and included co-founding an institution of higher learning in his adopted town of Las Vegas, New Mexico; overseeing the phasing out of the Board of Trustees of the old Maxwell Land Grant, which required several visits to the Netherlands; taking the land dispute that resulted in the Colfax County War all the way to the United States Supreme Court for final settlement (a landmark case for land reform); and most importantly, devoting himself to his scientific studies. These studies had culminated in the scholarly publication of his life's paleontological work and the museum-level archiving of his vast fossil collection that was his real pride and joy. Overall, Springer had become highly regarded within the world's scientific, legal, and educational communities.

María Consuela Delgado Carter had slipped away in her sleep one fall night in 1933. Jonathon had never in all those remaining years broken his promise to always return to her warm bed; and when he had suddenly awakened that night, she still had her head on his chest and her arms wrapped around him and her long, white hair fanned out across his shoulder.

At María's funeral, her elderly brother, Manuel Delgado, had taken Jonathon aside and handed him a small hand-carved wooden box. In it, Jonathon found that it contained all of the letters, news clippings, and photographs María had sent to Manuel over the years. The old men hugged each other and wept for a very long time.

"So why do they call us *squirrels*, Papaw Salal?"

Jonathon's sojourn with his memories ended abruptly. He turned slowly and opened his eyes. He wasn't sure how much time had past, but he smiled at his great-grandson. "Mi ardillocito," he said softly, the faintest of smiles appearing at the corners of his thin lips. He reached a trembling hand toward the boy's face. "I'm so very happy to see you again."

Walter Carter reached out and grasped his great-grandfather's hand and held it. "I'm very happy to see you too, Papaw Salal. How are you feeling today?"

Jonathon closed his eyes and shook his head weakly in silent response.

"Here, have a sip of water. You sound dry."

Jonathon took the proffered straw in his lips and swallowed a mouthful of cool water. It felt good as it bathed his parched throat. He opened his eyes and gazed fondly at the boy. "My, how you have grown, my little squirrel. You're not a little boy anymore."

Walter set the glass on the table and shifted in his chair. "Well, I am almost eight now. But I still don't understand why my nickname is *squirrel*. You never told me why, Papaw. Why a squirrel?"

The old man thought for a moment. "Well, since it seems so important to you—it's because many Indian names are given to people from the animal world. With my people—the Cherokee—a squirrel is much revered and respected. The squirrel is smart and fast, and can get itself quickly out of many bad situations and then live to enjoy another day."

"But why weren't we named after a wolf then? Or a bear?"

"Would you rather be a bear?"

Walter thought very hard. "Well . . . I think it might be a better animal. More powerful. A bear, a lion, or even a badger would make people listen to you." He stopped and looked away. "Maybe make some people want to be with you."

The old man looked at his great grandson closely. "You're thinking about your father now, aren't you, *mi ardillocito.*"

The boy nodded. Jonathon squeezed his great-grandson's hand as tightly as he was able to manage. "Do you worry about how your father feels about you?"

"Uh huh. Sometimes I don't think he wants me around. He's always angry with me. And now he's gone—to join the army. Like he really doesn't want to be around at all."

"Oh, I don't think he is angry at you, little squirrel."

"Then, who is he angry with? Mom? With you? I don't think he likes that I always spend so much time with you, Papaw Salal."

Jonathon pursed his lips and thought for a moment. "No, I think mostly your father is angry with himself. And then he doesn't know how to deal with his anger. And he takes it out on those he really loves the most—like you and your mother." He paused for a moment. "You were also named for your father—*Robert Walter, Jr.* That is a very deep honor that your father gave to you. It shows how very much he really loves you."

They sat for a while in silence. Jonathon suddenly felt another presence and turned again to the window. The Ute warrior smiled and waved again. But this time he wasn't alone. Another rider had come up beside him. *Someone very familiar . . .*

"You come from important people," Jonathon murmured, but for a moment wasn't sure if he was talking to the boy or to himself. A silence fell on the room for a while.

"What was *your* father's name?" asked the boy, finally.

"His name was Isaac Stand Watie," Jonathon answered, squinting curiously at the shadowy second rider out on his lawn, then turned back to Walter when he giggled. The boy stopped when he saw that the old man didn't laugh.

"That's sorta a funny name too," Walter said, sheepishly.

"Yes, I suppose it does sound funny. But many Indian names do sound funny."

"Was he angry, too? Your father?"

"Sometimes. But mostly, he learned to use his anger—to channel it—for good. That's what a wise man will do—learn to use his weakness. You see *mi ardillocito,* my father—your great-great-grandfather—was a Cherokee chieftain and a great and famous general. Did you know that?"

"No. Really? A general—wow! Did he fight wars and stuff?"

"Oh yes, he fought bravely in many battles. Why, he was the only Indian general in the Civil War—did you ever hear of that war?"

The boy shook his head, then thought quietly. "Papaw Salal—did *you* fight in the war, too?"

"Yes. I fought for my father. Side by side with him."

"What happened to the general? Did he get shot and die?"

"No. He didn't get shot. But yes, he finally died. A long time ago now."

The boy thought about this concept for a while and then looked at the old man. "Papaw Salal, did you ever get shot?"

Jonathon grew silent, touching the old scar on his side. "Yes. I got shot very badly, but not in that war. It was much later—in a very different war."

Walter was quiet. "Did it hurt, Papaw? Did you . . . did you worry that you were going to die?"

"Yes, for a while, I truly thought I would die."

The boy stared up at the old man.

"Why didn't you?

The old man smiled. "Because a beautiful woman nursed me back to health."

The boy thought for a moment. "Great-gramma María?"

"Yes."

The boy thought again. "I wish Great-gramma María didn't die. But I'm very happy you didn't die, Papaw."

Jonathon closed his eyes. For a while he thought he might have slept. When he opened his eyes, Walter was leaning his head on his arms on the side of the bed. Walter was staring into space, but then noticed that the old man was awake again.

"Papaw Salal, are my mama and daddy going to die?"

"Yes, *mi ardillocito*. Someday. All people die someday. It's part of our lives. We live, we die, and our hope is to return to the Creator."

"The Creator?"

"God."

"Oh."

"So, am I going to die, too?"

"Not for a very long time yet, my Little Squirrel. A very long time."

"Are you going to die, Papaw?"

The old man thought carefully before answering. "Yes. I am going to die," he said softly. "And very soon, my grandson."

The boy fought back tears. Then he raised himself and laid his face against the old man's sunken chest.

"But I don't *want* you to die, Papaw!"

Jonathon stroked the boy's hair lightly with his thin fingers. The street noises from outside caught his attention. He peered back out the window.

"We are waiting, Squirrel."

Even at this distance, the voice was clear and strong.

"We, Nämpäry? Waiting for me?"

"There are many buffalo for us to hunt together, Salal. Many fine horses to ride . . . and she awaits you, as well—on the other side."

"Mi preciosa esposa?"

The boy looked up with tears on his cheeks and worry on his face. "Papaw

Salal? Who are you talking to?" He craned his neck to see out the window but saw no one.

Jonathon patted the boy's head and then caught sight of something else.

"Walter, you see that box over there, on the desk?"

Walter stood up and turned. "You mean that old wooden one?"

"Yes. That one. And the big, framed photograph propped up beside it. Bring them to me, would you? Be careful. Don't drop them."

Walter brought the items over as instructed. He placed them on the bedside table.

"Here, bring the picture to me, here on the bed where I can reach it."

Jonathon turned the photo around where he could see the faded sepia-toned faces looking back at him. "You see these men?" Walter looked and nodded his head. "This one is me. And all these others were my friends." He looked wistful for a moment. "They are all dead now, too."

"But, they all look like cowboys. Does that mean you were a cowboy, too, Papaw? A real one?" Walter looked closely and touched his great-grandfather's image with a finger, then slid it down to the gun belt that he wore.

"Yes. And a soldier, and a gold miner, and a lawman, and a rancher." He chuckled. "You name it, I did it!"

"Wow!"

Jonathon let his gaze drift around the room, stopping briefly on some of the other old photos here and there around him—of him and María, on their wedding day; of his sons, José Isaac and James Allison, both of whom had been named after great men, and both of whom had died prematurely and tragically, one in the trenches of the Great War in France and the other in a coal mine explosion in a place called Dawson. *A man shouldn't have to outlive his children.* "But mostly," he continued aloud again, softly, "I was a husband and father—and a good one, I hope."

When he looked back, Walter had opened the box and was looking through it. "What are all these? Letters, Papaw?"

Jonathon picked up one of his wife's letters and an old newspaper clipping and held them gently. "These, Walter, contain the story of our family—your people; our history. Your great-gramma María wrote most of these letters, and she saved the news articles any time they mentioned me." Jonathon laughed, which turned quickly into a long, deep cough.

"Why? Were you famous, Papaw?"

"More like *infamous*." He quickly waved off the question forming on Walter's lips. "Let's just say I got involved with a lot of other famous people—even a few outlaws."

"Really? *Outlaws?*"

"Yes." Jonathon took the documents, replaced them carefully, and gently closed the lid and latched it. "And I want you to read all of this, when you have more time." Jonathon hesitated, then handed the box to the boy. "You might want to give them to your own son one day, when you have one. Teach him who he is—

where he came from."

Then Jonathon pushed the framed photograph over toward the boy. "These are all yours now, Walter. And you must keep them all very safe, especially this. Here is the real treasure," he said. "At least I was told that by the man who gave it to me—this man right here." He tapped the image of a stern-looking cowboy in the photograph. "His name was Clay Allison. And he said I was to protect it, at all costs. And now you should, too."

"Why? Is it valuable?"

Jonathon reflected for a moment. "Maybe—I'm not sure what he meant. Clay Allison always played his cards close to his vest."

"What does that mean, Papaw?"

Jonathon smiled. "It means he liked to keep secrets." He let his hand linger on the photo while a finger played with a torn edge of the backing paper. "I always meant to glue that corner down again. Oh, well."

Walter tentatively took the photograph. He then looked at the old box of letters and hesitantly rubbed the carved surface of the old wood. "They're . . . they're mine?" He swallowed hard and looked at the old man. "But why? Don't you need them anymore?" The boy's eyes glistened again and his lower lip trembled.

Jonathon Salal Carter sighed deeply, felt a deep-seated sadness well up from somewhere in his chest—a feeling of indescribable loss—and felt his own cheeks growing damp.

"Come, *mi ardillocito*. It's time for you to go." Jonathon took young Walter's hand and squeezed it again. "Are you too embarrassed to give your old Papaw a kiss goodbye?"

Walter leaned over and kissed the old man gently on his cheek. It felt like dry, wrinkled paper. As he turned to leave, a tear fell soundlessly from his eye and dropped onto his great-grandfather's gaunt cheekbone. Jonathon reached up and touched this new treasure with his finger, silently watching as the boy turned and left the room with his own treasures firmly tucked under his arm.

"Salal. It is time!"

It was another voice now that Jonathon recognized—one which he hadn't heard in more than seventy years; the last time he had heard it he was sitting on his warhorse just inside a grove of silver maple trees somewhere in Northeastern Oklahoma, ready to take his Indian cavalry unit charging into the guns of the waiting Yankees beyond the creek below.

"I am here, Father. I am coming, General."

Jonathon pulled the heavy covers off as if they weighed nothing, sat nimbly up on the edge of the bed, and looked out the window. Below, in the middle of the lawn, sat both of his adoptive fathers on horseback—Cherokee/Confederate General Isaac "Stand" Watie and Muache/Ute Chieftain Nämpäry "Walking Elk," both dressed in their finest war gear, ready to ride off and join battle. Jonathon leapt from the bed and floated out of the window—down, down, until he alighted firmly and spryly on the ground in his leather knee-high riding boots, his striped uniform breeches tucked neatly inside, and his captain's tunic with its freshly polished buttons. He looked in amazement at his young hands, felt the youthful smoothness of his face, and wondered at the newfound energy that now coursed through his body. He ran forward, grabbed the reins of his warhorse from Nämpäry, and sprang exuberantly into the saddle. Then he wheeled around, grinning from ear to ear at his mentors.

"Let's ride!" exclaimed Captain Jonathon Salal Carter—young, naïve, and hungry once again for glory—and spurred his stallion away into action.

#

A few minutes later, the door opened softly and Penelope Carter stepped quietly into the bedroom. Her eyes widened and a hand came up to her mouth as she saw the old man lying quite still in bed, staring vacantly at the ceiling but wearing a peaceful smile on his face.

CHAPTER 30
Septum

(Present Day – Amsterdam, the Netherlands)

Trent Carter sat at a small wrought iron umbrella table on the patio of the Café de Hortus, sipping coffee. The café was located in the middle of the *Hortus Botanicus*—the vast and luxuriant botanical gardens situated in midst of the historic, and touristy, city of Amsterdam. The waiter had just poured a second large cup of black coffee for him, and for the second time he had given his American customer a miffed look when Trent again declined the offer of added heavy cream and orange liqueur to the cup, supposedly a local delicacy. As the server beat a hasty retreat, Trent settled back to sip the strong brew while enjoying what had come to be his favorite pastime of the last week—relaxing and watching all the harried tourists as they scrambled from one must-see attraction to the next with guidebooks firmly in hand and exhausted, grumpy kids in tow. After four days in Amsterdam, Trent was more than happy to have staked out this small island of relative tranquility while he awaited the women's return from roaming the magnificent gardens that surrounded the café.

Trent and Maggie had flown to Amsterdam at Ilsa Bouwmeester's personal request to attend the formal memorial service for her father. Although almost six months had passed since his death, Laird Bouwmeester's remains had been held in the U.S. because of the circumstances of his violent end, the need for an autopsy, and the overall mysterious manner in which the follow-up investigation had been handled—or not handled, to Trent's way of thinking. He was still uncertain as to what agencies had ultimately been involved—FBI, CIA, State Department, Interpol, or the mysterious Septum—or perhaps all of them. He was frankly quite irritated that he, or anyone else who had been directly involved with the entire affair, had never been questioned or debriefed.

Ilsa Bouwmeester had greeted them upon their arrival several days earlier at Amsterdam's Schiphol Airport, accompanied by the illusive and mysterious Britt de Jaager. The women had been their ever-present guides since then, ushering them to all of the major sights, museums, and eateries, as well as to the memorial service and the gravesite of Ilsa's father. The beautiful park-like Zorgvlied Cemetery, in the southeast part of the city, was one of the oldest, most celebrated final resting places in the Netherlands, containing the graves of numerous famous Dutch citizens—mostly celebrities. It was not too surprising, then, that the popular Dutch Education Minister would find his final repose here among them.

"Yes. *Pappie*—my father—loved visiting here," said Ilsa as they had strolled through the cemetery. "He came for walks here many times, often alone, just to get away and think.

The large headstone of mountain red granite that lay flat over Bouwmeester' grave was polished to a flat finish so that it gave off no reflection. Its multicolored earthen hues suggested something rugged yet elegant. Maggie had brought a spray of tulips to add to the other flowers that adorned the grave. "It's a beautiful stone, Ilsa. Did you select it?"

"Yes. I chose it for its name, really. *Mountain granite* seemed to be the perfect stone, under the circumstances. It shows strength and beauty . . . but also spoke to me of the place where my father died, in your rugged New Mexico mountains."

"It was a very fine choice," Britt de Jaager agreed.

It had quickly become clear to Trent that Agent de Jaager continued to take her duties quite seriously where Ilsa was concerned. It was a level of dedication that had given him pause to think that the supposed danger to Ilsa may not have ended with the assassination of her father and the exposing of the rogue Dutch agents. When he had attempted to broach the subject, however, Britt had changed the subject.

In the days that followed as they had toured through the crowded historic city, Trent couldn't help but sense that something wasn't quite right. It had happened more than once, and it made him wonder if they were not being followed. He had put this suspicion to the test, using reverse tracking skills that he had learned over the years, but to no avail. He hadn't been able to spot the tail—but his caution remained.

He sat now, listening to the nearby jangle of bicycle bells and the hum of trolleys that defined the old town center, as he sipped his American-style coffee and reflected that if there really were any danger, then in Britt's and his company, Ilsa was probably the best-protected young woman in Amsterdam right now. He smiled to himself, glad that Maggie, at least, had been thoroughly enjoying herself on this trip, reveling in the history, the culture, and the expensive shops.

"You really should take the barista's advice," came an unfamiliar voice to Trent's left. He turned to find the source and saw a solitary figure seated at the next table. The man was of slight build, appeared to be middle-aged, and was well groomed; he wore a dark suit, button-down shirt, and maroon necktie, giving him the appearance of a successful businessman relaxing after an afternoon stroll to clear his head. The gray fedora pulled low over his forehead hid his facial features as he held his own steaming cup to his lips.

"Pardon me?" Trent resisted the need to scratch his forehead. The stranger sat with one gloved hand on his coffee mug and the other resting flat on the table. He was still turned away from Trent, and spoke just loudly enough to be understood.

"Dutch coffee is brewed with skill; it's an acquired art," the man continued without looking up. "The creams and the liqueurs can be quite delicate but also distinct and should be savored." The stranger finally turned and looked straight at Trent, who could now see the man's piercing blue eyes behind black horn-rimmed glasses. "One should always partake of the local foods and refreshments when one travels, yes, Mr. Carter? It is an important part of the cultural experience."

For some odd reason, even though his sixth sense told him something was definitely up with this man, Trent felt no immediate warnings of danger. He had never seen him before but suddenly had a strong suspicion as to who he might be. Trent leaned back, slipped a hand into his jacket pocket, and pulled something out. "This is you, then, I take it?" he asked, as he held up a dull black business card featuring the symbol of a fossilized shell.

The stranger continued to smile, and then shrugged.

"So. You found my calling card after all . . . and our little gift too, I hope." The man raised an arm and slowly pushed back his sleeve, revealing the identical fossilized shell icon tattooed on his wrist.

"*Septum* then, is it? You've been following us, I guess, ever since we got off the plane," said Trent. "So, I don't suppose you have a name—like, a real name."

The man shrugged again, continuing to smile. "Septum will serve quite adequately, for now."

Trent grunted. "Don't know why I expected anything else. Seems par for the course, where you all are concerned—big boys and girls, playing spies with code names, gadgets, and other James Bond crap. Quite honestly, I'm a little weary of it all." He flicked the edge of the card with his finger. "I don't suppose you want to tell me just what this has all been about—like, just how much more gold did you take out of that grave back home?"

The man pushed his metal chair back, slowly stood up, and straightened his overcoat and hat.

"First things first, Mr. Carter. Come. Let's walk for a bit." He looked around the crowded patio. "I get a little . . . bored, shall we say, in one place for too long."

Trent nodded toward the botanical park. "Don't know what my wife will do if she returns and I've gone. She may just feel the urgency to pick up her phone and call the authorities . . . or the embassy."

"Yes," said the man called Septum. "I see your point. And I agree that Maggie has often proven to be quite resourceful in the past."

Trent didn't know whether to be surprised or irritated at the man's familiar use of his wife's name. "Maybe I should just text her real quick."

"Oh, that won't be necessary. I shall have you back in no time at all. You will scarcely be missed." Trent still hesitated. "Oh come, Mr. Carter. I assure you, I mean you no harm. If I had wanted to harm you, I would have had numerous opportunities to do so before now."

"Here in Amsterdam? Or in New Mexico?"

"Why, both, of course."

"So, the fact that I am still alive, even after your man Karl tried to murder me, is supposed to make me feel all warm and fuzzy, and assure me beyond a doubt that you're to be trusted?"

"Hmmm. *My man, Karl.* As you say, Karl was indeed my agent—at one time— as they all once were. Of course, you only ran into the tip of the iceberg. Many others were involved in this little conspiracy . . . but please, Mr. Carter. We are getting ahead of ourselves. Come. Walk with me."

The man turned and moved toward the flagstone steps leading from the patio and onto a nearby graveled path without looking back. Trent watched warily for a moment, and then left some money on the table and followed. As he caught up to him he kept a good space between himself and the man known only as Septum.

"So. Down to business," the man said. "You are curious, no doubt, about the organization—about Septum, yes?"

Trent noticed that as the stranger spoke, his lips were stretched into a perpetual smile, as if he were very pleased to be sharing secrets. "It had crossed my mind a time or two."

The man pointed down at the business card Trent was still holding. "How familiar are you with marine biology, Mr. Carter? For example, the extant version of the cephalopod family *Nautilidae,* pictured there on the card?"

"Can't say that biology was ever my strong suit."

"Nor mine. But I can tell you that what you are holding there depicts what is known as a nautilus—a fossilized example. Indeed, there are only six remaining species of the genus alive today. The characteristics of this magnificent creature describe my organization so very well, and hence, make a fine representative of our purposes. For example, here you see a cross section of its shell and many chambers, increasing in size as the animal ages. These chambers, as you see, are separated by walls called *septa,* which allow the creature to grow out of its previously restricting habitat and then seal itself off to prevent bacterial growth or other infestation from the outside. Another feature is that the animal adapts quickly to pressure sensitivity. Do you know that it is the only known cephalopod that can be brought up from tremendous oceanic depths and not arrive dead at the surface from the implosion of pressure? The lifespan of a nautilus often exceeds twenty years, which is most unusual for a cephalopod. Scientists have also recently found that they grossly underestimated the short-term and long-term memory capabilities within the nervous system of the animal, given the lack of a conventional brain; its proven capability of learning from outside stimuli far exceeds previous expectations."

"You don't say."

The Septum agent paused. "I am boring you. I can see that I am becoming much too exuberant in my explanation, and possibly too clinical. I do apologize."

"No apology necessary. Just sort of waiting for you to get to the point."

By now, they had left the botanical gardens behind, crossed a bridge over one of the dozens of famous old Amsterdam canals, and begun strolling down one of the quaint old streets filled with ornate medieval merchants' buildings. The stranger gradually slowed down and stopped. He turned to look up at one of the buildings. Trent saw that they were now standing in front of the National Holocaust Museum.

"The point is, Mr. Carter, that Septum has existed for more than a hundred years now, dating back to a point right after the end of the Great War—World War

I. All of Europe was devastated by that horrific war, and the one after it, and rebuilding itself and coming back to some semblance of normalcy was next to impossible."

He paused and looked around the street, smiling at its pleasures. "Beautiful architecture, wouldn't you say, Mr. Carter?"

"Yes. Very nice." Trent glanced at his watch impatiently.

"Amsterdam was, thankfully, spared most of the destruction that ravaged Europe in the first two world wars."

"The first two?" Trent asked.

"Well, one never knows, does one? At least most countries realized that the old system of kingdoms and the old alliances could no longer be trusted for preventing such disaster. So, a small group of like-minded individuals, from many walks of life—business, politics, the military, science, and the arts—came together, in private, and forged the beginnings of an organization that could operate behind the scenes, across national borders, and above and beyond all political fluctuations and insanity."

"I've heard of such a thing, but mostly in the movies—a shadow government, or star chamber—a bunch of elite, wealthy snobs who think they know all the answers and what's best for everyone else, right?"

The man looked away and thought for a moment. "Yes. You are absolutely right. That's what it was, but only at the beginning. And perhaps that is exactly why it failed so miserably in its infancy."

The man gestured across the street, toward a beautifully maintained white stone façade of what appeared to be an old theater built in Romanesque Revival style. Its entrance was marked with high classic archways. "Shall we?" asked the man called Septum, before moving to cross the street. Trent looked up as they went and saw the name Hollandsche Shouwburg engraved at the top of the third story. He checked his watch again.

"You think we have time for the theater?" he asked.

The Septum agent ignored the question and walked up to the double glass doors, holding one open for Trent. "You would probably be surprised to learn that someone like Adolf Hitler was once associated with my predecessors."

"Not so much," Trent said, stepping into a narrow lobby and looking around. "Come to think of it, now that I've seen first hand what your bunch is capable of, on a smaller scale, I'm not really surprised at all that you'd count old Adolf as an ancestor of yours."

"Don't be so smug, Mr. Carter. Hitler fooled the entire world, for a while, including your country's isolationist leaders who, at first, hailed him as a possible savior of Europe. Let's just say that we all learned our lessons too late."

As they stepped into the theater, Trent was surprised to see that the lobby didn't lead into an auditorium; rather, the back wall was missing completely. The granite floor led to a wide outdoor courtyard with no roof and entirely open to the elements. Recesses lined both sides of the original walls and held dark stone tablets into which had been chiseled countless names. A few other tourists roamed the plaza slowly and conversed respectfully in hushed whispers. At the far end of the plaza stood an immense onyx obelisk, in front of which burned what appeared to be an eternal flame of sorts.

"What is this place?" whispered Trent. "An old church? I thought it was supposed to be a theater."

"It was, once." The man had removed his hat respectfully and brushed back his graying hair. He pointed toward one of the stone tablets on the wall. "The names belonged to 104,000 members of 6,700 families—Dutch Jewish victims of the Nazi holocaust. The theater became a staging area for the Gestapo as they processed them for shipment to the concentration camps." The man shook his head sadly. "No one tried to stop them—not even Septum. That is to our eternal shame, Mr. Carter."

Trent's mouth had gone dry as he pictured the hundreds and thousands of helpless men, women, and children who for hours and possibly days had been crowded into this relatively small space. He could only guess at their appalling sanitary conditions, not to mention the lack of food and water, while they awaited an unimaginable fate.

After a few more minutes, Trent's guide turned abruptly to the exit. A few minutes later they were back on the street and headed back toward the gardens.

"Why did you show me that place?"

"I cannot fault you for thinking unkindly of Septum and me, Mr. Carter. As I alluded to earlier, you met only the few bad apples. Unfortunately, most of the agents you had dealings with are exactly the ones we are constantly on guard to ferret out of the organization—to clean house, so to speak, and build a wall behind us, much as the nautilus does when it builds a *septum* behind itself as it grows. It's exactly that lesson that we didn't learn until it was too late again, when Hitler seized power and initiated a genocidal war against the world. After that, we said *never again*. We learned to operate more cautiously, go much deeper behind the curtains, if you will, to assimilate ourselves more expertly into the shadows, and to operate to solve problems that mere governments are too lethargic or unwilling to resolve."

"Sounds like the right hand never wanting to know what the left is doing."

"Yes! Precisely. I had never thought of it in quite that way, but yes."

"So, tell me—just who were all those supposed noble agents of yours, those murderers who tried to wreak havoc in my own backyard? How did you latch on to those model citizens? The one we did a background check on—the one called de Groot who was your agent murdered while trying to dig up that old grave—happened to have the DNA of a long-time dead UN peacekeeper. What's that all about?"

Septum was silent for a few moments. For some reason, Trent felt a deep sadness from the man.

"Try as we might, our profiling efforts in our recruiting do not always uncover the fatal flaws we would like them to. The traitorous men who assassinated Laird Bouwmeester were renegades—only after the money, in the end. But they were also skilled professionals. You and your friend Ferguson, quite surprisingly, did a magnificent job of giving them the final justice they all richly deserved."

"Surprisingly?"

"Yes. I must say, I am amazed that you survived."

Trent frowned. "Not all of us did," he replied curtly.

The Septum agent was quiet for a moment. "I apologize for being insensitive. Yes, your friend will be missed, I am sure. But it may be some small comfort to you to know that most of the other co-conspirators, at least on this end, have also been taken care of. Please don't ask me how."

"Taken care of—like Gert Vos was taken care of?"

"Yes," the man responded, his face passive. "Like Gert Vos."

"I assume, then, that you were also behind all the sudden confiscation of evidence—the disappearance of bodies, the computer drive, and the like?"

The stranger shrugged again and smiled but didn't answer. As they walked back through the botanical gardens, Trent looked across the way and spied Maggie, Britt, and Ilsa in the distance, walking toward the café. The two men stopped in the shadows and watched from a distance. Trent nodded toward the women.

"De Jaager, too?" asked Trent. "You recruited her?"

The man called Septum took a long deep breath and looked toward the patio, where Britt and Ilsa were laughing. "My best and most reliable agent, actually. I recruited them both, you know—Britt and her brother, Cobus." He turned his head and raised his eyebrows slightly at Trent, as if unsure at first whether to continue. "Another disclosure then, Mr. Carter; I am their real father."

Trent stared at him, clenching his teeth, then shook his head. "Nothing says *love* quite like teaching the family business to your kids." He nodded toward Britt. "At least she's still alive."

The stranger's perpetual smile left his face and a cloud darkened it. "Now who is being insensitive, Mr. Carter? That seems to be yet another thing we have in common—we seem to know how to drag our loved ones into our work—to their ultimate peril."

Trent suddenly knew the man was referring to Vicky, and his mood darkened further. "Yeah, well, you seem to know an awful lot about my family and our personal history," he snapped. "I'm just a little at a disadvantage there." He paused, then continued. "So humor me. Just what was this all about, really? I mean, I know about most of what was on that thumb drive—some old letters and documents referring to some 150-year-old political intrigue involving a corrupt governor of New Mexico. But that can't possibly have been of interest to anyone today, especially some clandestine society of spies from the Netherlands. So, I figure this all had something to do with, what . . . mining? Military secrets? Industrial espionage?"

The Septum agent paused. Instead of answering, he pulled another card out of his pocket, took out a pen, wrote something on the back of the card, and then handed it to Trent.

"I would have preferred for you to not have seen the information on that thumb drive, Mr. Carter, or to have gotten involved in any of this at all. Nevertheless, I suspect that no more intrigue will happen in your corner of the world. But knowing what you now know, I would ask that you help us keep an eye on what happens there."

"In *my* corner of the world, that is."

"Yes. You never know what may suddenly transpire unexpectedly. And if so, well . . . just call this number immediately if you sense anything out of the ordinary—anything at all."

"Like what?"

"You will know it when it happens."

"Like something that only a powerful, mysterious shadow organization can deal with effectively?"

"Yes. Something like that."

"Not too helpful, Mister ummm. . . . What did you say your name was again?"

"Good try, Mr. Carter. Good try. But here's a more helpful hint, perhaps: There was once an old land deed to the Ute Indian tribe. . . ."

"What about it?"

"Do you, by any chance, know its whereabouts? It's actually the one loose end my people have not been able to tie up."

"No, of course not. I don't even know what you're talking about."

"What about the old map to the Vega gold mine? I believe your department confiscated an old photograph with the map drawn on the back—from Gert Vos, I believe?"

Trent hesitated. "No. I don't have any idea about that, either."

"Oh, come now, Sheriff Carter. Please do not insult my intelligence.

"*Deputy* Carter—not Sheriff. And anyway, not even that anymore, since I retired from the department."

The man smiled again. "Of course you did. Perhaps, then, it was a slip of the tongue. Or perhaps I speak of those things *which are not as though they were*—something from the Apostle Paul's writings, yes? Romans 4:17, I believe. Or, perhaps my sources, which are better than you could ever guess, inform me that you are about to be appointed by your governor to a certain office that has remained vacant for far too long, since the loss of your friend, Sheriff Ferguson. So again I say, please do not insult me. After decades in this business, I know many things, and I can read a lie as well as I know that you can. I'm not yet sure whether you know anything about the old deed, but you *do* have knowledge of the photograph and its map, do you not?"

Trent stared silently at the agent for a long time, then reached into his pocket, and produced the old, dog-eared photograph with Clay Allison's faded treasure map on the back. He handed it to the agent, and then watched as the man studied the photo closely before pointing to one of the subjects standing at the bar. "You, of course, know who this is, don't you?"

Trent leaned forward and took a quick look. "That's a gentleman named Frank Springer, I believe. He was evidently involved in quite a lot in my corner of the world, as you put it, way back when—lawyer of some sort.

"Lawyer, rancher, educator, philanthropist, scientist. It may surprise you that Mr. Springer is also quite well known in my circles. It was he who discovered the fossilized nautilus shell I referred to on his ranch land near Cimarron. Springer was not only instrumental in setting legal precedence in land reforms, but he also put together one of the most enviable collections of paleontological findings of the past century. He also went on to form a society of like-minded individuals who were dedicated to—how did you put it so well—*the right hand not knowing what the left was doing?*"

"So, you're saying that Frank Springer founded *Septum?*"

"Not in its present structure, no. Septum is now much more far-reaching and, shall we say, operational than when it was created; much more than its original founders ever imagined. Yes, my agency dates back to Mr. Springer's visits to my country to meet with the Dutch land grant owners, in the early 20th century. But he was merely the catalyst that gave a few good people pause to think creatively, and gave them a springboard to grow from. World history, like the old Maxwell Land Grant's history, is rife with needless killing and overreaching—and greed—and so the world continues. Although the majority of the old land grant has by now dwindled and has been parceled and sold away, Septum has evolved into something much more important—a protective agency crucial to the world today. It is dedicated to maintaining balance, order, and a certain separation of powers in the world, and all while staying quietly in the shadows. We failed miserably when Hitler and his cronies came to power, but we didn't have the resources we now have. Since then, we have managed to keep things relatively quiet, allowing wounds to heal, for almost a hundred years."

"*Quiet*, you say?" asked Trent incredulously. "You mean like Korea, Vietnam, the Middle East? That sort of *quiet?*"

"Well, yes. There continue to be *wars and rumors of war*—isolated conflicts, at worst."

The man called Septum adjusted his hat and coat. "I must take my leave of you. But look around us, Mr. Carter. People all over the world are busy living and dying. And people like you and me will always be touched by death. You have experienced it on several levels already, as have I. But my job—and now yours too, it would seem—is to help keep things relatively calm for at least another hundred years or so. A noble venture, wouldn't you agree?"

Trent's forehead began to tingle. *That's all bullshit!* came a sudden voice in his head that sounded an awful lot like Ben Ferguson's.

"That's all bullshit," Trent duly repeated, his voice low and calm.

"What was that?"

"You heard me. Life is much more than good guys against bad guys, or trying to figure out who's who in that regard. It has to be. We have the ability to overcome evil—true evil—to face the real enemy who roams the earth. And what's more," he paused, looking over to Maggie and Ilsa as the music of their laughter reached him as they admired each other's purchases of the day. "I don't believe your bullshit story about what really happened in New Mexico. I think you have conveniently glossed some things over. In fact, I think I deserve to know the real truth."

"The *truth?*" The stranger laughed, and then tapped the side of his head with a forefinger. "Here's the only truth that I know: *'Be sober, be vigilant; because your adversary the devil, as a roaring lion, walketh about, seeking whom he may devour.'* First Peter 5, verse 8, I believe. Yes, I know my scripture also, Mr. Carter. And Peter wrote some eloquent truth, don't you think? So let's just be satisfied with *that* truth, shall we? Goodbye, *Sheriff* Carter."

The stranger turned and walked away. Trent called after him. "It was you, then, wasn't it? You who had Bouwmeester's security detail infiltrated, and the helicopter sabotaged, and had him killed, along with the others on that aircraft? Almost killed his daughter there, too, who you have supposedly sworn to protect! You, who found the gold at the bottom of the grave? Why didn't you just take the gold at the beginning, huh? Why all the killing, the subterfuge?"

The stranger stopped in his tracks and turned around, staring at Trent as if reassessing him. He slowly walked back toward him, his hands thrust deep in his overcoat pockets. "Not all of us are the enemy, Mr. Carter. Some who walk among us want to blow up the world and all of us with it. And I think that you know why—for money. The old sickness is on your side of the ocean as well as mine. Others of us—I, and I hope you—know just enough of the danger to build barriers—like the *nautilus*, if you will—to try to hide the sins of the past and cure the infections of the present, to try and close the doors others have forced open— the doors that should always remain shut—and then to try to help the world to move on."

The man from Septum stopped just a few inches from Trent. "But those sins don't always get contained, do they, Mr. Carter? You want to know about the real enemy, then? The one who still hovers, back in your world? Hasn't it occurred to you yet? Haven't you guessed it?"

"No. I was hoping you would enlighten me."

"Wasn't it convenient and timely that Laird Bouwmeester visited Colfax County at the exact moment that an old outlaw's grave had been discovered? Not because of some supposed interest in American Western history, or delving into his grandfather's tales of some old Spanish land grant that had been pretty much powerless for the last fifty years. No, Bouwmeester had to do what he was going to do, but go about it legally—at least on the surface. Wasn't it oddly coincidental that he would choose that exact moment to meet with your current state governor, Cha'risa Thompson, to discuss some mysterious business—a deed to some old Indian land that you claim you have no knowledge of, but that possibly involves you more than you might think? Was it just coincidental that Bouwmeester then chartered a helicopter, the flight plan of which just happened to follow the same route as the one on this mysterious, long-lost treasure map?" He held up the old photograph and waved it.

"And isn't it curious that he would give his own daughter the computer drive for safekeeping that just happened to contain the details of that lost mine and an old gunfighter's grave where Clay Allison's gold horde lay hidden; a piece of information that could end up costing his daughter's life? Tell me, Mr. Carter. What sort of a monster would do all that, if not perhaps another Hitler in the making?"

Trent remembered his conversation at the governor's reception with Bouwmeester regarding Chunk Colbert's grave and what had been found there—and more importantly, what had *not* been found there, because the authorities had no idea that treasure lay another 18 inches *under* the corpse. He looked at the agent.

"So spit it out, already. You're still not tying it all together for me. What are you saying—Bouwmeester was behind it all?"

"Very good, Mr. Carter. I had almost given up on your deductive skills. You see, Laird Bouwmeester needed a great deal of wealth to pursue his political ambitions. So, he fell in with a group of mercenaries who helped promulgate and prolong a civil war in the Balkans years ago, hoping to gain the bounty and spoils of that war to fund his dreams; but the spoils never materialized, and the debt that he now owed these men still existed—a hundred-fold. And unless they got their money, they were going to expose him to the world as a fraud and a political terrorist. His promising chances of one day becoming President of the European Union would have disintegrated in his hands, and possibly along with his life as well. So, the proverbial *Lost Gold of Colfax County* was to become his last chance at paying off his blood-soaked debts to those lost soldiers of fortune, to save his own selfish neck. Very romantic, adventurous, and heroic of him, don't you think?"

Trent stepped over to a nearby bench and sat down, somewhat shocked. "Except, he never counted on you and your people showing up to put a stop to him, did he?" he said. "He had your son Cobus murdered, didn't he? That's why you had Bouwmeester killed—in revenge."

"No, not revenge," said the man. He glanced over toward the café, where the three women sat now drinking coffee. He nodded toward Britt. "My children knew the risks when they were recruited. Yes, Laird Bouwmeester was the one who orchestrated Cobus' murder—but the others turned on him when he couldn't produce the gold. Oh, we pointed the way to him, but his own mercenaries murdered him."

"And now he's being hailed in this country as a national hero. Where's the justice in that?"

"No one will ever need to know what he did. It's not part of our mandate to expose the tyrant, only to neutralize him. Therefore, we orchestrated his downfall, and now he is a much-needed hero of the Dutch people. . . ." He looked over toward Ilsa. "Yes, the ultimate irony, but not entirely a bad thing.

"Except now, Septum has all the gold, doesn't it? So just who are the mercenaries now, Sir? In the end, you are no better than any of the rest of them were—the old Santa Fe Ring, Clay Allison, the land grant regulators, your soldiers of fortune, . . . Bouwmeester."

"No. No better, but certainly no worse. Just as I said, not all of us are the enemy. But some of us have to continue to live in the shadows and be prepared at a moment's notice to act—to save our respective countries from the embarrassments they cause themselves, from the Bouwmeester of the world; to build more barriers around the sin and hide it behind a firmly locked door—a septum—and bury it deep. It can be very expensive work. But be assured that it will always be money well spent."

The man called Septum turned to Trent one last time. "I know you are not fully convinced, and I know you are a dedicated man of the law. But in case you are tempted to try to ensnare me, Mr. Carter, you will never be able to prove any of this; and you will never see me again." He turned and began walking away into the deepening shadows of the afternoon, calling back over his shoulder. "Time for us both to shut this particular door, Mr. Carter—shut it, lock it, and move on. For me, back to my shadows. For you? Well, back to your beautiful Maggie, your ranch, and your father Walter and daughter Sophie. And again, I believe congratulations are in order—very soon."

Trent's mouth dropped open and he wondered again at just how much the stranger really knew about him. *Sheriff*, the man had said to him. *I wonder.*

#

After Britt and Ilsa walked Trent and Maggie back to their boutique hotel along a quiet canal, Britt turned to them both. "I must also say my goodbyes, Mr. Carter—Trent." She reached out and shook his hand warmly.

"Also?" asked Trent.

"Yes," Britt smiled knowingly. "I understand you met my father earlier."

Trent raised an eyebrow. "It wouldn't surprise me at all if you had arranged that little meeting."

Britt responded coyly. "You deserve to know the truth."

"I get the feeling I only learned the slightest bit of it. Seems like you people still have plenty of secrets to wrap around you and keep you cozy and warm at night." Trent nodded toward Ilsa, who was hugging Maggie goodbye. "What about her? She still in danger?"

"Don't worry," Britt said, keeping her voice low. "Ilsa will be quite safe. She will always be under our protection, and she will never know the truth about her father. That would be too cruel to her. I do hope you will not think too badly of us—of me—and what we do. I know you do not completely approve."

"No, I do not. Your little secret society can only lead to anarchy and chaos in the end."

"Yes, perhaps. But sometimes a little chaos is required to break apart what doesn't work, before you can build what does. I prefer to think of chaos as often being a necessary part of justice, something I know that you believe very strongly in also, Trent—sometimes at whatever cost, yes?"

Trent didn't answer, but instead began thinking of all that his dedication had, indeed, cost him, and wondered whether it was still worth it. His reverie was suddenly broken as Britt stepped up and kissed him lightly on his cheek.

"Goodbye, Trent Carter," she whispered in his ear. "It has been . . . interesting." He was only slightly aware that she had discretely slipped something into his coat pocket.

Britt smiled and nodded to an equally surprised Maggie as she walked slowly down the steps of the hotel, where she stopped and waited as Ilsa rushed up and also hugged Trent around the neck for a long time. Trent embraced her and looked over her head to spy Maggie watching and shaking her head with a raised eyebrow, crossed arms, and a bemused look on her face. Ilsa suddenly broke free without a word and ran to join Britt. Trent watched her leave with an unexpected mixture of concern and emotion. "Watch out for the roaring and ravenous lions, Little One," he murmured after her.

Maggie walked up and nudged her husband hard in the ribs.

"Ouch! What was that for?"

"I think that it's way past time I got you back home, Cowboy, where I can make you forget about these pretty Dutch girls."

Trent grabbed her, took her in his arms, and kissed her long and deep.

"What Dutch girls?"

#

(Santa Fe, New Mexico)

Five weeks later Trent and Maggie walked into the New Mexico State Capitol building in Santa Fe, where they were ushered into an upstairs antechamber just outside the governor's office and offered seats.

"The governor will be with you shortly," said the young and overly efficient male assistant who had escorted them. "May I offer you a coffee, or a sparkling water, perhaps?"

"You may offer," answered Trent. "But no thanks."

"Excuse me?" the assistant asked, clearly confused.

"Don't mind him," Maggie responded, smiling warmly at the young man while kicking the edge of Trent's boot with her foot. "He's just being an ass." The assistant composed himself, gave them both his perfunctory and insincere smile, spun on his heel, and disappeared down a narrow hallway. "You behave yourself!" Maggie murmured to her husband once they were alone. "What's gotten into you?"

"Sorry," Trent answered. "Guess I just don't appreciate official unctuousness. Never have, never will." His fingers drummed the arm of his chair impatiently as he looked around the richly decorated room. Expensive-looking wood-paneled walls were hung with massive works of Southwestern art depicting scenes from various geographic areas around the state. His eyes rested on one particular oil landscape of a sunset exploding through the thunderheads rolling over what had to be the Sangre de Cristo Mountains. The painting seemed to pull him into its overwhelming vista, and he was momentarily transported to the horrific events that he had been embroiled in the previous autumn, somewhere up in those same rugged canyons and mountains. He leaned forward slowly and squinted, having made out what seemed to be the tiny figure of an Indian on horseback, silhouetted along one of the distant ridges. For the briefest moment, Trent could have sworn that the figure turned his head and smiled at him. He shook his head, and then turned back to Maggie, who also seemed lost in thought and was chewing absently on a fingernail.

"You sure you're okay going through with this?" he asked.

"Hmm? Oh, yes. I am more than okay with it. This has to been dealt with, don't you think?"

"Yes, I certainly do. But I'm just thinking this might be hard on you, being friends and all."

Maggie picked at a thread on her dress. "Yes, I've thought of that, too." She looked back at her husband, a look of calm self-assurance on her face. "But this needs to be confronted—once and for all, friendship be damned." She nodded at his jacket. "You have it with you, right?"

Trent smiled at his wife and patted his jacket pocket. "Yep. Right here."

The wait was not long. Five minutes later, one of the heavy double doors carved with the great seal of the State of New Mexico swung open and the unctuous assistant appeared again, holding it open and gesturing for them to enter, as if it were an invitation to the inner sanctum. As they did so, Trent returned the young man's forced smile with one of his own, and mouthed an exaggerated but silent *thank you*.

"Sheriff and Mrs. Carter to see you, Madam Governor," announced the assistant before shutting the huge door silently behind them, as if closing a vault.

"Maggie, and Sheriff Carter! So wonderful to see you both again." Governor Cha'risa Thompson was rounding the corner of her huge mahogany desk, which was surprisingly bare save for a small, neat stack of paperwork, a laptop computer, and on one corner a set of small sculptures of Navajo dancers exquisitely carved from exotic wood. She met her visitors halfway across the large expanse of rich, dark plum carpeting, whose deep pile seemed to beg Trent's boots to sink into it. She was dressed in a modest but finely tailored gray pantsuit, accessorized by equally modest but exquisitely designed turquoise and silver earrings and a matching necklace.

The governor, with a slightly more sincere smile on her face than had been on her assistant's, shook hands firmly with Trent and gave Maggie a big hug before motioning them to a plush loveseat placed strategically in the middle of the floor. She then took the matching loveseat across from them. Between them sat a massive, irregularly shaped wooden coffee table that looked as if it had been hewn from a single huge log. It was five inches thick, seven feet long, and roughly three feet wide; and it sported an almost obscene mirror polish. To Trent, it seemed like a bastion between them.

"I am thrilled that you have come all this way just to say hi," said Governor Thompson. "And may I say, Sheriff, that I am equally thrilled that you agreed to accept my appointment as the newest senior law enforcement official of Colfax

County. In all honesty, I had been led to believe that you probably wouldn't take the job—after all that you have been through, that is."

"And who would have led you to believe such a thing?" Maggie asked, rather pointedly. Trent noticed the governor's dutiful smile start to slip. He resisted the urge to chuckle.

"Well, I suppose it was more of an assumption on my part. I can't say that anyone in particular actually advised me of that—just a figure of speech, I guess." She put her official smile back on. "But still, I can't be happier that you accepted, Sheriff. The state doesn't have a more qualified person, in my opinion. And, of course, I was deeply saddened by the untimely death of Sheriff Ferguson—a fine and dedicated public servant."

"Thank you, Governor," said Trent, with a quick glance at Maggie. "I was truly surprised and honored by your appointment. And I do not—and will not—take my duties lightly . . . in the least."

"And I would expect no less. So, how else may I be of help to you today? For some reason, I sense that this is somewhat more than a social visit." She flashed Maggie another bright smile, which Maggie did not return, instead holding her gaze.

Trent unbuttoned his sports coat, reached inside, and pulled out a single sheet of paper folded length-wise. He laid it on the coffee table and pushed it gently across the polished surface.

"What's this?" Governor Thompson asked, glancing from Maggie to Trent, then back to the document. She picked it up and unfolded it. Her eyes suddenly widened and she sucked in her breath.

"Just a little something we thought you would be interested in . . . *Governor,*" said Maggie coldly.

"Yes, and on behalf of our mutual friend, the late Minister of Education and History, Laird Bouwmeester, of the Netherlands," added Trent. He hated to admit to himself that he was rather enjoying the sight of Governor Thompson's face suddenly draining of color.

She looked up in shock. "Where the hell did you get this?" she asked, her voice husky with emotion and dropping almost to a whisper. "Do you know how long I have been looking for this?"

"Yes, I can well imagine," said Trent. "Of course, you will notice that this is not the original—merely a copy, which, I might add, you are most welcome to keep."

"But how did you get this? Where is the original?"

"The original is safe and sound, Madam Governor, I assure you."

As Trent and Maggie were flying home from Amsterdam, he had begun to wonder about the whereabouts of the supposed deed of land to the Ute Indian Tribe mentioned by the Man Called Septum. Something about it nagged him, until he remembered the mysterious document, hidden behind the torn paper backing of Walter's old 8 X 10 framed photograph—a frame that Clay Allison had gifted to Jonathon Carter almost 140 years earlier.

Governor Thompson suddenly stood up and glared at Trent, her face flushed and eyes flashing. "What is the meaning of this? Is this some sort of joke?"

"Sit down, Cha'risa," said Maggie, her calm, steady voice matching the cold steel of her eyes.

"What? You're in on this, too, I suppose!"

"I said *sit your ass down*—Governor! You haven't heard one quarter of what we came to say, yet." Maggie's voice had dropped to a menacing growl. Trent raised his eyebrows, then smiled, and looked down at his hands. He had learned that when his wife got serious, it was best to let her get it out of her system.

"How dare you speak to me that way, Margot Van Ryan!" Governor Thompson protested; but Trent noticed that she promptly sat down. "After all of our years of friendship!"

"No! How dare *you* abuse the authority and trust of the people that put you into this office!" continued Maggie, finally venting what she had held pent up since walking into the room. "I was so proud to have served on your election campaign, Cha'risa; so very proud that we had finally elected the first Native American woman governor in this state. I remember when we were in school together, how we both talked about how wonderful it would be to one day have the interests of our indigenous peoples protected by the government; then to have that dream actually become a reality. And not only to protect and preserve Indian culture, but to fully represent it, through you, Cha'risa. I was never so proud—and then . . . this." Maggie gestured toward the document. She then looked down, grasped her husband's hand, and looked back up at the governor. "And by the way, the name's Mrs. Margot Carter."

"This means nothing, proves nothing," muttered Governor Thompson, tossing the paper onto the table. "Simply a photocopy of some nebulous, outdated historical document, the true existence of which I fully doubt! And even so, what significance does it have to me?"

"Well, you're right about that, Governor—on the surface it would appear to have no significance whatsoever." Trent paused as he reached into his jacket pocket and pulled out a small device. "Until you listen to this." He laid a small digital recorder—the one Britt de Jaager had slipped into his pocket in Amsterdam—on the table and switched it on. Soon, the immediate space between them was filled with the undeniable voices of Governor Thompson, the late Laird Bouwmeester, and two representatives of the Southern Ute Indian Tribe. Trent sat back and watched the governor for a reaction, and she did not disappoint him. Her face gradually deflated, and she leaned back heavily on the couch as the recorded discussion of a supposed private meeting began to lay out the details of a plan being hatched between the two leaders—a plan that involved the locating and executing of an old deed from Lucien B. Maxwell. This special deed, dated just before his sale of the Maxwell Land Grant to a consortium of British and Dutch investors in the early 1870s, supposedly had carved out more than 180,000 acres of prime land and gifted it to the Ute Nation. Before it could be properly recorded, however, Maxwell had fallen ill, and the document was thought to have been lost to the ages. But recent research obtained by Bouwmeester himself indicated that the document had, indeed, survived Maxwell, and had been traced to Governor Samuel Axtell's Santa Fe Ring. After that, it had somehow come into the possession of the famous Gentleman Gunfighter, Clay Allison, who, rumor had it, had hidden it somewhere in plain sight—supposedly in the possession of one of his close friends.

Further research produced a list of Allison's presumed friends, which had proved to be quite short but had included such prominent names as Frank Springer, Henri Lambert, Tom Stockton, and a certain Jonathon S. Carter, a local county sheriff. Bouwmeester suggested that a methodical and clandestine search of the former homes and business properties of these people—and more particularly those of their present-day descendents—might prove fruitful in producing the original deed. He had indicated that his hired team of professionals could accomplish the task with minimal consequences.

"Turn it off," said Governor Thompson softly.

"Why? It's just about to get interesting," said Trent.

"I said turn it off! I don't need to hear anymore." She had put a hand up to her mouth and was staring into space. She finally looked back at Trent. "Where did you get that?"

"Ah, that would be telling, now, wouldn't it? Let's just say that, like you, I have my impeccable sources."

"You've listened to it all then, I presume?"

"Yes. Every last word."

"Then I don't need to tell you that my part in this was only with the best of intentions."

"What I do know is that, if Bouwmeester had indeed been successful in locating the original deed, you were to be given the document to record in public record, thereby nullifying a portion of the Dutch claim to the land known as Ute Park, and its environs. In exchange, you pledged to give Bouwmeester all the mineral rights—which would have included a certain old gold mine that he had been feverishly looking for."

"Except," added Maggie, "we all know that such a recordation, after 150 years, would, at best, cloud the title to all that land, and, at worst, might have been looked on as a fraudulent filing."

"So, how could that have possibly benefitted me?" asked Governor Thompson.

"Indeed," said Trent. He reached over to turn the recorder back on. "Shall I again refresh our collective memories?" The governor shook her head and waved her hand at him. "No, I thought not. Because what you actually planned to do—and still could, of course, if you had the original deed—was to goad the various concerned tribes into creating such a political outcry and eventual shit storm surrounding the Ute Park land, that it would have to eventually be dragged into the court system to be resolved, perhaps again all the way to the Supreme Court. By that time, the cost to the taxpayers and the current landowners would be astronomical, until they were forced to settle, or quitclaim their interests."

"With our noble, Native American governor herself, selflessly leading the charge," added Maggie, "and giving you a glowing legacy in return, as the savior of the tribal heritage, along with enough political currency to take you ever higher. Who knows? Perhaps all the way to the White House—as the first indigenous woman president."

"Yes," said the governor. "And giving the Ute people back what they had already been given! What is so wrong with that? You don't believe that land reparations are reasonable, after hundreds of years of genocide and injustice?"

"Depends on what you call reasonable," said Trent. "Is it reasonable or just to arbitrarily take the land away from its current owners, who weren't at all to blame, without a thought or a methodical plan to compensate them? Or maybe even allow the owners to make that decision themselves and maybe donate back part of the land in exchange for some sort of a tax consideration?"

"That's not the point," exclaimed the governor, standing up and glaring down at Trent and Maggie. "It's long past time for white America to make things right— and be forced to pay for its violent crimes against my people!"

"Against *your* people? I thought you were elected to represent all the citizens of the state."

"That's a pathetic, short-sighted, and frankly racist answer, Cha'risa," said Maggie. "Two wrongs don't make a right. It took hundreds of years of wrongdoing to get to this point. It isn't going to be resolved overnight. And yes, it's a very noble cause, but one that deserves a well-thought-out plan."

"This *was* a well-thought-out plan!"

"No," said Trent. "It wasn't. It was a well-thought-out conspiracy. You started out on the right path, but then it turned into burglary, robbery, and finally murder and a cover-up, to which you are, at best, an accessory after the fact. At worst . . . well, let's just say you went way too far, Governor."

Governor Thompson was quiet for a good while, then looked back at Trent with contempt. "If this is the way you intend to exercise your new authorities, Mr. Carter, I will have no choice but to have you declared incompetent and stripped of your office, immediately. Your past mental and physical disabilities are well known. I should have taken them more into consideration."

"You're not stripping anyone of anything, Cha'risa," said Maggie, finally standing up and walking around to face her former college roommate. "The stories of my husband's past professional problems are anecdotal, at best, and his medical history is, of course, protected by law. So, please don't create yet one more legal and political blunder by trying to open that particular can of worms." Maggie lowered her voice to a menacing whisper. "But here's what you *are* going to do . . . *Governor*. First, you are going to create an executive panel to begin formulating a completely realistic, and legal, long-term plan for the gradual repatriation of tribal lands throughout the state. Secondly, this committee will be bi-partisan and will also be made up of representatives from all the major tribes in the state."

Maggie walked back around to stand next to her husband. "And thirdly, since modern land disputes are now fought in court rather than by a lynch mob, you will announce shortly your endowment of a new annual scholarship, in perpetuity, to the state's schools of higher education, for members of any tribe who wish to pursue a degree in tribal law." She paused and folded her arms. "Can you remember all that, Cha'risa, or should I write it all down for you?"

"Just one more little thing," added Trent as he finally stood up, buttoning his jacket. "After you have put all that in place, Governor, you'll also announce that you have no intention of running for a second term and that you are stepping down permanently from politics. In fact, if you decide you need to step down earlier, that would not hurt my feelings at all."

Governor Thompson glared at them both. "And just why would I do such a thing, pray tell?" She spread her hands to indicate the copy of the deed and the recording device. "Why in hell would I be compelled to do anything that you've demanded? None of this will actually stand up in court, you know?"

"Perhaps. But if you don't, Cha'risa, then I won't even need to take you to court to begin making your life a living hell." Trent took out his wallet, removed the business card that the man called Septum had scribbled on, and tossed it on top of the image of the deed. "And if you have any more doubts at all that your political aspirations are over, just give the number on this card a quick call."

"Oh. And for the record, Governor," added Maggie, "I'd make it a private call . . . and be prepared to pay international phone rates—out of your own pocket this time."

EPILOGUE
Field Of Holes, Part 2

(18 months later – Ponil River Valley)

Trent stood on the side of the slope and gazed out across the broad meadow of blue-green grama grass that gently rippled below him in the spring afternoon breeze. Behind him he could hear the wind sighing through the high branches of ponderosa pine and aspen trees. Farther to the south and east he spied the intermittent silver threads of Ponil Creek, which snaked its way and peeked through the scrub oak and piñon pine that crowded its banks. Beyond that, the distant canyon walls steadily diminished in height until the pastures contained within them spilled out upon the open plains that stretched toward Texas, which lay somewhere over the eastern horizon that was silhouetted by ancient volcanic mounds. He bent down, pulled a long stem of grass out of the ground, and stuck it between his teeth. Thrusting his fingertips into the pockets of his jeans, he smiled as laughter drifted back uphill to him.

Fifty or sixty yards away, in the middle of the meadow, an eleven-month-old boy toddled and giggled as Sophie and Maggie playfully chased him through the ankle-high grass and budding wildflowers. Trent chuckled and shook his head as the boy occasionally tumbled headlong into Maggie's arms, squealing with delight as she then swooped him up into the air before pulling him close to nuzzle his neck. Nearby lay the remains of a picnic lunch spread out over blankets on the ground.

A little farther, near the ruins of an old adobe house, Hector and Walter slowly walked and searched the area intently, stepping carefully and poking the ground with walking sticks. Hector stopped suddenly and called out to the older man, who walked briskly over to join him. Walter excitedly pointed with his stick before slowly bending down on a knee. Trent squinted, started to go join them, and then stopped himself. *Better to let him have a moment or two first,* he thought to himself.

Trent groaned and slowly lowered himself to the ground, stretching his legs out in front of him and leaning back on his elbows as he looked around and took a deep breath of the clean mountain air. Spring had decided to come early to northern New Mexico, especially up here in Ponil Canyon, four miles or so north of the sleepy little town of Cimarron. The heavy runoff from the winter's snow, coupled with the early spring rains, had brought abundant new life springing forth all around them, like a testimony to the Creator's magnificent plan—a perfect cycle of hope, life, aging, and finally death that had repeated itself over and over, year after year, ever since the dawn of time.

The family had decided that it was a perfect day to get out of the confines of the house after a long, cold winter and to get up into the foothills of the Sangre de Cristo Mountains. It was also a good excuse to pursue a long-desired dream of Walter's—to come search for his great-grandparents' final resting places here on the former homestead once known as the Delgado Rancho. Trent had called the current landowner and gotten permission for them to come exploring. On their drive over here, Walter had explained his vague recollection, as a boy, of the small private funeral for his great-grandfather—Papaw Salal, he had called him—that had occurred here, somewhere behind the old house. At that time, one could still find a couple of the weathered old crosses that had marked the older family graves located here. Now there was very little left of either the house—save for a couple of low, fallen-down adobe walls—or of the sad little family plot.

It had also been a great day for a picnic and for letting Sophie and Hector's son, Robert Trent Armijo, run off some pent-up energy. Trent looked up and smiled broadly as he saw Maggie making her way up the slope toward him, the giggling child in her arms stretching his hands out to his grandpa. The boy had his father's black hair and coloring and his mother's hazel eyes and cute pug nose.

"Bobby insisted on coming to play with Papaw," said Maggie as she stooped over and deposited her grandson squarely onto Trent's lap. He grunted, and then wrestled the happy toddler to the ground, growling like a bear as he rubbed his whiskered face against the child's smooth cheeks. Maggie plopped down next to her husband and gathered her flowered dress around her knees. She looked back down to where the others stood looking at the old graves. "It was sweet of you to bring Walter out here. He needed this, I think."

Trent sat up again and pulled Bobby back into his lap. "Yes, I know he did." He took a long breath and then let it out slowly, looking around reflectively. "I think I needed it too, after reading all those letters of his. It gives me a definite place in time where all of that family history happened, right here—or at least all within a few miles of right here. I mean I am embarrassed, and frankly ashamed, at how little I knew of my own family's story—how important it really was." He paused and readjusted his grandson on his lap, cradling him now as the boy snuggled into his arms and gazed up sleepily at him, slurping contentedly on a thumb. Trent gazed back, his heart swelling into his throat. He looked over at Maggie and held her beautiful eyes with his. "Whataya think, Grammie?" he asked.

She smiled and then scooted next to him and leaned her head against his shoulder. Trent could feel her warmth all along his side. "I think that it hurts so good, doesn't it?" Maggie asked.

"What? What do you mean, *hurts?*"

She turned her head slightly and nodded at Bobby. "That precious little thing right there in your arms. I mean, did you ever imagine that love for something so small could be so powerful that it actually hurts?"

"So that's what I've been feeling," Trent murmured, leaning his head down against hers. He allowed his nose and lips to move over her hair and caught its lemony scent. "Guess I've been *hurting so good* for a long time now—long before this little guy came along."

"Easy, Cowboy," she said, softly elbowing him. "The children are watching."

"Why? Do you think they might know?"

"What, that we're sleeping together or something?"

"Yeah. Or something. . . ." Trent leaned down and kissed the soft wrinkles at the corner of her eye. He then peered over her head and saw his daughter looking in their direction and waving.

"Come on, you guys," Sophie called out. "You should come see this."

Trent waved back at her and then placed the palm of his hand in the small of Maggie's back and pushed to help her up. "Your turn. Come on, old man," she pronounced as she bent to gently take her now-sleeping grandson from Trent. She cradled him in the crook of an arm and used her other hand to help her husband up. Trent groaned and grimaced as he slowly made it to his feet. His latest wounds had gradually healed, but his joints and muscles still ached more than ever.

She slipped her arm through his, and they slowly strolled back downhill. As they joined the others, Trent saw where Hector had cleared away some of the grass and dirt from a group of barely discernible mounds of weed-choked earth. The evenly spaced lumps unmistakably defined the long-abandoned Delgado-Carter family cemetery that they knew had been there somewhere. Trent smiled as he saw that someone had already fashioned a new small rough-hewn cross from small branches and pushed it into the ground at the head of the largest mound, presumably Jonathon's grave. Walter glanced up as Trent and Maggie stepped near. Trent thought his father's face was a little drawn and pale. "You okay, Dad?"

Walter looked back at the graves and nodded quickly, then brushed his nose between a thumb and forefinger. He let out a ragged sigh, reached into this jacket pocket, and pulled out a folded paper. As he unfolded it, Trent recognized the old five-by-seven photograph of Jonathon Carter and his four friends, taken in the saloon of the old Clifton House a century and a half ago. Walter held out an arm and Trent grasped it to help his father kneel slowly to the ground.

"Here you go, Papaw Salal," Walter said gruffly, swiping his nose again and this time also wiping something from his cheek. "Time you got this back. Thanks for loaning it to me. I did what you asked, Papaw—kept it all safe all these years, just like you told me to." He turned his head to indicate Trent. "Oh, but the boy here knows, too. But I suppose it's okay. After all, he is my son. And guess what? He's also a sheriff, just like you were—and a damned good one, too!" He leaned over as he continued to talk and scooped away some of the dirt from the base of the cross. He then propped the photo against it before shoving some dirt back to hold it in place. "And Hector here is a cop, too. Guess it runs in the family, huh?" He sat quietly on his knees for a few more minutes.

A slight breeze picked up and moved through the grass like waves on a lake, the scent of wildflowers and pine wafting over them as they all stood silently around the burial ground. Trent looked across the meadow toward the forested ridge to the west, broken by a pile of ancient boulders there. He narrowed his eyes as he imagined a slight movement in the shadows there.

"I miss you, Papaw," Walter continued. "But I know you're with Great-Gramma María now, and that you're happy. Give her a big hug for me, will you?" Walter paused and looked away, down toward the creek that chattered in the near distance, as if he were listening to something. He bowed his head for a moment, then looked back at the image on the photo. "One other thing, Papaw . . . if you see Robert Senior there. . . ." He paused and took a deep breath. "If you see my daddy, tell him it's all okay now." Walter looked up at each of his family members in turn and smiled. "*We're* all okay."

"*Sublime gracia del Señor. . . .*" Hector began singing softly, his strong, clear tenor voice floating away on the waves of shifting grass. The tune was quite familiar; only the language was different.

Amazing grace, how sweet the sound was almost audible as Maggie and Sophie began softly humming along with Hector.

Trent squinted at the deep shadows in the trees and rocks, then suddenly opened them wide, and caught his breath. The movements he thought he had seen were still there, and the shadows were solidifying into shapes.

"*. . . que a un pecador salvo. . . .*"

Three horsemen materialized just outside the trees and stopped to be silhouetted along the ridgeline, about a hundred yards away. They held their reins loosely and sat quietly watching the little ceremony. Two of the men sat their saddles easily on large, fit horses and were dressed smartly in some sort of military uniforms from another era. They now slowly removed their broad-brimmed hats, as if with a sign of solemn respect. But it was the third man in the middle who really caught Trent's attention. He had seen him many times. The young man sat stoically, majestically, his back ramrod straight, and he rode bareback on his painted pony. His dark long hair was braided and adorned with feathers, and he was dressed in ornately beaded deerskins. He carried a longbow strung across his shoulders along with a quiver filled with arrows.

"Oh my," Trent murmured under his breath, and took an involuntary step forward and stopped. The warrior smiled and slowly moved one arm across his chest, his hand resting over his heart. He then thrust it out toward Trent, palm-side down and fingers straight, as if in salute.

"*Fui ciego mas hoy miro yo. . . .*"

"Nämpäry?" Trent whispered. He could hardly believe his eyes. His old friend was no longer old, as he had last seen him, but young and vibrant, and he sat his pony well, controlling its nervous energy expertly with his knees. He smiled down at Trent and nodded once before swinging the pony around and nudging it with his heels. Horse and rider suddenly leapt away to disappear back into the trees. "Wait!"

"Hey! Stop muttering to yourself and help me up." Feeling Walter tug on his pants leg, Trent braced himself and reached down to give his father a hand. As soon as he saw that Walter was on his feet and steady, he turned back to the shadow horsemen. But they were all gone now, like mists dissolved on the wind.

"*Perdido y Él me halló.*" Sophie had stepped over to her husband and had taken his arm as he finished singing.

"That was just lovely, Hector," said Maggie softly, swaying slowly as she rocked her sleeping grandson in her arms. "Don't you think so, Trent?"

Trent didn't answer but continued to stare off into the trees, his mouth hanging open. He willed the riders to appear again, but something inside told him that they were gone for good. Trent could only guess who the two military men were, but it was a pretty good guess. Given that they were dressed as Confederate Civil War officers—and that they had bothered to appear to him at all—he suspected that he had just seen ghosts of his own ancestors.

"Maybe we should arrange to exhume the bodies," suggested Walter.

"Why would we do that, Grandpa?" asked Sophie.

"You know, take Jonathon and Maria back and bury them in town, with the rest of the family."

"No," Trent murmured, searching the shadows along the trees once more—shadows that held more than a few secrets now. "I think that Jonathon is home right here—right where he belongs."

He took a slow, deep breath. Walking Elk—Nämpäry—had come to say goodbye. Almost two years ago now in the shadow of Mt. Baldy, the ghostly chieftain of the Southern Ute Nation had not only guided Trent through his own version of a spirit walk, but had also saved his life there, and more than once. And just as when the spirit of his first wife Vicky had said farewell to him years ago, Trent knew that he would never see the warrior again—not in this life.

"What are you looking at?" Maggie had walked over to him and leaned against his shoulder. He felt hers and Bobby's combined warmth through his shirt. "Ghosts again?"

Trent turned and smiled at them both, a lump rising again in his chest—one that hurt so good. He wrapped his arms around his wife and his grandson and held them close for a very long time.

THE END

HISTORICAL NOTES

Although this book is a work of fiction, a continuation of *Act of Contrition,* and takes a similar format in skipping back and forth between two separate timelines, the historic touchstones in *Land of My Sojourn* are much more distinct and . . . well, *historic* than the first novel.

The fictitious characters of Trent, Maggie, Walter, Hector, and Ben Ferguson should all be very familiar to readers of the first book. The most important new fictional characters introduced here include Trent and Walter's ancestors, Jonathon Salal Carter and Maria Delgado Carter as well as her father and brothers, the elderly Ute Indian Walking Elk, Ben Ferguson's daughter Jennifer, the Dutch Minister of Education and History Laird Bouwmeester and his daughter Ilsa, and their bodyguard Britt de Jaager.

It should be noted that the characters of Minister Bouwmeester and New Mexico Governor Cha'risa Thompson are *not* modeled after anyone living or dead.

Most of the other larger-than-life characters who populate the late 19th century part of this book were very real people. These include Confederate Cherokee General Isaac "Stand" Watie—who was the only American Indian promoted to the rank of general in the Civil War, and was the last Confederate general to surrender after the end of the war.

Charles Goodnight and Oliver Loving were real cattlemen who forged a major cattle drive trail from Texas through New Mexico and on into Colorado and Wyoming. (And if the episode regarding Loving being wounded by Comanche arrows and dying of gangrene sounds suspiciously similar to a scene straight out of Larry McMurtry's novel *Lonesome Dove,* it's because McMurtry modeled his characters Call and McCrae after Goodnight and Loving. Oliver Loving really did die of gangrene from a Comanche arrow, after forcing Goodnight to promise not to leave him in the New Mexican desert, and was dragged back to Texas for burial. I suppose whatever's good for Larry McMurtry is good enough for me!)

Juan Francisco "Pancho" Griego was a real settler in Colfax County, and at one time an advocate for the other Hispanic settlers' rights against the Santa Fe Ring. He was thought to have switched allegiances after his nephew, Cruz Vega, was lynched for murder, and after Griego was indeed given a slap on the wrist for gunning down members of the famed Buffalo Soldiers U.S. Cavalry in a shootout at the St. James Hotel in Cimarron.

Robert Clay Allison and his brother John did come West after the Civil War to hunt for gold in Colfax County, where he soon built a reputation as "The Gentleman Gunfighter." His exploits in real life were even more outrageous than I have depicted in the book. I deviated from history with him in that he did not actually join Goodnight and Loving in driving cattle up the Trail, an action I fabricated so that he could meet and befriend my fictional character, Jonathon. Allison is generally thought to have been in the mob that lynched the serial killer George Kennedy in Elizabethtown, and reputedly cut off the corpse's head and carried it Cimarron, much as I depicted in the book. He also was heavily involved in fighting the Santa Fe Ring during the Colfax County War, was thought to have headed up the "posse" that also lynched Cruz Vega, one of the accused assassins of Reverend Franklin Tolby, and is also thought to have assassinated Manuel Cardenas before he could stand trial for the same murder. Although Clay Allison did shoot and kill Francisco "Pancho" Griego inside the St. James Hotel, the gunfight on the street I depicted with Allison, Jonathon, Griego, Chunk Colbert, and David Crocket III did not really happen that way (although Crockett, a great nephew of the one who died at the Alamo, really existed, but was later actually killed by Sheriff Rinehart's posse in a stable in Cimarron and not by my fictional character Jonathon, obviously).

Robert Clay Allison bought a ranch in Pecos, Texas, where he finally hung up his guns, had a family, and was later found dead after his wagonload of supplies supposedly ran over him and broke his neck.

The rancher Tom Stockton really existed, and built the Clifton House, at one time one of the finest hotels/stagecoach stations on the Santa Fe Trail, south of Willow Springs, NM (now the site of the city of Raton). The gunfighter Chunk Colbert actually was shot and killed in the restaurant of the Clifton House by Clay Allison, after they shared a steak dinner, and was buried in an unmarked grave behind the hotel. To my knowledge, his grave still lies undisturbed there to this day. Any gold buried with him exists strictly within my fertile imagination. The Clifton House was abandoned when the coming of the Santa Fe Railroad put an end to the stage lines, and it did burn to the ground at the end of the 19th century; most people think it was an accidental fire set by vagrants and not from the sparks of a passing locomotive.

Richens "Uncle Dick" Wootton really did operate a toll gate on top of Raton Pass, and truly angered Charles Goodnight with his exorbitant toll of 10 cents per head of cattle, to the extent that Goodnight's subsequent cattle drives bypassed Ratón Pass entirely.

Reverend Franklin J. Tolby actually was a staunch and outspoken advocate of the settlers who homesteaded the Maxwell Land Grant, and was assassinated in Cimarron Canyon for his stand against the Santa Fe Ring. His murder touched off what became known as the Colfax County War, which lasted for twelve years, becoming the longest land dispute in American history.

Attorneys Stephen B. Elkins, Thomas B. Catron, and Governor Samuel J. Axtell (among others that I have chosen to omit from the book, for brevity) were generally considered to be the ringleaders of the infamous Santa Fe Ring, which was guilty of fomenting the conflicts that became known as the Colfax County War and the Lincoln County War (of Billy the Kid fame), two of the biggest land conspiracies in U.S. history. As depicted in the book, Governor Axtell was thought to have actually penned a letter that amounted to a "hit order" against Frank Springer, Clay Allison, and William Morley, among others.

Frank Angell was a real investigator assigned by United States Secretary of State Carl Schurz to get to the bottom of the Colfax County War. His findings were instrumental in having New Mexico Governor Samuel Axtell removed from office.

George Curry was a Colfax County rancher who was shot and wounded in the shootout at the Colfax County Courthouse yard in Springer, New Mexico, involving local ranchers and sheriff's deputies. I have taken the liberty to alter some of the details of the actual incident to fit the fictional narrative of my story. Curry went on to serve with Theodore Roosevelt's Rough Riders in the Spanish American War, served in various government positions in the Philippines, served as Governor of New Mexico from 1907 to 1910, then as one of the first congressman from the newly admitted state in 1912 in the U.S. House of Representatives. Curry County, New Mexico, is named after him.

Bosque Redondo at Fort Sumner, New Mexico, was (unfortunately) a very real place of incarceration for members of the Navajo Nation during and after the Civil War. The tragic "Long Walk" I have described, as well as the concentration camp itself, was a dark blot on the story of the United States' misguided attempts to handle the "Indian situation" in the territories during westward expansion. I believe I have described this segment as accurately as possible, given the broader arc of one of the book's major themes of race.

The St. James Hotel was built and operated by Henri Lambert, who at one time really was President Abraham Lincoln's personal chef in the White House. Many celebrities and outlaws of the day, including "Buffalo Bill" Cody, Annie Oakley, Jesse James, Wyatt and Morgan Earp, and Black Jack Ketchum, frequented the hotel. The hotel and saloon was the site of many shootouts and murders. When Lambert's sons replaced the roof in 1906, they found numerous bullet holes, and presumably the double thickness of hardwood kept any of the guests sleeping upstairs from being accidentally killed. The St. James Hotel has been restored to its former glory, and thrives today as a popular hotel, restaurant, and saloon in Cimarron. Over 20 bullet holes are still visible in the tin ceiling of the saloon.

The Maxwell Land Grant and Railroad Company, at one time the largest of the old Spanish land grants with over 1.6 million acres, previously owned much of the other geographical areas that are described in the book. The company is still owned by a group of investors from The Netherlands, though the remaining holdings are small. Large parcels of the land previously held by the company were liquidated throughout the intervening years. Vermejo Park Ranch, the Carson National Forest, the NRA Whittington Center, and the Boy Scouts of America currently own the largest parcels.

The Boy Scouts happen to own the environs I used for the location of the helicopter crash, north of Ute Park and on the eastern side of Mt. Baldy, all the way up to the Colorado state line. The Scouts have been fine stewards of the land since it was deeded to them by the Waite Phillips family (of Phillips Petroleum) decades ago, and still operate a vast encampment called Philmont Scout Ranch there. I have chosen not to include this fact in the story line, more for ease in story telling than for any other reason. I just could not find a realistic way of including them in the novel.

The idea of the existence of an old, unrecorded "Ute Indian Deed" is entirely my fabrication.

Finally, I must make mention of Frank Springer, a major historical character both in real life and in my book, and a true Renaissance man of his time; a lawyer, rancher, land reformer, philanthropist, and scientist, Springer really did migrate from Indiana following his university studies to seek his fortune in the proverbial "wild west." He not only worked his trade as an attorney for the Maxwell Land Grant and Railroad Company, but also edited the local Cimarron newspaper for a time. He often stood up for the rights of the common man whenever he felt an injustice was being done. After relocating to Colfax County, New Mexico, he and his brother Charles founded what later became known as the CS Land and Cattle Company, an enterprise that still thrives today and is managed by their descendents. He was instrumental in bringing an end to the Colfax County War, the bloodiest and largest land dispute in American history, and the only one that went all the way to the United States Supreme Court to be resolved. But perhaps Springer's greatest passion was his work in the field of paleontology, specifically the study of invertebrate fossils known as crinoids, including the Nautilus crinoids. It is from this aspect of Frank Springer's work that I arrived upon the idea of the "Nautilus shell tattoo," and its depiction of the *septa* cross-section used as a symbol by the fictional secret society *Septum* in my book.

Although the dialogue that came out of Springer's mouth and the actions that he took in my story are completely fictional and attributable solely to me, I owe a tremendous debt of gratitude to David L. Caffey's excellent biography entitled *Frank Springer and New Mexico: From the Colfax County War to the Emergence of Modern Santa Fe* (© 2006 by the author, and published by Texas A&M University Press). Not only was this an indispensable reference on Mr. Springer's life and accomplishments, but also a remarkable account of the Colfax County War, its causes, participants, and the aftermath. For story-telling brevity and author's prerogative, I have excluded many of the historical incidents and people who were involved in this incredible chapter of New Mexico history. If you, the reader, are interested in learning more, I would urge you to avail yourself of Mr. Caffey's fine book.

Richard C. Trice
Raton, New Mexico
December 2019

AUTHOR'S BIOGRAPHY

Richard C. Trice has worked as an actor, astronomer, banker, business consultant, butcher, choir director, editor, freelance writer, grocery clerk, janitor, journalist, movie projectionist, musician, novelist, nurse's aide, pastor, photographer, poet, preacher, ranch hand, oilfield supply salesman, roofer, securities broker, shoe salesman, singer/songwriter, stage producer and director, strategic planner, summer camp counselor, teacher, wildfire fighter, and worship leader, but not necessarily in that order. He's an incurable traveler of the world and a lover of family, guitars, drums, motorcycles, the outdoors, history, other peoples' pets, other peoples' points of view, an occasional good cigar, good books, good art, good movies, strong coffee, red wine, vanilla ice cream, any food with green chilé, and is a follower of Christ Jesus. He and his wife Linda have three grown and wonderful children, lots of wonderful grandchildren, a few wonderful friends, and live in a wonderfully rambling 135-year-old Victorian house in Northern New Mexico.

Land Of My Sojourn is the second volume of a planned trilogy; Trent Carter will return in *Hearts of the Earth*.